THE PROPERTY OF A GENTLEMAN

THE
PROPERTY
OF A
GENTLEMAN

———◄═◆═►———

Catherine Gaskin

DOUBLEDAY & COMPANY, INC.
GARDEN CITY, NEW YORK
C 1974 350p.

92B8819

Facsimile signature of Philip II
courtesy of the Granger Collection, New York

Library of Congress Cataloging in Publication Data

Gaskin, Catherine.
    The property of a gentleman.

    I. Title.
PZ3.G2125Pr3   [PR6057.A75]   823'.9'14
ISBN 0-385-03934-4
Library of Congress Catalog Card Number 73–15341

In loving memory of Lee Barker,
editor and friend

AUTHOR'S NOTE

AUTHOR'S NOTE

I wish to acknowledge my immense gratitude to Christie's for their kindness and generosity in allowing me a behind-the-scenes view of the way they work. However, the Hardy's of my story is not Christie's; nor are the characters based on any living people. If the demands of fiction have required of my characters certain actions which are at variance with the principles or practice of a great auction house, the responsibility is entirely mine.

C.G.

THE PROPERTY
OF A
GENTLEMAN

PROLOGUE

About half of the ninety-three passengers, those in the tail section, of the flight out of Zurich bound for Paris and London survived when the plane ploughed into a mountainside shortly after takeoff. Among those killed was a Junior British Cabinet Minister, half of a Dutch football team, an antique dealer from London by the name of Vanessa Roswell, and a man, presumed to be a Dutchman, whose body no one came to claim, and whose passport the authorities, after close examination, found to be forged.

Within hours of the crash the daughter of Vanessa Roswell and a friend, Gerald Stanton, were on their way to Zurich, with the desperate unspoken hope that Vanessa might be among the survivors; they had only just learned that Vanessa had been on that flight. Before he left London, Gerald Stanton put through a telephone call to an associate in Mexico City, who in turn managed the difficult feat of reaching by telephone a remote hacienda in the mountains south of Taxco; then a man who hated cities, and hated flying, went to Mexico City and took the first plane to Europe—any city in Europe which had a connection to Zurich, he wearily told the booking clerk. It was the day after the crash when he arrived, and it was snowing, the snow blanketing the terrible debris. The man shivered and longed for the Mexican sun. The bodies of the victims were in the school of the small village near to where the plane had come down. The body of Vanessa Roswell had already been identified, so he went to a hotel five miles away to which the police directed him. There he found, sitting in silence before a fire in a private sitting room, Gerald Stanton and a young woman, a beautiful young woman, he thought, gauging her with his painter's eye, whose face now wore the numbed expression of shock and grief. She looked at him without recognition. That was not surprising; he hadn't seen her for twenty-seven years.

"Joanna," he said quietly. "I'm Jonathan—your father, Jonathan Roswell."

CHAPTER 1

I

But it was not of my father, Jonathan Roswell, we talked that day at lunch more than two weeks later.

"A year in gaol would change any man, I suppose, but when it is a sentence for the manslaughter of your wife and son, it must have been a particular sort of hell for him."

Gerald drew slowly on his cigarette, not at all hurried by the thought that we still had a long way to travel that afternoon; I refrained from looking at my watch. He would have seen the gesture, and disliked it. He had deliberately sought out this well-recommended restaurant far off the Motorway, had had his martini to the exact degree of dryness and chill his cultivated palate demanded, had had his wine with lunch. Because I was driving I restricted myself to one Tío Pepe. It had been the kind of disappointing, heartbreaking morning one too often experienced in the auction business, and the tension of it still stayed with me. I had hardly begun to focus on what lay ahead of us.

"His father and grandfather were well established in the pattern of English eccentrics—and Robert added his own bizarre touch. They were recluses and autocrats within their own world —it must have seemed like their own kingdom in those days, being so isolated and remote. Robert quarrelled with his father

—Birkett fathers and sons seemed to make a habit of that. And then Robert committed the heresy of joining the International Brigade during the Spanish Civil War—and yet while he was there he married a girl from an aristocratic Spanish family, who, of course, fought with Franco. A Catholic, naturally. Robert returned to Thirlbeck only for his father's funeral. It seemed all of a piece with the strangeness of his life, somehow, that he was actually on his way back there when the accident happened. So he attended his father's funeral, and then the funeral of his wife and son. Afterwards they charged him with manslaughter—said he'd been drinking and lost control of the car. A year's sentence, and remission for good behaviour."

"And I suppose he's kept to the pattern himself—a recluse in his own little world ever since." I said it absently, thinking of the journey ahead, half my mind back with the momentous journey into another country and another age, almost, that I had just completed.

Gerald had stubbed out his cigarette and he added to my impatience now by pausing to light another. I realised I was fussing again, worrying about small things—after all, this was a restaurant, not the auction house of Hardy's in St. James's, the place that was the centre of both our lives. In Hardy's one was not permitted to smoke in the public rooms, or the great salerooms, and this restriction of time and place had been hammered into my head since I was eighteen, the most junior on the Front Counter. Gerald, who had to observe the rule also, smoked incessantly at other times; he was in his late sixties, and a lifelong devotion to good wine and food had produced only a pleasing roundness of face, and the slightest thickening at the waist. He didn't even have a smoker's cough. I suppose if I had to name my closest friend I would have named him. Friend, that is. I was twenty-seven. It was nice to have a friend who had never even remotely threatened to become a lover.

"Quite the contrary," Gerald answered. "He got out of gaol just after the war started in 1939, and immediately enlisted in the ranks. I suppose he was anti-Establishment before anyone heard the word. Nothing would persuade him to take a commission. Perhaps he intended he would just serve out the war as anonymously as possible. But he wasn't born to be anonymous. He won an M.C. at Dunkirk, and a V.C. in the Western Desert. He received his V.C. from the King, and that must have been one of the few times an ex-convict has ever been invited to Buckingham Palace. People who knew him said he wasn't really the stuff of heroes—just lacked imagination, and he was so numb after prison that he really didn't feel anything. Certainly not danger. Myself, I think that's a slander. I remember Robert at Eton—a terribly shy boy, only moderately good in class, but superbly endowed as an athlete. Of course, being good at games pushed him into prominence, whether he wanted it or not. I've seen him literally shaking in the dressing room after making more than a century at cricket, and he would come off the rugby field looking blue with cold, as if he'd never run half a yard, and yet in his last year he was captain of the team. I think he didn't last more than a year at Cambridge, but in that time he got his Blue in several sports. People without imagination just aren't like that—their guts are in whatever they're doing. If Robert ended the war as probably the most decorated private in the British Army, it wasn't because he didn't know what he was about. And he stayed a private, right to the end. It was almost an embarrassment. When it was all over he made a determined effort to disappear. But people like Robert find it difficult to disappear."

"What happened?"

Gerald frowned a little. "I know he tried to go back to Thirlbeck, and I think he might have stuck it out there for perhaps six months. Then he left it, and so far as I know he's never been back. He began to travel—some of the usual places, the Caribbean, Italy, Greece. He was always among the first to find the newest watering place, and then moving on when the herd arrived. He was part of the Jet Set before anyone knew it existed. He helped to make it. But when I've encountered him in one of the more usual places—I mean the *comfortable* ones, he always seemed just to be back from some odd spot like Yucatán, or the Falkland Islands—or sailing round Cape Horn the wrong way. He's managed to talk himself onto a couple of archaeological digs—doing the donkey work and getting none of the glory." Gerald barely repressed a shudder at the thought of such discomfort. "I don't think he ever had a permanent home—always rented villas. He never married again. That might have been too permanent for him also. But he probably has had a dozen-odd mistresses in that time—some rich, some famous, some both. All of them beautiful, those that I've seen. He could always attract women, could Robert, and do it without seeming to make any obvious overtures. Robert has style—which is something different again from charm. He always has had it, even in the days when he was that painfully shy schoolboy. He could melt the hearts of every girl and woman watching just by the way he walked out to bat. You'll see, he'll be wearing his historic millstone with grace."

Outside, the bright April morning had darkened to a grey, rain-threatened afternoon. "Odd, I don't remember ever hearing of him. And I'm not quite so stodgy that I don't look at the gossip columns."

Gerald shrugged. "Well, put it down to the fact that he's probably—well, he's in his early sixties now. He hasn't lived in England since the Forties. He's not one of the *young* Beautiful People. And add to that the fact that in the last few years it's been common knowledge that he's been short of money. Let's just be blunt and say he's probably broke. He doesn't buy jewelry for beautiful ladies any longer, nor give any parties. He may yet become the recluse you imagined. By necessity, not by choice."

"Unless he decides on a sale, and then goes off and lives off the proceeds."

Gerald's lips tightened just a trifle. He lifted his fingers to summon the waiter for the bill. "My dear Joanna . . ." From the way he said it, I knew I had displeased him. "I really am surprised that by now you do not display more discretion. There is not yet even the whisper of a sale. All we know is that he is financially embarrassed, and that he has returned, hardly a week ago, to a house he has not been known to visit since 1945." He gestured with a touch of irritation. "After close to thirty years of an absentee owner, who knows what sort of state the

6

place is in. For all we know, there may be nothing to make a sale of. These old houses . . . who knows . . ."

"Then why are you going?"

About to rise, Gerald settled back into the chair again. "I have been invited, that's why. An invitation always means something. I was leaving Eton the year he entered. I once remember doing a small favour for him—the very lightest gesture that a Sixth Former might make to protect the very rawest entrant into that rather barbarous system of education. Whether or not he remembers it, I don't know. Neither of us, of course, has ever mentioned it since." Now his irritation was gone. "In this business, Jo, as you know, we go anywhere we're invited socially —and keep our eyes open because there's always the off-chance that in twenty years' time someone may want to sell their Constable, or their set of Sèvres, and they'll think of Hardy's before they think of Christie's or Sotheby's. But this invitation wasn't quite like most others. Perhaps I'm wrong, but I sensed a kind of desperate need of a lonely man returning to a place he dislikes, a man with few friends left in England, and perhaps a fear of what he goes back to. When he asked to meet me at the club about ten days ago I had the impression of a man twisting in some kind of uncertainty. He needs advice . . . perhaps he needs help. I believe that is why he asked me to come." Now he did rise to his feet, looking down at me. "And that is why I asked you to come with me." He gave me his smile of restrained affection. "We all of us have need of our friends, Jo."

I stayed until he had paid the bill, just slightly overtipping as was his habit; then he wandered off to the Gents in a leisurely fashion. I was both warmed by his love, and rebuked for my lack of sensitivity. I went out to the car park, and spent the waiting time emptying the ashtray, wiping the windscreen, dusting the instrument panel, studying the map yet again—all this, and cursing myself for being a fool. Was I going to spend my life emptying ashtrays, because that was what they had taught me? But they'd taught me a lot more than that at Hardy's— along with it a kind of reverence for people like Gerald who seemed to know far more than I could ever hope to. So I was

7

willing to empty ashtrays, carry his suitcases, chauffeur his stately Daimler, because Gerald didn't like to drive, just for the experience of being with him, of going over a house, as we had done that morning, of seeing his discerning eye run over a library, a few pictures, a ceramic collection, while I made notes. I was privileged, and I knew it; and I also couldn't bear what was so often too evident—I couldn't bear the hope, pitifully revealed in the anxious hovering of the owner, who pretended indifference. But I could see the shabbiness of once-elegant rooms, feel the chill of unheated houses, the encroaching neglect of gardens. But even I, whose subject wasn't pictures, could tell that the painting was only of the school of Reynolds or Romney, and that under the grime of another large canvas was only a bad copy of a Rubens. When paintings like these came up for auction at Hardy's they would, just possibly, be labelled under those names, but that only meant that Hardy's considered them to have been painted at about the period of Reynolds or Rubens. If Hardy's decided upon putting the initials of the painter in the catalogue, it would have meant that one of his pupils or a close associate of the master might have done the work. To have labelled a canvas Sir Peter Paul Rubens would have put the full weight of the authority of a great auction house behind it—and it would have been a major art sale. We had known there would be no major art to discover when Gerald and I had gone to Draycote Manor that morning. "After all," Gerald had said as we had driven up the weed-grown drive, "we already know where everything is—south of the Wash, that is. There's very little to discover, and I don't expect anything here. But if people pay for us to come to do a valuation . . ." He shrugged, as if to dismiss it, but privately I had always considered Hardy's fees for travelling to do a valuation very modest.

I had rather liked the owner of Draycote Manor, a gentle, sad man whose wife had died a few years ago, and who wandered his house now like a lost soul, wondering how to find the money to keep it in repair. I would have liked if there had been something we believed would justify his hopes. What he had to offer would fetch some money—but cause no excitement. There wouldn't be enough out of his sale to halt the decay around him. My eyes had fallen instantly on the baluster vases and covers in the hall that his letter had mentioned. *Famille Noire*, he thought they were. They weren't. They were rather poor copies, made in England, during the last century. His grandfather had told him they came from China, he said. I felt wretched over his disappointment. I had been hoping they would be *Famille Noire* too. My subject was ceramics. But of course I had left it to Gerald, who was senior, and a former director of Hardy's, to tell him. I was furious with myself for feeling his disappointment—and yet if I hadn't been disappointed that there was no *Famille Noire*, I wouldn't have served those years at Hardy's, wouldn't have been emptying Gerald's ashtrays for the privilege of learning from him, wouldn't have passed through the ranks of the novices, edging my way towards being fairly knowledgeable, towards developing an eye, and keeping the distant hope that one day I would be an expert, *the* expert, the one whose name could authenticate a piece. That was still a long way off.

As I waited I swung the driving mirror down and combed my hair. The face I saw always seemed to belong to a stranger —was it because I tried to please so many people too often, and had never given myself a chance to let my own personality come through on it? It was a good-looking enough face; that much I knew from other people. On the Front Counter at Hardy's it had been part of the show, and plenty of men had smiled at me, young and old. Gerald liked me to drive him not only because I drove well, but because of the way I looked, just as he liked his martinis dry and cold. When I had ended my probation period on the Front Counter some wit at Hardy's had made a remark about Jo Roswell disappearing into the dust of the ceramics department, never to be seen again. Twenty-seven. Not old, but not so young any more either. I worked more determinedly at my hair, and paid some attention to my lips. Was all my passion, and were all my young years to go on *Famille Noire*? Then I saw Gerald strolling across the car park and, like a dutiful Girl Guide, I sprang out of the car and rushed to open the door for him. I did it before I could stop myself. Damn it! Hadn't I got any blood in my veins besides what Hardy's had put there?

But Hardy's was in my blood, whether I liked it or not. There had been no thought of refusal when Gerald had suggested that I join him on this visit, seemingly casual, unbidden so far as I was concerned, to Thirlbeck, home of Robert Birkett, 18th Earl of Askew, where we might find treasures, or perhaps—in Gerald's favourite phrase—a load of old rubbish.

II

Gerald had told me to take the turnoff from the Motorway at Penrith. I had thought there might be a stream of cars heading for the Lake District this Friday afternoon, now that the M6 had made access from Manchester so much quicker; but it was spring, and still cold, and the traffic, except for the long-distance lorries heading for the Border and Scotland, thinned out; a slashing rain closed the horizons, and the lorries flung dirt on the windscreen as we passed. The wipers clicked monotonously; Gerald dozed, as I thought he would, and I was left to my thoughts.

Gerald had been so much of my life, and was still so much of it, guiding me, nudging me, pushing me where I seemed to falter or hesitate. He had been probably the closest and oldest friend my mother had ever had. They had met soon after I had been born, when she had been trying to set up in business in Kensington Church Street; he had introduced her to other dealers, taught her a great deal of what she had known about antiques, had kept a friendly eye on her rather chaotic business methods, tried to hold her back from the excesses of her own temperament, and sometimes hadn't succeeded. He had watched her indulgently through a series of love affairs, and had always been there to comfort or humour her when they came to their inevitable end. He had never lectured or tried to change her. She had been a beautiful, passionate, exuberant woman, and in a world that too often contained dull, safe people, Gerald had prized her. For what he had done for Vanessa I loved

Gerald, and now it seemed almost as if I had, with her death, slipped into her place, though I was unlike her in so many ways. Gerald had sat beside me on the plane to Zurich, and never offered me false hope that we would find her among the survivors. He had stood beside me when I had identified her body. It was his telephone call which had brought my father from Mexico. He had been a universal presence in the lives of both Vanessa and myself.

Gerald had, of course, been my introduction to Hardy's—that and the fact that Vanessa had been there every week, viewing, attending the sales when something interested her, sometimes stealing a good piece away for a low figure, sometimes seeing it go to another dealer who had a particular client in mind for its resale. Some buys had been inspired, some good, some foolish; the foolish ones bordered on mad extravagance. This quality in my mother had been well known, and hadn't, I thought, helped when I went for my interview with the directors of Hardy's. But there were other things that helped. At her best, Vanessa had been brilliant, with a sharp eye when she bothered to use it. The interview hinged, I thought, on whether the directors believed I might have her brilliance, without her hasty excesses. I was the right age then—eighteen. Better, in their eyes, to have too little education than too much of the wrong kind. "If you're right," Gerald had said, "we'll teach you what you need to know. It's hard work, unless you coast, in which case you'll be gone long before your probation time is up. If, in the end, we take you into a department, you'll work the way Vanessa never has. If you stay . . . well, I don't have to explain why you'll think it worth while. By the way, the money gets better later—later, when we're sure we've got you." They reminded me a little of Jesuits, bent on capturing the minds of the young, secure that afterwards there would be unquestioning devotion, almost fanaticism. I had come through the interview, Gerald carefully absenting himself, and had taken my place on the Front Counter, as everyone who worked for Hardy's did for some period. Except for the beginner's salary, it had been wonderful. I had everything going for me—my brilliant, flamboyant mother giving me an airy little wave as she ascended the great staircase to the salerooms, nearly always deeply engaged in conversation with some other dealer, nearly always, I noticed, a man; there was Gerald who was my friend and my mentor, and there was also the fact that it was no hindrance to be the daughter of Jonathan Roswell, some of whose paintings were even then beginning to appear in the salerooms, and were bringing very respectable prices. In my time on the Front Counter men smiled at me, and Vanessa had noticed that and approved —she would have felt let down by a daughter whom men hadn't taken to. And then after a year on the Front Counter someone had decided where my aptitude might lie, and I went into the ceramics department. I saw rather less of Vanessa for the next few years because I had taken a flat on my own. I went on working, growing up, making a life for myself, and somehow waiting for something to happen—perhaps waiting for myself to turn into another Vanessa, or to become identifiably my own self. Neither of these things happened. Until the day of the plane crash I seemed purely the creature of Vanessa's and Gerald's influence—and Hardy's.

The rain drifted off into mist. The lorries were fewer. I enjoyed the sensation of power in the big car, the sense of being virtually alone on that fast, straight road. I had to keep watching that I didn't slip over the 70-mile limit. Gerald liked fast, smooth driving, but he would have been mortified if I had been booked for speeding; to him it would have seemed a breach of good taste. Strange how he liked big, powerful cars, and yet had never willingly driven himself since he had come out of the Army at the end of the war. Impossible to imagine him in some vehicle that laboured or rattled. Smoothness was Gerald's way in everything, his whole life style. Of course I had not been there to witness how he had met the crises of his own young life; I had seen the portrait of the woman who had been his wife, and whose death had left Gerald childless, with not only his own quite respectable private income, but her considerable fortune as well. So besides what he earned from Hardy's, moving always upwards and taking on a degree of administrative work along with his position in the valuations department, he had money for a way of life that had thrown him into the company of people who had trusted Hardy's with the sale of some of their treasured possessions, people who didn't want publicity for such sales. Who would know, except Gerald and a very few other people, if the Georgian silver was sold from the bank vault?—who would know if a replica was made for a necklace, which only the eye of the expert could detect? Naturally, there was always more interest aroused if some piece coming up for auction were known—the more publicity, the more people were drawn into the bidding; the provenance of the work, if it existed, always gave clues to the owner, and some pieces were too famous for their sale to go unmarked. The world of art sold publicly at auction was becoming very small. What went on in the rooms of private dealers was held to be their business alone; Hardy's could afford no shadow of doubt on their transactions. Discretion was everything—discretion and judgement. Who came and bid for what, and on whose behalf, was also the business of the client. But Hardy's displayed for public scrutiny what was for sale, offering what provenance existed, placing the whole weight of the reputation of the house behind what they backed as genuine, leaving alone, and to the decision of the buyer, that which was doubtful. It was a game of risk and gamble, and often of high excitement, hidden under a façade of enormous calm. So much was revealed, so much must remain hidden, and in the area of hazard. But in these days of inflation more and more people seemed willing to take the gamble that the work of art they bought was more valuable than the money they paid for it. People, like that sad man we had seen at Draycote Manor that morning, rummaged through their attics as newspaper items appeared telling of the staggering amounts of money some seeming trifle had brought at auction. The miniatures were looked at again hopefully, and the fussy collection of china dogs; they carefully took down a plate or two of the dinner service which had been put away in the top cupboards of the kitchen in their grandmother's time. There could be heartbreak behind the sale of some single item, or a whole collection, cloaked, the owner hoped, by the discretion of Hardy's and under the obscure designation of "The Property of a Gentleman," or some other kindly shield and salve for pride. Of course it was all there, recorded in the auctioneer's day books—the sale, the price, the owner's name, the buyer, and if the object had ever passed through Hardy's hands before—all of it there in the leather-bound books kept since Hardy's had opened in St. James's almost two hundred years ago. Those books had miraculously survived the bombing of the premises during the war. I often thought that there might be those who wished they hadn't survived. It must be painful to remember that it was on record that what had been sold in the Thirties for a bare hundred pounds or so, now, as inflation rushed on, went for many thousands. Pride would have liked the records of some of those sales wiped out—especially those who pretended that the silver was still in the vault, or the jewels remained there for security reasons. How much of all that Gerald literally carried in his head—Gerald, who seemed to me at times the epitome of Hardy's.

He had gone to the right schools, had spent his life among the rich and the powerful. Just too young for the First World War, he had been A.D.C. to a famous general in the Second. No medals for Gerald, but useful contacts, political as well as military. "I never was the stuff of heroes, my dear," he had once said of his war service. But he had turned it all to advantage, and used it for the advantage of Hardy's. He was fluent in French and Italian, was part of the scene wherever the rich gathered. His quick, discerning eye had fallen on many art works in houses which were open only to invited guests. His wartime journals would never be for publication; my mother had told me that they were a record of the advance and retreat of armies, and unique in that they concentrated on the houses of the rich and the noble which stood in the path of those armies. No one really knew how much advice Gerald had given to the Allied Arts Commission on where they might search for the plundered masterpieces, the vanished treasures. It was not the sort of thing he would ever talk about. He had kept his own private record of those whose houses and fortunes had been destroyed. In his urbane, patient fashion, without a hint of patronage, he had spent his spare time searching out such people, gently probing to find if any of the treasures had somehow survived the holocaust, the destruction, the hungry years that followed. For some, the years were still hungry, but hunger had not eroded pride. It needed someone of Gerald's tact to suggest how the problem might be alleviated. It was often through Gerald, his journal and his fabulous memory, that some dazzling piece had turned up in Hardy's salerooms.

This venture today lay in the same province, brought about by Gerald's instinct for timing, his patience and tact, his long-reaching contacts. And I was with him now because he had wanted me with him, and because I was only two days back from Mexico, and the shock of my mother's death, and the spell of the man who was my father was still upon me, as the sun tan of Mexico showed on my wrists above the driving gloves.

It was Gerald who had urged on us the decision to bury Vanessa's body in the churchyard of the tiny Swiss village. "She wasn't religious," he said, with truth, "and this is surely a more pleasant place than Highgate." And when Jonathan had turned to me after the service, with its harrowing row of graves newly made, and said, "Will you come back to Mexico with me—for a few weeks? A few weeks of sun, Jo, and quiet. There's nothing else but that—it's all I can give you now," it had been Gerald who had pushed me towards the decision. "You should go, Jo. I'll make it all right with Hardy's. You're due some holidays, aren't you?—and any rate, they'd give you time off, I know. Better not to come back to London just now. Time enough in a few weeks."

"But . . . I . . ." I looked at the stranger who was my father, never seen before, who was proposing that I should go with him, learn to know him after this space of twenty-seven years. "I don't have any clothes with me . . ." I said lamely and stupidly.

"We'll get some in Mexico City. You won't want much. San José is very remote, and completely unfashionable. Coming, Jo?" A question, almost a challenge I had then answered with a nod, and had not regretted.

San José had been what he had said—simple, remote, an almost peasant style of life lived by the numerous descendants of the Martínez family who had had the original land-grant of its huge acreage from Isabella and Ferdinand, licences to mine its silver from further kings of Spain. They were proud and very poor, and clinging stubbornly to the myth that they were still wholly Spanish, that no drop of Indian blood tainted their veins —which was what everyone in Mexico claimed, and none believed. Their sprawling hacienda was nearly in ruins—Jonathan told me that twenty years before he had stumbled across it, and had asked to rent one of the nearly ruinous outbuildings as a studio and living quarters. They had given the studio only for the price of the materials to mend the roof, and Jonathan had lived as a member of the family ever since—the most prosperous member, paying for expensive items like electricity, transport, and the food they couldn't grow themselves. In those days it had been a large expenditure; these days, for him it was a pittance. They didn't understand his world-wide reputation for painting what they considered were not true pictures at all, and so they didn't take his work seriously. What they did take seriously was his almost tender concern for them, to keep their way of life going, even though the silver mines had long since passed from their control, and they lived as best they could from the poor land. So, close to fifty dark-eyed children followed him everywhere he walked—his *niños* he called them—chattering, vying for his attention. El Inglés they called him—not a Yanqui. And there was the beautiful, dark-eyed woman about thirty years old, who I guessed was his mistress, a widow with three children, none of them his, and the family considered it yet another aspect of his strangeness that he should treat her with such generosity and gentleness. So he had stayed, and worked, and lived as part of their family group for twenty years, and as his daughter I was regarded as an object of curiosity and nearly veneration. At first I found it strange and uncomfortable—and in the end succumbed—to the place, to the gentle courteous people, to the atmosphere of life centuries ago.

I could remember standing beside him staring up at the great stone sixteenth-century aqueduct which still fed the hacienda its water, turning my face to the sun. "How clear the air is— and the light's so harsh."

"A painter's light, Jo. I see everything in it—shapes and forms, everything I need. Bright, fierce colours and black shadows, this landscape says everything I want to say. I never have tried to paint what I see—just what the shapes are." And it was that, and his singleminded concentration, which had made him one of the foremost abstractionist painters of the world. "I'll never leave here," he added. "If I left here, I'd die. And I'll die before I leave here. They'll bury me with all the rest of the family, Jo—there in the ground beside the chapel. You'll understand, won't you, Jo?—the way we left Vanessa on that hillside. It isn't alien ground. Here is my home."

I had somehow, in that short time, both known and understood, in some degree. I had known at last why he and Vanessa had parted, had known why they never could have remained together. Impossible to imagine Vanessa in this setting, except as a transient visitor. Impossible to imagine him anywhere else. And when I witnessed him cough as soon as he got to the polluted atmosphere of Mexico City, I had understood much more. He only remained alive in that high, clear atmosphere of the mountains in a tropical climate, with heavy blankets and fires banked high at night against the sudden chill. In this serene, clear air he breathed, and lived, and worked. He had been right to ask me to come; now I had a father whom I not only knew, but had begun to understand.

And then back to London, and hardly with my bags unpacked, Gerald's phone call that he wanted me to come with him to visit two houses, and that I had the permission of my director, Mr. Hudson, to stay with Gerald however many days were required. I read the accumulated letters at my flat—mostly they were letters of sympathy about Vanessa, and I had no heart to begin to answer them. I visited Hardy's, and everyone was kind, and said nice things about Vanessa, even those I knew hadn't really admired her. I talked over the arrangements for this trip with Gerald, I wandered around in the basement of Hardy's for a while, poking my head into departments I didn't often visit—how long was it since I had been in the arms and armour section?—or stopped to give some time to the line of costumes accumulating on the rack?—or the row of dolls waiting for their particular sale? I went upstairs and spent twenty minutes in the largest of the salerooms where they were auctioning English pictures—quite important pictures. The sale was packed, with closed circuit television to another room, and the prices were running high; as usual it was all carried out with an air of nonchalance and familiarity, the various dealers murmuring caustic or deprecating remarks about what other dealers bought. It was all very far from the clear, calm silence of San José, and from the snow-covered mountain in Switzerland. I was back to my old world, but something had changed. At a coffeeshop in Jermyn Street I found myself greeted by two young men from the coins and miniatures department of Hardy's. At first we talked about Mexico, and then the talk drifted to Hardy's—upcoming sales, expected prices; we couldn't help it, any of us. We were all that way. I wondered for how many years we'd be doing the same thing, only the prices would be different. Afterwards I went and gave my routine donation of blood at St. Giles's Hospital—a card had been waiting as a reminder among the pile of mail. And then I went home and cooked some chops for supper, and sat and willed the telephone to ring and that it would be Harry Peers; but no call came from Harry. He had sent three cables, long, extravagant cables to Mexico, but no message waited for me here. I began to repack for this trip with Gerald. A kind of hurting ache came into my throat at the thought of Harry Peers. Gerald had told me he had flown unannounced to Switzerland on the day I had left with my father for Mexico, and had missed seeing me. That was Harry. In the end I finally did telephone his flat, and his manservant told me that Mr. Peers was out of the country; he didn't know when he would be back. So I would wait, and sometime he would phone. I wished I could feel angry with him, but I couldn't. Harry only operated by his own rules, and everyone who knew him came to understand that. I either could accept him as he was, or do without him. I didn't want to do without him.

And then Gerald's voice came to me over the soft clicking of the windscreen wipers. I had thought he was asleep.

"It's wonderful how the excitement comes back," he said. "I was beginning to think I was too old for this business." As if

18

he knew I would bridge his thoughts he continued. "Robert hasn't been in the house himself since 1945. I can't find a record of it, or its contents, anywhere. I had one of our people go through the indices of *Country Life* the other day. It must be the only house of any size in England which hasn't been photographed and written up. They must have been eccentrics with a vengeance, his father and grandfather. His father never even bothered to take his seat in the House of Lords. I doubt if Robert did, either. I wonder who the heir is . . . ? The line nearly died out in his great-grandfather's time—the title and estate passed to some farmer-merchant who wasn't expecting it. I begin to wonder if they were collectors of anything, or will the place be filled with Victorian junk? Well—who knows, there might be things there from before his grandfather's time, though if there are I wonder why we don't know about them. I must say, for an Earl, Robert's inheritance is very obscure. I should have thought to look up the newspapers at the time of his trial, and then again when he got the V.C. Newspapermen have such a talent for worming their way into places no one else can get a nose in." His voice sharpened as he straightened himself and took out a cigarette. "All those years—and a house unvisited, unrecorded. What shall we find, I wonder?" Then he added: "It's good to feel excited, eh, Jo?"

He went on: "He won't be expecting you, of course. But perhaps he remembers I don't like to drive. I remember that he was faintly amused that I had a chauffeur and a car brought all the way from England last time I came across him at a house party in Italy. As if I'd place myself in the hands of an Italian driver! But of course Robert will accept you. He is charming, always, with women—even when he's furious with them, or worse, quite indifferent to them. Heaven knows what state the place is in . . ." His tone grew lower as he considered it. "One can hardly hope to be warm, but it won't kill us for a few nights. I'll know soon enough why he's asked me to come. Either he just needs a friend about, or he needs to be told what there is to sell from his house. I'll pretty soon know whether it's worth sending up our young geniuses from the various departments to do a detailed valuation. We shall pretty soon know if this old man's eye is still as good as he thinks it is."

He spoke with no false modesty. Because of his age, he now worked only in an advisory capacity for Hardy's. He was, therefore, more free than he had ever been to indulge his passion and his hobby—the quiet search for what was still unknown and undocumented, and which one day might appear in a Hardy's catalogue. He specialised in nothing; he had the all-round knowledge of a lifetime among rare and beautiful things. But on his advice the experts followed, and not very often had he been seriously mistaken.

"I indicated," he said as the signs for Penrith began to appear along the Motorway, "that we would be looking over a property reasonably close to the Lakes. He knows Hardy's well enough to know that we would never say whose property. It won't be necessary to say we have spent all afternoon driving to reach Thirlbeck."

He continued in a low tone, as if his words were almost for himself. "We'll see . . . we'll see. If there's anything worth selling still there, I could perhaps persuade him of relieving himself of the insurance costs. Of course, there *is* something there, something so superlative that even the Birketts haven't been able to hide its existence. But who would ever buy it? I wonder. No one in his right mind, I think. But still, what an auction La Española would make . . ."

His voice trailed off into the sigh of weariness of a man who has done enough work for the day, so I kept the pace steadily at seventy, and asked no questions. In good time Gerald would tell me. "Dear God," he said a minute or so later, "I hope the place isn't too run down. I hope there's ice for the drinks . . ."

III

We edged towards Thirlbeck by miles of those torturous, magical roads of the Lake Country; the mountains humped about us, fantastic shapes, like a strung-out menagerie of child-drawn animals marching along the skyline—not mountains, really—shapes, heaps, crumpled-up folds of earth, not high, but the rises and descents so sheer and sharp that they felt as if they towered forever above us. Then suddenly, within a mile, we would have topped that humpback, and another valley, cupping its own secret rain-dark lake, was below us.

"Theatrical," was Gerald's comment. Clouds spilled over unseen mountaintops, in other places the sky was clear and great glittering shafts of sunlight struck down, amethyst, amber, opal; the brown bracken was beginning to uncurl its green tentacles, the larchs were assuming the brightest of green that a tree can wear, the birch trunks were pale, slender forests of wraiths; there were sombre green rectangles of conifers.

"We'll have to remember to call them fells," Gerald said, nodding at the mountains; I was silent, concentrating on the difficult, narrow road, hemmed by the most beautiful stone walls I had ever seen. "And the small lakes are tarns. Well, we shall make mistakes, but we won't be here long enough to matter. All visitors are tourists, and therefore rather contemptible. Anything not Cumbrian-born is something less interesting than the animals. They care about sheep here. I know an art dealer—odd sort of man. He comes up here every year and spends two weeks fell-walking. He says he's getting past it, and it nearly kills him, but he lives just to come back. He's angry now because the Motorway has come. Says the whole area is so crowded in the season that you can spend a weekend on the road looking at the back of a caravan. Only way to be alone is to get out on the fells and walk, and even then you're lucky if you don't see a dozen others on the trail before or behind you. Twenty years ago, in spite of Wordsworth and his daffodils, it was a different place, still hard to get to, completely out of the world. Oh, yes . . . I took the trouble to telephone my friend before we left. I did remember *that*. He's heard of Thirlbeck, of course. But he doesn't *know* anything about it. It's just a name on a map, in a valley that's almost completely bounded by the National Park, and trespassers, walkers or picnickers are neither invited, wanted, nor permitted. And when they say 'trespassers will be prosecuted' they *mean* it. Of course as an art dealer he's curious—but the locals don't talk about Thirlbeck. The memory of Robert's father and grandfather, and their passion for privacy must die hard . . . and, rather naturally, the young ones don't care. If there's the odd poacher or two on the property, they'd be the last to talk. That there *is* a house, they know. What's inside it, no one seems to know or remember. My friend once wrote asking for permission to come onto the estate . . . I suppose he hoped he might be able to talk his way into the house. He got a less than polite letter warning him of legal action if he tried it. That was all he could tell me, and I suppose it speaks for itself. Oh, Jo, I wish we'd *get* there. It's been a long day. I've never much cared for the Lake District. Too violent. Too much rain. I think you really have to be born to it."

"And this is my first time here. Funny, except for expeditions to do valuations of houses"—I glanced across at his weary face affectionately—"mostly thanks to you, I really don't know England at all. I don't think I've ever spent a whole holiday in England. That's pretty shameful to have to admit, isn't it? When I could afford to take holidays I shot off to Paris and Rome and Madrid—and later I started to borrow Vanessa's car and wandered around country districts all through Europe. And it's always been to look at museums and churches. I must be the only person alive who spent *weeks* in Venice, and has never been to the Lido." The thought came sharply, like the great blades of light striking the stony sides of the fells. "Gerald, I'm twenty-seven. Have I spent too much of my life with my nose pasted against the display cases in museums? I want badly to go to New York and Washington—and do you know why? Just to see the Metropolitan and the Cloisters and the National Gallery. When someone says California I don't think of the sun, I think of the Norton Simon Collection! Twenty-seven— don't laugh, Gerald! It sounds young to you. But quite suddenly I'm beginning to feel that I've missed out on something. And I haven't really any idea what it is."

"Why don't you marry Harry Peers? You could have the Metropolitan and a suite at the top of the Pierre at the same time. And if you don't care for the Venice Lido, there are still private beaches in the Aegean with little Greek amphitheatres as a backdrop. You could *buy* those little pieces of Chinese porcelain, instead of just looking at them. Your answer to being twenty-seven and feeling you've done nothing is to marry Harry Peers. He can give you all the worlds you think you might have missed."

"Apart from a few other things, such as a lot of beautiful girls he knows, what's wrong about that idea, Gerald, is that he hasn't asked me to marry him. If he does—*if*—it will be done quickly, over in a day. The shares will be rapidly acquired, with a minimum of fuss. Until then, he'll be as secretive as he is about all his deals. He's out of the country now—New York, I'd guess. I don't know whether he's gone to try to buy the Empire State Building, or just because there's a girl he rather fancies. He won't bother to go to the Metropolitan. He's *been* there. But he'll come back with some precious little thing or other, bought from a dealer. And he'll show it to me. And he'll see me want to lick my lips over it . . . that's Harry. Does anyone like Harry really have to marry *anyone* these days? Isn't everyone available?—all styles and sizes, and, for Harry, all degrees of intellect. And don't say, 'Everything's available—at a price.' Yes, I know. In a sense, we're all up for auction. But I'm not being fair—that isn't Harry. He's better than that—has a much more subtle sense of what he's after. There is more to the game than the price. And me—the trouble with me is that I'd just be too dull for him. Too earnest. Why couldn't I have been like Vanessa? He adored Vanessa, and she him. Yes . . . I do think I would marry him if the day ever came when he finally decided that the property was right. He's got an oddly old-fashioned streak like that. He'd want it to be for good, and forever. His values are still working-class in that way. He thinks if a marriage comes to a divorce, it's all been a waste of time—and of course he's right. He'll never gamble on marriage the way he does in the property market."

"Well, then, he's a bit of a fool, which is something I didn't think I'd ever say of Harry Peers. Marriage is the least safe institution in the world. Real gamblers love it. And if he won't gamble on you, he *is* a fool."

I smiled. "Gerald, you're kind. That will make reading his

doings in the gossip columns a little easier." And I didn't add that I had been glad, for this reason also, to be away from London for a few days. It might have a little shock value for Harry if I were not at the other end of the telephone line when he decided, at whatever hour suited him, to call from New York, or the Bahamas, or wherever it was that some empty beach or city-centre property was tempting him. I told myself angrily that he was utterly selfish; in justice he also was generous and kind, in odd, unexpected ways. He was also capable of the sort of flashy, showy gestures that at times made him seem vulgar, and at other times reminded me so much of my mother. It was true that Vanessa had liked Harry; she had applauded the sheer guttsiness of his vulgarity, and admired his style.

Perhaps I was thinking just a little too much of Harry, but then the bend at that particular point was very sharp. I wasn't driving fast, but even so I was almost on top of the other car before I even saw it, and applied the brakes sharply. "Sorry," I said to Gerald. "But he's absolutely crawling along."

"Yes . . . it would have been a pity."

"What would have been a pity?"

"If you'd run into the back of a . . . well, I'd guess it could be about a 1931 Bentley. Beautiful condition, isn't it?"

"Gerald—*you* know what kind and year it is!"

"Well, my dear, when they made that sort of thing, there weren't so many about. These days I can't tell one new one from the other . . ."

I dropped back a little. We were within ten miles of Kesmere, which was the town closest to Thirlbeck, and for all I knew there wouldn't be a stretch of road safe enough to pass before then. Certainly it was not to be done where we now were—with bends every few yards, and a drop down a sharp slope of scree below us. I sighed; it would soon be dusk.

Then the car in front, a drophead with the top down, slowed even more, and then, at the first place where the width of the road permitted him to draw over, he stopped completely. I saw him signalling me to pass with, I thought, a rather impatient gesture. I had the impression of a rather youngish man with careless, tow-coloured hair, wearing a thick jersey. He looked cold, seated there in the height of that splendid anachronism—and he was probably a bit wet too, since we had just passed through a shower which must have hit him as well. I saluted to thank him, but even in the driving mirror I saw no more of him; the bends were sharp and numerous.

We went about two miles farther, dropping down almost to the floor of the valley, and once again I had to touch the brakes quickly. Both of us had almost missed it—a break in a section of the high stone wall we had followed for about half a mile, a clear semicircle of ground off the roadway, and between crumbling stone pillars, unpleasantly topped by barbed wire, a strong pair of galvanised iron mesh gates. Behind the wall, which was also spiked with barbed wire, was the ruins of a gatehouse on which the slate roof had collapsed. A bleak, rather crudely lettered sign hung on the gates.

THIRLBECK

STRICTLY PRIVATE

TRESPASSERS WILL BE PROSECUTED

I looked at Gerald. "This is it?" The road that led beyond the gatehouse seemed barely more than a half-overgrown track, rising at an impossibly steep angle, between hand-cut stone walls and a forest of larches, feathering green.

For once Gerald seemed non-plussed. "Has to be." He drew a deep breath. "Good God—do you suppose this is the *main* entrance?" He was fumbling in his jacket pocket. "Must say his directions weren't very explicit . . . where's that letter? But I do remember he said something about Kesmere . . ."

I was out of the car by now, and Gerald had wound down his window. "Well," I said, "this has to be his back door—and very firmly padlocked." I was rattling the heavy chain and lock that secured the gates, and looking beyond to the rather sad desolation of the ruined cottage, which must once have been quite beautiful; then I saw, propped against its side wall, the rusted remains of heavy wrought-iron gates, a tracery of design through them, and what might be part of a crest. "I hope his front door is more welcoming. We'll have to go on, Gerald. I'm sorry . . . and you're tired."

He had found the letter. "Yes—he says go through Kesmere, and take the right . . . oh, well, we'll ask when we get there."

I took one last look up the larch-lined road, and saw that its paving had been hand-laid, as were the walls. There was a kind of lordliness in that, a memory, even, of the days when labour had been so cheap; and now the weeds grew through the stones, and the noble emblem on the great gates had rusted into anonymity.

For all its splendour, the Bentley had a noisy engine; I heard it coming before it rounded the last bend. It slowed and stopped, pulling off the road in front of us, into the curving space before the big gates. The man got out. He looked less young, less sporty, now. He wasn't old, or even middle-aged, but it was a tired face, a thin, straight-cut mouth and weather wrinkles about the grey eyes. He had heavy brows darker than his tow-coloured hair. With the thick sweater he was wearing stained corduroy pants.

"Do you need help?" It was said rather brusquely as if he didn't want to waste any time on pleasantries.

Gerald spoke for me. "Lord Askew is expecting us. We wondered . . ."

"Lord Askew is *expecting* you." He didn't even attempt to disguise his sarcasm. "Lord Askew hasn't been here since God-knows-when."

"Then you're misinformed." Gerald's tone grew terse. "Lord Askew is in residence, and we are expected this evening—and his note says 'go through Kesmere.' We thought this might be a shorter way. I'm tired . . ."

The man came towards him, rounded the car to speak to him at the open window. Watching, I saw a strange softening of that strained face as he looked at Gerald. Suddenly, between them, all strangeness disappeared; they were such an odd contrast, that man, and Gerald; the one with the whiff of the farmyard about him, and yet driving that elegant Bentley, and Gerald still wearing his London suit, his city skin pale in contrast to the weather-beaten man who faced him. For some reason they recognised each other—not as known persons, but as people who trusted the basic honesty of each other.

"You know he's here, then? It's hardly been a week . . ."

"He asked me here. I might presume to say I am a friend."

The man looked at him for a moment longer. "A friend. I'm surprised to hear he had such a thing as a friend in England. Well, no matter. I believe you. And I might be able to help you."

"Yes?"

Now the man glanced towards me. "If the lady here is game . . . the road isn't easy, but it would save you about twelve miles. And quite a bit of traffic in the town. Saves you going into Kesmere, and about three miles out of it again. It's a loop. Gets you back a few miles from here."

"How?" Gerald said with characteristic directness. "The place is padlocked."

"Well . . . I rent a piece of land from Askew. I have to have access. And I have the key."

Gerald brightened. "Well, then, let's get on."

For the first time the man turned to me. "You used to driving steepish inclines?"

"I've driven mountain roads—I take it all carefully."

"Well, then, *take* it carefully. I wouldn't want the responsibility of sending you over the side of a fell." With this, he brought out a bunch of keys and selected one. "Watch it up there—it's slippery in places."

I was back in the car, the engine ticking over. I didn't want the man to change his mind, Gerald's influence to wear off. I was conscious of his weariness—and my own. We shouldn't have tried to do Draycote Manor and finish this journey all in one day. "Thank you," I said, as the man swung the gates open for us, and we drew level with him. "How far?"

"About three miles. Up over the rise, and down again. A valley with two narrow openings. Very private—as the Earls wanted it."

I gave him a salute in the mirror, and thought about his last words: "as the Earls wanted it." As if he talked about many generations, not this one man who had returned to England after so many years. The last glimpse I had in the driving mirror before we rounded the first bend was of him closing the

27

gates and beginning to padlock them again. Faintly reluctant to lose sight of him, as if he were the last contact with the outside world, I slowed almost to a halt again.

"Go on," Gerald said.

We went on, and the dim green beauty would have forced silence on us, even if we had not been so tired. There were moss-covered rocks among the plantation of trees, and all the time the sound of rushing water, as though a stream, or several of them, accompanied us all the way. We crossed several little dangerously humped bridges, and the water was white beneath them. A flash of the last of the sun came through the trees. I almost expected a temple bell, and the figure of a Japanese monk, motionless. It seemed the idealised scene in an Oriental watercolour, the mossy green stillness, the rocks, each seemingly placed with its own significance, each stone of these walls laid by hand. A thousand men could have taken a thousand years to create it. And it had grown here, naturally, in this remotest part of England, like some child's pictured dream.

The shock was all the harsher when we emerged from the larch plantation and topped the rise. Here was the roof of heaven. We were almost, but not quite, now among the clouds. The moorland was rough, wild, nearly barren. The fells slipped down into a narrow cleft to the green of pasture, to the dark beauty of a long, slender tarn; there were great scars on the hillsides where patches of scree had tumbled during the centuries, and those unbelievable stone walls still marched relentlessly up the sides, into the heights, the clouds—put there time out of mind to mark one man's land from another's, to keep sheep from straying. How could men have built such straight lines over the roughness of a mountainside, and how many hundreds of years ago, with no instrument to guide them but their own eye?

There was nothing to be seen, nothing but the intensity of the terrain about us. In all this secret place there was nothing but sheep grazing down by the tarn, and the narrow, stone-lined road, winding on, winding down, going on forever. It could have looked this way when the Romans came through, but as close as this strange country was to the ultimate line of

28

the Roman occupation of Britain, Hadrian's Wall, I guessed that this might have been one of the hidden places where no legion had ever penetrated.

"Go on," Gerald said again, because I had, once more without thought, halted—compelled, shocked almost. "It can't be much farther. God Almighty, what a forsaken wilderness! I haven't even seen a shepherd's hut."

I went on, taking the pace very gently on the steep grade. About a mile down beyond the crest, a copse of white birches, still only with the green catkins of spring hanging from their boughs, straddled two sides of the road. Here, we were getting into a lesser grade, the walls, tumbled and broken in places, had been left to lie as they fell. As we went down into the copse we were in the shadow cast by the opposite fells. The cloud finally spilled over their edges, and they were lost. I saw the cloud roll down like a silent avalanche. The tarn turned black. If the cloud came lower we would be caught in it. Suddenly, in spite of the car heater, it was cold.

It was then I saw it—that tall white wraith of a dog who stood for an instant's time beneath the birches, and then took flight straight across our path. I slammed on the brakes. Whether it was weeds beneath our wheels, or wet leaves, or just the suddenness of the braking, the car slipped perceptibly and sickeningly sideways, sliding too fast down the slope towards the next bend, the wheels locked in a skid. I corrected as much as I could, easing my foot off the brake, doing a kind of manic steering exercise through the bend and letting the car right itself. We grazed the wall with the back fender, and I heard stones topple. Then we were straight again; I put my foot very gently on the brake, and eventually we came to a halt. Without a word to Gerald I turned and looked back; the dog had crossed the road and was almost lost among the birches, the long high stride like a deer in flight.

It was a time before Gerald spoke. "My God, Jo! What possessed you? Is there something wrong with the car?"

I turned back to him. "You didn't see it—the dog? It took off from the trees straight in front of us! I would have crashed right into it!"

"The dog? *What* dog? I didn't see a dog. What would a dog have been doing up here alone? What sort of a dog?"

I shook my head, and I suddenly knew that I had to conceal from Gerald the trembling of my hands on the wheel. "Not a little dog, Gerald. A very large dog, a whitish dog with long legs. You had to have seen it!"

He took a very long time in replying, taking yet another cigarette from his case and lighting it. There was no possible way for him to control the trembling of his hands, but it was caused by a different reason from my own. I knew he did not believe me; he had seen nothing.

"I must have nodded off, Jo, dear. No, I missed seeing the dog. Let's get on then, shall we. It's getting dark." The words were spoken with infinite kindness. Whatever he thought had gone through my mind in those seconds when I had believed I had seen the dog, he would not comment on it further. He was prepared to give me the benefit of the doubt, or at least not to call me any further into question. But it was equally impossible to believe that at this stage of the journey, so close to its end, in such a place as this, he had nodded off in sleep. My eyes had seen what his had not. That also was hard to believe.

We went on, and very soon the road was down to the level of the water, and here it skirted one great pile of scree which tumbled almost to the edge of the tarn; the valley opened out. Then we saw the house, about another mile away. Neither of us had spoken in this time. I put on the windscreen wipers again because the mist had truly reached us now, and hung like rain. The house kept appearing, vanishing, and reappearing as the mist moved before us—a stone pile, a formidable and strangely beautiful outline in the settling dusk. I wished Gerald would speak; I began to think this perhaps was something I also had imagined.

He did, and his words reflected my own sense of unease, but at least he saw what I did. "I would feel better if there was even a light," he said. "I suppose they *do* have electricity." I remembered that I hadn't seen any power poles or lines, but I didn't say so now. He was already more nervous than I had ever known him.

"It isn't quite dark yet."

"It feels dark."

The valley floor widened farther as we drew nearer the house; here were meadows where cattle grazed, and sheep and their new lambs being given the higher, sparser pasture. Around the house itself was a parkland of ancient oaks and beeches, flushed with the first green of spring; the grass about them was cropped close by the cattle. The tarn drifted off into a slim dark finger, close to the walls of a sort of outer garden of the house, a garden dark and tangled with plants and hedges gone wild with neglected growth. The edge of the tarn was lost in a small forest of rushes.

There was, at last, at a ground-floor window, a light; but that was swiftly blotted out, as if someone had drawn a curtain. "I hope you saw it too," Gerald said. "And it looked like electricity. Perhaps, after all, there will be ice . . ." We passed over a cattle trap and the first of the walls that were meant to mark the formal garden. Little remained of it; great untamed masses of rhododendron and laurel sprawled under the beech and oaks. In the clear space, if there had ever been flower beds, they had given way to long grass where daffodils now held sway, thousands of them, rampant, wild, thin little things, growing weaker with the years, but always finding new territory to move into to re-establish themselves. Quite abruptly we reached a wide gravelled area, weed infested, in front of the house. Half obliterated paths led off towards the lake and the rhododendron forest. "Well," Gerald said, "this is where the road ends, so this has to be Thirlbeck. And . . . yes, by God, it *is* worth the seeing."

It was a magnificent piece of domestic Tudor architecture, loosely wedded to a rough stone tower that must have been some centuries older. It would have been mostly built in Elizabeth's reign, I guessed, when noblemen, even in these remote wild areas, were beginning to feel some security and peace in the land, no longer enclosing themselves in castles and fortresses. It was a house of windows, in those times a sign of wealth—everywhere there were tall mullioned windows thrusting out in square bays. It was symmetrical, save for the tower—

two huge bays to each side of the doorway, and rising two storeys, topped with a lacey stone frieze decorated with what appeared to be heraldic animals. It was perfectly proportioned —not too big, the height just right to the length. There were only three steps rising to the doorway, a modest disclaimer of too much grandeur. It was a great country house which made no pretensions to being a palace. Its builder seemed to have borne in mind that its origins were firmly rooted in that crumbling stone tower which must once have been the refuge of the whole manor, beasts as well as people, at the times of the Border raiders. There was still a strong sense of the wildness of Scotland across the Solway Firth even in this graceful structure; its stone matched the dark slate colour of the tower, as if it knew where its strength lay.

"And to think it's been here so long, and no one seems to know about it—or care . . ." I said softly.

We had sat feasting our eyes on what we could see in the growing darkness, the last outlines fading rapidly. And, as we sat, the door had opened. A light shone out on the steps, and suddenly what seemed like a dozen or more enormous shapes came bounding towards the car with a silent, deadly kind of speed. Within seconds the hounds were all about the car—not really more than eight, I thought, though they seemed more. They planted themselves there, perfectly still, the largest dogs I had ever seen—I guessed that at their shoulders they must have been three feet high; they stared at us, great heads on long necks, deeply whiskered brows, with hairy, bristly faces and little beards. Long thin tails curled over those powerful but slender backs.

Gerald said faintly, "One might have expected it. These, without doubt, are the hounds of the Birketts."

We didn't attempt to move, and the dogs remained motionless and uncannily quiet, those eyes under bushy brows fixed intently on us. It seemed an interminable time before another figure started down the steps, a tall lean man with faintly hunched shoulders, hands in pockets, and the air of someone who doesn't often hurry. As he drew near, Gerald risked rolling down the window a few inches.

"Is it safe, Robert?"

The man bent to the level of our own, and the dogs', faces.

"The dogs? My dear Gerald, they're gambolling puppies. I'm glad you made it before dark. I saw your lights up on the edge of the fell. The drive over from Uskdale is not for the timid in the dark. But this driver doesn't look at all timid, and is a great improvement over that one I saw in—was it Italy? How are you, Gerald? It's good to see you. Good of you to come. Come in—come in! No, really, the dogs are all right. They'll just annoy you by being overfriendly. Here, let me help you with the bags. You're both staying, of course."

He was, as Gerald promised, completely charming. He spoke with the nonchalance of someone who has a staff of twelve, and bedrooms always ready, and that could not have been so, if the neglect of the garden was evidence. But I warmed to him because he behaved as if my coming had been entirely expected and welcomed. He was round at the boot of the car before I had slid from the front seat. The dogs moved silently away to let me pass. He took the keys from my hand and undid the lock. The great hounds hung about us, their heads seemed to reach almost to my shoulder; with endearing curiosity four of them thrust themselves forward to sniff the suitcases in the boot. Even in the fading light I was aware of the man's curious combination of silver hair which must once have been very blond, with a rather dark complexion and brows, a seamed face whose lines were all vertical, still an incredibly handsome face. The eyes were a light colour, grey or green I couldn't yet tell.

"Gerald seems too paralysed to introduce us. I'm Robert Birkett."

"Joanna Roswell, Lord Askew," I answered. "I work at Hardy's, and Mr. Stanton and I have been on a valuation job this morning. I often drive him. We thought . . . well, we expected that I would go on to Kesmure. There must be rooms there so early in the season."

"Of course you won't. We've rather a lot of rooms here. We'll be delighted to have you. I wouldn't dream of parting Gerald from one of his comforts—if you don't mind my describing you that way." He smiled as he spoke; I could take no offence.

"It's been my privilege to be . . . one of Gerald's comforts. He's been a friend since I was a child . . ."

I stopped because he had put the suitcases down again, among the whole pack of hounds, and was staring at me with strange intentness. "You said Roswell, didn't you? Roswell . . . Are you related to the artist, Jonathan Roswell?"

"His daughter. You know him, Lord Askew?"

"I used to. But that's years ago. It must be—well, it must be close to thirty years since I last saw him. Of course he's become famous since then. But he doesn't live in England, does he? I read somewhere . . . Where *is* it he lives now?"

"Mexico." I smiled now, pleased. So few people seemed ever to have met my father.

He answered my smile. "And your mother . . ." He stopped abruptly. "How clumsy of me. Please forgive me. She died in that plane crash. I was shocked to read her name in that list. Forgive me," he repeated.

He bent to pick up the cases, and I sensed real distress at what he thought was his blunder. He added quickly: "If you'll let me have the keys I'll put the car away after we've had a drink. There isn't much lighting around the outbuildings, and although it looks respectable enough here in front, round the back the ruts would challenge a tractor." And as Gerald emerged warily from the car, and all the hounds in turn moved to sniff at him, "Well, then—welcome to Thirlbeck." And in a different tone he called to the dogs. "Ulf, Eldir, Thor, Oden—mind yourselves now!" They moved back obediently.

We followed him, I left only with my handbag and our two coats to carry. I looked up towards the house. The double doors had now been opened wide, and more lights had been turned on. I knew, without being able to see her face, that the woman standing there in the doorway was beautiful. She carried the assurance of beauty stamped on her in the indelible lines of bone structure. A little sharp wind blew from the tarn which moulded her long thin pale dress about her body. Her long hair was dark, with the sheen of blue caught from the light behind her. She was like something captured and transplanted from those birch woods, a creature of black and white, with hands whose incredible grace and form I could already see and marvel at. She was the sort of woman whose feet would be beautiful too.

We had mounted the steps, and now her face was half-turned to the light. Yes, beautiful. Lord Askew paused.

"Carlota, may I introduce Miss Joanna Roswell. Miss Roswell, this is the Condesa de Avila. And this, Carlota, is my friend, Gerald Stanton."

She murmured something in a low voice. Gerald was gazing at her, enchanted. She smiled, knowing the effect she had had on him, and being accustomed to it.

"Please . . . you must both be tired after the drive. It is a fierce one, over that mountain, is it not?" Her voice was almost accentless, but if there was an accent, I guessed it was Spanish. She moved before us into the hall. The dress, high-waisted and long-sleeved, low-cut on a beautiful bosom, was pale champagne in colour, not white as I had first thought. Several of the dogs flanked her silently; they seemed, for these moments, like creatures from a medieval tapestry. Uncannily, she belonged in this setting. We followed through a second pair of doors into a great and splendid hall, almost bare of furnishings, but warm with the richness of the panelling which reached the height of the full two storeys. The carving of the balustrade of the staircase, which split and went off on two arms to an upper gallery, was deep and intricate. The whole place was lit only by a few electric sconces, and the ceiling carved, beamed, was nearly lost in the shadows. There was the scent of flowers from a large jar filled with daffodils on a long oak table. There was the brightness of two fires burning in opposite chimneys. There was little else—a few tall carved oak chairs, one silken rug—and this graceful creature gesturing towards an open door. "Here is a fire—and the drinks. Roberto remembers that you like martinis, Mr. Stanton . . ."

I was conscious of two things as I followed: that Gerald had said all Robert Birkett's mistresses had been beautiful, and that the great white dog that had appeared like a phantom in front of the car at the birch copse, the dog that Gerald had not seen, belonged to the family of these great hounds.

CHAPTER 2

It was grandeur, and the beginning of decay. We sat in the library, and Gerald had his martini exactly as he liked it—the Condesa was expert at that—and my heart ached over the ominously dark stain of damp in the plaster over one corner of the huge room. Save for the fireplace wall, and the great oblong windowed alcove, it was lined with mahogany bookcases, with faceted glass fronts. They had been built in place, probably some time in the middle nineteenth century, and behind the glass was the dull gleam of gold-stamped bindings. Under the windows were great monsters of ugly iron radiators, which gave out a faint heat. The velvet curtains above them were crimson, faded to a pinkish white in the folds; the covers of the chairs and sofas were thin to the point of shredding, the flowered patterns of fifty years ago all faded to a uniform greyness. I was not part of the conversation; Gerald was explaining how we had happened to come over the mountain instead of through Kesmerc. I roamed the room, glass in hand, now, at last with the drive over, a martini like Gerald's. There was a single tall prunus vase on top of one section of the bookcases, and I was trying to look at it closer, but the room was lighted only by two sconces on the fireplace wall, and two rather ordinary, cheap standard lamps; the vase was lost high in the shadows. I moved slowly back to my chair, walking the perimeter of the room, and seeing, with a sense of sickening disappointment, that under the corner where the stain of damp was, the books in the cases also were marked with the telltale stain; pale vellum bindings bore the same horrible mark. I wondered if they would survive handling. But that was not to be tested, not now. Lord Askew must have watched my progress. "They're all locked, I'm afraid. I must ask where the keys are." Then he shrugged. "Perhaps no one knows any more."

A lifting of Gerald's eyebrows told me to mind my own business. But of course, this was our business. The room held more than books. Despite its size, it was crowded. Interspaced between the decaying sofas and armchairs with the creaking springs, arranged with no eye to displaying them to advantage, were some of the most beautiful single pieces of furniture I had ever seen. Mainly French, I thought—Louis XIV and Louis XV —marquetry tables, writing tables and *bureaux plats,* even two magnificent bow-fronted commodes, placed awkwardly back-to-back, a delicate little tricoteuse mounted with porcelain plaques shoved, almost cheek-by-jowl with a tall brass-mounted secretaire whose marquetry work was like a song in wood. They all stood about, like pieces in some phantasy furniture shop, unrelated, none with space to show itself off, a collector's dream, a guardian's nightmare when one remembered the fatal combination of the invading damp, and the big iron radiators. The sale of almost any one of them, I guessed, would have brought the money to find and fix the place where the damp seeped through the wall, or the weak spot in the roof where half a slate could be missing, or copper or lead peeling back. Under our feet, and as slight cushioning for the great dogs who lay about, were rugs, most of them Persian, but the big main one before the fire, and the one, I thought, in imminent danger of the spluttering, careless sparks, was surely Aubusson. Everywhere my eyes moved there was beauty. A matched pair of mirrors with carved wood and gilt oval frames, some carved wood gilt chairs with rough string tied across them so that no one should inadverently sit on them. The damask covering on the seats was aged and splitting. Altogether it was a room to

37

send one wild with the thought of seeing its treasures displayed in the salerooms of Hardy's—a sale that would, I judged, make the category of Highly Important in the catalogues, and bring buyers from all over the world. I began to be impatient. What else was there in this house? And why had no one ever known that these pieces were here? Great collections were not made in the dark, or with dealers being ignorant of them. But then, given Gerald's story of the kind of family Askew was sprung from, given the location and isolation of this hidden valley at the top end of England, what might not have come to it unknown and unmarked? Hardy's itself had not begun keeping their own day books in a serious and detailed fashion until about 1820. All this could have been the result of some quick buying when the stream of French émigrés flowed over to England to escape the Revolution, selling what they had to, holding onto what they could until poverty forced the sale. I knew that as long as forty years after the Revolution, articles in the Hardy's day books recorded some sales under the simple designation of "The Property of a French Nobleman." I wondered if any bill of sale existed for what I saw about me. But whoever had purchased these beautiful things had done so through no one single agent, or Hardy's and the rest of the art world would know something of their existence. I began to realise even more fully the implications of Askew's invitation to Gerald, his own return to this house he had not entered since the end of the war. The thought was enough to bring the heat of excitement to my cheeks, and to drive out the fatigue. I returned now to my seat near the fire, more anxious to listen to the talk.

The firelight lovingly played over the carved wood of the great mantel, reached to touch the smooth oval of the Condesa's face, the outstretched forms of the great dogs, one on each side of Lord Askew's chair, the others as close to him as the spaces between the furniture permitted—at his full length outstretched, each dog could have measured seven feet. They seemed extraordinarily content, as if in the presence of their master, and yet Askew had returned only a week ago. Surely this great pack must belong to the house; no one could have travelled the world with them. I mused on it as the talk went on about me—places, Rapallo, Mabella, Ocho Ríos, Gaastd—friends recalled, acquaintances mentioned. I wasn't part of the talk, but I didn't mind. Suddenly, like the dogs, I felt content just to be here.

It was strange then to see the Condesa shiver and lean further towards the fire. Of course the filmy dress was not suitable for this house; but whoever brought clothes sensible enough for unheated English houses? Askew also had noticed the gesture, and he was on his feet at once, laying more split logs on the fire. He was smiling at her faintly, that only half-committed smile of his, as he spoke.

"My poor Carlota—it seems a long way from the sun, doesn't it?"

He said nothing more, but she seemed warmed by his words. The look which passed between them was its own communication. She was about forty, I guessed, but she had all the smooth grooming of the international beauty whose age is difficult to tell. She had to love him, I thought, or she wouldn't be here with him—away from the sun.

The door opened then, and a man stood there, not advancing farther into the room. "Mrs. Tolson wishes to tell you, my lord, that the rooms are ready. She's put the young lady in the Spanish Woman's room."

I glanced at the Condesa, wondering if this was some kind of insolent gibe offered to her, not able to believe that such a thing could be said to her in Askew's presence, or that her own dignity could have permitted it. But neither reacted with any sign of outrage—she was even indifferent, as if it mattered not at all to her where I slept. Evidently the Spanish woman referred to was not she, and all of them understood that.

"Has she, indeed?" Askew said. His brow knitted for a moment as he considered it. "Not the cosiest place, is it?"

The man half shrugged. He didn't look in the least like a servant. He was tall and very powerfully built, with a mass of dark hair thickly frosted with grey. His big shoulders were stooped and his arms hung forward. He wore flannel trousers and a tweed jacket, and it was difficult to see his eyes behind the heavy pebble glasses; he had a long, dark, rather melancholy face, a face closed against the coming of strangers. I judged that he was a few years older than the Earl, but he seemed rocklike and monumental by contrast.

"Can't be helped, my lord," he answered. "It's the driest— at short notice. It's reasonably close to the bathroom Mr. Stanton will use. It hasn't got water laid on, but there wasn't any possibility of getting hot water to any of the other rooms—at short notice," he tacked on again. His brief glance at me was accusing; I had caused trouble. I was not the expected driver, for whom they had probably prepared a much more comfortable room in the servant's quarters. "At any rate, I've got the fires going, and there's three hot water bottles in the bed. Be comfortable enough, I should say. It stays quite dry, that room. I've put the young lady's bag there—and Mr. Stanton's is in his room. Anything else, my lord?"

It was the most curious mixture of familiarity and deference. That he was the man in charge of this establishment there was no doubt; that he respected the presence of the titular owner was not questioned either. It was almost the relationship of a tutor to his pupil, patient but not willing to suffer fools gladly.

Lord Askew gestured with his glass. "Nothing, Tolson, nothing. You've managed very well, as always. Thank you."

The man stepped back and closed the door without another word.

"That was George Tolson. You'll get used to him—Cumberland independence and all. The place couldn't have held together without him all these years. He's seen to everything. Steward and handyman and bookkeeper all in one. It's a nuisance for him that I've come back. Mind you, he believes I never should have left. But my coming this way . . . it makes problems. More fires, more hot water, an attempt to push some real heat through the radiators. And, of course, we have to eat, as well. He's never been a butler, though he's trying his best now. He was brought up in this house . . ." Askew paused, and in that small instant I saw his eyes scan the room, and seem to go beyond it to the whole house, the lake, the surrounding fells and dales.

"There must have been Tolsons here as long as there have

been Birketts. Two of his sons have tenancies of land within this valley; two more have farms at Thirldale, just beyond the gates. That's about the area of the original estate. It was much bigger once, but we've sold off a lot . . . I'll like it if the entail would allow me to sell to the Tolsons, because of anyone, they've deserved to farm their own land." He nodded, as if reinforcing his own words. "The Tolsons—they're strong men, all of them, intelligent and competent. Tough, if you like, as farmers in this area have to be. I wish I could say I'd served any one thing as well as Tolson has served this house, but that wouldn't be the truth. He and his brother Edward were just a few years ahead of me. My father sensed the good material he had under his hands, and he saw that they both got to the Grammar School in Kesmere. Edward went on to become a solicitor—my father got him articled to a London firm. He made more than a success of it. Handled all the estate business until he died about two years ago—that, and a lot more important things. But George Tolson never had any idea of leaving Thirlbeck. This was his home. He's become quite a patriarch over the years—I swear he must have chosen all the wives for his sons. If he did, he showed eminently good sense. They're a clannish lot, but then, there *are* a lot of them and they like to hang together. Between them, with their tenancies of the estate, and the way they've worked together, they've kept this valley just about totally closed off from the world. That's the way my father wanted it though, that's the way he trained Tolson. I've sometimes thought how much better it would have been for my father and Thirlbeck if Tolson had been his son. Things seldom work out that way, do they . . . ?" He brought his lips together in a wry smile, something that switched the subject off.

"Now, Carlota, my love, would you be kind and mix another martini? I'm no good at it, Gerald—too heavy with the vermouth, Carlota says. How can she know when she never drinks them herself? Well, we could all stand a topping up. And then I'll take you upstairs."

She did it with those graceful, almost indolent movements. The chill sharpness of the fresh drink stung my palate, and renewed the sense of warmth that I had experienced before in this strange room. I was oddly at ease, relaxed, almost drowsy. I watched the fire, and the shadowed parts of the room seemed to grow darker; the voices of the others were low-toned, blending sometimes with the gusts of wind that blew down the long funnel of the valley. One of the great hounds licked a muddied paw; all of them seemed to doze, and yet I sensed that they were alert to every movement, and were waiting for the second that Askew would rise. I watched the firelight heighten the colours of the rug, and I looked at my suntanned hand holding the glass; I dreamed of Mexico and the magnificence of the landscape in that high, clear air. Suddenly, with a choking sense of loss, I wished Vanessa were here.

And then the noises began—a heavy clanging as if metal doors had closed shut. Both Gerald and I straightened, and glanced at Askew.

He gestured to dismiss the sound. "That will be Tolson closing the shutters. He's contrived to have metal shutters put on all the windows of the rooms on this floor. Part of his idea of security. One of his sons is a very handy mechanic as well as a farmer—knows about tractors and electrical things. I told Tolson that Ted could have made a fortune just fixing things for people—as things go these days. But he farms, and helps to take care of the place, and the shutters were his idea. I think he actually fitted them himself. Very few strangers have ever been in this house—in the valley—since I went away. The Tolsons are almost self-sufficient. George Tolson's grandchildren are helping run the farms now—some of the boys have left, of course. Not enough farming land to go round. One of the granddaughters lives here in the house, and the others, the daughters-in-law, and the girls who are old enough, have come in to help out since we arrived. Of course it would have been impossible to keep a staff here all these years. So long as this house has to be taken care of, I'm grateful to the Tolsons— all of them. I let Tolson do as he pleases. Nothing has ever gone seriously wrong yet. Carlota thinks—"

His words were stopped by more sounds of shutters being closed, a hollow ringing sound that echoed across the hall.

Askew rose, and the dogs all scrambled to their feet. It was like seeing an army come alive. He had evidently decided against telling us what the Condesa thought on the subject of Tolson and his family.

"Shall we go up, then? Take your drinks, if you like. Helps to keep the chill out." Then he looked down at the Condesa. "You stay, my love—no need to leave the fire. I won't be long."

She stretched her slender body in the big chair, and the shining black hair fell forward catching the light of the fire. There was an incredibly sensuous quality to the movement. "Yes, I'll stay. But will you pour me a whisky before you go, Roberto—please?"

She accepted it from his hand with a lazy, charming smile, and then her eyes went back at once to the fire, as if it were a substitute sun to which she was drawn.

As we went into the hall we heard another set of shutters clanging with its unmistakable metallic ring.

II

Gerald and Askew went ahead of me—talking, and I was taking my time, quite deliberately. At the landing where the two arms of the staircase branched, they waited for me.

"Mostly sixteenth century—except for the pele tower, which might go back to the twelfth. From the top of Great Birkeld up there you can see to the Scottish Border. In the old days they used to keep watch up there for Border raiders. From the church tower at Kesmere, you can just see the top of the pele tower here, if you know where to look—they used to light a beacon if the raiders were sighted. It gave the town a little more time to prepare, and from Kesmere the beacon lights would be passed all along the valleys so that the cattle could be rounded up into safety. Some of the townspeople used to come out here to the pele tower for protection. Very feudal. The Birketts exploited their power in every way possible, I'm afraid. The title dates from Elizabeth's time, and the first Earl built this house—more fitting, I suppose he thought it, for a nobleman, than sharing the accommodation with the cattle." He gestured to the hall below us. "They messed up parts of it trying to introduce modern conveniences about fifty years ago—electricity, and bathrooms, and the heating, which never really has worked. But it's better than outright freezing. But when something goes wrong—and that happens constantly—there's a devil of a job fixing it because they didn't leave any plans of what they did. No one knows exactly where the drains go, and all that sort of thing. If you try to repair a wall, you may find the ceiling about to come down on you, or else you've blundered into the flue of the chimney of the next room, which has got an unaccountable bend in it. I'm afraid the whole place needs a complete overhaul —but it won't be done in my time. If it is ever done . . ."

"What will happen to it?" I couldn't help saying it. We looked down on this hall of a beauty to match the exterior of the house, and upward to the sculptured ceiling which I now could see more clearly, and I couldn't bear the tone of detachment in Askew's voice, as if he cared not at all what happened to it.

He shrugged now. "I expect it will fall down. It will fall down when there isn't enough money to keep it together and when the Tolsons' ingenuity and energy is exhausted. Who knows—perhaps the National Trust will take it. I haven't offered it, and I don't know that there's enough money to endow it, or that I care to spend that much money on it. Perhaps you can end up giving too much to a mere building. Well, it doesn't concern me very much. Shall we go on?"

I felt myself almost hating him as he led the way up the rest of the stairs, and to the room that Gerald would occupy. He had treasure all about him, the building itself as well as the pieces of furniture we had already seen, and he didn't care. I hated his lack of interest, lack of caring. Had the blood gone thin and cold in those veins—was he truly as weary as he looked, too weary to make any effort to save his great inheritance? I didn't even try to think of what Gerald had told me about him, the tragedies of his life connected with this place, the gallantry he had shown during the war. He didn't deserve what he had inherited; he hadn't won it, or earned it, and so it gave back nothing to him.

Gerald's room, the first on a corridor that led off the gallery, was comfortable rather than imposing. It was stuffy—the windows and curtains closed. I thought the fire must have burned here all day—and an old-fashioned electric fire added its small warmth. It was furnished in a muddled, red-plush Victorian style, obviously a man's room. "My father used it," Askew said. "He moved over here after my mother died. I suppose it was warmer than anywhere else. He brought his desk up here. I thought you'd find it more comfortable than most we have to offer, Gerald. Bathroom's through here. Miss Roswell, I think Tolson means you to use this bathroom too—there's a door from the passage. I don't think there's a bathroom nearer your room than this, but if there is, then obviously it isn't usable just now."

Gerald waved airily. "Joanna will manage, Robert. At Hardy's we bring them up to manage. And she's been *very* well brought up. I saw to it myself. If there's a chance of Joanna finding an old bit of pottery or something of the kind, she'd climb into one of those chimney flues of yours."

I felt my anger at Askew extend to Gerald also. Gerald didn't have to make me appear such an earnest child. And yet, I supposed that was how I often did appear. I tossed his coat onto the bed, instead of hanging it as I would normally have done. "Not just now, Gerald . . ."

I was aware that I was tired and hungry, and despite two drinks and the relative warmth of this room, I was cold. I had probably sounded peevish, and so had let Gerald down. All at once it seemed an incredibly long time since we had left London that morning, and if I was tired, then Gerald must be more so. I glanced apologetically towards him, but he had chosen to pay no attention to my acidity. So I went and hung up his coat. Then I followed silently when Askew, after a few more words to Gerald, gestured to show me the way to my own room.

We came out on the gallery above the hall again, and then turned off into another corridor, closer to the front of the house.

Askew paused. "Let me see—yes, this is it. I haven't had time since we returned to get to see all the rooms, and there are far too many of them. I'd better leave this door open so you won't lose your way." It was yet another passage, a short one, with two doors opening off it at right angles to each other. Askew fumbled for a light switch, but there was none—only the light from the outer corridor showed the way. Even here, and all along the corridor we had left, was the same perfection of wood panelling and pointed arches above each door, the same carved cornices which were miniatures of those ones in the great hall. The passages were red-carpeted, and dusty; a few iron radiators had been spaced about but they didn't give off any heat. There was no furniture, no pictures, no mirrors. It was like walking backwards in time into an age where such things, even with the rich, were rarities.

Askew had opened the door facing the one we had come through, and was waiting for me to precede him. But there was a kind of involuntary stiffening of his body that warned me something had disturbed him.

"I hadn't remembered it quite like this." His tone was very low, as if he were talking to himself.

It seemed an immense room—its size perhaps increased by the fact that only one light burned here—an absurdly modern lamp perched, like a hurried afterthought, on a stool by the bed. The shadows, therefore, were black and deep, and the glow from the leaping flames of two opposite fireplaces didn't seem to bridge the darkness between them.

"Oh, God," he said softly. "Can you stand it? Perhaps I should ask Tolson . . ."

"Please, don't." I moved past him, fascinated. It was a room of sombre magnificence. A huge four-poster bed hung with dark blue velvet curtains hardly impinged on its space. There was a long oak stretcher table in the big rectangle of windows, and a straight-backed chair at one end. Another tapestry-covered chair stood before one of the fireplaces, with a footstool beside it. There was a carved oak chest, and a tall clothes press flanking each side of the second fireplace. A few pieces of blue Delft-ware stood about as the room's only ornaments; the biggest piece, a deep bowl, stood in the middle of the table. I moved towards it, and quite distinctly came the sad-sweet smell of last summer's roses. The bowl was full of petals, and I couldn't stop myself running my hand through them.

Askew had advanced a little from the doorway with an awkward diffidence I wouldn't have believed possible a few minutes ago. He noted my suitcase on the oak chest, and beside it, a bowl and jug of hot water, covered with a towel.

"A bit primitive," he said. "Better use the bathroom . . . I suppose the modernisations didn't get this far. Only one electric light—and even that's surface mounted."

I stared around the room again. It did not seem like a place just in this last hour disturbed from a period of long neglect. The wax polish on the table shone lustrously, as did the floor of wide oak plank. The Delft pieces had been recently dusted.

Askew paused before one of the fireplaces, the one where the solitary chair stood, placing his hand on the brick. "I suppose Tolson's right. It's dry enough. The chimney probably has a common flue with one of the ones in the hall. Tolson keeps fires in the hall all year round, he told me, so I suppose a certain amount of heat reaches here. There are some cupboards—oh, yes, here." He was opening wide doors in the panelling, one each side of the fireplace—in the sheer size of the room and the dimness I hadn't noticed how they broke the line of the wall, nor the carved wooden knobs to indicate the doors. "Shelves this side—hanging on this side." He shrugged and gestured at me. "Well, that's about the extent of the comfort we have to offer you—some padded hangers that look as if they came from the village fête, and a sachet of lavender. It's very English, isn't it? I know I'm back in England when I see that."

"Yes . . . it's England." It was here, solid and real as the arms beaten into the fireback, and the crested firedogs, long houndlike creatures, similar to the dogs that followed Askew, their thin limbs bearing the same shield as the fireback.

"Well," he said again, "I suppose it will do, though I wish Tolson could have managed something a bit less forbidding . . ."

"Do you think it's forbidding, Lord Askew? I like it."

He glanced at me curiously. "Do you? Funny, I never expect young people . . . Well, I'm afraid I don't know so many young people any more." He cut short his own line of musing. "At least the rain has cleared for the night. Shall I draw the curtains? It would make it cosier for you."

"No—leave them, please. One gets enough of drawing curtains just for privacy in London. There can't be anyone out there . . ."

"There shouldn't be." We moved at the same time towards the windows. I realised now that this room was directly over the library, and it was about equal size, and shared the same oblong bay of leaded-glass windows that faced out across the lake and the valley. The wind had blown the clouds clear of the mountains, and an icy moonlight struck obliquely through, bathing the whole area where the table stood in pale light. "Look," I said, "there's snow on the mountain."

"That's Great Birkeld—the highest around here. It catches all the weather. Quite often you can't see it for days at a time because of cloud. The word 'changeable' must have been invented for this country—mist, bright sun, pelting rain, clear moonlight—and in winter it can get so choked with snow Tolson uses a Land-Rover to get out of the valley. Heaven knows how the people stand it. I couldn't, not any more. No wonder poor Carlota is bewildered."

Three of the dogs had now crossed the room to join him. He stood staring out at the tarn, and the moonlight turned his hair to bright silver. Before us, the valley was shadowed in part, magnificently highlighted in others, and the snow on Great Birkeld laid a kindly cover over its formidable rock slopes. I literally saw a gust of wind ripple along the surface of the lake, heard its moan about the building, felt a draught from some unsealed window in the big bay. Askew hunched his shoulders as if he were cold.

"Mr. Tolson called it the Spanish Woman's room, Lord Askew. Why is it called that?"

He looked at me, and then moved slowly back into the centre of the room. He took his time about answering. Two more dogs had now moved in from the passage, and were squatting before one of the fires. Even the huge size of them belonged here. Askew fidgeted for a while without attempting a reply, checked the hanging cupboard again as if he were counting the hangers, went over and put his hand on the jug of hot water, lighted the candle on the mantel and carried it to the oak chest, so that its flame lighted a small, wooden-framed mirror above.

Then he came back to the window as if all the delays were exhausted.

"The Spanish Woman . . ." He took a deep breath. "The Spanish Woman was the second Countess of Askew. It was a kind of derogatory term given to her in this household which didn't welcome anyone both Catholic and Spanish. Her husband, the second Earl, was Catholic—many of the landowners still were Catholic, or were changing from Catholic to Protestant and back again according to who was on the throne. But this was Elizabeth's reign, and the house and the title were relatively new. The second Earl was somehow implicated in the Babington plot against Queen Elizabeth, accused of plotting to put Mary Queen of Scots on the throne, and so he lost his head on Tower Hill. He was a relic of the Old Faith, rather a fanatic, I'd judge. He spent some years abroad before he inherited the title, in Italy and in Spain—at the court of Philip the Second. When the news came that his father was dead he was urged to start back home, but before he left he committed, at Philip's urging, the supreme folly of marrying a Spanish bride. It may have been love—but much more likely it was politics. She was a noblewoman, distantly related to Philip, and of course Philip had never given up his hope of bringing England back to Catholicism. I wonder how well the second Earl weighed his choice. Of course, Philip was already preparing to send the Armada—it would be a great help to have a Catholic nobleman and a Spanish ally here in Cumberland. If Philip should successfully invade—or if Elizabeth should die and Mary have the throne—then he would have become one of the premier Earls of England, instead of a minor Border Lord. And then, along with his Spanish bride came a dowry—some in kind, a large amount promised in cash. The cash, incidentally, never was sent. The Spanish bride journeyed with a few ladies to join her husband and was just in time to see him arrested and taken off for trial. Philip might have had other plans for his little protégé, another Catholic lord, perhaps. But in the little time she and her husband spent together she had become pregnant—pregnant with a possible male heir. And her husband's brother, who would have succeeded if the marriage had been without issue, was Protestant.

"The stories were spun about her during the years, how many true, one doesn't know. It seems that her own servants were sent away, and she was left entirely alone—no friend but a young English serving boy from this household who had been with her husband on his travels and who spoke a little Spanish. How much hung on that pregnancy—with her brother-in-law probably hoping for a miscarriage, or the death of the mother and child at birth. There must have been precious little comfort or kindness for her. One imagines . . . I've imagined . . . how frightened she must have been, not knowing if Elizabeth's commissioners were riding North to question her, or if the next mouthful of food was poisoned. They say she took to walking as high and far on the Brantwick road as she could without danger—she never mounted horse for fear of losing the child. 'The Wanderer' was the name they gave her."

Suddenly he turned and motioned to me. "Look at the tarn down there—white and silver and innocent, isn't it? Well, she drowned in the tarn. Some were prepared to swear that she had been murdered by her brother-in-law. Her body was never recovered, nor the body of her husband's serving boy who rowed for her when she used the boat. If her body was ever recovered, it's buried in an unmarked place. Poor, lost, lonely little Spanish Woman—poor little bitch."

It was the first time I had really liked him. Now I began to see the shy young boy of Gerald's description, dreaming his dreams of a Spanish bride of nearly four hundred years ago. As he spoke I knew that the Spanish Woman had been a real person to him, not a dry family legend, repeated without thought. He had pictured her, 'The Wanderer,' growing heavy with her child, a political pawn, probably longing for the sound of her own language, the dry fierce heat of the Spanish plains. She must have written her sad letters at this table here, have sat in that chair by the fire, the chair that had no companion. Then I shook my head; I was falling into the Earl's mood. It was impossible that no one had disturbed the arrangement of this room in all these years, that new bed curtains had not been made, that that had really been her chair, with its footstool, suggesting that she had been a short, small woman. How did we know?—and yet Askew thought he knew. Could there ever have been anyone so alone? The tarn, black or silver, reflecting the sky above it, had known her final loneliness.

Beside me, Askew stirred, as if he really were waking from a dream. "You'll be all right here? You're sure? Perhaps I shouldn't have told you—"

"I'm glad you did. She has to have some friends, doesn't she? —the Spanish Woman?"

His smile now thanked me for sharing his dream, for not shattering it by ridicule, for not being afraid of whatever small, harmless ghost might sit by that fire. And I was lost to that smile, as I was sure many women had been, and I began to understand very well the presence of the other Spanish woman, the modern beauty who had followed him to this remote, cold world, blocked by the mountains, torn at by wind and rain. It would be easy enough to follow Robert Birkett if he had asked it.

"Come, dogs." They all rose as one and went with him. He gave me the same smile as he closed the door. I think he meant it.

III

Tolson hadn't become so much the butler that he attempted to unpack for guests. I sorted my clothes between the two cupboards Askew had opened—the hanging cupboard had a wooden rod on which the padded hangers rested, and at the back were the stout old oak pegs which served as hooks, probably there from the time the room and the cupboards had been panelled. There was no piece of furniture with drawers, so I laid my underwear and accessories in the cupboard that contained the shelves. I wasn't without a sense of clothes—no daughter of Vanessa's could have been. I even had a touch of her flamboyance in that respect which Harry Peers found amusing and unexpected. "For a girl like you, Jo, I mean—" and left me to decide what he did mean. Unlike the Condesa, though, I dressed for the English climate; the long skirt was of brilliant orange quilted cotton, and I wore it with a yellow high-necked sweater, and tied about the waist was a long black sash I had bought for a few pounds in one of Hardy's auctions of Victorian costume. I also wore the amber brooch which had been part of the contents of Vanessa's handbag discovered in the snow on the day of the plane crash. I wore it for her, and with love, thinking of the day she had bought it at another Hardy's sale of minor jewelry years ago. "It shall be yours, my pet," she had promised, but I had never had the heart to remind her of the promise because the gold and amber had seemed so much a part of Vanessa's personality. My thoughts slipped back to Hardy's—the sash, the brooch. It was one of the diversions and delights of working there—to spend one's lunch hour on the view days before the sales selecting the things one would like to buy for oneself, asking, as any member of the public could, what they thought a particular item would go for, and then watching the clock on the day of the sale to gauge when the lot number would come up, slipping up to the saleroom for a few minutes, and either getting the piece, or seeing it go beyond one's price to someone with more money, or more determination. That was another of the disciplines one learned at Hardy's—never to give way to the temptation to exceed the limit, to hold back the eagerness and the desire to possess. That had been Vanessa's weakness, and she had often bought without knowing how she could resell at a profit. Sometimes there was the excitement of bidding with someone else's money—for a client who couldn't be present in person, or who didn't want to be identified because their very interest in the object would push up the price among the dealers. And so they telephoned someone they knew on the staff, a price was set, and then the client would almost always say, "You can go a little over, but not too much." The nicety of discretion always came when one had to decide when too much was too much.

Then I remembered sadly what Askew had said. "You can end up giving too much to a mere building."

The gong sounded for dinner, a hollow sound that came from a long way off. I wasn't ready—I had slipped into the dreaming, dawdling habit that was too much my way. So I combed my hair quickly, and added a little more pale lipstick. It wasn't a beautiful face that looked back at me from the mirror, not beautiful in the way Vanessa's had been, or in the classic mould of that silken beauty downstairs at the library fire. It was a face that a hundred years ago might have been considered downright plain, but which now had come into fashion. "A twentieth-century face you've got, Jo," Harry had once said. From someone, perhaps my father, I had received the blessing of dark brows and lashes, looking odd with the light-coloured eyes, neither green nor grey nor blue. From Vanessa came the mouth, but wider than hers, and curving—perhaps to my detriment—to every mood. My mouth would always betray me—to laugh or to cry, and I never could control it very well. I made a mad sort of grimace at myself in the mirror for wasting time bothering about what couldn't be changed, and then I hurried downstairs to answer the gong.

* * *

The dining room was not crowded as the library had been. There was another long oak table which could only have fitted into a house of this size, Jacobean, I guessed, and in very good condition; there were a dozen or so chairs which matched it, two long sideboards on which the red pilot lights of electric hot trays shone eerily. There were more of those beautiful gilt-framed mirrors, and some very ordinary Chinese vases. There was here the same feeling of serenity that the almost-bare hall possessed, a sense of rightness. The dogs, all eight of them, were once more grouped about the fire.

The food was, unexpectedly, very good. There was onion soup with hot garlic bread wrapped in a towel, chicken in some kind of sauce that only a serious cook could make, the sort of pastry that one saw on the trolleys of the most expensive restaurants, and a single piece of marvellously flavoured Wensleydale cheese. We helped ourselves from the dishes on the sideboards; none of the Tolson family made an appearance. There was a beautiful hock, poured in Bohemian engraved glasses with green stems. I hardly spoke through the whole meal; I was hungry and the food was delicious. When it was finished I said so with no trace of false politeness.

"Tolson's granddaughter does most of it," Askew said. "Jess—Jessica. She's brilliant, really. A natural cook, and quite a brain, too. Won a scholarship to Cambridge. She's one of those geniuses who lap up all their A levels—or whatever they call it—at sixteen. Tolson said she came out of school at Kesmere with one of the best passes in the whole country."

"She's here now, though?" I said. "I thought term hadn't ended yet."

Askew frowned. "She never did take up the scholarship. I'm not sure why. Perhaps she overdid it a bit. Tolson said she was quite seriously ill about three years ago. Perhaps they thought she was too young—or not well enough—to send away from home. Undoubtedly, she's her grandfather's pet. He says she just prefers to stay here. Highly strung . . . I suppose they're afraid of what will happen to her out in the world. A pretty little thing, too. She must be going on twenty now."

The Condesa smiled. "She will marry, Roberto. She will marry someone her formidable grandfather approves of, and live very near to home. This house is more her home than the farm she comes from. Wherever one goes in this house, there she is—"

"But she does help with the housework," Askew interrupted. "Does a great deal of it as far as I can see. So why shouldn't she be around?"

"Is there housework on the top of the pele tower? I've seen her there."

"I wish you hadn't, then. The pele tower isn't safe. But then a bright, imaginative child—why shouldn't she go where she pleases? She probably has all sorts of romantic fantasies about this house."

"She is not a child, Roberto," the Condesa said quietly. "Highly strung, brilliant—a wonderful cook. Yes. A child? I do not think so."

He shrugged. "Well, let's not upset her. It may mist and snow and rain, but at least we have good food. Don't we, dogs?"

At his word all the hounds turned and lifted their ears expectantly, and then settled down again as they realised that no movement was coming from Askew. Askew laughed at the kind of mirrored image they all gave of each other. "Extraordinary lot, aren't they?"

"More than that," Gerald said. "I almost had Joanna turn the car around when they appeared. It's hardly . . . well, it's hardly *decent*, my dear Robert. So many of them, and so huge!"

"Don't blame me. It's Tolson's hobby. They're his dogs, but since the instant I arrived they've unaccountably attached themselves to me. I've never even fed them—in fact, it's one of Tolson's strictest rules that they must never be fed from anyone's hand. He doesn't want them being a nuisance at the table—or, for that matter, taking food from a stranger."

"Does he show them?"

Askew looked surprised. "Why . . . no. I suppose I don't realise how strange they must look to outsiders. But there have always been Irish wolfhounds at Thirlbeck. There was in my young days an even bigger pack than this. Somehow Tolson managed to feed and keep alive at least one breeding pair during the war—not the easiest thing to do with food rationing as it was. I suspect they often got things that were meant for people. Tolson wouldn't put his patriotism before his care for Thirlbeck. The farm made record yields in those years, so I think Tolson must have worked like three men, and all his sons worked, though they were only kids then. I suppose he thought he'd earned his right to keep the dogs."

Gerald leaned forward. "There's something particularly important about them?"

Askew looked rather embarrassed. "I don't really know. It's just that tradition has it that there have always been wolfhounds at Thirlbeck. They're a very ancient breed, and were very nearly extinct in this century. They're said to be the largest dog in the world—and the only one that hunts by sight as well as smell. They're famed in Celtic literature, Tolson says, for bringing down enormous stags by their own power—when you consider the size of them, the height, well, I suppose you can believe it. This lot doesn't seem to go after the deer, though. They stick pretty close to the house, and since I've been here, they've stuck pretty close to *me*."

He extended the hock to refill my glass. "Do they always stay together?" I asked. "None of them ever goes off alone?"

"Not that I've noticed. There's always eight about whenever I bother to count them. They seem to enjoy each other's company. In any case, they all stick to me like shadows . . . sometimes I wish they wouldn't."

Then I was aware that his look hadn't been one of embarrassment, but unease. He was gentle with the hounds, and offhandedly affectionate. He wasn't afraid of them, but I had the feeling that he wished they weren't there, which was exactly the same feeling I experienced when he had said they never went off alone. I shivered, and hoped that no one had noticed. This was the dog—one of these dogs, I would swear—which had dashed across the road before my eyes at the birch copse that evening, nearly causing me to crash. I wondered if Gerald was also thinking the same thing. But Gerald hadn't seen that dog, and neither of us had had any foreknowledge that this pack of wolfhounds, with their amiable, shaggy faces and gentle eyes, were the traditional hounds who had for centuries guarded the Birketts and Thirlbeck. I had caught some of Askew's sense of unease.

"I don't know why Tolson bothers with metal shutters when there's this lot around," Gerald said. "They're better security than anything short of armed guards."

"Double insurance, Gerald. I suppose he thinks that if his electrical gadgets fail, the dogs won't. For whatever reason, I wouldn't dream of interfering with his arrangements."

"Nor would I, Robert. They're admirable . . . admirable." Gerald beamed over the hock. He was at his best at this time of the evening, with good food and wine inside him. His pleasant, well-preserved face glowed; good-will came from him visably. All he needed now was a little Mozart.

The wine had brought other thoughts to the Condesa. "Roberto tells me your father lives in Mexico," she said to me. "Myself I do not care so much for abstract painting, but Roberto says he is very good—famous."

"He is good," I conceded. "I don't think *he* would agree that he was famous. He just keeps painting—and in the last ten or so years he's begun selling very well. That's the only difference for him. It hasn't changed his life . . . not at all."

She shrugged; her amused look indicated that if a man didn't care whether he was famous or not, then he was more than an eccentric. "He is fortunate living in Mexico—always the sun. There is quite amusing society in Mexico City and in Acapulco. You remember how it was in Acapulco, Roberto?"

"Yes, my love, I remember. For once you had enough sun. You have Spain in your bones, Carlota, and you're not really happy without that eternal sun."

She shrugged again. "And this is in your bones? This mist and damp? Then give me Spain." She suddenly remembered me. "Does your father go to Acapulco in the season?"

I almost laughed, and it wouldn't have been fair because she could not possibly have known what my father was like. "No —never. He lives in the mountains south of Taxco. A very remote hacienda. He never leaves it if he can help it."

She shuddered delicately at the thought. "Never . . ."

"He doesn't like cities. For him to go to Mexico City is a torture because of the smog. It starts him coughing. He's no good in damp places either, and down at sea level it's too humid in Mexico."

"I remember he didn't like damp places," Askew said slowly. "He still has that weak chest, then? A bad legacy from a German prison camp. I remember it rained so much when he was here, and he was trying to paint, and not succeeding at all. That autumn was very wet—and there were some leaks in the roof . . ."

"He was here?" I repeated. "*Here*—at Thirlbeck?"

"Of course. That's when I knew him." He looked at me in

puzzled surprise. "He and Vanessa rented that little lodge up there by the gate where you came in. The roof did leak, but it wasn't a ruin at that time. I would have fixed it if they had been going to stay on. But it wasn't right for either of them—for different reasons. I was grateful to them for being here then—it was my one attempt to try to live at Thirlbeck, and they were good friends. They made the attempt bearable, even if in the end it didn't work out. I remember they left with the first snow —and I left soon after." He looked directly at me. "They never told you they were on the Thirlbeck estate?"

I shook my head. "My mother said they had rented a cottage in the Lake District the summer the war ended. And my father—well, I didn't really know him until a few weeks ago. There were so many other things to talk about."

"I can imagine." He looked around the room, this red-curtained fastness against the wind that blew outside, the firelight lapping the dogs on the rug. "We shared many a bottle of wine in those few months. We had all survived a war, and we were pretty heady with the triumph of just that simple fact, so we were pretty reckless with what remained of the cellar my father laid down. There wasn't much else to be reckless with—petrol and clothes were rationed, and so was food, but we didn't do too badly with that—this being a farm and the valley alive with game. We made a bit of a thing about trying to put some weight on Jonathan—he'd been repatriated from Germany and discharged almost at once, with orders to find himself a place in the country, and get some fresh air and rest. I think the Army kicked me out very smartly because I was a bit of an embarrassment to them. So we were all celebrating survival on the contents of my father's cellar—pretty good, it was too. I suspect we forced the gaiety at times. Or perhaps I forced it—they were both quite a lot younger than I, and I suppose I wanted to show I could keep up. But even while we drank up the cellar and ate illegal venison, I suppose we all knew that nothing was working out—for any of us. We knew we were all going to leave."

I couldn't help seeking Gerald's eyes across the table. His rosy face had become almost pallid; I hoped I hadn't betrayed the same shock while Askew had been speaking to me. We had, Gerald and I, been thinking of Thirlbeck as uncharted ground, and already we had seen treasures here. And Vanessa, whom we both had believed we had known so well, had once spent a whole summer and autumn among these lovely things —she had known Thirlbeck as only, perhaps, the Tolsons knew it. And she had said nothing of this place—nothing.

IV

We went to the drawing room for coffee—again a pot kept hot on an electric plate, and we served ourselves. By now I think both Gerald and I had come almost to expect what we found —a room only a little less crowded than the library, but still holding almost the same amount of beautiful pieces arranged without any thought of display, but simply for the convenience of herding them into this room. This would be one of the rooms with the metal shutters, I thought, as I ran my finger over the dusty top of a magnificent *bureau plat* mounted with porcelain plaques which I made a rough guess as being from the Sèvres factory. There were other pieces almost as fine in the room—commodes, pier tables, marquetry writing tables, gilt-wood and tapestry chairs with the same rough string tied across them. A few sofas and chairs of about the Thirties vintage, covered in the same faded chintz as those in the library, were there to be sat on. The rest of the contents of the room would have made one of the most exciting sales of fine French furniture Hardy's had ever mounted—if it ever came to auction. I could have cried out with impatience at the elaborate game we all played—no one mentioning even the smallest item of furnishing while we drank coffee from inexpensive earthen-ware cups. Gerald talked with the Condesa, avoiding my glances towards him. If he was as shaken as I was by the thought that Vanessa must once have seen all this splendour he had managed to recover himself. Perhaps it had not been like this in Vanessa's time; perhaps these pieces had been scattered through the whole house, and she had never seen them in this way, heaped together like a miser's hoard. But if she had known Thirlbeck, and even with the limited knowledge she had possessed in those days, she would have recognised the best of these pieces—and who could have forgotten them? Who would not remember them as the prices of works of art shot up higher and higher? Had she given no thought at all to this treasure trove on the day that Mrs. Dodge's Louis XVI *bureau plat* sold for 165,000 guineas, more than double the previous world record price for a single item of furniture? I didn't think so. She had been at the sale and had been as astonished and as breathless as everyone else at the prices reached. And yet she had said nothing.

I looked again around the room and found the thing that seemed missing from the whole house. While there were several beautiful mirrors, there were no pictures. There were not even the usual dull, crudely executed portraits of the Birketts through the centuries. Their total absence made me think that in some other room with metal shutters there would be frames and frames stacked against the walls, and among them there might be just one picture that came up to the quality of the pieces we saw about us here. Then, thinking of the prices rising daily at Hardy's and other auction houses, knowing as much as a reputable house did know about the more dubious side of the business, and what went on between private and not honest dealers, I began to be afraid for Thirlbeck. It needed now, much more than metal shutters, the remote loneliness of this valley, the pack of wolfhounds and the barbed wire. With every day that passed it would become more and more a target for those who knew what treasures it possessed. And Vanessa had said nothing.

There was a sense of restlessness in the room, as if we were all holding back from saying what we most wanted to say. Gerald and the Condesa were seated on a sofa, talking, both of them using their smooth sophistication to cover the fact that they were talking of nothing that much interested them. The Condesa, improbably, had produced a small travel bag and taken a frame filled with fine canvas from it. Gerald watched, in evident fascination, as she stitched at the intricate petit point of the design. Askew smiled a little as he stood beside me at the table where the coffee service was laid out, nodding towards the Condesa. "Unexpected, isn't it? I always see her as the sort of person who should be carrying skis, or skin-diving equipment—and she does both those things expertly, and a lot more besides. But wherever she is in the world out comes the piece of tapestry, and you can be sure that every man in the room will eventually gravitate to her side to watch the progress of the work, and compliment her. I accuse her of using it as a secret weapon, but she swears that there are twenty-four chairs in her mother's house near Seville which need new covers, and it is almost a life's work. How demure she looks, doesn't she? —like a girl in a convent. No doubt that was where she learned it."

"Yes," I said lamely. And yes, I thought, one could easily imagine her skiing and skin-diving and doing all the sportive things that the rich did to pass the time. Why did I suppose she was rich? Only because she moved and spoke and dressed as the rich did, and she had that carelessly elegant look that is only produced by a great deal of time and money.

Did I let my small jealousy of her show too much? Askew turned at once and refilled my cup, holding out the cream and sugar, attending to me as if he thought I had been neglected. As he poured brandy he said, "So they teach you well at Hardy's, do they?"

What did he mean? Was he expecting that I, the least experienced of them here in this room, would be the one to break the silence, to make the first remark about the furniture. Did he want that? "They do their best," I said carefully. "They try to find out what you might be good at—if you're going to be good at anything, that is. Then you learn what you can by handling, seeing, listening."

"And are you any good?"

I shrugged. "Who knows—yet? Oh, I'm long past my Front Counter training, which I suppose first of all is a drilling in manners—there are so many different kinds of people to deal with, and all of them carefully. We spend all our time on the Front Counter answering little questions, and when someone brings something for a valuation, phoning for the experts to come from the various departments to the interview rooms. Sometimes the oddest things turn up—and the oddest sorts of people. But one has to be polite, even if *they* sometimes aren't. And there's the sort of person whose feelings can be hurt quite easily by someone being offhand, or hurried with them. They might have brought in something they believe is quite valuable, and you know yourself—even without getting the expert's opinion—that it isn't worth five pounds. But you must never let them think it's been a waste of time—for us, or them. They might have something really valuable that they will someday bring along. And there's the other side of it. When you get some experience and are called up to give an opinion on something, you can sense sometimes that what the person is thinking of selling is something very precious to them—something they'd rather not part with. That's when the most tact is needed, making them feel easier about it, if possible making them think it will be bought by someone who will cherish it—even if we know it's most likely to go to a dealer who will resell it."

He nodded. "Pride—yes, the most difficult quality to deal in." Then he added: "What do *you* handle mostly—pictures?"

I wondered if he said it to keep polite conversation going, or if he wanted to know how expert I might be in something that would be of particular importance here and now. "Ceramics. It was my decision. I stayed on the Front Counter until an opening came in the ceramics department. My father wrote from Mexico to Vanessa and offered to pay for me to go and study art history in Italy for a few years, but I was already hooked on bits of Meissen and Chelsea and tin-glazed earthenware. It must have disappointed him—but he never said anything. What I'd really like to do is Oriental ceramics, but that's very specialist, and there was no place for me in that department. I suppose everyone who gets interested in ceramics ends up by going back to the Oriental things—and if they're really hooked, I suppose they'll spend their lives searching for Attic vases. Oh . . . I'm sorry . . ."

He inclined his head, as if what I had been saying had absorbed him, which I doubted. He had his own style of good manners. "Sorry? . . . why?"

"I'm talking shop. Once you get touched by the mania you're apt to run on, forgetting that other people aren't as crazy about the subject as yourself. Gerald thinks it's the worst form of bad manners. Fishing, he says . . . trying to smell out if someone has something they might be persuaded to put up for sale."

He laughed aloud, a spontaneously genuine sound that caused Gerald and the Condesa to raise their heads, and I could see a faint flush on the Condesa's pale olive skin. She didn't much like me, I thought, and it made me feel better about my own burst of jealousy of her.

"Gerald, your protégé here has just told me she's been fishing, and that you wouldn't approve. Shall we make her fishing worthwhile, Gerald? Do you think she'd like to see La Española?"

Gerald leaned forward. "It *is* here, then?"

"Of course. Where else would it be? It will stay here now as long as it exists or the house exists. Of course I won't be alive when it happens, but I wonder if the curse will finally leave La Española when this house tumbles before the bull-dozers, or gives up to the weather."

Gerald was controlling his excitement, but I knew him well enough to know it was there. "I would very much like to see it myself, Robert. You surely know, don't you, that the Gemological Institute of America has it listed as 'present whereabouts unknown, but believed still to be in the possession of the Birkett family.'"

"The Birketts don't possess it—they're possessed by it."

The Condesa gestured impatiently. "Roberto, you make too much of this silly superstition. If you were determined, it could be sold tomorrow. Many people would prefer to have La Española in the bank than money." She slipped the embroidery frame into its bag. "Come then, show Mr. Stanton. If it is never to leave this house, it may be his only chance." She got to her feet, and Gerald rose also. She had neatly cut me out by making this showing of what they all called La Española for Gerald's benefit and pleasure, not for mine. But it was my arm Askew took as he headed towards the door.

He led us to the fourth room of those which opened directly off the great hall, opposite the dining room. There were wide passages between the rooms probably leading to the other square bays of the house, but no lights burned there, and they seemed dusty and disused. The room we came to was panelled like the rest, in a severe, beautiful, linenfold. One wall had had shelves built against it at a later date, and most of this was filled with thick boxes—not books—bound in identical red leather, with dates stamped in gold that had dulled with the years; they probably were estate records, I thought, and household papers filed there for convenience. And then at some date in this century the binding had stopped and ordinary box files, the inexpensive kind found in any stationer's shop, filled the lower shelves. There were two desks in the room—a large carved one whose handsome bowed-legged chair had its back to the fireplace, and another, close by one of the red-curtained windows, a humbler, roll-topped one, rather battered, as if it had once served a schoolroom. It had a swivel chair whose cushion was torn and shedding its stuffing. The big desk had only a blotter on its leather surface, an unused blotter. What went on at the roll-top no one could tell; it was closed.

"Just a minute," Askew said. He left us and hurried off across the hall to open a green baize door under the staircase, revealing what seemed to be a service passage. "Tolson, are you there, Tolson?" We heard their voices, and a minute later Askew was back with us. All the dogs had made the short journey with us, and they all crowded into the room as Askew came back. I had a brief glimpse of Tolson's figure in the passage; I thought there was disapproval in the stare he gave to us, then he gave a kind of a shrug, and turned back.

The room was lighted only by a single lamp on the big desk; the coals of a dying fire glowed in the grate. "This is really Tolson's room," Askew said. "He does most of his work here." He nodded towards the telephone on an oak stool beside the roll-top desk. While he spoke his hand was feeling for a known spot at the side of the carved mantel; then he went and touched another place in the panelling itself.

"Such elementary precautions," he said, "but Tolson insists on them. I had to have him turn the alarm system off." He had opened a small door cut in the panelling itself, its dimensions fitted exactly to a natural division of the panel, so that no unnatural line showed. "My father had this little cubbyhole made after La Española became too famous and troublesome." He fumbled again within the cavity, and a light came on, showing a velvet-lined interior behind a thick glass screen. Wordlessly, the three of us watching moved closer.

It was a blue-white stone, roughly octahedral in shape, about an inch and a half at its widest part. It was touched at four points by simple cage grips, and strung on a gold chain of medium weight. It seemed as if only its natural planes had been polished, and the stone itself relatively uncut, and yet with only these large surfaces revealed, the refraction of light from its heart, the inner facets, was of extraordinary brilliance. It seemed too awesomely big to be a gemstone. There was something almost crude and stunning in its size, and yet it lay there so quietly, so innocently on its black velvet cushion. Askew swung open the glass screen, and gently lifted the cushion out. Even with that simple movement the light sprang from it as if it were a living flame. He lifted the massive thing on its chain and swung it gently.

"La Española—the Spanish Woman," he said softly. He watched it himself as it moved in its pendulum swing. "Oddly, it was the serving boy who had been in Spain with the second Earl who gave it its name. He spoke Spanish rather badly. When the Countess came to Thirlbeck from Philip's court she and the jewel which came as part of her dowry were called the same thing. How crude and barbaric she must have thought the manners of this household."

Gerald leaned closer. "May I . . . ?" He gestured, and Askew slipped the gold chain over his hand. Gerald took the velvet cushion and carried both to the desk where the light fell directly upon it.

"I wondered if I would ever see it again," he mused, turning the great stone in his fingers. "I remember the time in the Thirties when your father sent it to Hardy's for auction and there were no buyers."

"Yes—and there were lines of unemployed outside on the day of the sale protesting about rich Earls with diamonds to play with while they were hungry."

"You were fighting in Spain then," Gerald said, without ever looking away from the stone.

"I was, but I still heard about it—not from my father, of course. He was right to try to get rid of it, but it wasn't the time to sell, and the reputation of the wretched thing went before it. So 'believed still to be in the possession of the Birketts' is all too true."

"Yes, but that same book on diamonds from the Gemological Institute is studded with entries of famous stones which gives their history and simply end 'present whereabouts unknown,' or 'the such and such bank deny knowledge of the stone.'" All the time he spoke he was bent over the gem, turning it, moving it in his fingers, apparently fascinated, as I was, by the uncountable rays of light thrown back from its great heart. "You might have taken it somewhere and had it cut into small stones and disposed of. None of the buyers of the stones would have known they were buying part of the reputation of La Española." He glanced up enquiringly at Askew. "Somewhere about two hundred carats it runs to, doesn't it?"

"The last jeweler who examined it gave it a few more—but significantly he admired, sighed, and shook his head. He made no offer. That was after the Terpolini affair. That really was the kiss of death. There had been stories before, but only stories. After two attempts to steal it went wrong, the underworld began to believe the stories, and they'll probably make no more attempts until the next generation comes along to laugh at the superstition. With the Terpolini affair the publicity was enormous. After fifteen years people still remember. So that entry 'believed still to be in the possession of the Birkett family' is right because there's been no chance to make it otherwise. Here it lies, in its primitive little cave, uninsured, because I can't afford the insurance, guarded by nothing more than a few electric wires and alarms, with a small emergency generator to use in the event of a power failure. No one to guard it except Tolson and the dogs. It would be absurdly easy to steal, except that no one wants to touch it. No one *will* touch it."

"Why not?" I asked.

Askew looked at me. "Ah, yes—fifteen years would be too long for you. What does a child care about diamonds? You see . . . the story still circulates that a curse was put upon this stone. Sounds ludicrous, doesn't it? No one really believes in curses, do they? And yet no one has come near it in fifteen years."

"Two hundred carats," Gerald mused. "Worth . . . well, with a stone of this quality, blue-white, flawless . . . at about four or five thousand pounds a carat. There's a million pounds, and its value rising every day as money devalues. Properly cut, it could make two or three big gems, and a lot of smaller ones. Could actually be worth much more, even with the carats lost in the cutting. And no one wants to steal it, much less buy it."

"That's about it, Gerald." Now Askew touched it, his long fingers tentative, slightly reluctant in the movement. "So here she lies, poor, neglected, lonely little bitch. She was meant to shine on the neck or hand of a beautiful woman, and here she lies, closed in her dark little tomb, unseen, unloved. La Española . . . the Spanish Woman. She brought it to the Birketts, and it seems she means to keep it forever."

"How so?" I was now spellbound by the sight of the gem, feeling it a living thing, almost.

"This," he said, "was intended as a portion of her dowry, the Spanish Woman's. A dowry assembled in a hurry for her by Philip the Second, because her family could not provide one. He wanted to send her to her English husband with something substantial as evidence of good faith. The rest—the money was to follow. It had just come into his possession, and he had it polished just a little, and mounted virtually in its rough state. That, of course, makes it more valuable now. An antique cut, and the inevitable loss of parts of the stone would have brought down its size and shape. As it is, it's ready for all that a modern cutter can take from it. Well, it might have been her dowry, intended for her husband and his family, but she never let it go—the little Spanish girl. About seventeen, they think she was when she came here. Old enough for those times, I suppose. Then Elizabeth's men took her husband away, and beheaded him, and she was alone, except for the child she carried. She was in mortal danger, and she must have known it."

His voice now had taken on the tone it had had upstairs as he had gazed out over the silvered tarn, a distant tone as if he repeated the tale he had gone over many times in his mind, a part of him. "The story goes that each day in calm weather she would have the serving boy who had been her husband's favourite row her on the tarn. He must have grown attached to her, though I suppose they could exchange few enough words. They say she wore the jewel always, a kind of talisman because it had come from the hands of Philip, whom I suppose must have already seemed a saint to her. They say she waited endlessly for word from him—instructions as to what she must do, where she must go. She would have married anyone he had commanded—but I can't help thinking she must have, more than anything, longed to be summoned back to Spain. So far as we know, Philip sent no word. She just waited—waited for her child to be born, and waited to know if it would be a boy, and therefore Earl of Askew, displacing her Protestant brother-in-law. The brother-in-law, another Robert Birkett by name, evidently intended that the child should never be born, and the mother should not survive to marry another Catholic nobleman in the North, and join two important families. They say . . . well, who really knows how it happened, because no one ever wrote it down, and almost four centuries is a long time for a story to twist upon itself."

It was odd, how detached he sounded, as if he weren't speaking of his own family. "They say, though, that he waited for a calm, but misty day—October. The tarn can be totally visible one minute, totally obscured the next. When she was out on the lake he rowed after her, taking a younger brother with him. The Spanish Woman was not to have a chance to survive, nor the boy with her. She was almost back at the landing stage, here at the shallows at this end near the house when the two boats came together. No one precisely knows what happened, of course. They must first have beaten the boy from the boat, and clubbed him so that he drowned. And then they turned on the Spanish Woman. The story goes that they could hear her cries from the mist, but no one could see what was happening. They wanted the jewel, of course. They couldn't let her drown and the jewel go with her. She must have struggled fiercely, but the thing was finally taken from her neck. We aren't certain that this is the original chain, so God knows how brutally they might have treated her to get it. The stories must have varied. You know . . . fog distorts sounds so much, and most of the serving people were hugging the kitchen fire that day. But there were gardeners about, and shepherds and herdsmen. The sound had to have reached them. And someone whispered afterwards that he had heard the Spanish Woman's voice, as if she knew she was finished, without hope for her life or her child's. And then she shouted what sounded to them like the motto of the Birketts—probably she reverted to Latin, the only language she had in common with anyone in this country. I would think she had mouthed it to herself many times after she was married and sent to England. It's as wild and aggressive a motto as any untamed Border Lord would wish. The gentler manners and ways were for those in the South then—"

"The motto?" I asked.

" 'Caveat Raptor'—roughly, 'Who Seizes, Beware.' Perhaps she interpreted it as 'who takes . . .' Did she mean the jewel, her life, the life of her child? Did she even say it? The Earl and his brother said nothing. They swore they were riding towards the other end of the tarn. They heard cries, they said —nothing more. The boat had overturned, and the two had been drowned. But her body was never recovered, and they had the jewel. The new Earl simply said she had not worn it that day. No one believed that part of it, but they began to believe that the boy had not been drowned at all. He survived, a living witness, and perhaps the origin of the stories that began to fly about."

Askew shrugged. "One wonders if this part of it isn't pure fantasy. They say the boy was hunted, but never found. His family was put off the estate, forced to seek work in Carlisle, where most of them starved. The story fattened, though, and more began to attach to a curse on the jewel, especially when the Earl broke his neck after a drunken tumble on the stairs. He had been, they said, displaying the jewel to one of Elizabeth's council members who was riding through from Scotland. By this time the jewel itself was being talked about as La Española, and they were trying to forget the Spanish Woman herself."

Askew leaned back against the desk. "They didn't succeed in burying her, did they? Here we are, still talking about her. The story goes that the lad who had been with her in the boat that day lived still in this valley as a fugitive, raiding the Earl's cattle and sheep, and waiting for the day of vengeance. He didn't have it. After the Earl's death, his brother, the fourth Earl, died peacefully in his bed, but not before this house had been raided and the jewel, along with anything else portable— sheep, cattle, plate—and the young women—had been taken by Borderers. It was the last time the Borderers ever came this way. The odd thing was that the leader of the raid never got beyond the limit of this valley. When they were through the worst part of Brantwick, and the way out seemed easy, his horse stumbled and rolled on him. There seemed no reason for it. He was left there alone to die, and none of his raiding party would touch the jewel. There was blood from his pierced lungs on La Española when it came back to Thirlbeck."

Now I could make myself touch it on its velvet cushion. Somehow I had expected it to feel warm, as if it had just left the throat of the Spanish Woman, or the hand of the Borderer. "Could they really have left something like this with a dying man?"

"So they say. They must have begun to feel pretty frightened of it, and no one really wanted it back at Thirlbeck. They had begun to believe the motto, and the curse . . . and the Spanish Woman, whom they wanted to forget, was a permanent legend. In their memories, she never died. Perhaps it was the boy who was with her, or perhaps it was just someone, still a Catholic, who wished her passage to be marked, because she had no grave in consecrated ground. A stone marker appeared by the tarn, with some crude letters on it. As many times as the Earl removed it, it reappeared—it, or another like it. He began to see that he could not lay the ghost, and so he left her monument alone, to let the grass grow up around it, and the winds wipe out its legend. And La Española stayed on. They say that in her old age, Elizabeth herself was offered the jewel by the fourth Earl, as some sort of bribe for favour—you remember she had a passion for jewels. But this one she refused. The family history has it that there were several attempts on it over the years—nothing very serious, and none successful. This is a remote valley. Travel by road was difficult and slow—too slow for thieves. Until the First World War help was easy to come by, and cheap. There were plenty to guard it, in a haphazard sort of way. There was a serious attempt on it in the Twenties, but the thieves took the way out of the valley that you came in by today. At the worst bend, where the road cuts through the birch copse, they went out of control. The car crashed and burned, and they with it. The diamond, of course, survived. Tolson says to this day there are a few scraps of rusted metal with the bracken growing through it, which are the remains of the car. After that, my father lodged it in a safe deposit vault in Manchester. It was there three years before there was an attempt, by tunneling, on the vaults. Someone from this house must have given them information, because no one but my father was supposed to know where it was. And they were selective. The security guard was thought to be involved, but that was never proved, because he died with them. It was something about the tunnel—what they hadn't reckoned on was meeting part of the old Roman Wall, which no one knew was there. It collapsed on them on the way out. They had been through a few strong boxes besides ours, but La Española was by far the most valuable part of the haul. It came out covered with dirt, and shining just as ever."

He touched the gem again on its cushion. "It sounds odd, but I think you'll see the point. La Española wasn't especially important to us. No one wore it—its value didn't represent nearly as much as the land we owned at the time. No one thought too much of it until my father died, and it was assessed for death duties as part of the estate."

What he passed over in that slight pause was what I remembered Gerald had told me—the period in prison, the war, the decorations, the return to Thirlbeck, and his absence until barely a week ago.

"I myself made only one attempt to sell it after that. It had come back to Thirlbeck, and it stayed here. The Manchester bank wasn't anxious to have it again, and I—well, perhaps I hoped someone *might* take it from Thirlbeck and relieve me of all its responsibility. But no one did try. From time to time the newspapers would rake up its history in lurid detail, and people were frightened to make the attempt. But finally I negotiated a sale, and Tolson brought La Española to Milan. And that was where the Terpolini affair burst on the world. The publicity was too much—all the old stories of the curse were revived, and a few tacked on. The underworld, as well as those who buy diamonds as an investment, were scared off again."

"The Terpolini affair?" I said. "What was that?"

Askew looked at me. "I keep forgetting you're so much younger. You've heard of Terpolini?"

"The opera singer? She's dead, isn't she?"

"Not dead, but she might as well be. She was at the height of a very sensational career. She had the gift of star quality, as well as a wonderful voice, and everything she did was news. She was the mistress of the oilman, Georgiadas. He was—still is—strongly superstitious, but it was his belief then that the gods looked with particular favour on him. His every endeavour was blessed with good fortune. In fact, he was the darling of the gods. Until he encountered La Española. I sold it to him, you see—well, I had sold it to him subject to expert examination, which was why Tolson brought it to Milan. It was everything they had hoped for. It was to be cut, naturally, and everyone supposed that Constanzia Terpolini would have the biggest stone that came from the cut. But just to emphasise her triumph, her dominance of Georgiadas, who isn't an easy man to dominate, she asked to wear it, just as it is, uncut, on its simple chain, when she opened the season at La Scala, in *Turandot*. The papers were full of the story, she was photographed in costume, wearing it. But the next day the papers all over the world were full of the story of her fall down that long flight of stairs in the last act. When it became clear to everyone in the opera house that she couldn't rise, they brought down the curtain. She never saw another curtain go up. A fractured spine, which paralysed her from the neck down. On the same day, Georgiadas's only son was lost in a sailing accident off Crete. That was the day the gods really turned their back on Georgiadas. Terpolini still exists in a private sanitorium near Geneva. Georgiadas stopped visiting her a long time ago, though he still pays her bills. He is more superstitious than ever, only now he fears the gods—keeps looking over his shoulder. La Española was returned to me, the sale incomplete—and Tolson brought it back to Thirlbeck."

Once again Askew's forefinger went out to touch the gem, that blue-perfect gem which seemed now to cry to me with the cries of that little Spanish girl in her last moments. I glanced quickly at his face, the lines in it appeared sharper now as the light from the top of the shade struck them. He did not regard the gem with bitterness or distaste, only a trifle ruefully.

"What's the capital gains tax now, Gerald—thirty per cent? I could still live quite a long time on what was left if I could sell it—if La Española were not a priceless, valueless piece of carbon drenched in superstition and greed. Myself, I don't believe in the curse—but I'm a Birkett. Others do. And so my unfortunate heir will have to scratch about for the death duties on something *he* probably won't be able to sell, or insure, either. It was quite a legacy she left us, the little Spanish Woman. I wonder if her spirit mocks us now, when we have come to this?"

Carlota spoke. "And you say you don't believe, Roberto? I think you believe more than anyone else. If you had only the will to carry it to Amsterdam yourself and find someone to cut it, it could be sold and there would be no more money problems for you—and the Birketts would be rid of La Española at last.

It is so simple . . . no publicity, no auction, no more stories . . ." Her tone had grown fainter though, and I think we all had noticed that even as she spoke she had shivered.

It wasn't really cold, and we were all crowded close to the fire. But the gem on the velvet cushion seemed to radiate an influence both benign and malignant. It lay there, in its nearly matchless splendour and purity, and for the hands of the Birketts only. "Who Seizes, Beware." I moved back, closer to the fire.

Askew gathered up the cushion, and ended one of La Española's few moments of exposure to light and admiration, the thing that all great gems seem to exist for. It would shine alone in its dark sanctuary for how long more?

"And will you drive to London in the car with me if I do that, Carlota? Will you fly in the plane to Amsterdam? And will you find the cutter who will touch it?"

He snapped the panel shut. "I think we might just leave La Española in peace, Carlota—and ourselves. That is not all I have to sell." He turned back to us. "Gerald, what do you think?"

"Of what, my dear Robert? Of course there are many things here that we would be happy to handle for you . . . without publicity, if you wished it that way. It would be a pleasure . . . I don't know how a house like this and a family like yours, which has not been known as collectors, has come by such pieces, but most of them are first-class. Yes, first-class. It would make a beautiful and exciting sale, Robert."

"What—the furniture?" He seemed surprised. "Yes . . . well, I wasn't thinking so much about that." He sounded rather disinterested, as if he didn't know or care much about the value of what was under his roof.

"I have just one thing that could stand beside La Española in importance and value. Possibly it's much more important. If it went to a great museum instead of a private collector it would be seen, in time, by millions of people. Beside it, even La Española becomes relatively lifeless and unimportant. What would you say to a Rembrandt, Gerald?"

"A Rembrandt?" As quickly as his tone had changed, Gerald

looked across at me, as if to warn me to stay quiet. A kind of charge of excitement ran between us, excitement and—yes, it was fear, almost. I felt my mouth go dry. It was not that we had discovered something, Gerald and I. It was being discovered for us. And even in that second I thought again of Vanessa, and wondered if she had known of this also.

"A legacy which has come to us in a perfectly honest, ordinary fashion, Gerald. I don't know if you ever knew that my grandfather was only a cousin to the fifteenth Earl. He never expected to inherit—there was a son and a brother before him. They both died. The Birketts often seem to be unfortunate in losing their direct descendants. Twice the title almost died out because there seemed no obvious male heir, even though the country hereabouts is studded with Birketts. Well, my grandfather was a prosperous farmer, with an interest in some small mines, and he ran a few coasters out of Whitehaven. He liked to travel with them himself—often went over to the Continent, and most often to Rotterdam—and even more after he had met Margeretha van Huygens. She was the daughter of one of the burgomasters of Rotterdam, an only child, and they didn't think the match to an obscure English farmer was nearly good enough for her—she seems to have been pretty as well as rich. They thought of it rather differently when he rather suddenly became Lord Askew. In any case, the marriage took place, and like any good Dutch housewife, she brought furnishings to her marriage home, as well as money. And naturally she inherited everything on the death of her parents. All the French furniture came from the van Huygens—things they'd picked up quite inexpensively after the French Revolution. And with the furniture came a collection of Dutch pictures—most of them pretty dull, I think. I'm perfectly certain, though, that my Dutch grandmother preferred her scenes of cows and windmills over the one great treasure of the collection. I can remember her, my grandmother, living on to a great age, long after her husband had died, still speaking pretty bad English, and continuing to live at Thirlbeck with her son and his Scottish wife. Both of them were rather afraid of her. I remember I was. She was full of all the characteristics we think are Dutch—thrift, good management, a rather phlegmatic temperament. It just wasn't in her nature to admire the self-portrait of a man in his old age, dressed in nondescript clothes. She judged a man by what money he had accumulated, and she despised those, like Rembrandt, who having had money, wasted it and ended in bankruptcy . . . even if he was Rembrandt. I suppose at the time she was growing up, Rembrandt wasn't even in fashion. We don't know how the van Huygenses came into possession of the picture. To my grandmother it was just one of the many she brought over, and in her day it hung in a dark passage because she didn't care to see the face of old age looking back at her. She never, that I know of, paid any attention to the picture, never talked about it. We just knew it was there . . ."

I had crept closer to the fire as he had talked, but still the chill persisted, a cold excitement twisting in my stomach, the kind of moment in which one either laughs hysterically, or clamps ones lips tight against their tendency to tremble and go out of control. Now that La Española no longer engaged our attention, we had both of us, Gerald and I, begun to look in the direction that Askew faced. It was a long room, as long as the dining room across the hall. In the darkness of that panelling we could see only the dull brown outline of the frame of the picture that hung on the farthest wall. Its subject was totally lost.

"It is possible, isn't it, Gerald, that a Rembrandt could exist that has never been catalogued? Something overlooked by its owners because they were too familiar with it?"

"It's entirely possible, Robert. The art world, while running to fluctuations and prices that every year begin more and more to resemble the stock exchange, is in almost total chaos. There is no central registry of works of art, who owns them, when they are sold, and to whom, who has them locked in a bank vault because they are stolen and they're too hot to display until the statute of limitations has expired. Even the museums don't have to tell us what they buy and sell. And, above all, they don't have to tell what they pay. You can't look up the price of your Old Master in the daily newspapers. That's why record sales of any art object at auction make such news. In America it's no-holds-barred in the scramble to get the best. It's a state of anarchy which would send the normal businessman mad. And yet we live with it, because there is a general unwillingness to admit that art is big business. And because in the scramble and rush to acquire, there is always the hope, the possibility, that in someone's country house, hung in a dark corridor, there may be a Rembrandt. We actually *expect* several Vermeers to turn up. A Rembrandt—one that had always been in the hands of a private family, never sold or exhibited—yes, entirely possible . . ."

Gerald's words trailed off as he began to walk down that long room. Askew said, "I've had Tolson bring it out and hang it. It can't have seen the light of day since Tolson shut it away at the beginning of the war."

I thought Gerald walked with a kind of stiffness, as if the same cramping excitement had gripped him also. If what Askew had said was true, then this remote country house would suddenly witness the coming and going of the experts to authenticate the picture, photos of the whole painting and details would appear on the desks of museum directors all over the world, it would arrive at last in the special rooms on the top floor of Hardy's which were used to house with greater security the special treasures which came for auction there. The television lights would go on in the great saleroom, and the world's press would gather. And if the buyer was foreign, there would be the usual appeal for a fund to save it for the nation, and one more man, in this case Robert Birkett, would be condemned for selling away a national treasure. There would be questions in the House of Commons about refusing an export licence. No wonder Gerald walked warily.

He stopped. "I can't see it, Robert," he said. "Aren't there some lights?"

"Lights? Oh, yes." Askew crossed to the switches by the door, pressed one, but that only activated the modern extension arm lamp perched on the top of the roll-top desk. The sconces on the wall remained dark. "Damn!" he said. "There's never been enough places for lights in this house. Well, I was stupid to let Tolson hang it there—I forgot about light. Perhaps we could plug Tolson's lamp into one of the outlets down there. Just a minute, Gerald."

I moved ahead of Gerald. "There aren't any outlets close enough, Lord Askew. And the lamp's on a very short flex—perhaps we could tilt it—"

"No," Gerald said. "No, don't. I don't want my first sight of it spoiled. We'll look at it tomorrow morning, Robert. We can put it on a chair facing the window . . . Yes, tomorrow morning would be better." His tone was curiously flat.

Suddenly the excitement was gone. I was more than ever conscious that I was tired and chilled, and as I looked across at Gerald he carefully avoided my glance. The rosy glow he usually wore had faded completely. He seemed now what he was, an aging man who had had too long a day. We said good night to the Condesa and Askew at the bottom of the stairs, and I could feel them staring after us as we went up. When we reached the gallery Askew said something, and the Condesa's voice rose in sharp protest. As I glanced down she had already started up, but at the landing she turned to take the other arm of the staircase leading to the opposite wing of the house. By the time we reached Gerald's door she had vanished in the shadows of the corridor.

"Can I come in for a moment, Gerald?"

He nodded, as if he had known I would say that.

v

He shook his head wearily. "I just don't know, Jo. It's no use asking. I *don't know* why Vanessa never said anything. As ignorant as she was then, she must have known these were good pieces. She can't have forgotten, even if it is a long time ago. For some reason she chose to say nothing. It must have been a very good reason, but we'll never know what it was—not now." He pulled on his cigarette wearily, his eyelids drooping. I felt I was forcing him when he didn't want to talk, but I had to go on.

"Perhaps he *asked* her not to. Yes, that would be it. The

Birketts all seem a bit touched to me—at least, *he* is. All that business about staying a private during the war, and winning every medal in sight. That's cracked—that, and all this secrecy about the house, not letting anyone in, keeping a Rembrandt hidden away where no one would ever see it. Do you suppose Vanessa saw *that*?"

"Jo," he answered with exaggerated patience, "I don't know what to suppose. I agree that Robert is an oddity—but what does it matter? There will be a sale—one of the most splendid sales we've ever had, whether that is a Rembrandt or not. Robert needs money, and he's not going to stay on at Thirlbeck."

"Do you doubt it is a Rembrandt?"

"My dear Jo, don't jump on me. I haven't seen it, have I? There's no reason why it shouldn't be—the van Huygenses could have been of the same family of Constantijn Huygens who wrote about Rembrandt in his autobiography. This is how these things happen. Pictures and furniture are passed on, all taken for granted by the family, until some new headline about soaring art prices makes them take a second thought about what's in the attic. Robert needs money . . ." He sat, half hidden behind the haze of cigarette smoke. "A Rembrandt . . . I wonder . . ."

I couldn't help the words coming out. "I don't much like Lord Askew, Gerald—or at least I keep changing my opinion of him. He hates this place, doesn't he? He doesn't care if it falls down. The bulldozer or the weather, he doesn't care which gets to it first. I almost felt he could sell his own grandmother—after all, it was her furniture and pictures."

"And now they're his, to do as he likes. Never forget it, Jo. It's his property. In any case, does liking him matter? In this business one doesn't always have to like ones clients."

I shrugged and moved towards the door. "Of course it doesn't matter. And what if the house does fall down? It must just happen to be one of England's least known, most hidden architectural treasures, and stuffed with wonderful furniture—and it would cost the price of a Rembrandt to preserve. Who *would* want it, after all?" I wondered why I was arguing with myself.

I had answered my own question, hadn't I? "Good night, Gerald. I hope you sleep well."

"I shall, Jo—I shall."

At the door I turned back. "Will I disturb you if I have my bath tonight? If we all take baths in the morning the hot water will probably run out. I'll be very quiet . . ."

He squashed out his cigarette. "Nothing, dear Jo, would keep me awake tonight . . ."

I suddenly thought that I had never seen Gerald look old before. The idea frightened me. I couldn't lose him now—not just after I had lost Vanessa. I think I would have gone and kissed him then, but for the fact that he might have guessed what was in my mind. So I just smiled at him. "Good night . . ." I was aware of a sense of unease growing upon me as I made my way back to the Spanish Woman's room; outside the wind had strengthened; it slashed through the bare boughs of the oaks and beeches with their barely budding green, and stippled the silver surface of the tarn with black; it had a desolate, soughing sound as it beat at the building, and all the old wood of this house creaked and shuddered like a living thing.

* * *

I was back in the Spanish Woman's room after bathing in the marble tub of Edwardian proportions when I realised that my handbag and my only cigarettes were downstairs. I had managed to cut down to ten cigarettes a day, but the last and best of them was something I looked forward to. It was too late now to disturb Gerald to ask for his. I went out to the gallery and looked down. The Condesa had gone upstairs, I knew, and probably, by now, Askew also. But the lights in the sconces still burned, fires had been newly made up. Except for the wind there was silence. What time was it?—after midnight by now. Would Tolson have gone to bed, and locked the drawing room where I had left the cigarettes? I went downstairs, hesitating just a little at the thought of the dogs. There was no sight or sound of them. The door of the drawing room opened at my touch, and the lights were still on, but someone had placed a guard against the fire. I found my handbag eventually, not on the sofa, where I believed I had left it, but on a table near the door; someone had been through the room—the used ash-trays were removed for washing, the cushions plumped up, and here also the fire had been banked, as if in an effort to keep its embers alive until the morning. Did they leave the lights on all night—or was turning them out Tolson's last duty as he locked the rooms? I was beginning to be aware that even if Vanessa had appeared to be supremely indifferent to the value of what was housed here, Tolson was not.

I was halfway across the hall when I saw her. She stood in the shadow thrown by the stairs, and for a second I wasn't quite sure whether or not she was a child. Then she turned her head towards me; I saw a girl of perhaps eighteen or nineteen, with a shower of silvery-blond hair framing a face whose features had a childlike delicacy. She seemed very tiny, standing there in her short skirt and plain blouse, and she had the porcelain look of a figurine, a complexion which glowed even in the shadows, slender white hands, red lips that curved upwards in a half smile that seemed almost fixed, as if her face rarely wore any other expression. Now that she was aware of me she regarded me calmly, neither with curiosity nor surprise; in that she was not at all childlike. I knew then that this was Jessica, Tolson's granddaughter. I moved on towards the stairs, meaning to nod to her, and speak some greeting, and wondering why it was I, and not this slender, tiny girl, who should feel discomforted. I just caught myself on the verge of explaining my presence in the drawing room at that hour.

It was then that the door to the room which housed La Española was flung open. The murmur of voices I had caught as I crossed the hall was suddenly loud and sharp. It reached me now as an outburst of anger, as if the speaker were at the end of patience, a voice I remembered.

". . . had enough of it! I'm telling you now, Askew, if I so much as see a hair of one of those dogs on my land—whether it's the land I rent from you, or my own—I'll shoot it. Or all of them. I'm a farmer. I need my lambs. I'm damned if I'm going to have them slaughtered as playthings for your bloody dogs."

"Nat, you haven't a shred of proof that these dogs are responsible for your dead lambs. In any case, I think it's a matter to be taken up with Tolson. They're locked in the house at night—and by no stretch of the imagination could they be called *my* dogs."

"They stopped being Tolson's dogs the minute you set foot here—by what magic I'll never fathom. So it's you I'm giving warning to. You're the owner of this house—you're responsible."

"I think you're being hasty and unreasonable, Nat. And what of those eagles of yours? Don't they—"

Askew was cut short. "Shows what you know about golden eagles—or dogs! Just try looking at the difference between the damage a dog does and the way an eagle attacks. Eagles almost never kill lambs—they feed off the carcase as carrion."

After a pause Askew spoke again. "I accept your warning, Nat, but I refuse to believe these dogs are responsible. However . . . look, won't you sit down again? There are things we should talk about. Stay and have a drink with me—"

He was cut off again. "Some other time. I've things to see to now. When you feel like it, you come to *my* house. Or don't you unbend with the locals? Any rate, it'll be a long day before I sit comfortably in this hellish house!"

"Nat—!"

Now the door was flung wide, and closed again in almost a slam. I saw the angry face under the tow-coloured hair. He was wearing the same clothes he had had on that afternoon when he had opened the gates to the valley of Thirlbeck. Then he had merely worn the look of an overworked man, weary, too busy to spend time in talk. Now he had the appearance of agitation, of being near desperation. If he remembered me he gave no sign of it. His glance swept over me almost as if I weren't there, and then on to the girl.

"Nat," she said, also ignoring my presence, "there's no need to carry on so. You've a right here as much as he has. This house is yours . . ."

"Oh, hush, Jess," he said impatiently. He was walking towards

82

her. They both turned without another glance at me, and started down the passage that opened under the stairs. I caught the last of his words as the green-baize door swung closed. "Be a good girl, will you, and make me a cup of tea. I've got to go out and look at some ewes . . ." There was a homely acceptance between them that excluded this whole world of run-down grandeur on the other side of the door. They would drink their tea in the kitchen, and talk of practical, familiar things, and his voice would probably lose its edge of anger as he sat with this porcelain creature who seemed to know him so well. Unreasonably, I felt troubled by the exclusion.

"Oh . . . there you are . . ." I turned and looked at Askew. He stood gripping the doorframe, his lips trying to force a smile, but producing something that barely covered a grimace of pain. I could see the dogs standing behind him. He didn't seem to think it strange that I was in my dressing gown, or that I was there at all. "Do me a favour, please? Go into the dining room and bring me a brandy? It should be in one of the sideboards—and the glasses will be somewhere about. A large one . . ." He made to turn back into the room. "Oh, get one for yourself, of course . . ." He was gone from sight before I could reply.

I found it easily enough. The glasses on a tray on the sideboard were still warm from washing. I poured one large drink and carried it back to him.

It didn't seem possible that the exchange I had overheard could have produced such a reaction in him. He was stretched in the chair behind the desk, as if trying to straighten his body from cramp, but then, almost at once, he doubled over, clutching his stomach, his eyes closed. Sweat stood out on his forehead. I went to his side and set down the glass.

"Lord Askew—are you ill? Shall I call . . ?" Whom would I call?

He opened his eyes and looked at me. "Back already. Clever girl . . ." His hand was reaching for the brandy, and while he took the first long swallow, my fingers held it also; his hand felt terribly cold on mine, but his palm was sweating. He straightened and leaned back in the chair. Now he could control the glass himself, and I withdrew my hand.

"Not supposed to do this. Terribly bad for me, the doctors say. And I shouldn't be smoking, either. But they don't tell me what to do in place of it. I've got some tablets upstairs, but it's a hell of a long way upstairs."

"If you tell me where, I'll get them."

He shook his head. "No, I'll get there eventually. And in the meantime this"—he gestured with the brandy goblet—"does as well as the tablet. They tell me I'm burning out what's left of my stomach, but what's the odds. To live and enjoy—or not to live at all? I've done what I'm doing now all my life. I don't know how to do anything else." Then suddenly he seemed to focus fully on my face. "Oh, for God's sake, don't look so stricken. It's an ulcer—a bloody great ulcer. It kicks up from time to time. Tonight is one of the times."

"I'm sorry."

"Sorry? Ridiculous. You've never seen me before. Why should you be sorry?"

"Sometimes one is."

"Do you like me? Is that why you're sorry?"

I took time to think, and in that instant all of Vanessa's, of Gerald's, of Hardy's training was thrown out. "I like you for some things—and decidedly not for others. I'm sorry, though, when people are in trouble. That man—he's in trouble about his lambs. And you're in trouble about your dogs. I'm sorry for both of you, and for the animals."

Now he took a large gulp of brandy, and made a grimace of pain and distaste. "I hope you're not a little Miss Goody? Do you know who that was—that righteous farmer with the dead lambs?"

"No, but of course I remember him. He was the one who let us in at the other end of the valley."

"That—*that* is a cousin, God knows how many times removed. Nat Birkett by name. He is also my heir."

"Your heir—but you really don't know him? I heard you—"

"I know, I know. It isn't his fault he's next in line. He didn't ask for what's going to be thrust on him, and he doesn't want it. This last week is the first time we've met. And it hasn't been a happy occasion. The title and the entailed part of the estate—the nucleus of the land here in the valley, the Tolson farms, the house—they go to Nat Birkett whatever we both might wish otherwise. Of course he doesn't want them. A pretty sorry inheritance. But I thought he'd come here tonight as a friendly gesture, and now I find it's about his stupid lambs . . ." He gave a half laugh that was meant to cover any trace of regret he might have had, but it ended in a short gasp of pain. He gestured with the brandy glass. "Where's yours? I'll have another. We'll drink to happier relations with my heir."

I shook my head. "No—and you shouldn't be talking to me like this. What's between you and Nat Birkett is your business. It can't possibly be mine—"

At the same instant she spoke I became aware of her presence in the doorway. I didn't know how long she had been there. "You are right, Miss Roswell. It isn't your business . . ."

I smelled her perfume, watched the graceful sway of her body in a robe of amber silk, her long black hair tumbled over her face as she came towards us. She disregarded me completely as she went to Askew. "Roberto!" Her voice shook a little, a mixture of anguish and anger. "Why do you do it?" She leaned over him, peering down into his face, her fingers feeling for the pulse at his wrist. "Why do you do it?" she repeated. She took the brandy glass from him. "There are other ways to kill yourself beside this madness." His face was white and beaded with sweat. He made a weary gesture as if to ward off her reproaches.

"Carlota—don't!"

She turned and looked at me. "Go," she said, very simply. And I went.

* * *

I had my cigarette by one of the dying fires, thinking of what I had done, and seen, and learned that day. But I was also very tired, and when I got into bed I felt the warmth of the hot-water bottles gratefully, and I was asleep almost at once. I hadn't drawn the curtains, so I woke, startled, to the sense of a changed atmosphere. The straight, cold direct rays of the moon were gone. From the changing pattern of light I knew that clouds must be scudding swiftly across the valley. I heard the wind moan in the chimneys. What else did I hear? What did I think I saw? Was it the rustle of paper, or the sound of stiff petticoats moving, or perhaps the sound of the claws of a small dog, or a cat, against the big chair? Or was it simply mice behind the panelling? Did I actually see a small dark shape seated in the chair—hear the sigh of loneliness and waiting? No—both fires had died now to a bed of embers, giving little light; the moon was darkened. I saw nothing, I heard nothing. It was no more than the remembrance of a dream, imperfectly remembered. If the little Spanish Woman was there, I did not feel she resented my presence. Perhaps she only wanted recognition of herself. I slept again, easily and deeply.

CHAPTER 3

I

She was in the room before I was properly awake; there was the faintest rattle of the spoon on the saucer as she put the tray on the long table in the window bay, and I opened my eyes to the sight of her silver-gilt hair and that tiny figure silhouetted against the blaze of morning light. She turned to me at once.

"Hello—I'm Jessica. George Tolson is my grandfather. I expect Lord Askew told you I live here, and help my grandparents." She spoke with cheerful familiarity; not for her the reserve of her grandfather, though her voice was light and whispery, almost on the edge of excitement when there seemed nothing to be excited about.

She surveyed the tray expertly. "I've put it over here. It's never very comfortable having things to eat in bed, is it? At least I don't think so. I hope you like the bread—I bake it myself. Grandmother's getting on a bit, you know—she has bad arthritis. So I do most of the things upstairs here. Saves her a lot of walking. Do you like this room?"

I wasn't fully awake even then, but I struggled to find an answer—something to stem this rush of words. "Yes—I do. Very much."

"I love it." She was bending now and scooping the faded rose petals from the big Delft bowl, smelling them, and letting them flutter down from her doll-like hand. "This is my favourite room at Thirlbeck. I often come up here to read or study. I like to sit in the window here where I can see the tarn. I've written about it—how it looks in each season. It's not very good poetry, but it will get better."

I knew then whose hand had kept this room so immaculate, kept the table at such a high polish, who had gathered the rose petals of last summer and let their scent linger on here. "I build up the fires in the winter and sit here and imagine how it must have been when she had this room."

"She—the Spanish Woman?"

"Oh, of course. I can't think of anyone else using this room, though I suppose they must have. Most of the Earls seem to have used the room opposite this in the other wing—the one Lord Askew is in now. The last Earl, his father, only moved into the room Mr. Stanton has now after his wife died. This was meant to be one of the—well, one of the state rooms of the house, but they say that after the Spanish Woman died no one wanted to use it, and it was shut up for a long time. I expect they wanted to forget about her. Perhaps the third Earl felt a bit uneasy sleeping in her bed." She seemed to take it for granted that I must know the whole story.

"I've slept here myself just to see what it was like. But then, I've tried out most of the rooms in the house. This is the best."

She spoke of the place as if it were her own, and I suppose it often must have seemed that way. No one had lived here but her grandparents since she had been born. She had never set eyes on the present Earl until this past week. I sensed a slight impatience in her as she spoke of the Earl, as if she couldn't wait for him to be gone again, for all of us to be gone, so that she could have back her own world—the world of her dreaming. She was moving around the room now, touching things with loving familiarity, the carving on one of the mantels, the pewter candlestick. Her eyes quickly skipped over my toilet things lying on the big chest, alien things to her, and possibly resented. She was like a piece of quicksilver, whispery, her eyes large and Dresden blue in translucent skin, her cheeks touched with the faint pink flush of a painted doll, her lips sweet and red. And none of it was artificial. As she moved round in the morning light she was clean and scrubbed, and entirely without make-up, and the colour of her hair was her own. She was just slightly fey, I thought, and she couldn't resist this chance of an audience. She was brilliant too, Askew had said, and not strong enough to take up the scholarship at Cambridge. It seemed to me that she walked the delicate line of nervous tension, which threatened to spill over on the wrong side.

And then she was around near the bed, and on her way to the door. "Well—I should drink your tea before it gets cold. I hope you like the bread." And she was smiling at me, but as if I were an object, not a person.

"Mr. Stanton—"

"Oh, I've taken tea to Mr. Stanton. What a sweet man!" The air of sophisticated judgement in the remark infuriated me—what business had she making comment on Gerald, whom she had never met before? And then I felt like laughing, because I recognised the jealousy in my own reaction. "Breakfast will be ready when you come down. Just help yourself . . ." She bestowed that enchanting, unreal smile upon me, and closed the door very softly.

I lay back on my pillow, forgetting for the moment how badly I wanted the tea, and reaching for a cigarette instead, something I rarely did at this time of the day. I could laugh a bit, but it really wasn't funny to be trapped for some days between the two opposites of ideal beauty—this tiny, perfect English rose, and the haunting, dynamic presence of the Spanish aristocrat. It was a situation in which Vanessa would have revelled; not by any means as classically beautiful as either, she would have outshone them both by sheer flamboyance.

I flung back the bedclothes. Better try this maddening little girl's tea and bread; the tray gave me no reassurance that she ever made mistakes. The tea was kept hot in its little teapot by a knitted cosy; the china was delicate, and the wafer-thin slices of bread tasted like something that everyone had forgotten how to make fifty years ago. And this girl-child wrote poetry as well. I scowled at the morning-blue surface of the tarn—not the best beginning to the day.

* * *

Gerald greeted me in a rather subdued way when I entered the dining room; he was eating a piece of toast with a very thin scraping of butter on it. "Finished already?" I said. "Would you like more coffee?"

"I haven't begun," he answered.

"Unlike you. There's everything here." I was lifting the lids off silver dishes. "You can have bacon, kidney, sausage—three kinds of eggs. There's even something that looks like kidgeree." I didn't mention the oatmeal—that wasn't Gerald's dish.

"Thank you, this is enough." His tone was so unusually remote that I turned to him swiftly. "Didn't you sleep well?"

"Well enough, I suppose. Yesterday was a long day—perhaps we were overambitious. Should have taken two days to come up. It is pretty well the end of the world, isn't it?"

"You don't like it?"

"I didn't say that, Jo. Just pour me some coffee, would you please?"

I settled at a place opposite him. "You're missing something in this sausage."

"Cumberland sausage," he said briefly. "They make a thing of it up here."

"I suppose you were awake enough to see the fairy-child who brought the tea?"

He brightened a little. "Yes—lovely little creature, isn't she? Can't imagine that dour old giant Tolson is her grandfather."

"Stranger things have happened. She's a little bit spoiled, and is certainly Grandfather's pet. She likes to think she owns Thirlbeck, too."

For the first time that morning he smiled fully. "Jo, you sound rather like the Condesa. Little Jess hasn't many friends among the women here."

"All right," I answered, "so I'm jealous."

"That's better. Always better when you face the truth."

"The truth is she could put on a drawstring bodice and a

Bopeep hat and she'd be the ideal model for a porcelain shepherdess. Not really my taste in china."

"She drew my bath for me," Gerald answered. "I think she's charming."

"That leaves the Condesa and me to our own opinions. And where," I said, "are Lord Askew and the Condesa? Do you know?"

"Robert's been and gone. The Condesa, being a Spaniard, probably doesn't like to rise before eleven. I think our charming little Jessica might get a pillow thrown at her if she attempted the early-morning-tea routine with the Condesa. Coffee black and strong, I think, would be to her taste." He snapped a piece of toast in two. "And I've remembered about the Condesa."

"What about her?"

"I was thinking last night—couldn't remember where I'd ever encountered her before, or if it was just her name I remembered. Her face, of course . . . but then, one dreams of faces like that. Or you see them in glossy magazines. But I was thinking . . . remembering. She's the daughter of a Spanish nobleman—someone who was once in Franco's cabinet. I think he's dead now. She was involved in some scandal. I can't remember the details. The usual thing, I suppose. She took up with another man, and there was no prospect for a divorce from a Spanish husband. And when *that* relationship fell through, she was on the international circuit, with barely enough money to keep her afloat, I imagine. Cut off from her family, to whom, naturally, she is a disgrace. How old do you think she is: thirty-five—thirty-seven?" He was giving her the benefit of a few years, I thought, but I did not object. What mattered was what Gerald felt about her, not what she actually was. "Her relationship with Robert can't be of very long standing. She wasn't with him when I chanced to meet him in Venice last spring. She can't like it here. It's not her sort of place, is it? They can't be planning to stay long. An international beauty can't afford to retire for too long from the scene—she wastes her fragrance on the desert air."

"Perhaps she loves him," I said. "It may be as simple as that."

"It may be that she is forty," he answered, with unusual ruthlessness. "Or more. And she is growing a little afraid. She has come here with Robert because she doesn't want to let him go—and there is no other place at this time for her. And probably not much money of her own. Naturally she can never marry him, not so long as her husband is alive—and Robert is so much older."

"Now that she has seen what is in this house—the furniture, the one painting on display—will she let him go?"

"Will it be her choice? Was it ever the choice of the others? I really don't know. He is a man of great charm—and kindness, in his fashion. But I also think that since the war—since the death of his wife and son, he has become a man who hasn't allowed himself ever to become completely involved with, or committed to anyone or anything. But, well, there comes a time. Perhaps if she would agree, he might be willing to settle with the Condesa for the rest of his life. A man grows tired of endless pursuit . . . In fact, a man just grows tired." His tone dropped to a musing quiet, as if he were thinking of the tiredness of age. "Who is the heir, I wonder . . . ?"

"His heir, Gerald, is that tousled young man in the Bentley we met yesterday. And my impression is that he can't bear the thought of Lord Askew and the whole idea of an inheritance—"

We stopped. Tolson stood at the door.

"Miss Roswell. There's a telephone call for you—from London. A Mr. Peers."

I smiled, not able to help myself. And I was hurrying towards the door. I didn't care about the tone of disapproval from Tolson, or about Gerald's knowing smile. Harry did that to me. I wanted to hear that lighthearted, slightly mocking voice, the grin that was implied in it—all the things that were so opposite to my own approach to life.

"If you will take it in Lord Askew's study, Miss Roswell— I'll show you."

"Yes—yes, I know. We were there last night," and I hurried across the hall ahead of him. He followed me, and for a wild moment I thought he was going to stay with me while I talked. But he watched me for a moment as I picked up the phone near his desk, his heavy brows drawn together as if he didn't feel it was altogether right for me to be receiving calls on Lord Askew's phone, and how had the caller known I would be there, in any case? Then, with a kind of a shrug, he withdrew. I waited for a few seconds, listening to his steps fade away into the service passage before I spoke.

"Harry?"

"Fine one you are! Leaving me stranded—alone—all weekend. Didn't you know I'd be rushing back to hold your hand?"

"Liar! You never rushed anywhere to hold my hand. You just happened to come back. Had a good time?"

"A good time?" His Manchester accent, slightly overlaid with London, rumbled at me sternly; it was one of the things I liked about Harry that he had never tried to do anything with his accent. It wasn't public school—it never would be. At times its implication of Northern hardheadedness was a valuable asset to him. When he spoke, his listeners knew that shrewdness and success spoke; how the words came out didn't matter. "It was business, luv—not a good time."

"Since when has business ever stopped you having a good time?"

He laughed and made no more protests. "Well, it was profitable. I'll be able to afford to take you to dinner a few more times. What I'd like to know is when that will be. You're up there in those damned Lakes. I once knew a chap—he lived next door in Manchester—went up there and never came back. Fell down a bloody mountain plank into a lake. Dangerous, I call it. My old mum would never let me go up there."

"Harry, you fool. If only I could believe you sometimes."

"Honest, luv—cross my heart and hope—and all the rest of it. So when are you coming back from Lord Whatsits'?"

"I'm not sure. Perhaps tomorrow. And how did you know I was here?"

"Know? Listen, luv, when Harry Poore wants to know something, there's always ways of finding out. I telephoned around. Found out you were with Gerald Stanton. So then I found out where Mr. Stanton was headed."

"Hardy's isn't open. The security people wouldn't know where we were."

93

"Who said anything about the security people? I think I roused one of the directors from his bed to enquire about Mr. Stanton's whereabouts."

I sucked in my breath. "I wish you hadn't. One doesn't call the directors to find out where a minor employee is for the weekend."

"Cool it, Jo. I didn't mention your name. And the same director thinks I may be going to buy something quite big in a sale that's coming up. Which I might. He didn't mind talking —not at all."

"Harry, you're dreadful."

"You mean it?"

"No—you're wonderful!"

"That's better. *That's* my girl. And how is that madman, the noble Lord Askew? What's he trying to sell—that rock of his?"

"Rock?"

I could hear him sigh. "God bless your nice upbringing, Jo. I mean that bloody great diamond of his. Does he still have it?"

"It's right here in this room."

For once he had no immediate reply. Then slowly, as if he were speaking to a child: "You mean *there*—right in the room with you? Did you see it? What does it look like?"

"It's fabulous, Harry. It's hardly been cut at all—just polished on the natural surfaces so that you can see right into it. It's like a . . . a sort of mountain of light. It's so big you can't believe it's a diamond—"

"All two hundred-odd carats of it. Always wanted something like that myself."

"Not this one, Harry!" All at once I felt a sort of coldness about me, and I knew that I also believed the stories about La Española. "You wouldn't want this one."

"Who says I wouldn't? I'll bet anyone who bought it could make a tidy profit by the time it was cut into a few decent-sized hunks. Is that why you're there? Is he selling? What's Gerald Stanton doing there?"

"I don't know how you know so much about La Española, but you *ought* to know that I can't discuss Gerald's business, or anyone else's with you. Gerald is paying a call. He was invited—and I am driving him. So far as I know there *is* no business being done here."

"Luv, I don't believe you. But I'd think you were a fool if you said any more. I like a girl who can keep her trap shut." His tone changed. "Are you all right, Jo?—I mean all right." I knew he was talking about Vanessa's death. "I just missed you in Switzerland, and I didn't like to bust in in Mexico—not when you were just getting to know your dad. After all"—the flippancy returned to his voice—"after all, he might have thought I was trying to pick up a few of his paintings on the cheap. But it went all right with him, did it? I mean, you and your dad, you got on all right?"

"Yes, Harry. It was—it was very good."

"Glad to hear it. Nice to find a dad at your age, and one that won't breathe down your neck either. I'll miss your mother, though, Jo—she was my sort, Vanessa was. Smashing girl."

"I know." My voice came out thinly because of the tightness in my throat.

"All right then, luv. Take care. Try to stay dry up there, and don't fall down a mountain. See you."

"When?" I couldn't help saying it, even though I knew he hated to be pinned down.

"Oh—soon. Bye, Jo." Then there was the dull buzzing of the disengaged line. I felt more lonely then than at any other time since Vanessa had died. Harry had slipped away from me once more. There would be someone else for him to call now, someone else to take to dinner tonight. And with this sick emptiness upon me, I believed I loved him. But I didn't think he loved me, or any other woman. Love—that kind of love—had been beaten out of him as he had pushed and shoved his way to the top. Probably the only woman he had ever loved was the mother whom he had settled—his father was an adjunct with whom he liked to argue about soccer but whom he otherwise didn't seem to regard very highly—in a suburban semi only about a mile from the row of slum houses where he had been born. They hadn't wanted to go farther away, or to live more grandly, and Harry had the wisdom not to try to force them.

His knowledge of his origins was Harry's strength—more than any other man I had ever known. His women were the decorations of his success; no particular woman, it seemed, was essential to him. I wasn't essential to him; he was offhandedly fond of me, and in these last weeks, unusually gentle and kind. I replaced the receiver slowly, leaning back against the roll-top desk, hearing Harry's words again, the flirtatious mockery, seeing his half-ugly face, with its strong eyebrows crooked in amusement, a ruthless, eager face, his brown eyes quick and knowing.

I was remembering, as I too often did, the first time I had felt those eyes fastened on mine; I remembered it in every detail. It had been my first exposure to his brashness, his cocky good-humour, when it pleased him to be that way. I had been walking down from the bus stop in Piccadilly to Hardy's, taking note as I always did of the changes in the windows of the art dealers and galleries which lined the street below Fortnums. I had reached the one that specialised in ceramics; this day there had been a new pair of Chinese vases, of an early dynasty—which dynasty I wasn't expert enough to place absolutely, and certainly not without handling them—and I looked much closer. I was rooted, though, entranced by the colour, the pale green, the crackled glaze, the long tapering necks of the jars, their perfect proportion to the flare of the base. And then behind me, Harry's voice, unknown until that moment.

"What a beautiful pair . . ." I turned and his grown-up urchin's face, with the springing black hair, had been grinning at me, his eyes just a little above the level of mine, his stance like a game little fighting cock. ". . . of legs," he had finished.

And then he had walked on with me, talking about the Chinese vases with a degree of expertise which might have been the truth, or equally might have been meant to dazzle me and give me no time to probe his knowledge further. I made some stumbling replies as we walked, he turned the corner with me, and to my great shock, mounted the steps of Hardy's with me. I was utterly dumb now, wondering what to do with him. I had paused at the Front Counter, making some excuse to turn off and say something to Mr. Arrowsmith, who had presided there for more than twenty years, the man who began the training of every newcomer to Hardy's, the sons of directors, and the sons of dukes, the shy ones who had to be taught how to talk to those who came to the Counter, and the ones who had to be taught that two years studying art history didn't automatically make them experts. He was, in many ways, the face of Hardy's to the public, a jovial, courteous but shrewd face; I had trained under him, I trusted him—in a way I also loved him. I stood with him now as the urchin young man—not really so young since he was in his thirties—had continued up the great staircase to the salerooms, saluting me with an impudent wave of his hand. It was a gesture that, for all the world, reminded me of Vanessa.

Mr. Arrowsmith had acknowledged him with a smile and a benign nod of his head.

"Mr. Arrowsmith, who's that?"

"Who's that? But you came in with him, Jo."

"I'm still asking who he is."

"That, my dear, is Mr. Harry Peers. Clever young devil. He's got a good eye and he's learned very quickly. Jumped up from nothing, of course. But he's a millionaire, they say. Not that he's got his money from spotting good buys at Hardy's—that's just a millionaire's hobby. I'm surprised you don't know about him—haven't seen him in here before this."

"Why should I? These days I'm shut up in my cupboard with my bits and pieces of china, aren't I? It isn't like the old days on the Front Counter—I saw everyone then."

Mr. Arrowsmith had nodded; he thrived on every minute of his contact with the crowds of people who flowed through Hardy's door. He wanted his young people to get on in Hardy's, to find their place, but he felt sorry for them when they had to leave behind the vitalising force of this busy, colourful reception hall. Not for anything would he have spent his life in one of our storerooms where the items were catalogued and made ready for the sales. His passion was for people, not objects.

"Yes, true, Jo. You've moved on, and up—I suppose. One day

you might be very good. But you don't have half as much fun as you used to, do you?"

And I hadn't denied it.

I was remembering this now, the time, the passion spent, the love lavished on objects as I began to move slowly away from the desk, pausing about the middle of the room—the room that looked so different now as the morning light poured in at the long windows on each side of the painting. The same cold excitement gripped me as had done last night. I was hardly conscious that I was committing a breach of manners and discipline in staying to look at the painting without invitation, without Askew and Gerald being present. What was drawing me was the emergence from the shadow which the light from the two windows threw between them, of a face. I stared, and the face came more and more to life—the painted face of a man with an ugly, bulbous nose, a man with careless hair and a cap perched haphazardly on it, a man with brown eyes that registered age and suffering, had known the happiness of success, of his wife, the comfort of her dowry, the misery of her death, the taking of a kindly, undemanding mistress, the death of his only son. He had painted his own face so many times in his life, in great adornment, in the garish turbans and antiquities with which he had once loved to surround himself; now here he was in his old age, a plain man, revealing himself in the splendid beauty of his plainness. The portrait was unadorned, as if he had looked into the mirror and had been determined to record the pain and joys of his long life—Rembrandt van Rijn, son of a miller, painter of Leyden and Amsterdam, thrown from poverty to riches to bankruptcy—all of it looked from the portrait without self-pity or compassion. It was painted in the muddy browns of his later years, but it also wore the dirt of the years since it had been painted. I stopped at the point where the light from the two windows blinded me, and shadowed the painting too much.

"Ah, you're here before us, Jo." Gerald's voice behind me, and it had a tenuous quality about it, as if he wished he were elsewhere. I turned to see him and Askew coming down the room towards me.

"It's almost as hard to see as last night," I said. "It's here in the shadow between these two windows."

Askew sighed. "Yes . . . well, I asked Tolson to bring it out of the room where he's stored all the pictures, and we seem to have picked the worst place in the house to hang it. But Tolson insisted it should be this room, because of security . . ."

"Move it onto a chair facing the light," Gerald said.

It wasn't a large canvas—about three feet by two. I brought a chair, and Askew lifted it down off the wall with ease. I propped it against the back of the chair directly facing one of the windows, and Gerald moved around to look at it.

The Rembrandt of old age was now fully revealed, the period when life had nothing more it could use to hurt him. Close to, it was a daub of heavy ochre colours on a dark background; seen from a distance it was the marvellous face of a man who could even summon up a faint smile—almost a clown's grin— to reveal that the spark of life and creation was not yet extinguished. And yet it had been very near the end. The signature was there, almost obscured, and the date, 1669, the year he had died.

I glanced at Askew. At this moment, for all his sophistication, he was no different from all the others. Instead of looking at the painting, he was watching Gerald's face. In the end, for him as for others, the waiting became too much, the impatience and the eagerness too much to control. "What do you think?" he said.

Gerald spoke slowly. "Remarkable—very remarkable. An unrecorded self-portrait, but signed and dated. Perhaps it's not so surprising that your grandmother's family didn't regard it very highly. Rembrandt, at the end of his life, had fallen from the height of being Amsterdam's most fashionable portraitist, to the state of hardly being able to get a commission. They might well have regarded this particular picture as the portrait of a failure. This would have belonged to the period shortly after his son's death—he survived him by only a year. Of course, in three hundred years opinions have changed about the best of Rembrandt's work—this, at the time of his maturity and deepest suffering, says far more to this present age than his more facile works when his life seemed full of fruit and flowers and very theatrical costumes. Yes—very remarkable indeed." He turned to Askew. "Would there be any documentation for this—family papers, any record of its being bought, when it was bought—if anyone else had owned it or if it was acquired directly by the family and comes to you by descent?"

Askew shrugged. "I haven't the least idea. There may be, but I've no way of knowing." He gestured helplessly back to the wall filled with the filing boxes. "That's full of family papers—but there must be several hundred years of them—and mostly relating to estate matters. The estate once was quite sizable—and then there was the mining. I haven't any idea if Grandmother van Huygens brought over any papers relating to her own possessions. There may have been a marriage settlement. Dutch bourgeois families are pretty careful about such things, aren't they?"

"I would say they are. You see, any scrap of provenance—"

"But do we need that? It's signed and dated."

"Yes," Gerald said. "That's very significant. And it's been here as long as you can remember, Robert?"

"Of course, that's how I knew it was a Rembrandt. They always said it was. But Grandmother van Huygens had it hanging in one of the passages upstairs—a passage she didn't very often use. I told you she didn't care for it. Coarse, she called it."

"That was the way he was painting at that time of his life. He—"

"Excuse me, my lord."

Startled, all of us looked up. None of us had been aware of Tolson's appearance at the open door of the study; but I had the sense that he had been standing there for some time, listening as keenly as Askew to what Gerald had been saying.

"What is it, Tolson?"

"It's Mr. Birkett, my lord. He would like to have a word with you. I've put him in the library."

"Which Mr. Birkett? The place is full of Birketts."

It was plain from Tolson's expression that for him there existed now only one Birkett apart from Lord Askew.

"Mr. Nat Birkett, my lord."

"Damn—can't it wait? I'm busy now, Tolson. Ask him if he can come back. If he had telephoned first . . ."

"I should see him, if you can, my lord. It's about the sheep and the dogs."

"Not again! We've been through all that. Last night. Tell him what you know, Tolson. You know these dogs—"

"It isn't about *our* dogs, my lord. He's found the one who's been after the sheep. I think he's come to apologise. Not easy to ask a man to come back again to do that, my lord." I was astonished to hear the tone of pleading in Tolson's voice. Evidently Askew recognised it also. He shrugged. "Very well—I'll come. Can't have Nat Birkett forced to grovel. He *was* very sure last night, though. Won't hurt him to apologise."

"Not at all, my lord. But you see, he's a farmer . . ."

Askew was striding up the room. "And you're a farmer too, Tolson, and so are your sons. Well, I owe more than this to you. The library—?" He tossed a message back over his shoulder as he left the room. "Come and rescue me after a while, Gerald. Nat Birkett will welcome it as much as I will."

We waited for Tolson to close the door after Askew left, but he stayed where he was, great round-shouldered figure, the grey-black head, and black mat of hair on his hands somehow more forbidding in the daylight. "Is there anything I can do, Mr. Stanton?"

"Do . . . ?" Gerald looked bewildered. "Why—I don't believe there is."

"Well, sir, perhaps you would like the picture hung up again."

"No, not for the moment, thank you. I'll just look at it a little longer. If you don't mind."

"I don't mind, sir. It's just that several of the grandchildren are about today—supposed to be helping, but really just having a good time. They're not all as careful as Jessica. Just for safety, sir . . ."

"Yes, I see. Well, I'm sure Miss Roswell and myself will see it safely back on the wall. And then we'll do as Lord Askew suggests, and go and rescue him . . ."

"Very well, Mr. Stanton." The door closed gently.

I turned at once to Gerald. "What's the matter? The picture's all right, isn't it? I mean . . ."

He didn't even glance at me. His eyes were fixed on the painting, and his face was as grave as I had ever seen it.

"Remarkable," he said again. "Very remarkable. A wonderful piece of work. Pity it had to be a Rembrandt self-portrait that Robert owned—and that it was signed and dated."

"But that makes it better, surely? It proves . . ."

"It proves nothing, Jo. It's a very remarkable painting. But I just don't think it was painted by Rembrandt."

"Oh . . ." I felt the excitement leave me and a dull disappointment take its place—a sense of outrage too, that I had been so completely taken in, had believed in the man in the picture, had felt his life of suffering and joy. And then the second thought came. I turned swiftly to Gerald.

"But it's *signed*. And it's certainly a portrait of Rembrandt!"

"Yes, Jo, and I wish it weren't. If it had been some other subject, one might have believed it had been painted in his studio perhaps by one of his pupils—which would explain why the van Huygenses thought it a Rembrandt. Though I suspect when the real expert looks at it he'll say something about the cracking of the canvas being not what it should be—and of course there are X rays and the other tests. But that isn't the main thing. Here and now I don't, without anyone else saying a word, believe that Rembrandt painted it. There's just something it hasn't got—the quality isn't right. I have a feeling that I'm looking at a photograph of Rembrandt. Everything is here, and yet it isn't the real thing. I hope to heaven I'm completely wrong. I hope our people will come up here and tell me that I'm wrong. But if I'm right, then we're looking at the best piece of forgery I've ever seen." He shook his head, a gesture of sadness and wonder.

"Yes—remarkable. Very remarkable indeed."

11

We stayed looking at the painting for some time, Gerald's face unhappy and pensive. Finally he shrugged. "It's no use, Jo. I can't say more than I've said. We'll have to bring Lutterworth up here. In the meantime, what am I going to say to Robert? He believes it's the real thing—I'm sure of that. It appears to be the painting that his grandmother brought from Holland, one that he's grown up with. But I just don't think that at the time it came here anyone would have been bothering to produce forgeries—at least not forgeries of this calibre. Anyone who could paint like that in the nineteenth century would have made a good living signing his own name. Even the greatest artists weren't bringing such great prices then—I seem to remember as recently as the 1820s and '30s there are records of Rembrandts selling at auction for as little as twenty pounds. What matters is fashion—and he wasn't always very fashionable. But I don't need to remind you of what has happened in the last ten years. When the Metropolitan bought *Aristotle Contemplating the Bust of Homer* for over two million dollars the rush was really on. Anyone who owned a Rembrandt was rich, Jo."

"Then if this is a forgery, you think it's a recent forgery?"

"Has to be." He shook his head. "I'd love to know who's good enough to have done it. Remember van Meegeren? He painted Vermeers that Vermeer had never thought of. Even though they discovered what he was up to, and tracked down some of the fakes, there still must be a few reputable museums and collectors through the world who are proud of their Vermeers—painted by van Meegeren. When did he come out of jail, I wonder—or is he dead? Perhaps he—no, I don't think so. It was quite another style. I don't think this would be his work."

"But *how*, Gerald? And when? Has someone stolen the original and replaced it with this?"

He shook his head. "I don't want to know. And it could be that I'm wrong. For Robert's sake, for everyone's sake, I hope I'm wrong. And perhaps you could try looking through some of those papers. With Robert's permission, of course."

I looked with despair and disbelief at the wall where the files were stacked. "Gerald, there seems to be a lifework for anyone who takes that on. I've no experience . . ."

"Oh, just make a game of it. Anything so I won't have to

tell Robert here and now what I think. Time enough to break his heart later, when we're sure. We'll leave tomorrow, and I'll tell him I'm sending Lutterworth—and possibly someone else. Two opinions are better than one. If it's even faintly dubious, we can't touch it. But I wouldn't bet that some dealer couldn't sell it under the counter, without publicity. They can always make some story about avoiding the need to get an export licence. There are collectors mad enough and rich enough to lock a Rembrandt—or what they believe is a Rembrandt—in a safe for twenty years until there's a convenient way of having it 'discovered.' I don't think I'll tell Robert about that method. I'll just urge him to sell his furniture and live off the proceeds. What he does with this canvas—unless our people vouch for it—will be his own business. Damn, damn shame!"

"But who do you think . . . ? It's been locked up here for so long . . ."

He cut me short. "Don't ask, Jo. Better leave it alone. We'll go back to London tomorrow. I'll make some soothing noises to Robert. And you had better forget you've ever seen Thirlbeck."

"I don't think I ever can, Gerald . . . but I think perhaps I never want to come back here. There's so much I don't understand. Vanessa and my father being here, and my never knowing . . . Askew himself . . . it all disturbs me."

"Jo—this isn't like you." Gerald bent and looked for a moment into my face. "My dear, you're looking a little forlorn . . . and it certainly isn't a very cosy or comfortable house. I'll tell you what—while Robert is dealing with his Nat Birkett you and I will find where he's hidden the car, and we'll go off and find a pub in Kesmere."

"He has the keys. He didn't return them last night, and I forgot to ask him for them."

"Trapped—as they say. Well, never mind—" He stiffened suddenly. "Yes?"

It wasn't to me he spoke, but Tolson, again standing by the door which we had not heard open. "Mr. Stanton, Lord Askew would like it if you and Miss Roswell would join him in the library. Shall I replace the picture?"

I wondered if he was so possessive of everything at Thirlbeck, and then again wondered why he should not be. After all, he had tended it alone for so many years, had accepted the responsibility of it all. How would a man not come to believe it was his own, and that we—and I included Askew in this—were interlopers in his closed-off world, his treasure house of beautiful things? If that were so, then Gerald and I must seem to him even worse, the appraisers who descended on his kingdom and began to put a price on everything, a price that valued beauty, but not the devotion or service which had preserved the beauty. I suddenly saw us with the eyes of a person like Tolson, and we did not wear such an acceptable look as we were accustomed to.

He was beside us already, lifting the picture and easily stretching to rehang it on its hook. "There—" he muttered. "Out of harm's way now."

It was as though Gerald and I were being driven off, like a pair of thieves, and the threat to the security of Tolson's world was temporarily over.

*　*　*

The sound of the Condesa's laughter greeted us in the library. She hardly turned at our entrance, calling a "good morning" and then gave her attention once more to Nat Birkett. He stood in front of the fire, dressed in cavalry twill trousers and tweed jacket, a freshly laundered look about him, and the desperate air of a man who finds himself with a glass of champagne in his hand at eleven o'clock in the morning and wonders why he is where he is. He looked at Gerald with relief; they had made instant contact yesterday when we had encountered him at the back entrance to Thirlbeck, and it still endured.

Askew gestured to us with a bottle. "Champagne? Carlota's tastes run to it at this time every morning. But we've had to buy this little lot—much to Tolson's distress. We drank all there was in the cellars when Vanessa and Jonathan were here." He was holding a glass towards me. "Jonathan said it reminded him of the sun . . . is that what you feel, Carlota?"

"I feel gayer," she admitted. "I feel I shall very soon be on a terrace overlooking a blue sea, and the sun will be hot. But poor Mr. Birkett here thinks all this is a waste of time, I'm afraid. He'd really rather be getting on with his farming." But she smiled at him, and the words had no sense of sarcasm.

"Farmers never have enough time—but it's sometimes a good thing to remind them that they're never going to be caught up with work, and they should take a few minutes for . . . well, for this." He gestured to include the room, the champagne bottle, and even, I thought, the Condesa herself. She looked this morning exactly like Gerald's description of her as someone one saw in a glossy magazine; her pale cream slacks and the subtly toning cashmere sweater, Gucci shoes and the small Gucci travel bag that held her needlework tossed on the sofa beside her were the international badges of understated wealth and taste; if she was, as Gerald said, short of money, she didn't betray it. But there were different degrees of being short of money. I wouldn't have minded being short of money in the same way as the Condesa seemed to be. Nat Birkett's eyes were on her appreciatively, and she was enjoying that.

Then he looked across at me. "You managed to find your way last night, then? I thought afterwards perhaps I shouldn't have sent you over by Brantwick. The road's breaking up a bit in places . . ."

"Managed perfectly," Gerald said quickly. "Jo's a marvellous driver. We were grateful to you for saving us so many miles." Again I had the sensation of my skin creeping as I thought of the dog I had seen, and Gerald had not—the dog he refused to talk about.

"It was a great help," I said. "And spectacular views—before the mist came down. Formidable country, though. I wouldn't like to be lost up there."

He looked at me more closely. "You'd be surprised how many experienced walkers do just that. And this valley has the added attraction of being closed off—all private land, but bordered by the National Park. The trails on the maps lead them up near the top of the fells, and sometimes the temptation's been too great to see what the valley of Thirlbeck looks like. A few times we've had searchers out for days on those fells looking for walkers. One wasn't alive when we found him. Mostly it's their own fault. People won't believe how quickly the weather changes—some are not properly equipped or dressed, and they panic, try to find any way down they can. And they will cross over to this side, where the paths aren't marked. Every summer the Tolsons and I do what we can about replacing the signs along the walls that tell them it's dangerous, and to keep out—and every winter the snow knocks most of them down. And one or two people will always ignore a sign. This year we're getting volunteers from the district—hand-picked, to see that no one does stray across, by accident or design."

"Why volunteers?" Askew asked. "Why do you need them?"

For the first time Nat Birkett's face fully relaxed; he put down the glass of champagne as if he didn't want any more. "Because we've got a pair of golden eagles nesting up there on a crag of Brantwick—this is only the second pair to nest in the Lake District for more than two hundred years. And if it kills me I'll see no one gets near that nest, either for the eggs or just out of curiosity. Shepherds don't like eagles of any sort—they claim they take the lambs, which isn't true. But they try by any means they can to scare them off the nest so that the eggs will get cold and the young won't hatch."

"But you're a farmer—a sheep farmer, Nat."

"I'm that, but I like to think there are a few more things that interest me. The eagles really don't bother the lambs. If the lambs die they feed off the carcases, that's all. In any case I'd give a few lambs for the sake of having golden eagles back again."

His voice grew louder as if a pent-up frustration had to break through. "I'm so bloody sick of what's happened to this country—overrun with people, with their cars taking bigger and bigger chunks of the land, and their infernal plastic picnic litter making it look like a rubbish dump. And they're so bloody ignorant. They come out of the cities and treat the countryside like one big car park. They're actually eroding the soil in some so-called beauty spots by the sheer numbers of them. Places where heather and ling used to grow there's nothing but impacted subsoil now. No, by God, if I have to use a gun at least

I'll keep them away from that nest until the young can fly. I've phoned the Royal Society for the Protection of Birds, and they're rounding up a list of people in the district who'll take turns to watch." His light-coloured eyes were almost vengefully alive. The strain and worry that I had first noted in his stark, rather boney features, were transformed by a kind of messianic light, and I wondered what there was in the life of this young man which made him both attractive and yet too blunt, angry almost. "If I never do anything else in my life but make sure the golden eagles will continue to return to this valley to breed, then I'll have done enough."

Then he stopped and was aware of the silence about him. "Well, I'm assuming too much. It isn't my valley, of course. But with your permission, Lord Askew. And now I think I'd better go—"

"Wait awhile, Nat," Askew said. "Have another drink. And I'd rather like to have a talk with you . . ."

But Nat Birkett had already begun to nod his farewell to the Condesa, Gerald, and myself. "There can't be so much to talk about," he said to Askew. "Just so long as I know it's all right to organise watches."

Askew shrugged. "There *is* rather a lot I'd like to talk to you about, Nat—certain legal matters. But as to the rest—of course you must do as you wish. The Tolsons, I imagine, will co-operate."

"I can't do it without the Tolsons. They're already strengthening the fences along each end of the valley, and the young ones are being paired off to go and watch after school. In a sense, the birds made a good choice of nesting place—a valley that has no through motor traffic, where anyone who comes in without permission is trespassing. Oh, and I'll be paying for my part of the posts and fencing. Damned expensive these days, but neighbours usually share things like that. We intend to fence off the whole area around the crag so that no fool starts to climb it. I was hoping you'd agree to pay half of it, because it's on your land. Tolson says it can be managed. All right with you?"

Askew made a gesture of helplessness. "Anything for golden

eagles, Nat. And of course anything Tolson agrees to . . . well, who am I to say him nay?" Then I watched as Askew's air of faint amusement changed suddenly, his features twisted with a kind of distress. "Yes—I wish you *would* do it! There isn't much left in England to protect from the developers, and I'm for doing what can be done. You know . . . I've been to a few odd spots in my life, like the Galápagos Islands and seen the land turtles and the flightless cormorant, which exist nowhere else on earth. And places like the Coto Doñana in Spain which is the last refuge of the Spanish lynx and the imperial eagle. And I've been in the Seychelles while it was still a paradise, and it sickens me to think of what sort of tourist-trap mess they're going to make there. Yes, bring the golden eagles back, if you can, Nat. Do anything you can for this valley. I don't seem to have done much . . ."

Nat Birkett was already at the door, evidently not wanting to share any part of Askew's regret for what had been left undone in his time. "I'll fix it with Tolson, then. Good-bye."

We listened to the sound of his footsteps in the hall, and the impatient slam of the front door; then the motor of the Land-Rover parked in the gravel circle was started. Where I stood I could see that as the vehicle began to move, Jessica came running from the side of the house waving her arm. The Land-Rover stopped, and she leaned her arms along the open window, talking rapidly. I could see Nat Birkett nodding, and his face settled into a look of determined patience, as if he knew he must let Jess say whatever it was she meant to say. She held him there perhaps three minutes, and then stepped back from the vehicle; at once it roared into life and Nat Birkett drove it away at a speed that sent the gravel flying from under the wheels. But there was a smile on Jessica's face as she turned back towards the house. The great front door of Thirlbeck opened and closed so quietly that I couldn't hear it, nor the footsteps of that tiny creature cross the hall. I had the uneasy thought once more that we were interlopers, and that she might have been listening to our movements also.

And we were silent until the Condesa spoke. "That is a rather handsome young man, Roberto. What a pity he is so . . .

so . . ." She struggled for the English of the word she wanted. "So gauche—is that right?"

"Gauche? I wouldn't really call him that. In his own world he functions very efficiently. He's a hard-working farmer, and it must seem unbelievably frivolous to him that a group of people sit here and drink champagne at this time of day. Like a lot of well-heeled lay-abouts. He has no particular reason to like me since I'm saddling him with an unwelcome inheritance—"

"He doesn't want to be Lord Askew?" She smiled at the simplicity of a person who didn't want a useful social title.

"Why should he? There's no money with it. He has to have the title, but none of the perks that used to go with it. I imagine that when I die he will insist on being addressed as Mr. Birkett —or just Nat. He will need to go on farming his farm, and plain Nat Birkett goes down better at markets and fairs than Lord Askew. He can strike a bargain for stock on market days over a beer—not a glass of champagne, Carlota—rather more easily if he's the same man he's always been to the other farmers. Of course if he's got anything for the show ring, it mightn't look too bad to be Lord Askew in the programme."

"It's worth a little more than that, Robert," Gerald demurred.

"Is it? What am I going to saddle him with? Just this house, out of which, by then, I'll probably have sold anything of value, this valley, a lot of which is wilderness, a few stands of trees, which most likely he would hate to cut. There's the home farm here in the valley, and the farms the Tolsons rent. There might be a few acres here and there left of what was my grandfather's inheritance, but not much. The mines and quarries are worked out. There was some selling at the time my father died, for death duties, and then there came the time, after the war, when the income from the land wouldn't support my idle, roving life, so I instructed Tolson to sell what he had to. I didn't want to know any of the details—I just wanted the money. For that, I don't doubt Nat despises me. He comes of quite a different breed. His forebears were what they call Statesmen here in Cumberland. He lives in a house, carefully preserved, which has been handed down, father to son, for several hundred years. Not a grand house, but I'd bet anything it's a damn sight pleasanter to live in than this pile. He's in debt a bit—what farmer isn't? But he owns far more than his indebtedness. And the last time he borrowed money was on his father's death about six years ago and it was to buy—just imagine—it was to buy from Tolson a fair-sized parcel of land that runs right up against the wall of the estate which he needed to make his own farm more viable."

Carlota gestured in surprise. "Then he is simple-minded! He really is a very dull farmer with a handsome face. Why buy what you will inherit?"

"Not so simple-minded. It wasn't until after his own father died that he learned that he was next in line to me. That was when he began to worry about death duties, and what he was going to have to pay in taxes and so on, on this house. I think it was his effort to have something—a really prosperous farm—which he knew would be no part of the estate on my death. He went to enormous trouble to have it correctly valued at the current market price, so there would be no chance later for the Revenue Commissioners to say that he had it at a give-away price—or for nothing. Tolson wrote me all about it at the time. I was almost tempted then to come back, to see him and try to get something worked out. But I didn't. In the end, I didn't.

"So, Carlota, when he sees us sitting here drinking champagne, one wonders if he isn't remembering that it might be paid for with the money he had to borrow. Just imagine if he looked around here and translated everything he sees into so many sheep and cattle, so many tractors, so many bales of hay. Could you blame him?"

"And the estate is entailed . . ." Gerald ventured.

"The original estate is entailed. What was added after the creation of the Earldom is not. It's complicated, Gerald. I don't pretend to understand it. All I know is that I can't sell these farms—the farms all the Tolsons rent, what's in this valley and some land lying towards Kesmere. So Tolson tells me—or at least his brother did while he was handling the estate. The rest Tolson has been selling piecemeal over the years, as I've asked for more money and the rents haven't reached the figure I needed. In most cases, I suppose, the tenants were just too glad to be given the opportunity to buy. Most landlords won't sell. So what Nat Birkett will inherit is not only an unwanted title, but a very shrunken estate. Land is readily salable, but who in his right mind would want this house?"

Without thinking I spoke. "I would want it." I recognised the statement as the exact opposite of what I had just said to Gerald.

Askew smiled at me, disregarding Gerald's frown. "You're young still, and have the energy, and courage, I suppose. When one is sixty-odd you think only of the burden, not the romance." He went to refill his glass, and gestured with the bottle towards the rest of us. "We weren't meant to be here—my grandfather, my father, and myself. I think my grandfather was a great man, huge in body, and—I think—in spirit. He was a farmer and a merchant landed suddenly with a title he never expected. He was a reformer in his day—all kinds of new ideas about land drainage and reclamation. Before his time in all that. He went and took his seat in the House of Lords, and really thought it was going to be a platform for his ideas. New agriculture bills to be brought in, a better deal for the ordinary farmer and farm hand—rather than the landowner. He was howled down in the House. He never finished his maiden speech. My own father told me that when *his* father walked along the corridors of the House after that, some wit or other would set up the cry of 'Baa . . . aa . . .' after him. Not a noble lord at all. Just a farmer. So his son never went near the House —never even took his seat. Neither have I. It's funny how the sound of sheep bleating can echo down the years. Of course, if Nat Birkett ever chooses to go there, there'll be more respect for him. We've become very egalitarian since those days, and the man who really knows what farming is about is listened to. Well, I missed my chance. I didn't know anything. I haven't known how to do a damn thing since I left school except fire a gun. It may win medals, but not much else." He moved towards us. "Well, let's fill up the glasses again . . . and since the sun has come out, we might even walk down to the lake before lunch."

Gerald persisted. "What will Nat Birkett do with this place?"

Askew shrugged. "I haven't the faintest idea. I haven't done anything with it myself, so he'll hardly come to me for advice. Quite a few years ago Tolson started to worry about who would inherit, and so his brother got people working on it to find who was next in line. It turned out to be Nat Birkett's father, rather to everyone's surprise. He's about a fourth cousin—removed, at that. At that time, they didn't worry too much—there was always the chance that I might marry and produce an heir. I suppose it really came home to Nat Birkett when his own father died that the whole thing was more than a remote possibility. It became quite likely he would inherit, and he doesn't want it. He doesn't want the title, the taxes—or—" Abruptly he put down his glass. "And I assume he doesn't want any of the rest of it. The Earls of Askew don't have a happy history. Who could blame him for wanting to stay clear of it all?"

Even Gerald had nothing to say after that. Askew went around and refilled our glasses. It was surprising how flat champagne could taste. The first break in the silence came as the Condesa delicately and accurately tossed a cigarette end into the heart of the fire.

"And Nat Birkett has a wife?" she said. "The future Countess of Askew? He has children?"

"He has two thriving, beautiful sons, Tolson tells me—whom I've never met. He had a sweet, charming wife—a girl from somewhere over by Ambleside. The ideal wife for a good farmer who was going to become an Earl. Only she died. And do you know where she died? Right here in this house. She had a heart condition—serious, but not so serious they thought, as to cause her death except in rather extraordinary circumstances. But she died in one of the upstairs rooms here. No one even knew she was in the house. And this bloody place being what it is, they didn't find her until she'd been dead for almost a day, they think."

Now I heard his voice as it had sounded when he had looked over the wind-riffled tarn and talked of the Spanish Woman. "Poor little bitch," he said.

Lunch was an awkward meal during which Gerald uneasily skirted the subject of the Rembrandt; but it seemed that no one else wanted to talk about it either. I thought that Askew was so sure it was a Rembrandt that he felt no need for discussion. Only when Gerald mentioned leaving the next afternoon did Askew take any real notice.

"So soon, Gerald? Why not stay on a few days . . . you're looking far too much like a City gent."

Gerald set down his coffee cup. "I'd better ask it now, Robert. Do you want to sell the contents of this house? Do you want us to arrange an auction?"

Again, when pressed, Askew vacillated. "Well, I thought just the picture . . ."

"There is some very valuable furniture here, Robert," Gerald said. He hoped, I thought, to turn Askew's mind away from the painting, to show him that there were other things of value so that the disappointment, if it came, would be tempered. "I wonder do you mean to keep it as it's being kept now, or do you want to realise its worth?"

"I'd sell it tomorrow if I hadn't some qualms about it—about stripping the place before Nat Birkett takes over. It can't be worth all that much, surely . . . ?"

"It's worth more than you can afford to pay in insurance on it," Gerald said bluntly. Then, as complete silence answered him, he looked around, shaking his head a little. "It seems so . . . so wasted, somehow. Almost lonely." This was so totally unlike Gerald, who loved beautiful things, but was not sentimental about them, that I turned to stare at him.

Askew rattled his spoon nervously in the saucer. It was a long time before he responded. "Lonely . . . it's always been lonely." He wasn't talking about the furniture. "I've never been able to believe in this place. I've spent time here, but I've never *lived* here. When I used to come back on school holidays it always felt like some enormous hotel with no guests. If I could sell it—house and all—I'd gladly do it. As it is, yes, I suppose I'd better say I'll sell what I can. *You* tell me."

Gerald's face coloured slightly. "Well, I won't pretend that we wouldn't love to sell many things I see here. I thought that that was what you probably had in mind—to liquidate what you can while you're still able to enjoy the proceeds for yourself. After all, it will lessen the death duties on Nat Birkett. No one can tax him on what's been spent. You will pay your own capital gains tax, and that will be that."

"So what I'll be leaving Nat is the title, and the tax to find on La Española and the house, and what's left of the estate. They'll probably find ways to allow him to break the entail so that they can have their pound of flesh. What I worry about is placing the Tolson family in a bad situation. If the farms could be sold, would they be in a position to raise the money to buy them? I expect they might. Most banks will lend money on land . . . Perhaps I could even arrange in my will to help them —that is, if there's any money left that's actually my own when I die. I wouldn't like to see the Tolsons in difficulty. Nor would Nat Birkett. Well . . . it can be worked somehow, I'm sure. As for the house, Nat cares nothing for it, and I care less. I've no intention of living as a pauper for the rest of my life so that something like this can be preserved for a few more years. It's come to that. So what will you do, Gerald?" He said it almost defiantly, as if he dared anyone to say he might do differently. He was grateful to Gerald for seeming to thrust the decision on him. For this, perhaps more than any other reason, he had asked Gerald to come to Thirlbeck.

"Jo and I will leave tomorrow after lunch. I'd like to look at the other paintings before I go. And then I'll arrange for some of our people to come up here—they will have to take an inventory of every item, and you, Robert, must stay to tell us exactly what it is you want us to handle. You must stay here for at least that long." He glanced apologetically at the Condesa. "It won't be such a hardship. People come from all over England to spend a few weeks in the Lake District during the spring and summer. You see, it wouldn't do to enter into any disputes with Tolson over what could be sold and what couldn't. We must have your absolute authority for each article."

We sat for a while over coffee, and Gerald went on further about his plans, the whole apparatus of the beginnings of a great auction was set in motion. "You're aware of our scale of commissions for selling, Robert?"

"Commissions? Oh, yes, there has to be commission, of course."

"I'd just like to be sure you know it," Gerald said. "On individual lots up to five hundred pounds it's fifteen per cent. On individual lots from five hundred to ten thousand pounds it's twelve-and-a-half per cent. On individual lots over ten thousand pounds it drops to ten per cent." He glanced around him. "There are a great many items here which will, in my opinion, bring far more than ten thousand pounds. You may set a reserve price, of course, and if, at auction, the item does not reach that price, we, the house, buy it back in for you." He was reciting this almost by rote; this scale of charges was printed in every catalogue Hardy's issued. It was one of the ways the great auction houses held themselves above the dealer in modern paintings whose commission on living artists, and those who, dead or alive, were bound to him by contract, was often forty, and sometimes fifty per cent. I found myself for the first time wondering what commission my father's New York dealer charged for the sale of those pictures painted in Mexico, crated and shipped by air to New York, to buyers probably already waiting for them. Gerald was continuing, determined that Askew should know what expenses the forthcoming auction would entail. "If we were doing a valuation for probate or insurance there'd be a small charge—but if you, within a year of the valuation, send us the property for sale, the fee is refunded. On the contents of this house, which will, of course, run far beyond one hundred thousand pounds, the fee is one quarter per cent—refunded, naturally, since you have decided to go ahead with the auction. There are travelling expenses for the people who come to do the inventory, and a living expenses charge of five pounds per day." The mechanism, once started, went inexorably on. Gerald talked of sending up Hardy's two top Old Master's experts, and possibly another outside consultant. "It could be that there are other items of interest among the paintings from your Grandmother van Huygens. Are there other things locked away that we should see, Robert?"

He shrugged. "I lived here as a boy, Gerald, and after I left school I suppose I could count the weeks I actually spent in this house. There must be bits and pieces about, but as a boy I just wasn't interested. It was always a very uncomfortable place to live in—my mother went through one stage when she banished almost everything to the attics. Said she didn't want so many servants around eating their heads off just to keep the place dusted. A real Scot in that way, my mother was. She was completely dominated by my grandmother, who lived to a nice ripe old age. Our family were very unpopular in the county. No Edwardian house parties at Thirlbeck. They used to call my father 'The Invisible Earl.' He was very churchgoing—that's one of the few gatherings he was ever known to attend. He made my mother refuse all invitations—and she was allowed to issue none. No wonder she sent everything but essentials up to the attics. He never got over how the House of Lords treated *his* father. What he did was to thumb his nose at the whole system of which he was supposed to be a pillar, and yet when I went to Spain and joined the International Brigade he treated me as if I were a traitor. Perhaps the memory of that was what made me do such foolhardy things during the war. So you see, Gerald, there aren't many fond memories attached to this place. Might as well let it go." He twisted his cigarette into the saucer of the coffee cup. "Let it all go." He looked across at the Condesa. "We'll have some days in the sun left, won't we, Carlota?"

His answer was her hand extended to him. "Let us go for that walk we didn't have before lunch, Roberto. Yes, there will be days in the sun . . ."

They left us, and Gerald produced his notebook and was writing quickly, muttering to himself. I saw in my imagination the whole thing start up, the people from Hardy's I was so familiar with going over the place with interested, admiring—but stranger's—eyes. I saw the place stripped of what was preserved here, and what was left would be only that which was too large to move or to sell, and in the end the house might look as it had done when it was first built—very sparsely furnished with massive pieces, the long tables, the high-back chairs, the four-poster beds. The beauty of the house would shine through then, but it would be a house stripped of most of its history. For the first time in my life I felt a disloyalty to Hardy's. I wished Gerald and I had never come, had never recorded what was here. I began to understand the jealous possessiveness of Tolson and Jessica. I decided then that if I were invited to return to help with the inventory, I would find an excuse to refuse. I didn't want to see this house denuded, even for the most splendid sale I had ever been associated with. I suddenly understood the passion that invaded some men, so that they suffered any sort of indignity and invasion of their privacy to keep their ancient houses intact. And then, at that moment, I thought I began to understand Vanessa. If she had seen all this, and said nothing, then her reasons and feelings might have been what I was now experiencing. Once again I switched to dislike of that man, Robert Birkett, Earl of Askew, walking in the fitful spring sunshine with his mistress, planning their lives in a place where the sun always shone. Already I felt a sense of loss in what this house would suffer; I did not want to see it in the days when either the rain or the bulldozers would breach its walls.

* * *

Finally Gerald had finished with his notes. "I'm going up for a nap, Jo. You'll make some sort of start on that load of papers in the study, will you? Not that you'll discover anything in a few hours, but it will keep Robert quiet about the painting." He sighed. "Well, it will be my job to tell him what our experts think—but sufficient unto the day. You'll manage all right, won't you?"

I watched him go up the stairs, moving quite heavily. It was unlike Gerald to retire in the afternoon, but then I wondered if indeed he had really wanted to mingle with the first of the season's tourists in Kesmere when he had suggested the drive before lunch; Gerald's kindness sometimes overcame his innate discretion—about himself and others. Well, I wasn't ever going to see Kesmere. And I hoped I would never see Thirlbeck again.

Before I took the circular ladder from the library to begin my task in the study, I moved it so that I could climb up and inspect the prunus jar that stood on the top of the bookcases. Last night, lost in the shadows, it had given hope, but this morning even though my attention had mostly been focused on the people here, I still reacted to my training. Even to my inexpert eye it didn't look promising, and when I was up on the ladder and held it in my hand, it had no more virtue than the nineteenth century copies of the *Famille Noire* we had seen yesterday in Draycote Manor. These sort of jars were turned out by the thousand in Hong Kong. I shrugged. Well, what family didn't collect junk along with treasures? Or had this family ever collected anything? Perhaps all of worth and beauty, apart from the Elizabethan and Jacobean furniture which the house held, had probably come in the dowry of Grandmother van Huygens. I began to form an idea of the Askews—perhaps an unjust one. Lords of the manor in a small way, then owners of large tracts of land which gave them eminence, and then jumped-up to nobility, possessors of packs of hounds, and compliant women, and a great jewel. Until the event of a bourgeoise Dutchwoman, they had had nothing but their house and lands. I put the prunus vase back in its place with a shrug of half contempt. No wonder inherited titles of nobility counted for so little now. They were not earned nor even deserved. No wonder Nat Birkett fought against his inheritance. And Robert Birkett, for all his medals and his physical bravery, had lacked the courage to stay on and continue what had been begun so many years ago. He displayed a fatal weakness; it had needed only three generations for the vitality of his grandparents to decay into parasitical ennui. But as I climbed down the ladder I looked again into the bookcases, and noted the volumes—many titles in Latin, some in Greek, books on botany and anthropology, and there, in faded green leather, a set of the works of Darwin. This family had had its scholars, as well as its soldiers. What a mixed, odd lot they were. And I began to worry again about the stain of damp in the corner, and the mildew growing on the leather bindings. What else besides a possible first edition of Darwin could there be? In spite of myself I was growing interested in the Birketts again. Suddenly I felt more enthusiasm for the largely fictitious task Gerald had set me.

The enormity of it, though, struck me again when I wheeled the ladder into place under the wall of filing boxes in the study. I didn't even glance at the picture in its dark place down at the other end of the room; that was now for Gerald and the experts to worry about. I climbed the ladder and began staring at the dates on the boxes. When would Askew's Dutch grandmother have come to Thirlbeck? How old would she have been at the time? I allowed for Askew's age, and then gave fifty to sixty years earlier for the birth of his grandfather. When would he have married? At about the age of thirty—1880–1882? I took down a box marked 1880. When I opened the box by pulling on its red strings the smell of dust came strongly to me; there was dust already on my hands, and tickling my nose. I noticed with annoyance that although the box had been labelled 1880, the first few papers relating to rents due from variously named farms: Potter's Pasture, Bar End, Crossthwaite—were for the year 1883. The papers were brittle to the touch, and brown at the edges, and the ink turning brown. I glanced down the entries written in a copperplate, clerkly hand, and then a note thrust among the papers in this careful script in a thick sprawling hand, as though the writer had not the patience to spend much time at the desk. *See to the shipping of slate from Engle to Whitehaven. Dowson owes five hundred pounds. Start drainage of Torrister Bottom.* Askew's grandfather, the reforming farmer Earl?—the one who had been the butt of the House of Lords? Or was it the Earl he had unexpectedly inherited from? More sheets with accounts, then a surveyor's drawing of an acreage which contained three farms, one of them outlined in darker ink dated 1889. Something the Earl had sold—or wanted to buy. Then something written in a large, careful woman's hand—something that looked for all the world like a recipe and written in what I guessed was Dutch.

Then one absurd word at the bottom in English, in the same hand—*Gooseberries*. The prudent Dutch housewife putting down the store of jams for the winter? There might have been two hundred separate sheets of paper in that box. I looked despairingly at the boxes reaching over my head to the ceiling. It would make a fine lifework for someone—assembling the family history of the Birketts from their dusty, brittle papers. I sighed, and sneezed loudly.

"God bless . . ." It was Jessica, below me, and behind, standing in the doorway.

She wasn't fazed by my lack of answer. "Can I help you?" She seemed even smaller than before, and like a bright butterfly in this dim room, wearing her rather childish yellow sweater, something that looked as if it had been left over from school, shrunken from many washings, and outlining small, immature breasts.

"Well—I don't know." I wondered why she made me so uncomfortable, as if I had been caught prying. "Lord Askew and Mr. Stanton thought I might be able to find some references to the picture. But the papers are very mixed up. They don't seem to follow the dates on the boxes."

"No, they don't, do they?" she replied cheerfully, as if she didn't mind at all the difficulty of the project. "It's as if someone had the good idea of having all the boxes made, and then couldn't be bothered sorting the papers properly. You'll never get through them all this afternoon, will you?" So she already knew that Gerald and I would be leaving tomorrow. "What sort of paper are you looking for? I've been through a lot of the boxes myself—just for fun. Grandfather says I'll have to really settle down one day and put them in order. I don't see the point myself, but they're fun to look through. What sort of paper?" she repeated.

"Well, anything that might relate to the pictures Lady Askew, the Earl's grandmother, brought over from Holland. There might have been a list of some kind . . . anything. Anything about when the family might have acquired them. A bill of sale . . . some reference in a diary, perhaps?" She was already shaking her head.

"Is it important?"

"Quite important. It's always a help when something is going to be sold if there are some details of its history. Who bought it, who sold it, if it was ever exhibited. We call it provenance."

Her face grew quite blank. "No, I don't know anything. I don't remember seeing anything of the sort." She took a few steps towards me, coming round to face me. "Are you going to sell everything in the house?"

"Whoever told you that?"

"Well, you're from Hardy's, aren't you? Does Lord Askew owe some money? He shouldn't sell off what's here. It doesn't really belong to him—it has to be kept . . ." The blankness was suddenly gone, replaced by a passion which made her soft voice shrill.

"Jessica!" Tolson was walking through the hall and heard her voice. He came quickly to the door. "Jessica, what's the matter?" Then he took in the sight of me perched on the ladder. His eyes seemed to darken behind the heavy glasses. "Is there something I can do for you, Miss Roswell?"

I found myself explaining once again why I was there. His face remained impassive, and Jessica broke in before he could speak. "I've told her there's nothing. I would have found it, wouldn't I, Grandfather? I've been through almost every box that's there."

"Hush, Jess—hush. Don't excite yourself." His tone was deliberately calm. "I expect none of us ever paid much attention to what's in those boxes. But it's a big task. Far too big for Miss Roswell in a few hours. Perhaps when she's gone you and I, Jess, could start to look. Now, I think your grandmother would like some help. She's preparing tea. Lord Askew and the Condesa have driven into Kesmere." He looked up at me. "Jessica will bring a tray to the library in about twenty minutes. Perhaps you might be good enough to inform Mr. Stanton?"

I began to climb down the ladder. "Go, Jess, there's a good girl." The tone was placating, gentle, more full of emotion than I could have believed possible. There was the sound of her light running steps in the hall, and the unoiled squeaking of the service door.

"I'll carry the tray to Mr. Stanton," I said, "if that's all right. He's a little tired. It might do him good to rest until dinner."

"Of course, whatever you like, Miss Roswell." He appeared perfectly indifferent to what I did, the voice so utterly changed from a few seconds ago. He was about to turn when I halted him. I had to ask it now, because I knew it was possible that I would not see him alone again before we left.

"Wait, please." He waited, impatience in his stance. "Mr. Tolson . . . You—well, you probably remember my mother."

"Your mother?" He repeated the words as if I were a fool.

"Yes, my mother, Vanessa Roswell." I pressed him because he looked as if he were going to ignore my question altogether. "My father and mother, Jonathan and Vanessa Roswell. They were here for some months just after the war. They had the lodge at the other end of the valley, across Brantwick." I was using the name as if I had known it all my life.

"Yes, I do recall. Yes. What about it?"

He had drawn in upon himself even more. The eyes behind the glasses seemed to freeze me. "Oh, just . . ." He made it impossibly difficult. "Well, I wondered how much you remembered of them. Lord Askew said they were often here with him. It was before I was born—I didn't know they were on the Birkett estate. I knew it was somewhere in the Lake District, but not here . . ."

"What do you expect me to tell you?" he demanded. "I don't remember every little thing. It was the end of the war. Things were very difficult—rations hard to get. The Earl was in residence and there was a great deal to see to. Very little petrol. Mr. Roswell used to drive that Bentley that Nat Birkett has now, and it used too much petrol. The Earl used to give him *our* coupons. And then they had cream and eggs and even meat—from the lambs and bullocks we slaughtered. I had a terrible time accounting for it all with the Ministry of Food. The Earl didn't seem to understand about such things."

"My father wasn't well," I said. "Perhaps Lord Askew was trying to help him."

"That is as may be. But the Bentley and the petrol *and* the food."

I sighed. "I'm sorry to have revived unpleasant memories. You didn't much care to have them here, did you?"

"I let them the lodge—I was responsible for that. They just came here and asked, because they saw it was empty. Out of the blue, like a couple of gypsies. Lord Askew was present at the time, and he said at once that they could rent the lodge. It wasn't strictly legal. The Ministry of Defence had requisitioned the whole house during the war, but they never finally came to use it. I had no idea what they ever intended it for—some place to house some scientists, I think. It was very annoying. The North Lodge was included in the requisition order, and they hadn't de-requisitioned it at that time. But Lord Askew insisted that we could go ahead without permission. As it happened, the Ministry of Defence never knew anyone used the place. And they went off without paying the electricity bill. Lord Askew even wanted to give them the Bentley, but Mr. Roswell said he couldn't afford to run it. They just went off the way they came—like gypsies, moving south when the cold weather came."

Yes, it sounded like Vanessa—not to pay the electricity bill. It sounded like my father, too, who had a strange passion for old cars, a passion that he could now afford to indulge, his one indulgence I had thought it, when I had seen the three vintage models he maintained at San José, and which had excited such reverence and a sort of awe among the tourists who thronged Taxco. I could remember the two occasions he had driven me and several of the Martínez children to Taxco, and each time, in the main square, an American had wanted to buy the car. And looking at Jonathan Roswell, the way he dressed, the tourists might have been excused for thinking perhaps he needed the money. Yes, the Bentley would have been a joy he would have hated to leave behind. And he had said nothing about that, either.

I dragged myself back to Tolson's presence. He stood there, frowning, remembering, no doubt, the electricity bill, and all the wine and champagne they had drunk together that summer and autumn they had all been here. Gypsies . . . And Tolson's values were so deeply rooted in place and family. His loyalty was hardly to the man, Askew, but his idea of what the lords of Thirlbeck should be. And in his fashion, Askew had turned into a gypsy too. Did he blame Vanessa and my father for that? Well, he would never say so.

"Was the place—the house—like this when my mother was here?"

"Like this? Like what?"

"All the furniture about? All the good pieces?"

"Why do you want to know?"

"She would have enjoyed them. I hope she saw them."

"Why don't you ask her, Miss Roswell?"

I drew in my breath. Hard to believe the whole world didn't know that Vanessa Roswell was dead. But then, would someone like Tolson read the names of passengers killed in an air crash? Not likely. Who remembered names? Not at all likely unless it concerned Thirlbeck.

"She died a few weeks ago."

"I'm sorry." It was a barely polite formula, not an offer of sympathy.

"But was it like this?"

"You mean the furniture? I really don't remember. It was a long time ago. I had put most of it into one room when the requisition order came from the Ministry. I couldn't have a lot of strangers smashing up these things. Some of it was too big to move. Your mother might have seen them. I don't know. I was busy. I didn't have time to find out what pleased or didn't please her. She spent a good deal of time here. She didn't like the lodge very much. She was a poor housekeeper—not able to manage on the rations. Mr. Roswell was . . . artistic, wasn't he? He painted. Terrible daubs, I seem to remember. He actually gave Lord Askew one—as if he thought he would hang it."

"Were the others hung then, Mr. Tolson?"

"Others? What others?"

"There were more than the—the Rembrandt. Lord Askew said his grandmother brought over a lot of Dutch pictures. Perhaps I should look at them. My father's picture might be among them. I would like to see it."

"I don't remember seeing it after Lord Askew left. Perhaps he got rid of it. But the other pictures are . . . are put away. In safety. It doesn't do to leave things about. I didn't leave them about when the Ministry was coming in. Those people, they get a few drinks, and they start putting holes in things. No, I can't remember whether your mother saw the pictures. Why should I? She came and went. It wasn't important."

Then without another word he turned on his heel and walked across the hall. Unbelievingly I listened to the sighing squeal of the green-baize door. It didn't seem possible that anyone could be so deliberately rude. Tolson was a law unto himself. He cared for nothing beyond Thirlbeck. He had not cared for Vanessa and Jonathan Roswell; they had been a bad influence on the Earl. He saw things in very simple, clear terms, Tolson did. He had been one of the few people my mother had never charmed. I wonder if she had cared—or even noticed. She appeared not to have thought anything at Thirlbeck important enough ever to speak of it later.

And that was what was wrong.

*   *   *

It was while I was having tea with Gerald in his room that the next shock came. I told him nothing of the conversation with Tolson about Vanessa—why worry him with more detail of a situation which neither of us could explain nor fully understand. So I said nothing except to report on the muddle of the papers in the study, and then see Gerald's shrug of acceptance.

"Well, I didn't think you'd turn up anything in a few minutes. That would be too much to hope, after the way they've managed to neglect or hide away all these beautiful things. I continue to hope, though, that somewhere there exists an inventory of what came with Margaretha van Huygens . . . she didn't come penniless, and in those days people set store by a dowry. If she was the sort of housewife I imagine her to be, there would even be a list of linen . . . And the Birketts don't impress me as being very much different from other people when it comes to throwing out old papers. Can't be bothered to file them properly, but still never getting around to burning them. Well, maybe we'll see if we can't get someone from Hardy's onto it . . ."

I had been wandering around the room as he talked, looking at the things that Robert Birkett's father had gathered into this, the final room to which he had retreated in the last years of his life. There were a few photographs in faded ·brown tints. I paused before the photograph of an elderly woman, dressed in black, with lace collar and a lace cap, vaguely reminiscent of the later photographs of Queen Victoria. In her arms she held an infant, who wore robes of lace that trailed from her arms and fell over the darkness of her dress. Standing behind her was a young woman, slender and fair, dressed in unbecoming clothes, who seemed to cast a long and anxious look at the camera, trying not to mind that it was not in her arms the baby lay. "Robert's christening, I should imagine," Gerald commented. "Grandmother van Huygens very definitely ruled the roost, I'd say." And I thought what a strangely lonely little group it was. There was none of the bursting vitality of the large family groups of the Edwardian twilight, not aunts or uncles for the little infant, no cousins seated at the feet of their grandmother. How very alone Robert Birkett had been.

"And this?" I said. "Would this be Lord Askew and his father?"

"I imagine so. It looks like a small edition of the boy who turned up at Eton—and already carrying a cricket bat. Father seems a bit camera shy, wouldn't you say? Handsome, though, as Robert still is. I wonder where Robert found anyone to play cricket with?"

"Tolson and his brother, I expect," I said promptly. "And anyone else of about that age who lived on the estate. That was something the gentry and workers were allowed to do then, so long as the workers' children remembered to call him Lord Birkett when they howled him out—he would have been Viscount Birkett then, wouldn't he?" I moved on. "And what's this . . . ?"

"I wondered when you'd come to it," Gerald said. "Aren't they charming? Can you see if any of them are initialed or dated? My eyes . . . Almost certainly by Nicholas Hilliard, I'd say, and most likely he made the frames also, since he was a goldsmith as well as a miniaturist. I wonder what else there might be tucked away? I've a feeling, Jo, that there's a great deal below the surface, and we've only seen the tip of the iceberg. But, dear God, that painting down there—if it turns out to be a forgery, I think I'll regret ever having set foot in this place . . ." And he returned to his preoccupation with what concerned him most.

And I gazed in fascination at the four tiny oval portraits, none of them more than two inches high, encircled by a gold frame of highly skilled and intricate workmanship, surmounted by golden loops in the form of a bow studded with small diamonds, obviously meant to be worn with a chain or pinned to a gown. A man—dark, bearded, possibly flattered by the artist into a kind of lean handsomeness—and three golden-haired children, two girls and a young boy. They all wore the ruffs of the Tudor period, and the quality of each portrait, showing the family likeness, but each having its individual character, was extraordinarily high. Gerald's guess of Hilliard as the artist could very well be right. "Who are they?"

"I asked Jessica. They're the third Earl of Askew—I suppose that makes him the villain of the poor Spanish Woman's story —and his children."

"There's one missing." The four miniatures had been gathered into one group and framed together, the loops above them pinned onto a background of faded crimson velvet. There was space for a fifth, and as I looked closer, it was possible to see the faint oval of slightly darker red on the exposed velvet.

"The Countess, I suppose. Jessica said she didn't know what had become of it. It has been that way ever since she remembered."

"Yes . . ." I was suddenly possessed of impatience. When Gerald offered his cigarette case, I shook my head. "If you've finished I think I'd better take the tea things down. Are you going to rest a little longer, or would you like to take a walk?"

He shook his head, his eyebrows raised questioningly, indicating with a glance the rain that pelted against the window, the spring day changed again and the light beginning to fade. "Not now."

"All right—I'll take these down. See you before dinner—unless you need me for something?"

He shook his head and went and opened the door for me to pass through with the tray. "Thank you, Jo."

I left the tray on the long table in the hall—I didn't quite possess the courage to penetrate into Tolson's domain behind the baize door. And then I went hurrying back to the Spanish Woman's room. The scent of the potpourri greeted me; the fires burned in both fireplaces. I had the strong impression that Jessica had very recently been there. It was reasonable; someone would have to tend the fires once they were lighted, but why did I feel her presence like a light current of air? I went to the cupboard where I had laid my few things on the shelves, and I took from my handbag another of the things that had been in Vanessa's own handbag when they had found it among the scattered wreckage on that mountainside. I had carried it with me to Mexico, and looked at it often. There was something about the tiny, perfectly painted face that had reminded me of Vanessa, but I had never shown it to my father, because then I had believed it had been a recent and important acquisition of Vanessa's—some lucky, chance find which she had snapped up, knowing or guessing it was a Hilliard, and knowing what kind of prices such miniatures now brought. I had imagined that she had discovered the miniature during her stay in Switzerland. Vaguely like Vanessa, yes—this lady had rather wild red-gold hair, she was wearing a gown of dark blue, with a small ruff about her neck, and a single ornament, a bluish unset stone hanging from a gold chain about her neck. In the short time Gerald and I had been together in Switzerland I had never shown it to him, either. The contents of Vanessa's handbag had been almost too evocative of pain even to look at, much less discuss. But I had kept it with me, and all the other jumbled miscellany of her possessions, thankful that these few things had survived.

I carried the miniature to the end of the table and sat down, studying it now with an intentness uncalled for before. When the bag had been thrown from the plane it had hit the ground with sufficient force to tear the leather on one side. Inside, zipped in an inner compartment, the miniature had had the protection of its soft surrounds, and a little leather pouch which must have been made for it. But still, the force of the impact had broken one side of the delicate filigree of the gold frame, and the glass had cracked diagonally across its face. I placed it on the table and put the fragment of the frame where it belonged; I sat and stared at it, fingering the tiny loop of diamonds above it. I knew now that Vanessa had not found it on her trip to Switzerland, nor had she chanced upon it anywhere else. In every respect it was the companion piece to the miniatures in the frame in Gerald's room. I knew if I had carried it there it would have fitted perfectly the oval of slightly darker red, the vacant space in the frame.

Attached to the little diamond loop was a small white tag, held there by a piece of fine red string, identical to the price tags Vanessa used for small items in her shop. And a number—the price, I had supposed—scrawled in Vanessa's writing on the tag.

Had she taken it from here in the days when she had known Thirlbeck? Had she really stolen this, and even Tolson had not dared to accuse her to me? Gypsies, he had said. People who were light of passage. Had he been implying that she had been light-fingered, as well? And had she, after all these years, finally been hoping to sell it—to sell it out of England where there was less chance of its identity and its real owner being discovered? It was a new side of Vanessa perhaps revealed, and one I was too frightened to examine closely. I didn't believe what I was now thinking, and yet what else was I to believe?

The wind moaned softly in the chimneys, and the rain lashed with sharper fingers at the windows. I looked up, and the whole valley was blotted out, just the last point of the tarn still visible. Those giant messes of Brantwick and Great Birkeld, shapes that in only two days had become like known companions to me, had disappeared; the icy draught from the ill-fitting window found me once more. I shivered in the last light of an April day. And then, although I did not hear the car on the gravel below, the sudden uproar among the pack of wolfhounds somewhere down there told me that Robert Birkett had returned to Thirlbeck.

I put the miniature back in its pouch. It was probable that I would never know truly how Vanessa had come by it—I really didn't want to know. I wished I had a more secure hiding place than my own handbag for it. From that moment I knew I didn't quite trust the all-invasive presence of the little golden-haired girl who slipped through these rooms on soft feet. If I stayed at Thirlbeck much longer I was certain that Jessica would find it, and I couldn't bear that Vanessa's long-held secret should now, at this time, be violated.

IV

It is strange how quickly one becomes used to the unusual. Gerald and I went through the ritual of drinks in the library before dinner, dinner itself, and coffee afterwards in the drawing room, and our eyes hardly ever strayed to what was exhibited before us. Gerald had entered into a strictly professional mood, his afternoon rest had seemed to restore him. Neither of us was haunted by the thought of Vanessa here all these years ago; we were both used to the eternal presence, and gentle presence, I was learning, of the wolfhounds. In the vastness of those rooms, even their great size seemed to scale. In Askew's company they were supremely content, asking nothing but to lie, as best their size would allow, close to him, and close to the fire. Only in very general terms did Gerald refer to the auction; the painting was not mentioned. I assumed that Askew believed that Gerald had accepted it as it was purported to be, and no thought of the problem over the authentication to come troubled him. It was a quiet evening, even a dull one; the Condesa stitched at her needlework frame, we listened to the news on the radio, and went up to bed. As we climbed the stairs, much earlier than the night before, Gerald and I could hear Askew's voice as he spoke to Tolson. And then, again as it had been the night before, we heard the ring of metal on metal as shutters slammed shut.

I paused briefly at Gerald's door. "Good night, dear Jo. Sleep well."

"Sleep well . . ." And once again I felt the urge to kiss him, to offer some thanks for what he was, and had been to me. But I was not Vanessa, who would have done it spontaneously, so I moved on. I called over my shoulder. "All right if I take a bath? I won't disturb you . . ."

And his acknowledging wave was the answer I got.

After my bath I sat by the fire for some time, savouring the last of the ten cigarettes of the day. I was drowsy from wine, well fed, comfortable in this room that at first had seemed to overwhelm by its size. I noted the bed turned down, the three hot-water bottles in place, the fires well banked, and I told myself I was a fool for resenting and mistrusting Jessica's presence. Someone had to do these things. Because the doer was intelligent and imaginative, there was no reason to mistrust her. In this mellow mood, even the presence of the Hilliard miniature in Vanessa's handbag had other explanations. She had found it, as I had first thought. She had discovered it somewhere, and known where it truly belonged. If she had ever completed that flight to London she would have been on her way back here, to Thirlbeck, or in some other fashion she would have been in touch with Askew, and the miniature would have been returned to its proper place. When I stubbed out the butt of the cigarette, I went finally to stand by the windows again. Once more the scene had changed. The rain was gone, the wind had died; just the caps of Brantwick and Great Birkeld were now mist-shrouded. In the valley the moon was beginning to highlight all the ridges, to deepen the folds. Directly opposite the house, on the sheer slope of Great Birkeld, the icy stream of the beck, from which the house took its name, tumbled down in a thin sliver of water, over the silvered rocks. It seemed to go underground before it entered the tarn; I could see no disturbance of the still water. Everything was still, no wind in the chimneys, no movement of the feathering twigs of the beeches and oaks. And even as I watched, the mist moved higher and higher on the raw slopes of the two great shapes that dominated this enclosed world. In any other part of England I would have guessed that the morning would be fair and clear. I had learned, even in so short a space of time, not to predict such a thing for this country within a country. I turned back to bed, leaving the curtains undrawn, liking what the moonlight did to the room.

And if in bed I thought I saw the same shadow as the night before, the small, quiet shadow, perhaps of a young woman heavy with child, then it disturbed me no more than it had before. If Thirlbeck had a ghost she had no malice to those who wished her well. And the wine had been very good, and warming, and I was easily, and deeply, asleep.

It was all the more of a shock, then, to wake as if an arm had tugged me rudely from that sleep. I lay for a second frozen with fright. A look around the room revealed nothing unusual, but the sense of urgency still persisted; I was sitting bolt upright, shivering, and wondering why I was awake. I could never have described the force that impelled me from the bed. There was no shape by the dying fire, there was no sound in all the great house. No dog barked on a distant farm, no leaf stirred. But something was wrong.

I flung on my robe, and it was by instinct, rather than memory, that I found the light switch by the door. That left a dim light to reach to the farther corridor. Beyond was darkness—but once I had groped my way and turned onto the main gallery above the great hall of Thirlbeck, the moon streamed down through the windows, and I didn't need more light. I listened first at Gerald's door, and then, without knocking, I went in.

The bedside light was on, and Gerald lay half against the headboard of the bed, as if he had struggled to prop himself up with pillows, and had failed. One pillow lay on the floor. The pallor of his face was shocking; the sound of his heavy breathing reached me across the room. As I went near I saw the beads of perspiration on his forehead.

"Gerald—what is it?" I was bending over him feeling inexpertly for his pulse.

He wet his lips before he could speak, but I could see an

expression of relief and hope flood his eyes. "Pain, Jo. Rather bad, I'm afraid."

"Where?"

"Chest—and down the left arm. Very tight." I had by now picked up the pillow and placed it behind his head, and reached for another to pile on top of that. I put both hands under his armpits. "If I help, do you think you can push yourself up a bit. I think it's better to sit up. Helps you to breathe." His weight was more than I thought, but I got him almost upright, and wedged the pillows so that he wouldn't slip, and brought cushions from the sofa so that he could rest his outspread arms on them.

"I can't give you anything, Gerald, except a sip of water, perhaps. It might be the wrong thing. You'll have to have a doctor at once." I looked at the clock on the mantel. It was 2:20. "I'll have to go and rouse someone. Stay as quiet as you can. Don't try to move."

"Jo . . . ?" The whisper reached me as I was near the door. I turned back. "How did you know . . . ?"

I shook my head. "I don't know. Some . . . something wakened me." I had almost said "someone." "Be quiet, please, Gerald. It's the only way you can help yourself."

Outside I paused on the gallery, wondering what to do, where to go first. Askew's room was on the other side of the house, but which was it? And would Askew react as quickly as I needed. Tolson or Jessica would be the best—they would know which doctor to call; but where, beyond that baize door, would I find them? There was a whole wing of the house back there, as there was a whole wing on Askew's side. Then suddenly I saw in the moonlight a sight which almost froze my blood. Onto the gallery across the hall from me, their huge white shapes quite well-defined against the darkness of the panelling, had come the whole pack of wolfhounds. They lined up against the railing, in near silence—but the silence of the house about us was so great that I could actually hear their breathing. They didn't utter a sound, just stood there, watching, waiting.

For a moment I couldn't make myself move, and then the urgency of Gerald's situation reasserted itself. I couldn't call for help—I had to go for it, and would the dogs let me do that? I could see the row of white bearded faces above the railing, ears high, and the tall thin tails straight and erect, and still. I tried to remember the names Askew had called them. Strange names, from the Viking past, names that belonged to the ancestors of these dogs. "Thor—Ulf—Eldir—Oden." Strange how loud my whisper sounded in the stillness. I began to move along the gallery, walking slowly, to the head of the stairs. As soon as I moved, the hounds did also. We started down each arm of the stairs at about the same time, but then they all moved quickly, and they were waiting on the landing for me to come down. I felt my mouth go dry with fright as I began a very slow and deliberate descent towards that waiting pack.

And then I was among them. There was no growl from them, no sign of threat. Why were they not barking? If only they had set up their ear-splitting chorus, there would be no need for me to summon anyone—Tolson, Jessica, Askew—all of them would have come. But I was thinking of Gerald also, and realising that if the dogs set up their barking he might interpret it as an attack on me, and the shock might be more than he could bear.

"Sush . . . Thor . . . Ulf. Come now . . . come now."

They were all moving with me down the stairs, some ahead, some behind, their big paws and nails making scratching sounds on the wood. We reached the bottom of the stairs, and I made to turn for the baize door. Still there was no sound from them; they seemed neither friendly nor hostile; ears were still up, and no tail wagged. Then I remembered the study, and thought there might be a quicker way to summon help. The telephone by Tolson's desk had a small push-button system on it—it probably had extensions in Tolson's part of the house, and perhaps in Askew's room. I turned slowly, and with the delicate tread of a sleepwalker, I made my way, surrounded by the dogs, towards the study door.

As I touched the knob Tolson's alarm system was triggered. Alarm bells sounded through the house, and I could hear them ringing in the passages behind the baize door. I stood petrified, the sweat trickling down my arms. Very soon, within a minute or so, the lights began to come on—from the gallery above, and another shaft falling across me from the passage when Tolson swung open the door. But in that time the strangest of all the strange things which had happened since we had entered the environs of Thirlbeck occurred. Instead of adding their chorus of huge deep voices to the strident ringing of the alarm bells, the dogs, as if moved by one reflex, all squatted down around me, those odd whiskery faces almost smiling at me, the dark eyes intent, and the tips of the long tails beating the floor with pleasure. None of the heads turned as Askew appeared on the gallery above me, or as Tolson paused, rooted, in the doorway.

Though they were like some loving circle of protection about me, I thought once more of the great white hound who had been seen by me—and only by me—on the slope of Brantwick, and I was sick with fear and bewilderment.

CHAPTER 4

I

We followed the flashing blue light of the ambulance along the road that led by the South Lodge of Thirlbeck, past the high wall and iron gates, through the narrow pass to Kesmere, I seated beside Askew in his sports Mercedes, my hands tightly clenched, and my teeth clamped together to keep them from chattering with cold and tension. I kept watching the blue light, somehow believing that as long as it kept flashing, Gerald would still live. There were lights on at the South Lodge, and a man stood by the gates to see us pass, giving a slight nod to acknowledge Lord Askew, and then at once he closed the gates. About a mile farther along the valley we had passed another house, a dark shape set back from the road, and on a slope, where more lights burned at a lower window.

"Nat Birkett's up," Askew said. "Either going to bed late or getting up early. I thought all the lambing was finished. It might be a calf though . . . it's always something being born, or dying, with farmers."

"With people, too."

"Yes," he said.

We didn't speak again until we reached Kesmere Hospital—a modern brick building, sprawling in several directions on one level, a sort of overgrown cottage hospital. We saw Gerald only

137

briefly as he was wheeled to a room, but I was cheered by the smile he managed to give us. He was attended by a man who had shaken Askew's hand when he had come to Thirlbeck—a man of about Askew's own age, Dr. Murray. "Can't believe he's still here," Askew had said during the drive. "I used to play cricket with him. He attended my father before he died—even wrote to me in Spain to warn me of what was coming, but I never got the letter. The war . . . And then he came after . . . after the accident. Did his best. I was very grateful to him. Came to see me for a drink a few times after I came back in '45. Both of us rather in the same state—recently demobbed, and both of us inheriting from our fathers. He got a country practice, and I rather think he got the better deal. At least he was trained for his job. He must have thought I was a bit of a dead loss . . . Tolson says he's a very good doctor. He looks after all the Tolsons—the wives and grandchildren. Knows them all. Hard to find that sort of thing any more. I'm glad he's looking after Gerald."

We sat together in the waiting room of the hospital, and I broke my rule and smoked one after the other of Askew's cigarettes. A nurse came in and gave us some tea; she was middle-aged and curious. She stayed to arrange magazines on the table, and offered remarks about the weather, but no answers to the questions I asked about Gerald. I saw how she stared at Askew even when he'd given up listening to her. She would have been old enough to remember the return of the much-decorated Earl after the war, the brief stay at Thirlbeck, the absence that now had become legendary. I had watched her colour when he had spoken to her; in his sixties he was handsome enough to cause a woman to do that.

Then Dr. Murray came back. I jumped to my feet. "How—"

He gestured me to sit again. "Got a cigarette, Robert? Thanks." I could have screamed with impatience as he lighted it. "Well, now, things aren't at all bad. We've got a good little cardiac unit here. Quite new. Damn good little hospital, in fact."

"Gerald—"

"Mr. Stanton is all right. You're not his daughter, are you?"

"No, he's a very old friend. We work together."

"Well, he's doing well. It was quite a mild attack—or at least that's what the cardiogram is saying now. He says he's pushing seventy. In very good shape for his age. Just have to be a little careful. We'll keep him here awhile—do a work-up on him. Of course he'll have to rest. That's imperative. I hope he was here on a holiday, not for work."

"A bit of both," I said unhappily. "We did the drive all in a day. I suppose we should have stopped . . . and we did some other work on the way up here. The Motorway makes it seem easy . . ."

"Too damn easy. Whether you're flying or driving, it's all hard work, and he's not a young man."

"Should he go back to London, Alan?" Askew asked. "Would there be better treatment there? I don't mean to be offensive, but he's . . . well, a lot of us regard him as a rather important man. And a lot of us"—now he was looking over at me—"love him."

"What are you suggesting? That he should be in The Clinic? Just fashionable, that's all. He'll get everything he needs here, and fresh air as well. Probably better nursing—we're pretty well staffed here, and we've got a couple of good young men just joined the staff. No, leave him here. The journey back to London by ambulance wouldn't help him one bit—not screaming down that Motorway, breathing diesel fumes. I'll let you know if he needs a specialist from London. I promise you I won't hesitate about that. But he won't. When he's completely fit to travel he can go and get his specialist check-up in London. Until then, he's better here."

"Can I see him?"

He shook his head. "He's dozed off. We've sedated him. He has no pain now. Just tired."

"I'll wait then."

"I wouldn't if I were you. It could be hours before he wakes."

"I'd like to wait. I want him to know I'm here."

Murray stubbed out his cigarette. "Well, I can't kick you out. But are you going to keep Robert waiting here with you? We old men, you know, we need what sleep we can get."

"No, of course not. There's just the question of how I get back. Perhaps . . . perhaps one of the Tolsons will be coming into Kesmere in the morning . . ."

"It's morning now, my dear girl." Askew got to his feet. "Here's the keys of the car. Come to think of it, I've still got the keys of Gerald's car. You'll run me back, won't you, Murray? Not too far out of your way." He smiled down at me. "Try not to worry, and don't wait too long. It would be just as well if you came back and rested, and saw him later. All right"—as he saw me open my mouth to protest—"I don't insist. Just tell Gerald I'll do everything in my power for him. Thirlbeck is his home for as long as he cares to use it. And I will gladly stay on to keep him company. I hope you will, too. You're good for him. Oh, here . . ." He put his cigarette case in my hand. "You'll be needing these."

Through the window I watched them both walk to the doctor's car. They were deep in conversation. For the first time I was grateful to Askew. He had known that I could not have left without seeing Gerald; the time was still too close to Vanessa's death. I would wait.

* * *

One of the nurses let me sit near to the windowed area of the intensive care unit. From there I could see Gerald's every movement, the gentle rise and fall of his chest as he breathed, the occasional movement of his arm and fingers. His very heart beats were being recorded on a monitor. I was watching the second that his eyes flickered open. I went and touched the arm of the nurse on duty, but the monitor had already told her that much. "Can I . . . ?" I said. "Just for a second. I won't say a word. I just want him to know I'm here."

She nodded. "Be very quiet. There are other patients . . . don't excite him."

And then I went and did what I should have done before. I went and stood by the bed, and I bent and kissed him. In ordinary circumstances he would have hated it—the fact that he was unshaven, rumpled, showing signs of his agony and fatigue. Now he just smiled faintly. "Knew you'd fix it, Jo."

It was beyond all the canons of my time, my generation, but I no longer wanted to play it cool. I touched his cheek, that unshaven cheek, and pushed back a lank piece of hair from his forehead. "I love you, Gerald," I whispered.

And then, obeying the beckoning of the nurse, I left.

I went out into the air, to the strange car in the parking lot, to a new key in my pocket, jingling against the gold of the cigarette case. Against all that I had thought about the change-ability of the weather here, the morning had dawned as calm and fair as all the radiant night had promised.

II

The gates at the South Lodge were firmly locked, and no one came to open them when I sounded the horn. Smoke rose from the chimney of the lodge, a building very much like the derelict one over beyond Brantwick, except that it was in immaculate condition, and had a fairly recent addition at the back. Here the wrought-iron gates with the crest of the Birketts had been preserved—no doubt by the same Tolson son who was so skilful at making metal shutters. They were formidably high, beautifully worked, and painted a glossy black. The walls on either side ran straight across this narrow end of the valley, and were in good repair. The face that Thirlbeck showed to those who came venturing on this dead-end road was prosperous enough, and hostile. On the wall beside the gates was a starkly painted notice.

THIRLBECK
STRICTLY PRIVATE
BEWARE OF THE DOGS

And beyond, almost lost in the distance and by the budding cover of the trees, was the heraldic frieze topping the great windowed bays of Thirlbeck outlined against the backdrop of Great Birkeld, the plunging beck glistening in the morning sun, the lower slopes a mingled mist of larch and birch. An enticing, beckoning fairytale world to which admission was strictly forbidden. I rattled those closed gates in frustration, and returned to the car to wait until someone should come. Was everyone who used these gates expected to have a key? Or did they know the comings and goings so accurately that they could leave the lodge, and the unexpected arrival might just possess himself of patience until they returned? It was Sunday morning, but in a farmer's life that made no difference. The chores were there to be done, as always.

The thought of farming brought me back to Nat Birkett. His house was there, visible, on the slope about a mile back; if he had a key to the North Lodge, then he probably had a key to this gate. I turned the car; better to do something than sit and wait for one of the Tolsons to turn up and let me in.

Nat Birkett lived in a rather beautiful house, I thought. It was called Southdales, simply a geographical description of its location. There were two oaks by the gate, a short drive, and a house of the myriad colours of the stone and slate of the Lake Country—blues, purples, dull greens and greys, all laid with the precision and craftsmanship that these men of the stone trade had learned through generations. It was two-storied, quite low, an L-shaped building with dormer windows on the upper floor. Its position on the slope, the slate of walls and roof, made it appear to grow out of the ground. The vines and climbing roses that twisted about its length were just beginning to put out leaf, and they pulled it farther into the earth, and gave it the homeliness of a house that had never aspired to grandeur. I began to understand Nat Birkett a little more—he, in his independence, possessing this and good farming acres as well, what would he want of Thirlbeck?

He had opened the door before I was out of the car. He marched out to meet me. "Is there trouble?" he said. "Can I help?"

For the first time since the moment I had discovered Gerald ill I could have wept with relief. For a second it seemed that Nat Birkett would shoulder all my worries, that he offered me a welcome and a concern I had not yet encountered.

"Yes, there was some trouble. You can help, in a small way,

possibly. I'm locked out of Thirlbeck. I wondered if you have a key to this gate, since you have a key to the other one."

"Yes, of course." Then he looked at me closely. "What's happened? You look awful . . . Come in."

I found myself in a kitchen which felt as if it had been inhabited for a thousand years, and that all the domestic life of the house flowed from this room. There was a beautiful dark oak dresser displaying blue china, red striped curtains at the windows, two rocking chairs before a brick chimney piece that had a bright red Aga cooker set into it. There was an electric stove, and a big refrigerator, and a new sink, and someone had found panels of old oak from which to make cupboards to surround all this. There was a great old table in the middle which was worthy of Thirlbeck itself, and a set of beautiful Windsor chairs. I had rarely been in a room of such charm and warmth. I found myself seated in one of the rocking chairs, edging up to the gentle heat that came from the Aga, nursing a steaming hot mug of coffee into which Nat Birkett had splashed some brandy, and he was rapidly making slices of toast as he listened to me talk.

"Bad shock," he said. "But he's going to be all right?" Then he added as an afterthought: "By God, I don't think I would have wanted to face those dogs in that way in a strange house—and they *know* me, after a fashion."

"You just have to do some things, don't you?"

"Yes." He placed the buttered toast on an oak table stool between us, and dropped into the opposite chair. "You'd better eat. You must be famished. I'll be cooking some bacon and eggs for the boys in a few minutes, and you can have some of that."

After a night of cigarette smoking I had thought I couldn't eat, but the atmosphere of this house, and Nat Birkett himself, had broken down those kind of nervous defences one erects at times of strain. I felt it was now safe to lay down the night's burdens. I ate like a hungry child, licking the dripping butter from my fingers, and holding out the mug for more coffee and brandy.

"I don't suppose you have brandy for breakfast every day, do you?"

"No," he said. "But I don't have champagne at eleven, either." We laughed at the memory of it; it seemed much farther away than yesterday. "I felt a right fool, I'll tell you. That elegant pair, Askew and his beautiful Condesa, really put me off my stride. I've handled champagne glasses before—I'm not quite an oaf—but I suddenly felt as if the damn thing was going to break in my hand, or that I'd knock over one of those silly little tables. I was afraid to move. And then you and Stanton came in, and I felt even worse. The experts up from London— fine art dealers, knowing all there was to know. You looked as cool as the Condesa, only a bit more useful. And I felt as if I must still faintly smell of the cow byre or the lambing parlor."

I gulped the coffee. "I don't look like that now, though?"

He shook his head. "No, you don't. You don't look at all like that. You look . . . well . . . human. As if something got out of you that you've been keeping locked up."

Without meaning to I found myself talking about Vanessa, about the way the wreckage had looked in the snow, about the arrival of my father and the weeks at San José. "It's all been so unreal. I haven't had time to get used to it. Last night I was terrified I was going to lose Gerald. I didn't know I could bear that so soon . . ." The words were spilling out of me as if they had thawed from some place frozen at the centre of myself. I hadn't been able to speak even to Gerald of some of these things; it was not the sort of talk I would have offered to any of the people I knew in London. I remembered the day I had gone back to Hardy's, and everyone had been so kind, but I really hadn't been able to speak Vanessa's name, and had taken refuge in the shop talk which was our lives and our passion. But to this man, a stranger in a strange world, I was saying things I had not even known were there—the jumbled mosaic of Vanessa's life, the acquaintance with my father which had become a friendship in so short a time, a little even of my stumbling search to find my own self—the self that surely must exist apart from Vanessa and my bits of ceramic, my peregrination all over Europe to look at works of art, and somehow missing myself on the way. I think I even talked about Harry Peers—wondering if Harry saw me as the cool creature of Nat Birkett's description, but still a person who stood in Vanessa's shadow, and even could permanently be identified with my role at Hardy's. All this spilled out in the half hour or so that I sat there with Nat Birkett, and the sun grew stronger at the windows, a cat scratched at the door to be admitted, and a collie dog arrived with it, both of them taking their places without question near the warmth of the Aga.

"My God," he said at last, "you know what you need—you need a couple of weeks walking on the fells just as badly as you needed that couple of weeks in the sun in Mexico. But getting to know a father at your age is a bit of a strain—sun or no sun. So in the time you're here you just get yourself a pair of decent walking boots—real *boots*, not fancy gear—and an anorak, and get up on the fells and walk. Walk until you want to drop. You'll be too tired to think. Just one thing, though. Stay where you know your landmarks. Don't go too high. Stay on the trails. It's an awful waste of time going out and finding these daft people who think, on their first day out, that they're polar explorers. And remember it's always rather hard-working people who have to go out and find them—people who'd rather be back doing what they should be doing."

"You think I'm going to stay?"

"Askew said you should. And Stanton has to have someone with him."

"Yes . . . yes, I suppose you're right. I'll have to telephone one of the directors. Someone at Hardy's has to know at once what's happened to Gerald." I pushed myself from the chair with effort. "I'll have to go. I should telephone at once . . ."

I felt his hand pushing me back, so that the chair rocked wildly. "Time enough," he said. "None of your directors is out of bed this time on a Sunday morning. Stanton's all right, isn't he? So don't drag anyone out of their sleep. Might as well shove some breakfast into you while you're here. Judging from the elephant noises above, the boys will be down in a few minutes."

"You were up early yourself—or to bed late." I told him about seeing the lights on the way to the hospital.

He grinned. "I'd like to tell you to mind your own business, and pretend I had a roaring night out. But it wasn't—a heifer had a hard time calving. Our animals sometimes need more looking after than our kids. And if there's anyone a bit more hard-worked than a doctor, it might be a country vet. That's why we keep the brandy bottle around. Nothing quite like it after you've just pulled a calf out with the rope."

He was interrupted by a kind of rumbling noise on the stairs, as if a couple of rocks were being rolled down. The kitchen door was flung open, and two young boys stopped dead in their paces as their eyes fell on me.

"Strawberry had her calf," Nat said. "And this is Miss Roswell. She's staying at Thirlbeck and got locked out."

"Jo is my name," I said. "What are yours?"

The older one straightened himself. "I'm Thomas. He's Richard." And then added with complete seriousness: "We thought there might be a Harry, but Mother died."

"Shall we call the new calf Harry?" the younger one asked.

"You'd have to call her Henrietta," Nat replied. "No, I don't think you should call her Henrietta. We might sell her one day. And then Harry would be gone. You wouldn't like that."

"No, that's right. We wouldn't like it." Thomas looked expectantly towards the Aga. "Will we start breakfast? It's almost time. But Richard's lost his Sunday tie . . . I gave him one of my old ones." The talk flowed on, and I was accepted without question, as if I were the new calf who had walked in during the night. They were beautiful, these boys, as Askew had told us. The older was about ten years, the younger about eight, and they still had that soft rosy bloom that healthy children wear, their badly combed, still-damp hair was a wheat-coloured blond. They looked like their father, but I knew that their mother had had intensely blue eyes, and a spikey fringe of lashes. They moved gracefully, and yet had the slap-dash quality of young children. They each knew their appointed tasks as Nat got out the frying pan. The eggs and sausages and bacon came out of the refrigerator, the cups, saucers, and plates were set on the table, the bread ready for the toaster. They did it as if they were all used to it as a prescribed ritual, something they did every morning of their lives, not just on Sundays. At last the younger came close to me, patting the collie as he spoke, a gesture that protected his shy eagerness. "You're going to stay for breakfast, aren't you, Jo? I've laid your place."

We all sat down, and I ate as much as the boys did, and more than Nat. I watched him as he moved from stove to table, and the eggs were dished straight from the pan. "Sorry about all this," he said. "But this breakfast bit is done to a tight schedule. The boys have to get off to school every morning, and the bus doesn't wait for late-comers—Thomas, elbows off the table."

"Does the bus come this far?"

"No, just to the crossroads a mile up the road. They go to the elementary in Kesmere. Three of the Tolson grandchildren are young enough to go with them, so there's quite a bunch."

"Dad, here's Mr. Tolson now, coming up the drive."

"Then you're late. Get upstairs and get your jackets. Richard, try to get that egg off your mouth." There was a clatter again on the stairs, and almost at once it was repeated as the two came down again. They were struggling into jackets, hampered by the large Bible each carried. Nat gave a last-minute twitch to Richard's tie and straightened his socks. "There—out you get."

"Dad, you're not going to come?" Thomas said.

"Thomas, being up half the night to bring a calf into the world is as much the Lord's work as going to church."

"Can I *not* go sometimes?"

"When you're older you'll decide yourself whether you want to go. Until then, you'll go with Mr. Tolson—and me, when I decide I want to go."

"I'll bet I'm grown up pretty soon."

"I'll bet you are," Nat replied.

And then the door opened and Tolson stood there, clad in a severe grey suit that looked oddly out of place on his big body, as if a bear had tried to assume the camouflage of a mouse. His hair, also, had been greased in an attempt to tame it, without much success. He just stood there, without greeting, and stared at me. Jessica came to the door behind him.

"Miss Roswell . . ." His tone was a rumble of displeasure.

"I was surprised to see Lord Askew's car here. I thought you were at the hospital."

"You'd shut her out, Tolson," Nat said.

"There's a phone, isn't there?" Jessica observed. She looked like a spun sugar fairy in a pink suit which she managed to make look elegant, even though it wasn't expensive; her shoes and gloves and handbag were plain. Sensibly, she wore no ornament about her; she knew enough not to gild the lily.

"Yes—there's a phone. But I decided to invite Jo to breakfast." He cut off Jessica's talk as if to remind her to mind her own business. "Well . . . you've all had quite a night over at Thirlbeck."

Tolson still looked at me as if the trouble were somehow my fault. "Yes," he said. "Very unfortunate. But Lord Askew says Mr. Stanton is doing well. Will you be leaving today, Miss Roswell, as planned?"

"I don't know. Lord Askew thinks it would be better for Mr. Stanton if I stayed. But I must telephone some of the directors of Hardy's about what's happened to Mr. Stanton . . ." I was more than ever aware that none of the Tolsons wanted me at Thirlbeck; they possibly saw Gerald's illness as a great inconvenience, a reason why both of us would stay on. As I saw Tolson's dark eyes boring in on me through the pebble lenses, a sense of resentment grew. This man dominated too much at Thirlbeck; he was its guardian, not its owner, and he had no power to turn me out. My body, which until then had seemed limp with fatigue and strain, was recharged with energy. If I couldn't outface this man, for Gerald's sake and my own, then I was nothing, and I might as well crawl back into my cupboard at Hardy's. "I will make that decision when I have consulted Mr. Stanton's colleagues," I said crisply. "But I think you may take it that I won't be leaving at once."

"Well, *that's* nicely arranged." Jessica's heels tapped sharply on the floor as she moved back to the door. "Grandfather, we'll be late if we go on with all this talk. Thomas . . . Richard . . ." What she had to say to them was lost as the three moved to the car. Tolson stood looking at me for a moment longer, and for the first time I sensed a sort of helplessness in him. Something in his planned and careful world had been upset, and he did not know how to adjust. In that moment his strength seemed diminished, and my own grew.

"I shall need to get into Thirlbeck, Mr. Tolson," I said. "Would you be good enough to lend me a key?"

"A key?" His head went up like an old lion whose territory had been challenged. "That won't be necessary, Miss Roswell. My daughter-in-law, Jessica's mother, is now back at the South Lodge. All you have to do is sound your horn. Good morning, Nat. I'll see you when I bring the boys back from church."

"You might not," Nat replied. "I'll probably be in bed. But I'll be over during the afternoon . . . some things about the new fencing to discuss."

"In that case," Tolson said, as he turned to the door, "I'll keep Thomas and Richard with us. They can have their lunch with us. I'll tell Jessica's mother there won't be any need for her to come here today—leave you to rest undisturbed. My wife will have cold food ready for you to bring back for supper."

His big frame darkened the sunlight at the doorway, and then he was gone.

I waited until the sound of the Tolsons' car had died away. I went to where I had left my handbag on the floor by the rocker, and took Askew's cigarette case out. As I extended it to Nat I saw his eyes linger on it. "No—" I said. "I don't run to gold. It's Lord Askew's. He left it with me at the hospital. Thanks . . ." as he struck a match and held it for my cigarette. "They seem to have arranged things very nicely for us all. Do you always let them run your affairs like that?"

Nat pushed back his chair, and swung it on its back legs. "I suppose it does look that way." He shrugged. "It's difficult to see how *not* to do it. And it works. Things were in a pretty bad state after Patsy died. The whole centre was gone from our world—for all of us. I could have found a live-in housekeeper, or I could have married again quickly just to achieve the same thing. I didn't care for either of those solutions. As it's happened, the Tolsons—all of them—have provided a continuity for Thomas and Richard that no outsider could have given them. I haven't tried to thrust anyone into their mother's place.

In every crisis that's arisen the Tolsons—one or other of them—have been here to help, sometimes to cope completely. Jessica's mother comes up here every day and does some cooking and cleaning, and she's not a woman who would normally do that. Except that to the Tolsons the boys and I already count as family—that is, they're simply beginning a little early a service that they'd normally be giving to the Earl of Askew. And that's what I'll be some day, whatever I may do to try to dodge it. So why resist? It could be worse. The boys have friends in the younger Tolson grandchildren, mothers of a sort in the Tolson wives, uncles in the Tolson sons. And there's Tolson himself, the patriarch of the clan. Things could be worse . . . and I see no better solution."

The chair legs rapped against the floor as he swung upright again. "It isn't ideal. But then nothing's been ideal since Patsy died. I go along because they've made it easy for me."

"And that includes taking your sons to church every Sunday?"

"It includes about everything. Tolson has strong ideas about how my sons should be brought up. Church is one of them. School is another. He's even at me to send them to Eton when they're old enough. He's been dropping heavy hints about a prep school. Eton! My God! They'll just have to be good enough to get into the Kesmere Grammar School, and that will do them. But Tolson doesn't think that's fitting for the sons of the future Earl of Askew. And yet he knows my income and how much I owe the bank . . . and he's offered to finance the whole thing from the Birkett estate. I gave him a flat 'no' on that—and still, even in the last week, he's said that all he has to do is to get Askew to write to Eton, and there'll be a place at least for Thomas. He's got very old-fashioned ideas, Tolson has. And he really can't believe how much I loathe the idea of moving into that niche that's all carved out for me."

I was standing by the window while he talked, staying very quiet because I had not wanted the flow of his words to stop. There was the kind of anguish of a lonely man in them, a man who had surrendered a part of a cherished independence so that his children would have a family, and the roots which that family gave them. I saw the two rosy faces of those children as part of his sacrifice, and as a reward for it, and I couldn't blame him. I remembered all the years when all I had known of my father was that he sent money to Vanessa for me, and now when I knew Jonathan Roswell myself, I knew what I had missed. But Nat Birkett was not a loner as Vanessa had been, as my father was. He could not be expected to live all his life alone. And then, coldly, I wondered if Tolson had already selected the woman that Nat Birkett should marry—as he probably had selected the wives for his sons. In the warm sunshine of that window, I could barely repress a shiver.

"I didn't realise how well you could see Thirlbeck from up here. That frieze around the top, and the tower."

The sunlight had made the lake a shimmering cloth of gold behind the buildings, the pasture about it seemed soft green velvet, the animals like toy creatures beneath the great oaks and beeches—the England of storybooks it seemed now to be, and no one could have guessed the dark spots of its history. "Will you go and live there, Nat?"

"Live there! You're daft—just *daft*. You and Tolson might make a good pair. I'll never live at Thirlbeck."

"Then what will happen to it?"

"It isn't mine yet. I'll worry about that when it happens. Do you realise . . . ?" He paused, and poured himself more coffee. I heard the coffeepot banged angrily on the table. "I suppose all women are soft about things like that. They see a great pile of stones, and just because it's got a bit of history wrapped around it, they think it's got to go on forever, no matter what. Tolson got to Patsy that way. He began to get her over there . . . any excuse at all. When the boys were very small they used to play all over the house. Tolson wanted them there, wanted Patsy to begin to think of it as her home. He even got them crazy about those blasted wolfhounds of his. The boys actually used to ride on their backs when they were small enough. It was insidious, the way Tolson planted things in Patsy's mind. He meant it for the best, of course, but it turned out for the worse. She actually died there, my Patsy.

She died in that wretched place. And now it seems like a mausoleum to me."

His chair scraped the floor as he rose. I watched as he went and brought the brandy bottle to the table. Then he brought two glasses and poured some neat, and carried both to the window where I stood.

"Here, drink this, and then go back and get some sleep. And try to forget all this nonsense I've talked. It gets too much at times—times when I'm tired and I realise the boys are growing up, aren't babies any more. I've seen her stand there where you've been standing—she didn't look like you, though. She was fair, but she didn't look at all like you, and she didn't act like you. She was a nice little girl, unsophisticated, unspoiled, and given to dreaming. I suppose most people would have said she was sweet, and let it go at that. But she was generous as well. Oh, hell, what's the use of trying to describe someone you've loved. I remember she used to stand there at that window and look down at Thirlbeck—'many-towered Camelot' she used to call it. And I knew that Tolson was getting to her, and there wasn't a thing I could do about it."

He moved away from me, back to his seat at the table, and poured more brandy.

"I wonder if I'm getting drunk?" he said. "Well, it doesn't matter. I'll be sober enough when I go to pick up the boys. Setting a good example, Tolson always calls it. God, you're right. I *do* let them run my affairs. And sometimes when I begin to realise just how much they run my affairs, I think I'll never get out from under the whole load of them. Tolson, all the sons and wives, their calm assumption that I'll take it all over when the time comes. None of them wish Askew dead, but he isn't part of their world any more, and won't be. His time is past. *I'm* the future, and they've saddled me with the future, and I haven't—God, I haven't got the strength to think for myself." He cupped the glass between both hands. "I'm smothering under it. They cook my food, and do my laundry, and clean my house. They try to make it seem as if Patsy hadn't died. But they can't give her back to me. And there's Jessica . . . God, I *am* drunk . . ."

I put down my glass, and gathered up the cigarette case and my bag.

"I'd better go now."

He didn't hear me. I had grown cold again at the mention of Jessica's name, as if the sun and the brandy hadn't touched me. For a moment I stood and looked at him, and remembered some of the things that had spilled from me in that half hour when he had kept me sitting by the range, and had listened to the jumble of things that had poured out. I had lived through an extraordinary night in my life, and he had lived through a routine night and morning, and now he sat and talked of the loneliness, and the pressing sense of the future being shaped in a way he didn't want it shaped. Would we be able to forgive each other for the things we had spoken and told? Would we despise each other for the weaknesses confessed, the anguish of death still with both of us? Strangers who have talked too much were often better never to meet again.

"Good-bye, Nat."

I don't think he even looked up as I went. Outside the first cloud had appeared at the ridge of Great Birkeld. The radiance of the morning died slowly as I drove down once again to the gate of Thirlbeck.

CHAPTER 5

I

I fell into the routine of the next days and weeks with strange ease, as if I had somehow been waiting for this pause in my life, as I had waited, without knowing of it, for that journey to Mexico. The phone calls were made to Hardy's; the managing director, Anthony Gower, asked me to stay on at Thirlbeck. He had already, he said, been contacted by Lord Askew, who had asked the same thing. I was to do anything I could to make Gerald comfortable, and to telephone daily reports to Hardy's. There was a slight note of alarm in the director's voice; for him, also, the Lake District seemed far enough away to be in another country, and he had the Londoner's feeling that nothing at the hospital here could be good enough for Gerald. He had talked to Dr. Murray, he said, and been reassured, but it was my task to make certain Gerald had every attention he needed. And I was to think of coming back only when Gerald himself could return. My time, he implied, was of far less importance than Gerald's comfort.

Then, from a public telephone box in Kesmere, I talked again with Mr. Gower. This time, his correct, pleasant voice had taken on a faint note of excitement, as much as a man who has handled sales of some of the most important art objects known would ever permit himself. I told him what Gerald and

I had seen in the few rooms of Thirlbeck which were open to us, and that it was Askew's intention, Gerald judged, that it should all go to auction at Hardy's. But Askew was not to be hurried. He had insisted that nothing be done until Gerald was completely recovered, that no appraisers from Hardy's should come at this time, lest Gerald should become involved, and overstrain himself. Judging Gerald's mood myself, I said nothing, for the moment, about the Rembrandt.

I also telephoned Gerald's manservant, Jeffries. I had a difficult five minutes calming his first panic. Jeffries had been with Gerald more than thirty years; he and his wife had entered Gerald's service when Gerald's wife had been living. In the deaths of those two women they had grown closer, the remains of what had once been a family unit. "He really *is* all right, Jeffries. No, it isn't advisable for him to travel yet—he needs rest. Mr. Stanton would like you to come up here. I'd be grateful if you could drive my car up. Then you could take over the Daimler. Lord Askew would like you to stay on here until Mr. Stanton is able to leave, so you should pack suitable clothes for you both." I described where to find my car, and asked him to go to my flat and bring some extra clothes for me also; I would telephone the owner of the ground-floor flat, who had a key. Jeffries was the one man I could have asked this favour of, but Jeffries was the sort of man who could have bought an entire wardrobe for a woman, once given her size. He also knew that I was somewhat neater in my habits than Vanessa; he had been fond of Vanessa, but disapproving of her style. I gave him the number of the car, and said I would telephone the garage. "You remember it, Jeffries? It's a Mini."

"A *Mini?*" He cleared his throat. "Now that you mention it, Miss Roswell, I do seem to recall it." He didn't recall it with any pleasure. It would be a severe test of his loyalty to Gerald and myself to drive it all the way to Thirlbeck.

"I'll expect you late tomorrow then?"

"I'll be there first thing in the morning, Miss Roswell. You surely don't expect me to *sit* here all today."

I went then to visit Gerald, thinking about Jeffries, a man past sixty, driving all night up the Motorway in a car which rattled when it was pushed past fifty miles an hour. It would have been useless trying to dissuade him; he wouldn't have any rest until he saw Gerald for himself.

I was only allowed to see Gerald for a few minutes the first day, but Dr. Murray told Askew and myself that he would be out of the intensive care unit within forty-eight hours, if there were no further trouble. The Condesa came with Askew, and blew Gerald an airy kiss through the glass of the unit which separated them, and I realised I was jealous because Gerald looked so pleased. He was washed and shaven, and was wearing a pair of Askew's red silk pyjamas. The colour of life had returned to his face, and his eyes were bright. Then I was suddenly able to laugh at my own jealousy, and exult in the feeling of something won back from death.

I had arranged to meet Jeffries in Kesmere the next morning. He pulled his long length from my red Mini as the post office clock was pointing to ten, and his grey-suited figure was already registering disapproval of everything he saw. He was yet another who couldn't see anything of any merit outside London.

"How is Mr. Stanton?" was his greeting.

"I've telephoned the hospital. Doing very well, they say."

"We'll go at once, then."

"Jeffries, I don't think you should. You look tired yourself, and you probably need breakfast—even just some coffee. I know you'd like to freshen up. It won't," I added as he started to shake his head, "do any good for Mr. Stanton to see you looking tired after such a long drive. He'll start to worry about *you*."

He submitted, reluctantly, and we went and ordered bacon and eggs in a cafe that looked as if it did a large trade with fell walkers. Jeffries was supremely out of place here, and seemed happy that he so obviously was. He had a highly developed sense of snob values which only long service to a rich man could bring about, and yet he had remained kind. He said nothing about the Mini, just asked if the Daimler were running well. I thought of his night on the Motorway, and laughed. "Beautifully. Not a rattle in her."

Jeffries looked hurt. "I trust not. Not the Daimler."

He relaxed a little after he had eaten, and even asked if I minded if he smoked a cigarette. "What sort of people are they —who takes care of Lord Askew? I'll be staying there, I presume?"

"The Tolsons—good people, Jeffries. But not . . ." I didn't know how to express it; very few people had servants these days, though Jeffries always himself used the term. I hardly knew how to say it. "Well, Mr. Tolson has been a kind of steward for the estate, and all his family work for it, as well as for themselves. They're not actually *help*. It's more their home than it is Lord Askew's."

"Most irregular," he said.

"I don't think you'll find it at all irregular when you meet them, Jeffries."

Nor did he; he made a point of our driving round to the stable yard, which now housed only farm machinery, and entering through the back door. Before unloading Gerald's and his own bags, he first carried in the large red fibre glass suitcase he had packed for me. Its inexpensiveness, the very mass-produced look it had, must have pained him as much as driving the Mini; he was eminently a man for leather luggage. Tolson and Jeffries confronted each other in the kitchen— Mrs. Tolson was seated at the table mixing a batter with an electric beater, and Jessica came in from an adjoining pantry. Jeffries took one swift look at the spotless, old-fashioned kitchen, smelled the bread baking, his glance going quickly from Tolson to his wife, in her white apron, using her arthritic hands skilfully, to Jessica in her neat blouse and skirt, and his approval was instant.

"My name is Jeffries," he announced. "I am Mr. Stanton's man. I expect to take care of him while he's here, and of course to take over any of the extra duties which Mr. Stanton's and Miss Roswell's presence may involve. I am used to cooking, polishing and dusting, cleaning silver and valeting. I also drive Mr. Stanton and clean his car. Anything I can do for Lord Askew in that direction I shall be happy to do. I'll take up Miss Roswell's bag first, and then if you'd be good enough to show me where my quarters are, and if I might locate an ironing board . . . I understand Lord Askew doesn't travel with a valet . . ."

There was a tradition of service which made these people instantly recognisable to each other, as disparate as they were. This was not an age of servants, and yet each of them chose to give service to some ideal of how the world should be ordered. It was not of my generation or time, and so I turned away, and found myself walking back through the kitchen door, to the stable yard, where the Mini and the Daimler were parked. I knew what was going on between these people, but I was not part of it. Jessica in her way, out of her time, understood and knew, and she partook, just as much as pleased her. Then, for the first time since Gerald became ill, I found I was brushing tears away from my eyes. The Mini, which I remembered as perpetually dirty, only garaged because I could not take the time to feed parking meters, nor to find any permanent free place to park it, was transformed. It had been washed and polished, and even the dirt of the Motorway didn't obscure that; it had been vacuumed inside, the ashtrays emptied, the shelf which usually held half a year's accumulated rubbish had been tidied, but only the obvious things discarded. It was the innate reaction of an extremely tidy man to a car which he would drive, for however short a time. I felt somehow shamed as I looked at it. Other people's standards were higher than mine—and if they were old-fashioned standards, it did not make them invalid. I drove the Mini to a place in the outbuildings next to the Mercedes, and left it there. If I was to stay on at Thirlbeck, the Mini couldn't stand always beside the front door. I wasn't a passing guest any longer.

II

There was Harry Peers on the phone from London. "Why didn't you tell me, you idiot? I'd have come up. Listen, do those hicks up there know how to take care of him?"

"He's all *right*, Harry. He really is all right."

"Don't you believe it. He'll probably be thrown out with

the bath water and find himself in one of those bloody lakes. Don't trust that lot myself. They know how to look after animals better than people."

"He's being very well looked after, Harry." I was beginning to grow tired of making that statement.

"Are *you* being well looked after, luv?"

"How well is that supposed to be?"

"As well as your Harry would look after you. I'm waiting for you to come back, Jo. Don't make it too long."

And then there was the vacant dial tone on the telephone after he had hung up. I suppose it was part of Harry—that habit of never letting anyone else finish a conversation.

I gave a thought to Harry and how he would have disapproved of the idea as I took Nat Birkett's advice the next day about fitting myself out with walking boots and an anorak. I had been to see Gerald quite early, and although he had made a marked improvement, I knew it would be weeks, not days, that I would stay at Thirlbeck. I felt self-conscious in the shop, not really knowing what to ask for; they were unpacking new stock ready for the arrival of the tourists—stock that seemed to range all the way from fashionable raincoats to the most professional kind of camping equipment. I was looking without much conviction through the racks when Nat Birkett touched me on the shoulder. "Saw you through the window. You're in the wrong place, you know."

"But they said this was the best shop."

"It's all right. I just meant you're looking at the wrong stuff. Those things might look all right in Bond Street, but they won't keep the cold out up on the fells."

"I wasn't really planning . . ."

"While you're here you might as well use your time. And that means walking. So . . . you get a padded anorak with hood and zips, like this—plenty of pockets. Here—this your size?" He jerked down a bright yellow one from a hanger. "It'll get dirty, but it's easy to see if someone has to go and bring you down off the fells." He surveyed it critically. "Yes—that'll do. Have you got a heavy sweater—really heavy? Well, that can wait a bit. But you'll need boots . . ." I found myself, under his supervision, trying walking boots that laced firmly about the ankles, worn over two pairs of heavy socks.

"Am I supposed to *walk* in these?"

"You will, once you hit the right stride. They could save you breaking an ankle." We were outside, Nat carrying the package of heavy boots, and I wearing the anorak rather self-consciously. It was new, stiff, and the yellow was very bright.

"We'll break it in, shall we?" Nat said.

"How?"

"Take some sandwiches and go to the coast. That'll get some mustard on it, and put some sand in the pockets . . ." We were walking towards the small town square and the car park. Nat's Bentley was a conspicuous anachronism among all the other cars. "I'll just telephone the farm. I really should go out there and collect binoculars and vacuum flasks and compass, and really get you initiated, but as sure as I do something will have blown up, and I'll get nailed. Suddenly, I feel like a holiday . . . We'll make do with wine instead of sensible hot coffee and soup."

I sat in the high passenger seat of the Bentley, and stared down those who stared at me. I thought that some people, not tourists, looked at me with more than ordinary curiosity. To the regulars of Kesmere, Nat's Bentley was a familiar thing, but mine was not a familiar face. I was glad when he came back, his arms loaded with paper packages.

"I've been causing some gossip, I think," I said to him. "People have been wondering what Nat Birkett picked up in a bright yellow anorak."

"Let them. Do them good. That's the trouble with these little places—everyone knows your business. Of course, when you're in trouble, it helps not to be surrounded by strangers." He was going through all the routine movements, unfamiliar to me, of manoeuvring the ancient car out of the parking space. It made a lot of noise, and a kind of ominous shuddering went through the body. "Needs a bit of work done on her," Nat shouted. "Damn thing takes more time than she's worth . . . don't know why I bother." The top was full of holes, he said, and so it stayed down, permanently. I found myself zipping up the anorak as we passed beyond the outskirts of the town, and the pace increased to more than twenty-five miles an hour. "That's about all she'll do, safely," Nat roared at me. "Cold?"

"No." But I was. At the same time there was a kind of exhilaration about riding so high in the world, of feeling the stream of air flowing about my face, of being able to see over the stone walls and hedges. I got used to the stares of the motorists who passed us. All at once I pitied them because they weren't bowling along as if there were hours and hours of time to travel a few miles.

We headed west, over a series of passes through the mountains. The Bentley laboured a little on the steep grades. "Really does need work on her . . ." But then after an hour the scent of the salt wind came to us, and we stopped at the gate of a farm and a dirt track leading towards the dunes. I got out and opened the gate, closed it carefully; I didn't want Nat to stop the engine in case it wouldn't start again. He seemed to have no such worry himself. He drove down the dirt track as far as an empty shed, almost roofless, and stopped.

"This is far enough. I know the man who owns the place. He never uses it—it isn't much good for farming, this kind of land. Bit of sheep grazing in these next two fields, but really only for summer. I've often thought I'd like to buy this bit so that the boys and I could fix up the byre as a kind of beach hut— leaving camping and cooking stuff in it. Maybe come over some evenings in the summer. But somehow there's always something else to spend the money on." He looked at the place more speculatively. "Really ought to sound Marshall out, though. The land's not worth much. And he can't get building permission here. I have to," he added, "keep reminding myself that it's necessary to *find* time to spend with the boys. Time alone. I can't let them grow up completely with the Tolsons. I shouldn't let myself just become part of the background. I ought to mean something different to them."

He led us through the dunes at a place where a beck trickled down to the sea. "It becomes a torrent after heavy rain," he said. Then we walked about a mile until we rounded the rock pools at the foot of a low sandstone headland. A small beach glistened between that and another headland. "St. Bees is a bit farther on." The Irish Sea glinted greyly in brief flickers of sunlight, with the beginning of a swell on it. "Always in a contrary mood, the Irish Sea is," Nat remarked. "It doesn't have anywhere to go except to pound England on one side and Ireland on the other—a hell of a lot of compression in one small space." We ate hunks of bread with pieces of cheese and ham, and tried to smear on butter with plastic knives, and squeeze on mustard from a tube. I got both butter and mustard on the new anorak, and Nat said it looked better. We sat with our backs against a boulder and drank very good red wine, passing the bottle back and forth to each other because the paper cups spoiled the taste. Afterwards we walked along the beach and Nat showed me how to make my way up a small cliff face, using the new boots, how to look for footholds and handholds. "Definitely not to be tried on your own, you understand. A fall of ten feet is enough to kill you if it's in the wrong place."

As we climbed, Nat gathered the little flowers and plants that grew in the crannies of the rocks, giving them their names—thrift, scurvy grass, rock samphire, bloody cranesbill—marvellous names, I thought, and tried to remember them. I tried to memorise too the birds he named—the terns, the fulmars, guillemots, kittiwakes—but all that was really familiar were the gulls, and their haunting, piercing cry. Then suddenly Nat said, "We'll have to move, or we'll be stranded here. The tide's coming in." We went back down the rock face with careful ease, but there was a sense of haste in the way we packed together the remains of the picnic. Nat cleared the sand where we had sat of the last matchstick, and the first drops of rain began to fall. By the time we reached the ruined byre where the Bentley stood, it was a downpour.

"No use waiting," Nat said, surveying the leaking roof. "We'll get just as wet here as in the car." He showed me how to adjust the hood of the anorak so that it covered almost everything but my eyes, and then he took an old cloth cap and loose oilskin from under the seat of the Bentley.

As he climbed in he said, "This is one of the times when I know what a damn fool I am to be bothering with a kid's toy like this. I spend more time and money on it than I can afford, and the Land-Rover is a damn sight more efficient and more comfortable. I never bothered with it when Patsy was here, but afterwards Tolson sort of thrust it on me as if I needed something to play with. I'm supposed to be a pretty good mechanic. It was a bit of an embarrassment when Askew showed up and I realised I was driving *his* car . . . Well, keep your head tucked down. The wipers don't work, so we'll have to lower the whole windscreen. It's going to be a long, wet, cold drive."

It was all of that. And it was worse because Nat's mood seemed to have changed as quickly as the rain had come down. He didn't attempt to talk during the drive; I thought sometimes he cursed the labouring slowness of the Bentley on the grades, and the car seemed to him as he had described it—a silly child's toy. The tops of the fells had vanished in the mist. Kesmere emerged at last out of a sullen grey landscape. Nat was perfunctory as he said good-bye in the town's car park, stopped beside my Mini. The rain poured down, and the place was deserted. His mood seemed to have taken on the wintry quality of the day. He was regretting the picnic, I thought; all the way through that wet drive he must have been thinking how much better the time might have been spent. I tossed the bundle with the boots and socks into the back of the Mini, and prepared to get in. I didn't know if I should try to thank him; a starkness in his face froze the words. He had probably taken me to a place where he and Patsy had often picnicked, and with me it hadn't been worth the journey. As I got into the Mini he suddenly said, "Here—take these," and he turned away without another word. In my hand were the little rock plants he had gathered, and the feathers of dune grasses. I didn't know whether he gave them to me as a gift, or because he simply didn't want them himself. That night in the Spanish Woman's room I laid them carefully between sheets of a newspaper and put them away in my big suitcase. Then I shook the sand out of the pockets of the anorak.

* * *

In the next few days I eased myself into the stiffness of the new walking boots. In spite of the heavy layers of socks they raised blisters in a few miles' hike. "Tenderfoot," I told myself, as I soaked in a mustard bath that Jeffries had insisted on my taking. Jeffries knew all about such things as mustard baths, and when to drink brandy after a long walk. I began to wonder how Nat Birkett would have taken to him. Probably not at all, I thought, as I soaked myself, and then went back to the brandy poured and waiting in the Spanish Woman's room. Jeffries loved the Spanish Woman's room, as, by this time, he loved every part of Thirlbeck, even those parts whose untidiness and neglect troubled him. He deplored the lack of conveniences, the old-fashioned stoking of the heating and hot-water system, he worried about the state of the roof. "But it's a marvellous house, isn't it, Miss Roswell? And those pieces downstairs—they'd make you want to weep to see them all bundled together like that. But still, I suppose Mr. Tolson's right. He has to look after them in the only way he can. Actually, his security is quite good, considering it's a sort of homemade job. Would cost a fortune, though, to put this house properly to rights . . . pity." He didn't, however, like the dogs, and he was puzzled, as I was, even if I refused to admit it, that they had begun to hover around me whenever Askew was away from the house. "Ugly-looking great brutes, aren't they, Miss Roswell? When I saw you setting off for a walk yesterday and all eight of them trailing you I really wondered if you'd be safe."

"I think I couldn't be safer."

He had looked doubtful, but then brightened as another thought came. "Well, Mr. Stanton's in his own room at last at the hospital, and he'll be out in less than a week if all goes well. Remarkable recovery. He'll live to be ninety." I had the feeling that if Gerald did do that, Jeffries would feel obliged to live long enough to take care of him.

"Wonderful people, the Tolsons. There aren't many like them now. Perhaps there's something to be said for living in the country and keeping your roots. That little Jessica girl— very clever, she is. And very capable. Can turn her hand to almost anything. It'll be a lucky man who marries her. But I haven't noticed any boy friends around. Well . . . there's plenty of time. She wouldn't throw herself away on just anyone, that little girl."

The edges of life at Thirlbeck that had been a little ragged became smoother with Jeffries's presence. In his total devotion to Gerald he wanted to serve Gerald's friends. He seemed to take no time off for himself. If he was not with Gerald at the hospital, he took on any task that offered at Thirlbeck. "I like to be busy," he said when Askew demurred about him doing too much. And then he added quietly: "One likes to be needed, my lord." And so he waited on table, and pressed clothes, cleaned bathrooms, vied with Jessica in producing beautiful food; he shared meals and exchanged recipes with the Tolson wives, and baked and iced a triumphant birthday cake for a Tolson grandchild.

The Condesa in those days displayed a dimension I had not expected in her—why did one think that beautiful women like her would always be self-centred and helpless? She had an ability to amuse and charm Gerald, and she used it unsparingly. She had a knack for finding books and magazines which would interest or amuse him, without tiring him. She would even read aloud to him from some of the magazines, making sharply wry comments on English customs and manners which delighted Gerald. Every day she brought fresh flowers, which she insisted on arranging herself, and she was very skilful with them. The flowers that arrived from friends in London were handed over to her, and she brought vases from Thirlbeck to replace the utilitarian ones belonging to the hospital, which she knew Gerald loathed. And when she sensed Gerald was tiring, she would sit quietly in the room, saying nothing, working at her needle-work frame, and I was not the only one who knew that just the sight of her pleased and soothed him. Jeffries openly adored her. "A really elegant lady," was his comment. "What a pity she can't marry Lord Askew."

I found my own rather solitary place in the world of Thirl-beck in those days. There was the daily visit to Gerald, and a report to Hardy's. Between them, Jeffries and the Condesa seemed to have taken away many of the small tasks I might have done for Gerald, so I was free to walk, and to drive, wherever I pleased. For the first few days I drove far afield of Thirl-beck, becoming familiar with the range of this country that seemed almost a foreign place. At first I did the obvious things —Wordsworth's tiny cottage at Grasmere, the churches of the dales, the haunting ruins, stark against the sky, of ancient castles, the druidic circles of stones that had stood, their purpose unrecorded, from pre-history. Beyond Thirlbeck's closed valley there were the great sweeps of fells and dales, the long stretches of the larger lakes, the eerie flatness of Morecambe Bay when the tide was fully run out. I never went back to the stretch of sandstone cliff near St. Bees. Each day I turned back again to Thirlbeck with the sense of the history of this pocket of England more firmly impressed upon me. I had seen the worked-out coal mines and slate quarries, had seen Whitehaven from where Askew's grandfather had plied his coastal vessels, and won a Dutch wife; I had seen the flocks of sheep, the Herd-wicks, that were the wealth of this country, upon the dales and high on the fells. At Askew's insistence, Tolson had given me keys to the two gates of the Thirlbeck valley, so I had the freedom to come and go, but more and more, as the days passed, I found myself turning back to Thirlbeck after the morning visit to Gerald, because the valley, and the house, seemed to hold the whole essence of this country. I walked the road over Brant-wick, through the larch plantation, moving quietly to catch a glimpse of the herds of red deer that roamed its fringes. Once I had a glimpse of a stag, antlers briefly silhouetted. I stood by the ruin of the lodge where Vanessa and Jonathan had lived that summer and autumn when they had experimented with the new life that survival of the war had given back to them both, the experiment that had obviously failed. But it gave me nothing of them, just the renewed regret that I had known my father only after Vanessa was dead. I stood often in the copse of birch where the first evening the great white hound had appeared, but I never saw it again.

I found the stone marker that Askew had talked about. Half hidden by the tall reedy grass growing about it, it was set in the marshy area that ran down towards the lake, within sight of the crumbling balustrade that marked the line of what had once been Thirlbeck's formal garden. I came on it by chance, and for a moment I didn't realise what it was. It was a roughly hewn stone, about three feet high; it might once have been a lintel over a doorway, except that it tapered slightly, giving it the vague air of an obelisk. I brushed the grasses aside and deciphered the clumsily chiselled letters, almost obliterated by weather and the all-pervasive moss of this area. *Juana*. And then, beneath this, as if it were not identity enough, further words, slanting away crookedly. *The Spanishe Woman*. I squatted before it, tracing the lettering with my fingers, wondering if this had been made by the boy who had been with her when she died, the boy who had been at the court of Philip, and could read and write. Juana . . . I wondered if Vanessa had ever seen this.

The ruined chapel and the burial ground of the Birketts was totally unexpected. It lay to the east of the house, on the side where the pele tower stretched to the sky. I found it by following a path that was barely more than a sheep trod to a copse of beech, elm, and oak, planted more closely than through the rest of the park. The walls of the roofless chapel had almost disappeared under a cover of ivy and briars, an outer wall kept the sheep out; the little iron gate sagged, but still held its place. It looked as if some work had recently been done on the hinges; Tolson, no doubt, had qualms about letting the sheep graze the graves of the Birkett family, but I thought myself it would have done the Birketts no harm, and at least would have checked the worst of the rough growth. Little sapling trees were beginning to gain height among the graves, a slender young birch had raised itself twelve feet within the walls of the chapel. I could read very few of the headstones because the blackberry straggled and sprawled voraciously over everything, clutching at my anorak and slacks. There were enough headstones, though, to account for many generations of Birketts. They couldn't all have been here—some must have died in distant places. But there were enough, and from here, staring across the tip of the tarn that came closest to the house, I noticed that the place where I had seen the marker for the Spanish Woman seemed to form a roughly equilateral triangle with the chapel and the house itself. It might have been pure chance, its placing there, or quite deliberate. Who could say anything for certain now in the twisted story of the Spanish Woman?

* * *

In the brilliant sunshine of an early afternoon I followed a sheep trod that wound steeply upwards on the rough, heathery slopes of Great Birkeld and experienced the swift shock of seeing clouds quickly rolling down from the tops, the mist descending rapidly, the trail ahead and below blotted out, the tarn vanished, the sheep wall I had taken as my landmark gone. I knew at last the real danger of what Nat Birkett had warned me about, and I had not totally understood. I remembered, too, that I had told no one where I was going, what direction I was taking. They were used now to my wandering and no longer asked.

The mist changed everything. Now that I could no longer see the trail defined before me, every step was in question—had it gone up here, down there? Was this a fork, or some blind turning that might take me toward the sheer crags of rock, the dangerous slope of scree? I turned back, and the trail I had followed only minutes before was no longer there. Sounds came to me out of the mist—the sounds of sheep cropping at the sparse grass, a faint bleat, the rasping sound of my own breathing all thrown back and distorted by the white wall of vapour. I knew now that I had definitely lost the sheep trod—this was spongy moor grass, there were hollows and depressions filled with dark peat and little pools of water. I could have turned back on myself a dozen times in the next hour; I never found anything that looked like the trail again, and I was exhausted. I stepped beyond the shelter of a boulder, and my foot touched the edge of the scree flow; a few small rocks were dislodged and I listened to them rattle and bounce on their terrible journey to the bottom. I froze then, edged back a little, holding onto the boulder as if I hoped it would save my life. It would do nothing for me, only give me its hard rock surface to lean against. I sat down on the wet ground and prepared to wait—to wait until the mist might lift, or to wait until the cold of the coming spring night, the invading damp, brought the final exhaustion, the terrifying sleep of desperation. In the next hour I seemed to grow lightheaded with cold, with hunger, and sleep, that deadly sleep, began to seem a pleasant alternative. I remembered the stories, the pitiful little news bulletins of walkers found dead from exposure within a few miles of warmth and shelter, and I always wondered how such things happened, and why they were so stupid. I wondered if I would die here above the valley of Thirlbeck—or might someone find me unconscious but still living? How cold did it become up here before dawn? And how long could one survive without moving? A kind of dreadful, fatal calm settled on me; I could begin to acknowledge that what I might be waiting for was not the mist to lift, or for the rescuers to come, but death itself.

I first heard it as a kind of far-off howl, unbelievably eerie and desolate. Was it near, or something coming from the floor of the valley, sound thrown back and reflected by the water, the high rock walls, the mist itself? It seemed to come from every direction; I was suddenly in the position of a sightless person trying to distinguish one sound from many. Then, very suddenly, it was quite close, the sounds of small rocks disturbed, the sound of feet on grass, and that awful howling sound. I screamed as something wetter than the mist touched my face, and then, at once, they were all around me. Sobbing, I put out my hand and touched the whiskery faces, their little beards with droplets of moisture strung on them like beads. "Oh, my God . . . Thor . . . Ulf . . . Oden . . ." I found myself clinging about the neck of one of them—which one I didn't know—and sobbing, wildly sobbing. Several of those rough tongues licked my face. One of them thrust his great head under my arm, as if to urge me back on my feet. I got up slowly; one dog stayed beside me, the others went off into the mist— they might only have been feet away, but I could no longer see them. I didn't know at that time if all eight were there. Their voices called to each other and to me at intervals, as if indicating the direction I should move in. With my hand firmly on the collar of the dog who had stayed with me, I started down.

I don't know how long that journey lasted. I was nudged and pushed and pulled—up a little here, down at another point. I never really knew if we got back on the sheep trod. They were smelling and sniffing their way, hoarse barks of encouragement and guidance coming to me from the leaders out of sight. And then finally we reached one of the sheep walls that ran straight up the slopes of Great Birkeld—probably the one I had taken that afternoon as my landmark and guide. Step by step I went down, feeling my way, one hand on the rough piles of stone that were the wall, one hand on the dog.

We came to a place where the land began to level out, and the grass grew evenly, the bottomland soil of the dale. I could hear the sheep bleat out of the mist. As the mist grew thinner I saw the sheen of water, and the dog led me to the trail that circled the whole tarn. They all clustered about me then, the whole pack of them, as if somehow they had to convey the message that their task was over. Then they strung out again, the leader invisible, the last one at my side, all the way back to Thirlbeck.

The dusk had become darkness by the time we reached the house. I went in by the front way, and the dogs followed. They left me at once to go in search of Askew. As I leaned over the balustrade of the gallery, the last I saw of them was the trail of muddy footprints on the polished wood floor as Askew opened the door of the library to admit them in reply to Thor's insistent scratching. I could hear his voice. "Well . . . where have you been? I've never known you lot to wander off before. Better not let Tolson know, eh?" I was glad they could not answer; I myself could never speak of how they had come to find me on the mountain that afternoon.

*   *   *

Nat Birkett noticed the cuts and scratches on my hands. He found me, about noon, after my visit to Gerald, about to look for lunch in the same cafe where Jeffries and I had eaten breakfast.

All I felt was his hand on my wrist. "Well, then—you've been very quiet lately. I don't ever see you."

"I've been—I've been busy."

"So it seems," he answered, suddenly bringing my hand up, turning it palm upwards. "Were you stuck somewhere and couldn't get down?"

"More or less."

"Come and tell me." He jerked his head towards the cafe. "If you've no objection to beer and cheese I know a rather cosier place." He led me across the town square, and through an archway that opened into what would have been a stable yard in past days for the hotel which fronted the square. Now it was the inevitable car park, but the stabling had long since become dwellings and small shops. A hanging sign, THE DROVER'S REST, indicated a pub. There was an equally discreet sign at the door requesting walkers not to bring their knapsacks inside. Once inside I saw the reason for the sign. It was very small, lots of shining brass about, a fire burning in a brick fireplace, and there was an instant greeting from the landlord. "Morning, Nat, you're early today." Then the man glanced at the clock. "Well— it's after twelve. What'll it be?"

Nat looked at me. "A short? Or would you really like beer? It's local. Very good."

We sat over beer and a cheese salad—and great slabs of bread almost as good as Jessica baked. "Gerald's coming out of hospital tomorrow," I said. "I expect I'll be going back to London soon—after Easter, probably. With Jeffries here, I'm really not needed. But Hardy's keep insisting I stay. I seem to have been here so long, but it's only a few weeks. I've been doing so little I'm rather ashamed. Just a bit of paper-sorting at Thirlbeck and driving around . . ."

"And walking," he said. "And almost getting into trouble by the looks of it."

I told him a little of what had happened on Great Birkeld, but not the real trouble I had been in, nor the arrival of the dogs. I simply said I had found my way down by a sheep wall.

"It's always better to try to keep to a sheep trod. The trouble is it all can change every winter. The ice works on the rocks, and what was a good path the summer before can suddenly step off into scree. You've got to be very experienced to get across scree. I never imagined you'd go off the valley floor, or I'd have insisted you had a compass." He thrust out his legs and looked at the fire, as if he were trying to keep his patience. "God damn it, Jo! You could have broken your neck, and kept us looking for your body for weeks."

"I would have been a lot of trouble, wouldn't I?"

"You bet your life you would. You should stay back in the city where you belong."

"I'll see that I do in future."

He lifted his beer. "All right—all right. But I've every reason to be annoyed. You're a bloody fool, and you must know it. But if you've got any time to spare we can put you to work taking a turn on watching the crag where the eagles are nesting. It's on the Brantwick side of the tarn, where the road goes, so you'll be able to drive quite close. I've put up a sort of shelter at the edge of the woods there—just enough to keep the rain off. The thing is that no one, not even the watchers, must go near the nest. When the word gets out that golden eagles are nesting there, there'll be plenty who think they have the right to come as close as possible to have a look, and there are enough stupid clots who'll actually want the eggs themselves. So we're ringing the bottom of the crag with really ferocious barbed wire, and there's an outer fence a good distance away which is in plain view of the hide. There are plenty of old, weak spots in the estate wall on the North Lodge side which anyone could get over, and there might be a few who would be tempted to come over from the other side of Brantwick. It's a fiercesome walk and climb, but a few might try it."

"What do you do if someone does try to come over the top?"

"Well, if it's you who see them, you get in the car and come back and rouse Tolson—any of the Tolsons. They'll telephone me, and a few other people round in the district, and we'll have to deal with it ourselves. That's going to be a rough one though —just getting there in time. If the eagles are frightened off the nest long enough the eggs will go cold—and then we might as well give them to the egg hunters. The people who climb in by the estate wall would have to go by the hide, and you or anyone else could easily stop and challenge them. It *is* private property, and there's a law of trespass. It's a chancy thing. Tolson wants to co-operate, but he's edgy about strangers—the crowd I've put together to help with the shifts—having the right to come into the valley. Oh, we have it nicely arranged. They've all got written passes to show at the South Lodge. But still he's edgy. He never has wanted people in that valley, but Askew said I'm to have full co-operation, and that's law with Tolson. But in his turn he's rounded up every last Tolson who can spare an hour—sons, daughters-in-law, and grandchildren. Well, the Easter holidays have begun, so that'll be a help as far as the kids are concerned. The more Tolsons there are, the fewer strangers. Tolson's a man who should have had at least six sons. It would have made life a lot simpler . . ."

We sat over our beer, and ordered some more, and Nat's talk drifted on to the time in 1968 when foot-and-mouth disease had decimated the flocks and herds of farmers all over the country, the time of heartbreak when every wind that blew had been a threat to livestock a man might have taken a lifetime to build up. "I'll tell you, Jo, I was thankful for the way Tolson had kept that valley closed off then. Naturally he included my stock among the Tolson's own, and they were all rounded up—the ones outside the wall of the estate, and driven inside. That's the time when we strengthened the fences and gates over by the North Lodge. One of the Tolson ladies went to shop for the food for all the families each week. The car was hosed down before she left, and hosed down again when she got back. We had the kids wearing white Wellingtons the minute they stepped off the bus, and they had to wade in a trough of disinfectant before they went a step farther, and again before they got past the wall of Thirlbeck. It was a pretty grim time. We couldn't go anywhere—not to the pub, or to church, or a film, or to visit anyone. There wasn't nearly enough grazing for the livestock, and we had to hand-feed. Hellishly expensive. And all the while we didn't know if these precautions were worth the time of day. The Ministry just didn't know how it was spreading. It could have been passed by natural contact—so we lived and breathed disinfectants—or it could have been carried by the dropping of any silly bird that happened to fly over the farm.

I'll tell you, that was one time of my life I didn't care much for birds."

He put down his beer and took one of my hands in his, tracing the scratches and deeper cuts. "You know, I'm awfully glad you didn't tumble down Great Birkeld and break your silly neck. And I've been talking like an idiot—stupid things about farming and birds that you probably don't give a damn about. I can't talk about old silver and paintings, Jo. It's hard for me even to imagine what sort of world you live in. But I thought when you left Southdales that morning that I had bored you to death with my stupid rambling—and here I am doing it again."

"And here I am listening. You listened to me, Nat. Remember?"

"Yes, I remember. Even though it was sad about your mother, and then having to get to know your father like that, it still sounded way beyond my world. Switzerland and Mexico. And working for Hardy's. And knowing someone called Harry Peers who telephones you from places I seem hardly to have heard of. Afterwards I wondered if you really had been at Southdales, or was it some drunken dream I had. You really don't belong there. Thirlbeck is your sort of place, and when all those glamorous types disappear from Thirlbeck, you'll be gone too—then or sooner. I didn't have champagne for you, and now all I've given you is beer." He shrugged and dropped my hand. The picnic near St. Bees had not been mentioned. "I rather imagine the hay is sticking out all over me."

"Not hay—just prickles."

"Ouch!" He laughed. "I expect I deserved that. Well—I'll walk you to your car, and then I have to come back here. I know a man with a couple of good calves, but he wants too much money for them. If I get enough whisky into him he might drop his price . . ." He was helping me on with my anorak. "Farmer's talk, Jo."

"We talk shop, too. It's different shop, that's all. Don't bother to come with me. What time do you want me to help with the eagle watching?"

"Would two to five in the afternoons be all right? After that a couple of the Tolson kids will take over for two hours. Can you manage that? I'll be there early in the mornings—people think if they get up before dawn they might just beat us, but we'll be there even earlier. I'll tell Tolson. He'll be happy that there's one fewer outsider coming into the valley."

"I'm not sure," I answered, "that Tolson doesn't think I'm one of the worst outsiders of all."

And I left him, the two beer mugs in his hand on the way back to the bar, frowning in puzzlement. It was true. I didn't belong here, and he didn't belong anywhere else. I thought there was a kind of amazing innocence left in him that wouldn't have long survived beyond this world of his. Then I began to imagine him meeting my father, and how very well Nat would have understood and respected my father's need for the lost, remote world of San José.

III

Easter came and Gerald returned to Thirlbeck, and life took up yet another rhythm. He now talked on the telephone himself, so my daily call to Hardy's was no longer necessary. He had his breakfast carried to him by Jeffries, and then made a rather grand appearance a half hour before lunch. The days were mostly sunny, and one of Tolson's sons had come along, first with a tractor, and then with a power mower, and cleaned the long grass in the avenue between the trees that led to that open space, with its crumbling stone balustrade, which gave a view along the length of the tarn. Garden furniture of a bygone age—teak benches and chairs, a handsome teak table—had been produced. Drinks were set out there whenever the weather permitted. To see Gerald walking down that avenue unassisted, with all his old command of himself and his surroundings, was, for me, to step back to a time before he was ill. His conversation was brisk and sharp, but he still returned to his room after lunch and didn't reappear until it was time for drinks before dinner. I saw how Askew and the Condesa had grown to look forward to his coming; Thirlbeck itself, I thought, oppressed the Condesa, and she wanted talk of other places, something Gerald could well supply.

Tolson did what he could to relieve the ritual monotony of the days. He produced the key of the gun room, and the Condesa and Askew spent some time each choosing from the racks of weapons the one that suited them most, cleaning it, getting ammunition ready. When they used the guns the Condesa held a slight edge over Askew. "I've lost my eye," he said. That one session of target practice was all they ever had. Nat Birkett complained that the noise was disturbing the eagles. The guns were put away.

After that Tolson found two hacking horses. Perhaps they had been bought, perhaps they were on loan—Tolson had connections in that countryside which made either situation possible. It wasn't really a rider's country, being too steep and rocky in most places, but he found the horses and they were handsome enough, a bay and a chestnut mare, to complement their riders. Askew and the Condesa had come without riding clothes, and having seen the shops in Kesmere, they travelled to Carlisle to buy what they needed. I thought that both of them had been more accustomed to made-to-measure breeches and jackets and boots, but they looked very well in what came off the rack. They also bought the heavy raincoats used by everyone who rides in that climate; the Condesa hated that weighty outer garment, but since they only rode through the valley, using the path which skirted the tarn, and made no jumps, it only hampered her, not the mare. When the rain came down, she was glad of it. A trestle was set up in the service passage where she and Askew left, and dried, their boots, jackets, raincoats, and caps. After the morning ride came lunch, and for the Condesa, the siesta. After that, the time drifted to drinks and dinner. She seemed to have ridden off the nervous energy that consumed her; by evening she was relaxed and gracious.

But the riding did nothing to end their isolation. They remained always within the Thirlbeck valley. Askew didn't seem to want to venture farther, and the Condesa didn't insist. Askew appeared to have entered a sort of state of suspension while he waited for Gerald to recover fully. He cared nothing about re-establishing contacts with the past; he postponed the future.

* * *

I took my turn, as I had promised Nat, at the shelter on the edge of the larch plantation below the crag where the eagles nested. My eyes ached sometimes with watching through the binoculars but the hours never seemed long. They were mostly golden days, with only swift showers that passed over the valley where the spring was now in full flood. I was supposed to watch on every side of the crag, and above it, for the approach of strangers, simply from curiosity or with intent, but often I found myself just watching the flight of the eagles themselves. I learned to watch for, to anticipate, to love that heart-stopping moment when one or the other soared above the crag, and then swooped in a dive to earth or towards the nest. I began to understand how Nat felt about them—they became for me a new manifestation of all that was free, things that Nat would keep forever wild and free, free to soar above the valley, to mate and to nest, things that had not been for two hundred years, and might return again, in defiance of the car parks and the picnic litter, but wild things that needed a territory as big as this valley, and the peace to nurture their fledglings. I grew to feel about those two birds as I felt about the house of Thirlbeck itself—that once it vanished something quite irreplaceable would have gone.

I was relieved of my watch each afternoon by some of the Tolson grandchildren—good-looking, sturdy children, most of them, friendly, but independent, as I would have expected. They bore a strong family likeness—many of them had the dark, strong features of their grandfather; they handled themselves well, confident in their own environment. Tolson had created a well to draw upon in them, but of all of them I met, Jessica still stood out—the blonde, fairy-like creature, gifted with a high degree of brains and possibly ambition, but too highly strung to put it to work in the everyday world.

Those people I relieved were drawn from the pool of volunteers recruited from the lists of the Royal Society for the Protection of Birds. They were mostly housewives, able to spare an hour or two, or retired people, people who cared as passionately as Nat that the birds should breed successfully, and should return to the nest next year, and all the years to come. But there were a few who, after exclaiming at the beauty of the Thirlbeck valley, complained that this had been their only chance to see it. "It really isn't right," one young woman said to me; "all around is National Park, and we're allowed to use it. And this still belongs to Lord Askew, and I have to show a pass written out by Nat Birkett to get in here. I've lived ten miles away all my life, and I think this country belongs as much to me as Lord Askew. It would make a Socialist of anyone, it really would. Just imagine he's owned all this, and the house as well, and he's never bothered to come here. Damn shame, I call it. But I wonder if Nat Birkett will be any different when it comes his turn. You'd think he would be—but they're all the same when they get their hands on something like this. And Nat Birkett always did like his own company. Strange he's not married again. Oh, look, there goes one of them! The male, I think." And she raised the glasses to follow the flight of the bird, and I was forgotten. I drove back to the house also wondering what Nat Birkett would do when this became his. By then Askew would have stripped it of whatever could be sold, and Nat would be left with the bare, beautiful bones of it.

All the time Gerald had been in hospital, and during the convalescent period, I spent several hours a day working on the boxes in the study, and it was as useless as it had been the first day I had made an attempt to find any paper relating to the painting, or to the other parts of the dowry which Margeretha van Huygens had brought to Thirlbeck. It was an uneasy and difficult task Gerald had assigned to me; he couldn't know how hard it was to approach the door of the study, knock, and find that Tolson was busy with papers at his desk, or worse, talking on the telephone. Quite often he would summon me with a wave of his hand. "Please go ahead, Miss Roswell. I don't ever recall seeing such a paper myself, but then I've not looked into every box. There's always been too much present business with the estate to worry about the past. I'm sure it's all very interesting . . ." But his eyes seemed resentful behind those cruel glasses. "Jess should give you a hand. She's very quick and good with papers."

"Yes, I'm sure she is. She's good with everything. Jeffries has a very high regard for her, and *he's* extremely difficult to please. Mr. Stanton hopes she can be spared to come on a visit to London. There's so much she would enjoy . . ."

For only a moment his dark, almost scowling features relaxed. I despised myself for trying to charm him with praise of Jessica, to let him know that others, whose standards were different and more sophisticated, found her irresistible. But it was the truth. I wondered why I didn't like her myself—perhaps because she didn't like me.

"There's a great deal Jessica enjoys in London—the galleries and such . . . She's only been there twice, for short visits. My brother, her great-uncle, lived in London. His widow still lives there. But one hears such things about London these days—drugs and all the rest of it. Sickening, I think. It's so easy for a young person to be—to be *influenced*. I wouldn't like her to get it into her head to stay there."

"With this to come back to? I don't think so, Mr. Tolson. Is it all right if I go on now?"

He would nod, and continue for a while with whatever he was doing at the desk. But I didn't doubt that my presence was as irksome to him as his was unnerving to me. Perched on the ladder, my hands smeared with dust and cobwebs, I handled the brittle brown paper in those boxes, scanned the faded brown ink, and despaired of finding what Gerald hoped for. Indeed, there was almost a kind of malevolent disarray about the contents of the boxes—some would begin with the date stamped on the cover, and then skip ten years. Papers in others would bear no relation to the date on the box at all. I began to think, after a while, that someone in that house had been through the boxes before me. Each day they seemed to become more confused, the contents more wildly scattered. I had so far worked systematically along the boxes dated during the years I thought Margeretha van Huygens might have brought her precious dowry to Thirlbeck, and then I saw that this was too obvious a progress; it could be tracked and anticipated. So I began to select at random from those years, and I made a point of going only to the boxes whose undisturbed dust told me that they could not possibly have been recently handled. Then after two days of this, I came one morning to find that all the boxes in the row on which I had been working, and those on the shelves above and below, had been dusted.

Jeffries stopped by the open study door one morning as I was perched on the ladder. "Well, Miss Roswell, I'm glad to see you're looking a bit cleaner this morning. Your skirt yesterday— really terrible. I thought at least I could make your job a bit pleasanter for you."

"*You* dusted the boxes, Jeffries?"

"Yes—they were in a shocking state. Of course the Tolsons can't possibly see to everything in a place of this size. A pity, isn't it? Have you seen some of those rooms upstairs—nothing but dust sheets. Rather spooky, Miss Roswell, I think. And a little sad. One likes to see a house lived in, don't you think?" Then he added cheerfully: "Mr. Stanton's very bright this morning. I had difficulty persuading him to stay in bed. Soon be on our way back to London."

Curiously, Gerald seemed in no particular hurry to return to London himself, nor was Askew impatient to leave. Both of them seemed to have fallen into their own pattern at Thirlbeck. Perhaps it was that Gerald was more tired than he had known, perhaps it was that Askew was beginning to face without fear his own past in this house. Askew even took his turn at the shelter from which the eagles were watched, and became almost as zealous as Nat Birkett in the attempt to block all invaders of this valley for the next months. It seemed to me that only the Condesa chafed under the restrictions of life at Thirlbeck. She did not openly complain, but at times I sensed a growing desperation in her as each day followed its by-now established routine. I thought that she feared Askew's seeming contentment in his surroundings; it might be difficult to pry him loose. "You should have guests, Roberto," she urged. "A little cocktail party. Gerald could manage that for an hour—not too tiring."

Askew's brow wrinkled. "Need we, Carlota? You'd find the county people rather dull around here, I think. In any case, I can't remember anyone to ask. And they've all forgotten me, I'm sure. Perhaps . . . if you'd really like it . . ."

But nothing was arranged. They paid no calls outside Thirlbeck, hardly ever left the valley. No one came to call, or if they did, they didn't get past the South Lodge. Tolson kept his grip on his whole little community, and it might have gone so far as to give instructions at the South Lodge to tell anyone who called that Lord Askew was not at home. Since it was always Tolson or Jessica who answered the telephone, the same answer could have been given to those who telephoned. The doubt still nagged at me that Tolson wanted any of us here—even Askew himself. I remembered Nat's words about Askew and Tolson. "His time is past. I'm the future."

Time seemed almost suspended in those few weeks. We ourselves waited for Gerald to become stronger, and we didn't seem to care what happened after that. How odd it was that I didn't become excited any more as I moved among those beautiful furnishings in the ground-floor rooms. The time of the auction would come, but it was not yet. The time to bring the people from Hardy's would come, but it would wait a little longer. The picture which I now saw daily in the study was either a Rembrandt or it wasn't. Time would reveal that also. And the room where the other pictures were stored was not even discussed. Gerald didn't ask to see them—perhaps he feared what he would find there, and Askew acted as if he had forgotten about them. Sometimes I thought I sensed a kind of desperation of impatience in the Condesa—I watched her often as she stood and looked out across the lake, and the spring evenings grew longer. But she said nothing, and she would return to her needlework with that quiet grace of a woman who has schooled herself, against her own nature, in the art of waiting.

The telephone calls from Harry continued, but they were brief, and at less frequent intervals. And then there came one during which he said he was going to Australia. "Just for a day or two, luv."

"Don't be ridiculous, Harry. No one goes to Australia for a day or two. What are you going to do there?"

"Mind your own business, luv. That way I'll never be able to blame you for talking out of school and letting some other bloke in on what Harry's already got his eye on. Back in a week. See you—that is, unless you've decided to retire up there."

"No, we'll be leaving in a few days."

"That's good. Someone else might slip into your spot."

"What spot?"

"Your spot at Hardy's, stupid."

"I've been *told* by Hardy's to stay. I'm to stay as long as Gerald does."

"Yes, there's a good girl. You keep your eye on Gerald. Worth having around, he is. Bye, luv."

"Harry . . . ?" But he was gone, was already a world away from me. Suddenly I was possessed of the Condesa's sense of being trapped here. It had been a few weeks, only a few weeks. But I had fallen into step with all the others, and it was a slower pace. Tolson had long ago, at Askew's insistence, produced the keys to the bookcases in the library. I searched there, as I did among the boxes, but with the same sense of futility. No diary, no book that I could identify as belonging to Margeretha van Huygens turned up, no list of her housewifely possessions. But in the mornings the sun came into that room —with the metal shutters thrown back it was a cheerful place, the jumble of furniture even making it seem cosy, as if they were not all works of art and should be accorded a graceful display. I enjoyed being there, sitting up on the ladder, taking down books, making notes that this or that might be of interest to the rare book specialists at Hardy's. There were a few, mixed among the others, as the masterpieces of the furniture-maker's art were mixed with the chintz sofas, that I began to suspect could be of more than usual interest—books in manuscript, illuminated, some of them. I had no idea where they might have come from, these beautiful things with their paintings on vellum pages, and their stately Latin phrases. Askew had not given a picture of the Birketts as men of learning at the period when these books had come into being—before the time of printing when a book was a very rare thing, and very few people could read. I had a sense, as I touched them, that they had fairly recently been handled. They were dusty, but the dust was not something undisturbed for years. Perhaps Jessica had also found and enjoyed these treasures, trying out her Latin on them. As I carefully turned the pages trying to drag up for myself a phrase or two of Latin remembered from school, I wondered if I should go and talk to Gerald about them, or talk to Askew. Something held me back. I was beginning to get the same sense as Gerald had had on his first night at Thirlbeck, the sense that while all seemed on the surface to be all right, that much at Thirlbeck could be very wrong.

I found the Book of Hours on the top shelf of a case I had not previously been able to open—whose lock yielded only after I had eased its stiffness with fine sewing-machine oil I bought in Kesmere. No one had had this case open for many years; the dust was heavy and undisturbed. The Book of Hours had fallen down, or been pushed down, behind taller volumes. It was tiny and exquisite, this *Horae*, illuminating with those curiously medieval figures, the seven canonical offices of the day—my memory spelled them out as I turned those beautiful hand-wrought pages—*mattins, prime, terce, sext, none, vespers, compline*. So beautifully executed, this book could have been made for a princess of many centuries ago. And so it might. I could not, from my very small knowledge of such things, know for what historic personage such a book had been designed and made. But it once had been given, and the name of the giver, or the receiver, was written in a faded but readable script. *Juana Fernández de Córdoba, Mendoza, Soto y Alvarez.*

And there, as I turned the pages, the brittle parchment sheet slipped out, and along with it, a page which held Vanessa's writing.

I don't remember how long I sat on top of that ladder. I do remember staring out at the lake, and back at the book, and the two sheets of paper. And finally, carefully closing the bookcase, I climbed down the ladder and went to the door. There was no one in the hall. When I reached the privacy of the Spanish Woman's room, it was more than ever a sanctuary to me.

I sat there at the long table in the window alcove, and spread out the two pages—one a fine parchment, yellowed, with a flowing script in Spanish. The other was an ordinary piece of modern notepaper. Vanessa's scrawling hand did not compare favourably with what she had translated—but no, not translated—Vanessa had no more than a tourist's knowledge of Spanish. She had made a copy of the Spanish words, and the translation was written beneath.

Y éste os enviamos, amada prima, nuestro retrato, por la mano de Domingo Teotocópuli, un espejo de conciencia, para que lo guardéis celosamente con fidelidad y de encargo hasta el día de la victoria final y en la eterna unión en Nuestro Señor Jesucristo y Nuestra Santa Madre Iglesia.

Yo, el Rey

And this do we send unto you, beloved cousin, our likeness, by the hand of Domenico Theotokopoulos, a mirror of conscience, to keep close, in faith and in trust, until the day of the final victory and the eternal union in Christ and our Holy Mother Church.

I looked in awe at the hand which had signed it, because I had seen it before, recently, and it seemed burned into my brain.

I, the King
Felipe

It had been on a document, proudly framed and exhibited in the hall of the Casa Grande of San José, and the proudest possession, my father had said, of the Martínez family—the title deed of the lands of the Hacienda containing the silver mines from which their one-time wealth had sprung, signed by Philip the Second of Spain, using the majestic title, I, the King, as all sovereigns of Spain had done in the days of her power and glory.

And here it was again, on a scrap of parchment, addressed to no one, undated, but I knew quite surely that it had been sent to the Spanish Woman, to hold her loyalty to the political mission on which she had been sent, a pawn in Philip's hand.

Vanessa had found it—or someone else had found it—and Vanessa had copied it, and had it translated. How many years ago? Her handwriting looked younger—not quite the almost illegible scrawl it had become in her later, less patient years.

A devotional Book of Hours, a scrap of manuscript signed by Philip the Second of Spain. Beautiful, valuable. And Vanessa had known of them both.

But the vital importance of that translated message was in that name, the name of an ordinary painter of that time, one who had portrayed his patron in *The Dream of Philip the Second*, who was known not to have been greatly favoured by the King, but obviously used by him for this special commission. This likeness, this portrait, would have had to be quite small, or it never could have reached the Spanish Woman in secret. Domenico Theotokopoulos. By that name he had always been described in official documents. To the world who would now pay almost unimaginable sums of money if one of his pictures had been for sale, he would simply be known, as he had been to the Spaniards, as El Greco.

I grew weak at the thought that one of his canvases might exist here, in this house. And the thought that Vanessa herself had come across this slip of parchment in the Spanish Woman's cherished book, the Book of Hours—Vanessa had found it, copied it, and had it translated. And told no one.

I looked wildly around the room, the dark agedness of the panelling, the huge bed, the sombre bed hangings. I thought of all this great house, and the many rooms in which I had never set foot. I thought of the room which guarded the pictures of Margeretha van Huygens. Was it possible that among them, alien to those Dutch landscapes and faces and still lifes, there existed a small portrait of a Spanish Hapsburg face, the face of Philip, archenemy of Elizabethan England, the face which must forever be hidden by the Spanish Woman? Even though I had never seen the collection I doubted that it would be there. If it still existed, if it existed at all, if it had ever existed, it would be in some place where the Spanish Woman had hidden it.

And then I looked out on the calm, golden mirror of the tarn. It seemed to hold no fear, no mystery. But the Spanish Woman had taken to her death in that tarn the knowledge of a greater treasure than the enormous jewel she wore about her neck.

IV

That was the day at Thirlbeck when I opened doors I never had opened before. Until now a sense of good manners—perhaps misplaced considering the job I held—had kept me from prying into parts of the house where I would not normally have gone. And now I knew that in fact it was a slight apprehension about Tolson which had kept me back from this exploration; Askew would not have minded; he would have thought me dull for displaying so little curiosity in a house which encouraged it. Now I went and looked in the dust-sheeted rooms that I had never entered before, the rooms Jeffries had apparently not hesitated to enter. I drew back curtains which darkened these rooms, lifted dust sheets, saw the same heavy oak Elizabethan and Jacobean furniture which did not need the delicate care of the fine pieces of marquetry Tolson had gathered in the lower rooms. Often, along with the dust, there was the pervading smell of damp, the ominous smell of rooms too long closed, the crumbling brickwork and mortar in the fireplaces. There were some marvellous firebacks, and firedogs bearing the crest of the Birketts. There were a few pieces of pottery about, and some pewter. In some rooms, brocade or velvet curtains hung in damp-stained shreds. I opened presses and chests, and met only the softness of old curtains or bedcovers. There were no pictures, and few mirrors. In some rooms I saw fingerprints in the dust, a trail of footprints on the oak floors. On all the presses I opened the knobs had been wiped free of dust; there were fingermarks in the dust on the lids of the chests.

I seemed to follow a trail that someone had laid before me. It could have been Jessica, who walked the rooms of this house with loving familiarity; it could have been Jeffries, whose curiosity had obviously been greater than mine—perhaps Jessica herself had conducted him. But when I briefly opened the door of a room in the wing opposite the one Gerald and I slept in, I realised that wherever I had gone in that house the perfume that was so strong in this room had been with me, quite a separate thing from the other smells of dust and damp —this a flowery scent, one the Condesa used during the day. I took a quick glance at the untidy splendour of the room she inhabited, a room, despite its fussy Victorian furnishings, on which she had indelibly stamped her personality. Her amber silk gown lay across a chair, a table with a swinging mirror was strewn with silver-topped bottles and jars which belonged to a crocodile fitted dressing case. Louis Vuitton luggage was stacked beside a mahogany wardrobe, one tiny-heeled slipper lay on its side alone in the middle of the floor. There were books and magazines about, flowers and foliage in a big vase on a table by the windows arranged with the careless grace that the Condesa had made into a high art. She even had her own polished silver tray of drinks, and beautiful cut-crystal glasses. And the perfume. By now I had come to think that the perfume wasn't in each room because the Condesa had been there before me, but because it was unconsciously a background to this whole house. It was in the dining room, the drawing room, the library; it was something we breathed simply because she moved. It had impregnated these walls as if she had been here forever, not just a few weeks

It was strongly in the room Askew used, adjoining hers. But now I was realising I had no business looking in these two rooms, and I didn't linger here. There was little to see. It was a large room, almost as grand as the Spanish Woman's room, and almost as bare. There was a surprising severity to it.

Two brushes on a table, a book, a pair of gloves—nothing else of a personal nature in sight. Unlike the Condesa's room, it had the appearance of one belonging to a man who was passing through, a stranger who would spend only one night under this roof. None of his childhood or adolescence was visible here, no photographs, no trophies, nothing that declared that this man had been born in this house. I closed the door softly, remembering that nowhere I had moved had I yet seen any place that looked as if it had been used as a nursery or schoolroom.

The house, which from the front appeared to be two storeys, grew to three at the centre. There was a cluster of low-ceilinged rooms with half windows that looked over the roofs of Thirlbeck and through the stone frieze. Here was the litter of generations—old trunks, bedsteads, riding boots, a collection of cricket bats, a croquet set. If Askew had a childhood, it was here, but he had not sought any of it, nor wanted it about him. The narrow corridors all came back to a steep stair—a Victorian edition which must have led down to the wing on the rear of the house which the Tolsons inhabited. I turned back. This was territory which I could not invade, and there nagged the thought that somewhere in those rooms where they lived there might be a smallish, perhaps dark picture, a portrait of a man in a sixteenth-century tunic with a small, austere ruff, a man with the Hapsburg chin, the man who had ruled most of the world as Philip the Second of Spain, painted by the hand of the Greek, and sent to inspire trust and hope in his little Spanish protégé, the one he called "cousin."

As I retraced my way through the unused rooms of that floor, the Condesa's scent still seemed to go with me, but I knew I was now merely imagining it. She could not have been everywhere, nor so recently. It was the strength of her personality, not her perfume, that was so strangely pervasive.

* * *

For the first time since I had been in that house sleep did not come easily, and when it came it was fitful. The sense of the closeness of the Spanish Woman seemed at times to press on me; I woke to the faint noises that the rooms always held, and again the familiar shadow that had no substance. It was not fear I felt, but something that tugged at me with overriding urgency, a feeling akin to that I had had on the night of Gerald's illness. I even went to check at Gerald's room. He slept peacefully, a single shaded light burning, the flex of an electric bell, rigged up by the Tolson son who had a way with such things, trailing across the floor, into the corridor, and to the adjoining room where Jeffries slept.

I returned to the Spanish Woman's room, and, unable to sleep, I went and lighted a candle and took it to the long table. Then I brought the Book of Hours and the letter from Philip. I studied those words over and over, and Vanessa's translation, turned the pages of the book, felt the essence of the centuries in its pages, the faith and trust and great hope of a young Spanish girl who must have held these things among her dearest possessions, who must have sat as I sat now, the lighted candle on the table beside her. But where would she have hidden the portrait of the man whose words must have been almost as sacred to her as the text in this hauntingly beautiful book? *Juana Fernández de Córdoba, Mendoza, Soto y Alvarez,* the name written in her careful script. They had taken her life, and the life of her child, the great gem she wore; they had tried to take away her identity, but they had not succeeded. She had no known grave, but she had lived in legend as none of the Birketts had lived. If they had taken everything else, would they have left the portrait of the most hated man in England? To the Birketts of the time the name of the painter would have mattered less than nothing, and to keep the portrait of Philip would have seemed close to treason. Was all that had survived of the Spanish Woman just the great gem, and this book and the paper with the seal and signature of England's greatest enemy? And how had her little Book of Hours escaped the vengeful, frightened hands of the Birketts? I went and sat in her chair, put my feet on her footstool; the light of the flames of the fire I had kept up all night, and the paler light of the candle met across the room, and the presence of the Spanish Woman seemed a cogent reality. She had to have left more than these few things—she *had* to. I still held the book in my hands, and by the light of the fire I tried to understand something she had written at the back of the book, words I couldn't understand but which must have been important to her to have written them here. Was this a message she had meant to leave, and I couldn't read it? The Condesa could possibly have done so, but I had no intention of showing this to her.

I slept there in the chair and woke to the dying fire, the first sleepy twitterings of the dawn chorus of the birds on a spring morning, and to the sound of a vehicle passing on the road that led past the house and on up the valley to Brantwick. The eastern light was glowing over the top of the mountain, and that had been Nat Birkett's Land-Rover taking him to his watch at the shelter.

* * *

It was chill in the dawn when I walked to find him. Everything—the trees, the grass—was beaded with moisture, morning swirls of mist clung to the tarn. But it was a morning of great radiance, like the one I remembered coming out to when I had known that Gerald would be all right. This morning, though, my mind and feelings tossed in unquiet speculation. I was weary of it all; I longed to be free of the thoughts of Vanessa, of her strange connection with this place; I wanted to be able to go and talk to Gerald, to try to explain, or to have him explain to me about Vanessa. But this was impossible. Gerald could not be worried now by such things. So I walked out in the dawn to talk to Nat Birkett, still almost a stranger.

But when he greeted me it wasn't as a stranger. I moved quietly through the larch wood to the shelter, but he had long ago been aware of my approach. The shelter was a kind of three-sided hut, with the open side facing away from the crag where the eagles nested; the crag was watched by binoculars through a long cut in the other side, with a sort of shelf where the watcher rested his elbows during the long sessions holding the glasses. It had no floor but the forest ground. A little sterno stove was for making tea, and a few biscuit tins stored the provisions.

He came to meet me. "I've been missing you, Jo. Have you

done any more stupid things like climbing Great Birkeld? There's water for coffee on."

He had put his arm around my shoulders in a way that was warmly companionable, and I was instantly conscious that this was not enough. All at once, I wanted much more from Nat Birkett. He seemed to be treating me with the sort of absent-minded affection which he would give to his collie. The collie was there with him, his long soft snout thrust against my hand. From him I could take mere affection; he was a dog. I began to realise that soon I would be leaving Thirlbeck, and Nat Birkett as well.

"I followed you," I said. "I heard the Land-Rover and knew it was you coming up here."

"Yes, I saw the light. In the Spanish Woman's room."

"You knew it was the Spanish Woman's room? I thought wild horses wouldn't have got you on a tour of Thirlbeck."

"I knew it," he said. There was abruptly a chilling quality in his voice. Perhaps I shivered, even with the warmth of his body close to me. "You're cold. I'll make the coffee."

The night had been long. I could feel my eyes swollen from lack of sleep, the worries of Thirlbeck and Vanessa's connection were back with me, and now this added new dimension of being acutely, painfully aware of Nat Birkett, and feeling that I was being pushed aside into an affectionate friendship, which would be forgotten when I left. "Any brandy?" I said.

"It just so happens . . ." He brought out a hip flask. "Do you make a habit of vigils? You always seem to be wandering around in the dawn."

I ignored the question. The mug of coffee laced with brandy was comforting between my hands, the liquid warm on my tongue, in my throat. "Anything to eat?" He passed over a meat pastie; I suppose it was either Jessica's cooking or her mother's. "How did you know—about the Spanish Woman's room?"

"Who hasn't heard about the Spanish Woman?" he answered. "Patsy once said to me that the Spanish Woman haunted that house—she and that bloody great rock she brought from Spain to Thirlbeck. *That* I'll inherit too, and all the bad luck that goes with it. I hope to God Askew lives to be a hundred. With some luck I might be dead before him—but unless they've abolished the whole House of Lords by then, that would leave the bad luck to Thomas."

"Are they really unlucky—the Birketts?"

"The Birketts aren't unlucky. It's the Earls of Askew who are unlucky. You take a plain, ordinary but clever man of business like Askew's grandfather—a good farmer and one who wanted to *do* something for farming. Then he becomes Earl of Askew, and everything goes wrong. He has only one son who survived, and *he's* a bit off his head—enough to make him retreat into Thirlbeck and never see a soul. They were rich then, the Earls of Askew. He could have had any sort of life he wanted, but he couldn't seem to enjoy even the life of a recluse. No better place to be a recluse than Thirlbeck in those days, if that was your choice. My father's generation he was—a bit older, really, but my father knew him and thought him a poor creature, dominated by his mother. Then he quarrels with *his* only child. That child has covered himself with sporting honours at Eton, and more when he has the only year he manages to last at Cambridge. Then he dashes off to the Spanish Civil War, marries a Spanish girl, and a Catholic—and they all begin to think that the Spanish Woman is returning to take Thirlbeck back again—"

I sucked in my breath. "I never thought of that!"

"*They* did. You'd think almost four hundred years hadn't passed since the Armada. Then she had a son, and of course the Earldom would go to a Catholic. But it never did. That poor bastard, Askew, manages to kill them both before they ever reached Thirlbeck, but almost in sight of it. Then he goes to gaol, then to war, and tries, I think, to get himself killed—honourably, of course. Instead of being killed, he ends up with the Victoria Cross and the Military Cross. I've always thought he was trying to leave behind the bad luck of the Earls of Askew by leaving Thirlbeck. There's something that hangs on in that place . . . no wonder he's stayed away. He'll go again, soon, I expect. I would, if I were he . . ."

"Nat, at some time, sooner or later, you *will* be the Earl of Askew. What will you do? What will you do with Thirlbeck?"

"With Thirlbeck? God knows . . . tear it down, if I have the money."

"Nat—*no!*"

"Why not? Who wants it? Who can pay the taxes on a thing like that, or keep it in repair?"

"Who . . . who? I can't say who. But people want it, Nat. They *need* it. They pour out from the cities all over the country . . . from concrete housing developments. They drive hellish distances to *see* something different. Here, they come to see mountains they will never climb. With Thirlbeck they would come to see something that builders of four hundred years ago put together. Something that no one could afford to build today. That's why they come. It's a dream, Nat. They really couldn't say it's a dream, but they want it preserved."

"Why should it be preserved for *them?* That bloody stupid mass. They don't know what they're looking at."

"Nat . . ." I was desperate. I was pleading for something that was not my own, which I probably would never see again. The words burst out of me, not of my making. "Nat, why is it so important to preserve golden eagles? Why are we here, this minute? Why did you get up before dawn? Why do you want to see that eagle rise off that crag? Why—why? Preserve the eagles. Preserve Thirlbeck. Why not? They're both unique. You will never get either of them back again. If you lose this pair, perhaps in a hundred years or so another pair may come back to nest—there's always the hope. Perhaps the young will survive, and come back and stake out their own territory. But once you tear down Thirlbeck, it's gone forever. I'll tell you, Nat, when Thirlbeck is torn down parts of it will survive. But only parts. Chimney pieces, staircases, cornices, the furniture . . . oh, yes, they'll survive because museums are rich enough to buy parts. But who will have the whole? The whole won't exist. Could you buy a golden eagle, Nat? Would you *want* to be able to buy it? There's no price for an eagle. Who can pay for Thirlbeck? But somehow it has to be paid for."

Suddenly his mug of coffee turned over and the liquid ran over the ground. He rose slowly and went to the long viewing space in the wall, raised the glasses, and scanned the whole

193

foreground and the horizon. In time, after minutes, he came back, sitting on the ground close to me.

"Dear God, Jo, it *has* been paid for! Thirlbeck owes me everything. I owe it nothing. Do you know how Patsy died?"

"They said . . . yes, they said she died at Thirlbeck. Oh, Nat —I'm sorry. I shouldn't—"

"Unique? You bet it's unique! It can so seduce a sweet, simple little girl like Patsy that she will die there. Do you know how Patsy was found, Jo?"

I felt myself shrink into my own body. Nat's face was in torment. "They said . . ." I whispered.

"Yes, I'm sure they said. They said all kinds of things. But do you know where and how she was found? I'll bet no one ever told you that. No—it was agreed among us—the Tolsons and I, that it was an unfortunate accident. And when the person you love most dearly in the world is gone, you don't have feelings of revenge—not against people like the Tolsons. There can never be an acceptable explanation. And nothing will ever bring Patsy back. So we just . . . let it go."

He picked up the mug and placed it among the biscuit tins, as if he were trying to decide whether he should say more. He sighed, and looked back at me. "We thought she was lost. She just simply . . . disappeared. Her car was still at Southdales— she couldn't have gone too far. We didn't even know she was gone until she failed to show up to meet the school bus. It was Richard's first year at school, and she always wanted to be there to meet him. I started telephoning around—all the Tolsons, first, of course, and any other place within a few miles walking distance. No one had seen her. Every farmer around here searched outbuildings—any place at all it was possible for her to be. I thought I'd go out of my mind that night. It was November, and it had suddenly turned bitterly cold. A hard frost. If she were out in it, I just knew she couldn't survive. We organised a big search for the next morning at first light—all through the Thirlbeck valley, all around the tarn. It was a hellish day. It was so long I can remember every minute of it, and yet it got dark so quickly. Then, when the light was gone, Tolson suggested a search of Thirlbeck itself. We had no reason to suppose she was there—Jessica had been there all the day she disappeared, and she said no one had been at the house. The thing that made Tolson suggest it, really, was that La Española was gone from its safe—and yet the alarm system was still connected, and working. Thirlbeck wasn't the way you know it now. Try to imagine it with all those metal shutters always in place. Those downstairs rooms always dark, always needing electric light . . . Patsy wasn't in the Tolsons' wing, and there was nothing to indicate that she was in the front part of the house. But with La Española gone, and she missing as well . . . that was when Tolson suggested a complete search of the house."

"Nat . . . I'm sorry. Please, no more. I shouldn't have said anything."

"Be quiet, and let me talk, will you?" He was hunched on the ground beside me, his arms wrapped about his knees, his chin thrust down towards them. He lifted his head.

"She had a heart condition—something left over from rheumatic fever as a kid. The valves of the heart had been damaged —they'd narrowed down. It hadn't caused her much trouble until about that time, but she was getting breathless, and small things made her tired. We went to London to a consultant, and he said they could operate—and she might live to be an old woman. He said he could do it in about six to eight weeks— you have to wait for the really good guys unless it's an outright emergency. So we came home and we were waiting for her to be called back to London. That's why I didn't really believe she had set out on a long walk without telling anyone . . . she wasn't strong enough for that sort of thing. And she should never have been under really severe stress.

"We found her, Jo, eventually, in the Spanish Woman's room. She was lying against the door as if she had exhausted herself utterly by banging and calling. She must even have tried to break a window. Those old fastenings on the windows are very stiff and bent out of shape. I suppose she didn't have the strength to open any of them. Some of the diamond panes of glass had been broken, and we found pieces of some blue china under the window and down on the gravel below. But of course unless someone had been actually looking up at the window when she was trying to attract attention, there was terribly little chance of her being seen or heard. The lock of the door was jammed. We had to use a jimmy to break it open. At first we thought the door was locked from the inside, but Ted Tolson, who took the lock apart afterwards, said the whole mechanism had jammed because parts of the metal were worn. It was the original lock that'd been put in when the place was built. Patsy had made it worse, he thought, by trying to turn the key to free it. It just jammed tighter. Well, these things didn't concern me at the time. All I knew was that Patsy had died there alone—probably during the night, cold and alone, and frightened. Her heart just couldn't take the state of panic she must have gone into. Dr. Murray, yes, how did he put it? He said it was an inefficient machine that had been made to work too hard. That's a pretty technical way to describe how a girl died. She lay there, my little Patsy, and she had La Española in her hand."

"Oh, God, Nat! La Española . . . *why?*"

"Why—who knows why? We'll never know that. She'd been encouraged to go to that house, to walk through it, to get familiar with it and everything in it, as if it were already hers. Tolson encouraged it. The way he encouraged her to come and look at La Española, to take it, handle it. I suppose he thought she should learn not to be afraid of it—of those stupid stories they tell about it."

"Did he teach her how the alarm system worked?"

Nat shrugged. "He *said* he did. It's easy enough, I suppose, to learn something like that if you're in the house often enough. It's a pretty simple system, I'd guess. Oh, what the hell! Who knows about the why of it. Patsy must have walked to Thirlbeck, used the duplicate key to the South Lodge gate I always left in the house. I blame myself now as much as anyone for not checking at once to see if the keys were still at Southdales. But there she was, at Thirlbeck—dead. Tolson and I found her, and I had to force her hand to get La Española out of it. Even before I lifted her we had agreed, Tolson and I, without even speaking, that we would say nothing at all about La

Española. I just couldn't bear to have Patsy's death surrounded by the kind of horrible publicity it would have brought. And then there was the question I never really asked, but it was there, all the same. How had Patsy been in the house and no one knew it? Why hadn't anyone thought to go through the place sooner? Jessica said she'd been there all day, but she also said she'd been in the vegetable garden for a while. None of us imagined Patsy would have come in by herself and not let anyone know. When I was asking everyone to look in outbuildings, I should have thought of Thirlbeck that way—a gigantic outbuilding to the wing the Tolsons lived in. My fault, quite as much as George Tolson's. In fact, it was so far from *his* mind that for once he didn't even think to check on La Española for a whole twenty-four hours. He must have been distracted out of his mind to let *that* happen. He was just as paternalistic about Patsy as he is about his own family. How could I blame him? I hadn't thought of it myself."

I shivered, as if I felt that cold that she must have felt. I thought of the Spanish Woman's room and what a haven it had become to me; but it had been the death chamber of a young woman whose heart had not been able to bear the panic, the cold and loneliness of that night. I thought of the house as it must have been then, with the Tolsons living in the back wing, and all the front of the house permanently closed in its metal shutters, all the downstairs rooms in darkness, and the little shadow in the big chair had seemed no friend to Patsy, with the unreasoning panic sending a rush of blood to the heart whose valves were too weak and deformed to withstand it.

Then another thought came. "Nat, if she were able to try to attract attention by breaking some of the panes, why on earth didn't she at least switch on the light? Why didn't she light a candle? Why didn't she light the fire? There's a basket of wood always there. *You* saw the light as you drove through this morning. *Someone* would have noticed that night when you were searching."

He shook his head. "There *was* no light. That was something Ted Tolson put in there afterwards. The way he fixed the lock. Yes, there was a candle and a basket of wood. There were no matches. Patsy had given up smoking because of her heart. She had no matches. She was all alone. It was dark and very cold. And Murray said she died that first night. Don't you think I've thought about the matches . . . ?"

I knew he had. I knew he must have thought about such things as matches and lights a thousand times. It explained so much about his rather fanatical preaching about being careful —always being careful, about the need for proper clothes and climbing boots, and compasses. I seemed to experience the anguish of his thousand regrets myself. The bright morning appeared to have darkened. The birds went on with their spring song, but now the sound seemed strident, a noise that was an intrusion.

"The dogs," I said. "Didn't they try, somehow, to tell you that she was there?"

"They did nothing. The police had brought their own tracker dogs, and they told Tolson to keep the wolfhounds shut up because they thought they might confuse their dogs and start fights. So we shut them up in one of the stables, where they howled their heads off. They might have helped . . . who knows? Another mistake, I suppose.

"After that," Nat said, "well, after that the Tolsons sort of closed ranks around me. They tried to make it seem that Patsy had never died—as if they could. They did everything for me. I didn't have to ask. It was already done. For three years I've lived with it, and when Tolson and I look at each other now the question is still there. Why did we let it happen? We never speak about it. I've fallen into a kind of lock-step with them, and I don't seem to be able to break it. I can't talk about Patsy . . . to the boys I call her 'your mother.' But that really isn't the girl who died. She was Patsy."

"You're talking now. You're talking about Patsy. You're talking about the Tolsons. Do you understand, Nat?"

"I think I do, Jo. I'm talking to you. Finally I'm talking . . . there's been a kind of drought. I've dried up. I've become a dull stick who only talks about sheep—sheep and eagles. One of those earnest types. I've taken to tinkering with a stupid toy car. I wasn't always this way. For three years I've felt like an old man. I've acted like one. Then one morning you appeared at my door, sat in the chair that Patsy used to sit in, and I didn't mind seeing that. In fact I liked it so much I got drunk just in astonishment at myself. I felt like a kid, and I was trying to cover it up. Well, I'm not going to cover it up any more. Kiss me, Jo."

I wasn't sure I liked the way he kissed me at first. It was hungry, almost greedy and hurting. And then I realised that very few men kissed like that any more because so few were hungry. Kisses and everything else were given and taken as a matter of course. But there had been no matter of course for Nat Birkett for more than three years. I moved closer to him. It is difficult to kiss when two people are sitting on the ground. It was inevitable that we would lie together as lovers always have.

"God, Jo . . ." he said. "I'll stop in a minute."

"Don't . . ."

"Shut up. You're crazy and so am I. I want you in bed. But not for a one-night stand. And you're going away. You're going back to all that stuff down there in London, and your fancy young tycoon. Well, what the hell! You'll go, and that will be that. What's all that stuff about gathering rosebuds while you may? You're not a rosebud, Jo—on both of us the thorns stand out an inch each side. But we are what we are. Jo, I wish you weren't going."

"I'm going—you know I'm going. I'm all wrong for your sort of life, Nat. As wrong as you'd be for mine. But kiss me again— with all the thorns. Or are they nettles? They say they don't sting if you have the courage to grab them hard enough."

But this time it was easier, gentler, his lips dwelling on mine as if we truly tasted each other. And his hands were gentle, patient, exploring, and finally exciting. And then to my shock, my own deep hunger, which I had not recognised as being there unsatisfied. I heard my own voice. "Yes, I wish . . . I wish too, Nat. Nat Birkett, why?" And then again. "Why not?"

There are many places to make love. A forest of larch and birch a little after dawn is one of them. Not so different, or unique. Lovers have done such things for centuries. But for me it felt as if it were for the first time.

* * *

It wasn't that we heard anything. There was no sound, no movement that we could see. There was just the sense of another presence, and Nat's collie standing alert, ears up. For a moment there was a low growling noise in his throat, and then that changed into a deep, joyous bark. He was gone like a flash through the wood, and we saw a figure among the trees, a slight, fairy-like figure with spun gold hair; like a wraith of the mist she was in those seconds, and then she and the collie were running, running together, back towards Thirlbeck.

Nat crashed his fist down on my thigh. "God damn it! Will they never let me alone? That bloody Jessica—that damnable girl! Forever under my feet—every time I turn around, there she is. Don't they understand I loathe the sight of her? Tolson still tries to pretend none of it happened. He shields and protects her—I suppose he's terrified she may say too much one day, or something may happen again."

"*Again?* Nat, what are you talking about?"

He sat up, and he took his time about lighting cigarettes for us both. I noticed his hands trembled a little. Then he rolled over and rested on his elbows, looking into my face.

"I'm talking, Jo—as I shouldn't talk. But now I've begun I can't stop because this is the first time the words have been allowed to come out." The smoke from our cigarettes drifted together, and vaguely shadowed his face.

"Jessica? . . . who really knows what happened between her and Patsy? Did Patsy just turn up at Thirlbeck, as she so often did—as George Tolson had encouraged her to do? Did she wander around? Did Jessica find her looking at La Española and resent it? Or did they both take it out together? Why were they in the Spanish Woman's room—and still with La Española? All this time and we still don't know the answers. Probably never will. All we know is that when I carried Patsy's body down that night, Jessica went completely to pieces—screaming hysterically that she had nothing to do with it, that she hadn't *touched* Patsy. I heard it, and I'll never forget it—that brilliant, half-cracked kid who'd had a nervous breakdown that summer after whizzing through all her exams, screaming and screaming that Patsy had had no right there in the first place. We were to take her away. She hadn't seen Patsy the afternoon before. She hadn't been in the house. She *shouldn't* have been in the house. She had no right to touch La Española. On and on it went, and every word out of her mouth made it worse. Like some horrible obscenity.

"All the things she was denying, we knew had happened. She had known all along Patsy was in the house, and had said nothing. Not until she saw Patsy's body. Then her nerves cracked. The things she said about Patsy . . . I wouldn't have believed Jessica even knew words like that—vile words. Tolson got her to her room, but the screaming still went on. Dr. Murray came. He looked at Patsy and told me he believed she had been dead since the night before. Then he had to go and give Jessica a knock-out injection. But he must have heard an awful lot. Being a doctor, he never said anything. I didn't doubt that having tried to help Jessica when she'd cracked up that summer, he'd have said she was still in a period of diminished responsibility. So . . . we just told the police and all the searchers that Patsy had been found, and it was all over. That part of it was over . . .

"Later, as Jessica grew better, it was less and less possible to believe that we had really heard her screaming the things she did. She couldn't, of course, ever admit it herself. Who would confess, or want to admit to having shouted that vile stream of hatred and greed and jealousy? Not little Jessica, not that perfect little ice maiden! No, she couldn't have. It would be quite impossible."

"Nat, do you honestly think she *locked* Patsy in the Spanish Woman's room, and simply left her there?"

"The Spanish Woman's room never was locked. The key was on the inside of the door, remember. It had jammed. Patsy made it worse, probably, by fiddling about with the key. I imagine I suppose either Jessica found Patsy there with La Española, or they went there together. Some row blew up, Jessica flew out of the room in a rage, slammed the door, and that was enough to jam the lock."

"So she might not have touched her, just as she said."

He shook his head. "Probably didn't. What she didn't do

was *tell* us that Patsy was there. And she reconnected the alarm system so that her grandfather wouldn't notice, wouldn't start to think about Patsy being somewhere in Thirlbeck."

"But *why* do that to Patsy? She couldn't have known she was going to die. She must have guessed she'd be in terrible trouble when Patsy did get out."

"You've seen kids, haven't you, who do something wrong, and try to cover it up as long as possible, even when they know it'll be discovered in the end. They stall—they do anything to hold off the evil hour. You could say Jessica had a fit of madness. When all the searchers started combing the Thirlbeck valley, she couldn't admit she knew where Patsy was. She might honestly have had a mental black-out. Forgetting what she didn't want to remember. Scared stiff, I suppose, the way children get scared of what they've done. She was . . . well, she was only sixteen at the time. Too young . . . or at least too young for me to feel there was any sense in accusing her. And knowing damn well that it would do Patsy no good, and wouldn't make me any more at peace with the world. Murray told me that same night that he was referring Jessica to a psychiatrist in London. She went away for a while. Had shock treatment I think. Then she went to a man in Carlisle a couple of times a week for two years. I didn't enquire very much into it. I really didn't want to know. And all the time, since that night when she screamed those hideous things about Patsy, she's been the good little girl she is now. Intelligent, willing, very competent. At times when she's around I can even forget, because the creature I see and hear now bears no resemblance to the evil little demon who let Patsy die there alone. I almost think she forgets herself, because she doesn't seem to realise I have any reason to hate her.

"So, you see, it was for Jessica's sake as well as mine that the Tolsons have closed in so tight, protecting me, making things easier for me, trying not to let me miss Patsy in any practical sense. In a way, they've denied me the right to grieve for her, and I resent it. My life fell apart, and I'm not allowed to show it."

He carefully squashed his cigarette butt into a rusty tobacco tin that was almost overflowing with the butts from all the other watchers who used the shelter. "So there they are, the whole tribe of them, propping me and the boys up, plastering over the cracks in my existence, refusing to understand that at times I've been close to letting the whole thing go. It's the boys who are the hook, of course. I go along with the Tolson situation because of them. But sometimes I wonder if we wouldn't be better, Thomas and Richard and myself, if we were quite alone, even if the house was in a mess and they had holes in their socks. But do I punish them because of Jessica? Not *all* the Tolsons are cracked. I think they're mostly just very decent people, trying to make up for Patsy not being here. I've kept quiet, so they probably think I've begun to accept it. But I haven't. I haven't forgotten that night, and I don't know how to wipe it all away. I don't know how to get out from the load of kindness and care they've buried me under. I feel, sometimes, as if I haven't had a breath of really clean air for more than three years."

He sat up fully, and I felt his hand hard on my shoulder, saw the perspiration break on his forehead. "For just these minutes with you I almost felt I was breathing again—not just taking in air, actually breathing, Jo. I had a feeling I was coming out from under. Maybe there was going to be a way out, after all. But I've come to my senses and I know you're going. You don't belong in this world, and you're going. I know it."

I had no ready word to deny that. Because I also knew it would be easier if I went.

And in a little time I did leave him; I left him squatting there in the shelter, smoking again, making more coffee, gazing after me with a look that could have been hurt, or equally could have been anger. But some special warmth still lived in me as I walked away, a new feeling in an aftermath of love-making, a sense of having tasted something for which I would forever after be hungry. I felt, even, a flicker of intuition that while it might be easier to go, it might not be better. But then, Nat himself had said it. I didn't belong in this world.

When I reached it, the mist had lifted from the lake, and from the tops of Brantwick and Great Birkeld. I looked back, but the woods had covered the shelter in their shadow. Above the newly revealed crag an eagle soared, went higher and higher, across the valley and was lost to sight against the upward straining mass of the bald mountain.

*   *   *

I had thought I would find her in the kitchen, and there she was. It was still very early—I had seen no sign of Tolson, and Mrs. Tolson didn't leave her bed until later in the morning. So Jessica was alone, as I had expected her to be, and in the kitchen surrounded by pans and bowls, starting the day's cooking.

She looked up when I came through by the back passage. She was completely calm, not at all disconcerted by the fact that she knew Nat and I had seen her from the shelter. The collie must have made his way back to Nat. There was coffee gently perking on one of the stoves. She hadn't yet started the preparations for breakfast. There was more than an hour to go before Askew would appear, before Jeffries would carry up Gerald's tray.

She jerked her head towards the coffeepot. "It's ready now. Would you like some?"

"Yes—yes I would." I went to the big dresser and took a cup and saucer from the pile. "Are you having any?"

"Yes, thank you. Cream and sugar. Cream's in the fridge."

In silence I poured coffee, put in the two spoonfuls of brown sugar she indicated, and passed the cup to her. "Thanks . . ." She took a sip, and then went on with measuring the ingredients she needed for her mixture. "It's Bavarian cream—for lunch," she said. "Can you cook?"

"Not much."

"No—I didn't think so. I don't know what you do at Hardy's, but you're not terribly useful anywhere else. In a few years, if I keep reading I'll know as much as you do—much more, probably. And I'll be able to run a house as well."

I drew out a chair and sat down facing her across the big table. "What's all this supposed to mean, Jessica? And why did you hang around the shelter this morning? What were you looking for?"

"Why did *you* go there? What were you trying to do—fill in some time while you're waiting to go back to London? Nat Birkett's not the sort for someone like you to amuse yourself with. He doesn't go for smart London types."

"Who does he go for, Jessica? Your type?"

"Why not my type? I'm not a child any more. He's going to know it—quite soon he's going to wake up and know it."

While she was talking I had begun fingering a plain cream-coloured bowl which stood with her mixing basins and measuring cups on the table. It was slightly fluted at the edges with a thin brown rim, and carved in the centre and sides with a delicate line drawing of flowers and leaves—possibly peony and lotus. A very plain bowl, very beautiful. Jessica probably meant to pour her completed dessert into it.

"And how are you going to wake him up, Jessica? Doesn't Nat Birkett *know* how valuable you are? How clever and how good you are at everything?"

"He will," she said sharply. "Once I'm twenty he'll realise. He's been too used to thinking of me as a child. But he'll realise."

Her voice was still very soft, like a whisper. Both of us spoke as if this were an entirely ordinary conversation, our tones level and calm. But I had seen the colour come more strongly to her cheeks, which always had the texture and appearance of a wax doll, and her china-blue eyes were brilliant and at the same time stony and hard, staring at me across the table with a strange fanatical glow of which I would never, until this morning, have believed her capable. What had Nat accused her of—greed, hate, jealousy, a blind, possibly a murderous rage? I gazed at her in fascination, and then my eyes flickered back to the bowl. Now I took it in my hands and turned it over, looking at the faint marks there, examining the glaze, tracing the line carving with my finger. There was a serenity in its execution, a lack of haste; it almost seemed to possess its own sense of time. I looked back at Jessica, and I couldn't have told if it was she, so transformed, or the bowl I held in my hands that caused the tightening in my throat, the churn of excitement that seemed also mixed with fear, in my stomach.

Her voice again, whispery, silky. "Why don't you go? You know you're not wanted here. None of you are wanted here. You've no business being here—upsetting things, putting things out of order. It was all right until you came. But you'll go again, and we'll have everything back as it used to be."

"Nothing will ever be as it used to be, Jessica. Lord Askew has come home, and *that* has changed things."

"He'll go again. It doesn't really belong to him."

"Who does it belong to, Jessica?"

"To us. To my family, and Nat Birkett. Lord Askew might as well die and let Nat Birkett have what is his. Why do old men stay around, making other people wait for what should be theirs?"

I thought she had the blank look of obsession now, the fixed eyes, the voice completely without emotion. And I turned and turned that bowl in my hands because she seemed mesmerised by the movement, and my pulse hammered in my wrists.

I spoke very softly to her, as to a person in deep shock. "And did Patsy Birkett get in the way, Jessica? Did she make you wait too long for what is really yours? There was going to be an operation, and she might get well, and live for a long time, mightn't she? She used to come and see the jewel, La Española, didn't she? Your grandfather encouraged her to come—to see the jewel, to walk through the rooms. Your rooms, Jessica. Did you take the jewel out yourself that day? Did she find you in the Spanish Woman's room with it? Or was it the other way around? Did you leave her there—alone, frightened? And when she didn't come down, you didn't go back to find out what had happened to her. Not then, nor all the next day, when they were searching."

Incredibly, there was the faintest trace of a smile on her lips, turning upwards as if in remembrance. "I did nothing to her. *Caveat Raptor: Who Seizes, Beware.* She held La Española as if it were already hers, and she walked around this house as if she already lived here. These rooms—*my* rooms. I did nothing to her. I didn't even touch her."

"Jessica! No more! You're imagining things again!"

Tolson stood in the doorway that led from the service passage. His black, monumental frame seemed stooped, his shoulders rounded more than before, his arms hanging loosely like some great animal.

And at the sight of him the bowl fell from my suddenly nerveless fingers and smashed in many pieces on the flagstone floor.

CHAPTER 6

I

Then I was driving down the Motorway towards London, the pieces of the bowl wrapped in a silk scarf, and packed among my clothes in a suitcase. I kept pushing the Mini near 70, pushing until my teeth seemed to rattle with the vibration. I noted the stares of the drivers I passed, most of them driving much more powerful cars; often I got frantic and antagonistic blasts from horns when I did something especially stupid. But I kept pushing and sometimes taking foolish risks—except that in my present frame of mind, I really didn't know what was foolish. I stopped when I had to at the service areas, to go to the toilet, to buy coffee in a plastic cup, and a wrapped sandwich which I ate later as I drove. All of England was going by in those hours, down from the sparsely populated region of the North-East, through the Manchester-Liverpool overspill, on and on down until the prettily luxurious, but still overcrowded Home Counties came up. It began to rain, and the driving grew harder, but I didn't relax the speed. I got to Watford, and Hendon, and I could feel my eyes begin to sting and burn. And then I was enmeshed in the crawl of the evening rush-hour traffic, and there was nothing I could do but sit and stare at the lines of cars ahead, and those going in the opposite direction, listening to the *click-click* of the windscreen wipers; it was then I smoked the first cigarette since I had begun to drive, and let my thoughts deliberately dwell on what had happened to Thirlbeck.

Askew hadn't even seemed very interested when I told him—hadn't even wanted to delay his breakfast to look at it. "You don't seem to understand, Lord Askew. It *may* be very valuable, and I've broken it."

Unbelievably he had shrugged. "I'm afraid I have to talk in clichés, but I don't know what else to say. It's broken—plenty of things get broken. As well as people."

"But you *do* understand that I have to go and tell my director at Hardy's. For someone who works with ceramics, I've been unbelievably clumsy. They expect better of me."

"Look," he said, "just sit down and have your breakfast, and let me have mine, there's a good girl." He poured coffee for us both. "I really think you're being a bit hasty over this. After all, what does it have to do with Hardy's if something in my house gets broken? I simply don't see the connection. Why does it become their business? Here, at least have some toast with that."

"Well, you did say you were considering offering the contents of this house for auction. What I've just done could seriously prejudice that. You might decide to take the sale to Christie's or Sotheby's . . . or somewhere else. Whether or not this turns out to be what I suspect it might be, or quite worthless, is hardly the case. You wouldn't expect anyone from Hardy's to go round smashing things in people's houses."

"My God, you do take yourself seriously. You mean to say if you happen to put a chip in an old kitchen cup you might get the sack?" He laughed as he spoke, and plunged into a plate of scrambled eggs and sausage.

"It's hardly a matter of getting the sack. The thing is that I believed I might be handling something very valuable. There are degrees of carelessness, Lord Askew."

"You know you really are a bloody fool. You needn't have said a word about it. If it was in use in the kitchen, no one had any idea it might be especially valuable. You could just have kept your mouth shut, and no one would have been any the wiser." He waved his fork in the direction of the pieces on the sideboard. "Looks like a perfectly ordinary bowl to me."

"Well, it *doesn't* look like that to me. And I'm surprised you'd imagine I'd say nothing."

He looked at me hard. Then he laughed again. "Well . . . I'd almost forgotten what it's like to hear something like that. And especially from someone your age. No wonder Gerald sets such store by you. Noblesse oblige . . . Scout's honour . . . and all the rest of it. I'm sorry I'm laughing. I just can't help it."

"I wish you wouldn't. I don't like it."

"Then I'll try not to. But suppose I just say 'forget it'? There was an accident. It happened to my property. I overlook it. I forget it. Now, do you still have to go rushing off and confess all to your director?"

"I want to. I *will*. What I'd like to know is if there's a chance that there's any more—like that." I inclined my own head towards the sideboard.

"How should I know? The house is full of junk, isn't it?—with a few good bits scattered about. You know how a family picks up rubbish through the years, especially if there's a place to store it. Just take those damn boxes you've been going through. At least two hundred years of papers there, and probably not a single piece of it worth saving. Have you seen the attics? A real nightmare. If you combed them you might come up with a few more pieces like that. No doubt that's where one of the Tolsons found it and decided to put it to use."

"It would be unusual for something like that to be lying around in an English country house unless it had been acquired in China. Can you remember, Lord Askew, if any of your family were in China—well, let's say some time in the nineteenth century?"

"I don't know. I wasn't alive then." He went back and helped himself to more sausage, sublimely indifferent. "There was, of course, old Major Sharpe. He was married to my grandfather's sister. Used to come over from near Whitehaven every Christmas. He'd been holed up in Peking during the Boxer Rebellion, and he insisted on retelling the story every time he came. They lived in a small place, and I seem to remember falling over

Chinese swords and armour and all that sort of stuff. There were probably a few Chinese vases around. Since they didn't have any children it's quite possible all those bits and pieces came here to Thirlbeck after my great-aunt died. But I really couldn't say. Once I went away to school anything might have happened here and I probably wouldn't have noticed any change. It's all a long time ago . . ."

All a long time ago. That was how families did it—collected these treasures often in complete ignorance of them. And the thought nagged again and again of Vanessa, who hadn't been so ignorant. I remembered the prunus vase in the library which had been made in England, and my head ached with it all, and from the petrol fumes, and the daylong vibration of the flight down the Motorway in the Mini. I hoped very much I was mistaken about what lay wrapped in the silk scarf in my suitcase.

It was after 6:30 when I reached Hardy's. The director of the ceramics department would probably have left, but I decided to go in. The daytime crowds were emptying off the streets in this part of St. James's, where almost no one lived, but many worked. I rang the night bell at the back entrance in an alley where the big delivery doors were, and was routinely examined through a viewer by the security man. "It's you, Jo," he said, as he opened up. He'd known me since I'd begun visiting Hardy's with Vanessa at about age fifteen, and he's never called me anything else. "Mr. Hudson's still here. He said if you came you were to go straight up to him. Here, want to leave the bag?"

I rummaged around and found the silk scarf with the pieces in it. Hardy's wore an almost ghostly air at this time of day— with the big front doors closed, and the great stair empty, no voices, no buzz of conversation, no whisper of the supposed secrets and tips that dealers were thought to pass to one another, no sudden burst of laughter when someone told a good trade joke, no stiffening and overpolite courtesies between rivals who knew they would surely be bidding against each other at that day's sale. I paused at the top of the stair, which led on to the salerooms, and for an instant they were peopled and full of sound, full of the life that daily flowed through Hardy's. How long I seemed to have been away, and yet it was only a few weeks. Until a few weeks ago I could almost have wrapped up my whole life and believed it had been lived here, would go on being lived here. Then I heard the lonely clicking of a single typewriter coming from the outer office of Mr. Hudson's room. I went and knocked and walked in.

Bunny Goodman, his secretary, looked up. "It's you, Jo. He's expecting you. Go in." As I passed she asked questions about Gerald, and then added something about Vanessa. "I was going to write you, Jo, but it seemed too formal, somehow. I'm awfully sorry. But I hear you've been out in Mexico with your father, and now that place in the Lake District with that dashing Earl. What a life! And here I am bashing out the same old letters."

It wasn't going to be quite the same again, ever. The snow-covered mountain in Switzerland, and Mexico, and Thirlbeck, Askew and Nat Birkett, and my father Jonathan Roswell, all stood between. I was acutely conscious of the miniature in its leather pouch which had never left my possession since the day I had discovered where it truly belonged. "He isn't really so dashing, Bunny. Just a very sophisticated, but not particularly brilliant man, who loves women, and good food and travel. He's won medals and he shoots and rides—I suppose that's it. It really isn't all that glamorous when you live with it. And he's getting on a bit."

"*You* can say that. I saw a photo of him once. I wouldn't mind being around him. Well, better get on in to the Boss. He'll think we're chattering again . . ." She pulled the paper out of the machine. "That's that for the day. I just thought I'd stay on a bit since the Boss was . . ."

She was another who had almost grown up at Hardy's, working on the Front Counter, and then in the catalogue room, and finding her berth here as William Hudson's secretary. She didn't pretend to have the qualifications of any of the experts of the ceramics department, but she was, all the same, a very shrewd judge of whatever passed over her desk. It was the kind of learning that went on at Hardy's; by seeing, feeling, and recording one learned.

212

William Hudson rose from his desk when I entered. "Ah, Jo, there you are. I hoped you might come before I closed up for the night." He paused. "My dear girl, you look terrible! Here—" He went to a beautifully inlaid cabinet and produced a bottle and glasses. "A Scotch, Jo? I expect you've been on the road most of the day. Nasty weather for it, too."

I sipped the Scotch cautiously, but gratefully. "Mr. Hudson, I don't think you'll be half as nice when you know what's happened."

He leaned back in his chair, his gaze going fondly, as it often did during interviews with him, to the beautiful glazed pottery figure of a mounted drummer of the T'ang Dynasty which stood on top of the bureau.

"Jo, I've had a telephone call from Lord Askew. I must confess it made me most curious. He said I was to take notice of absolutely nothing you said. He said he thought you were . . . well, a little *unsettled* still after your mother's death. Jo, what has happened?"

I put the glass on his desk and brought out the fragments of the creamy-white bowl. "This is what has happened, Mr. Hudson. And I broke it. I dropped it."

He drew the silk scarf towards him gently, and took a long time examining the pieces. He put a few of them together, getting an idea of the shape of the bowl, his fingers traced the carving just as mine had done that morning. He fingered the glaze, noted its crazing, turned the pieces back and forth. His face grew long in concentration, and as I watched, I saw the dawning of regret.

"Well . . . without betting my life on it, it looks terribly like that Ting-yao basin we had last year. Sung Dynasty. Beautiful piece—if it were in one piece."

"That's it. I dropped it. It was in one piece this morning."

He looked across at me. "And Lord Askew wants me to pay no attention to anything you say. A slight accident occurred, he said. Nothing of any importance. It was his property, and he doesn't in any way hold you responsible. In fact, he thinks you're a little mad for being in such a state. Did you tell him, Jo . . . Did you tell him about this?" He prodded the pieces.

"I didn't say what I *thought* it was. I just said I suspected it might be very valuable. But I don't know if he has any idea of how valuable. His ideas of value—well, it's how much champagne it will buy, or how much does a horse cost, or a good car. I didn't suggest . . ."

He regarded me bleakly. "Well, he absolved you of any responsibility. Absolutely. He made that quite clear. But of course he didn't know that we sold that other one for forty-nine thousand pounds. That's an awful lot of money to drop, Jo, isn't it?" Again his fingers gently touched the fragments. "And a very beautiful bowl."

"That's why I'm here. I told him I had to come and see you. He didn't understand. He thought I needn't have said anything. No one would ever have known."

He sipped his Scotch, and took some time before answering; he seemed to be giving all his attention to the T'ang horseman. "And you and I know different, Jo. *You* would have known—and that, in my mind, is what makes the difference between a person who does a job for what's in it for him, and someone who does it because he can't help it—does it for love, almost. I have to deplore your carelessness, and congratulate you on having a good eye for a piece that really is pretty rare. You could go a long way, Jo. I must see if there isn't a place for you in Oriental ceramics. I fancy you might be getting a little tired of all those Meissen shepherdesses." He fingered one of the fragments again, carefully not looking at my face so that I had time to compose it again. "And as for this . . . well, it can be mended, of course, but it can never be the perfect piece it was. Pity . . . it would have been nice to offer another of that quality. They don't come along that often. By the way, I assume Lord Askew was thinking of disposing of it?"

"How could he? . . . He didn't know he had it! It's all in such a crazy state up there. He was ready to have us come up there and go through the whole house. And then Mr. Stanton got ill. Now Lord Askew seems to have settled in a bit. He doesn't want to talk about business, and he doesn't seem to want Mr. Stanton to leave, even though he's well enough now, I think. And this morning, when I broke this, I thought I might have ruined Hardy's chances of having a perfectly magnificent sale . . ."

We launched into the talk that was close to both of us. For a time, as I described Thirlbeck, the barrier of age and status between us vanished. I told William Hudson about the crowded attics of Thirlbeck, the big ground-floor rooms crammed with furniture, the books, even the metal shutters. I found myself even telling of the night I had triggered the alarm system in the room which housed La Española. We were two professionals talking about what we loved; but I found there were things I could not say. I did not talk about the Rembrandt which gave Gerald so much worry, about the possibility of other pictures in a room I had never entered; I did not talk of the great hounds which followed me, and I said nothing about the miniature in my handbag. I said nothing at all about Vanessa ever having been at Thirlbeck. If that part of the story was ever told, it would have to come from Gerald. I said nothing, either, about the Book of Hours of Juana, and the translated fragment in the hand of Philip the Second. From this well-lighted office in St. James's, with the sound of the slackening evening traffic outside, the world of Thirlbeck seemed incredibly remote. I began, almost, to wonder if my imagination had not coloured too highly some aspects of that great house in its closed, hidden valley. But the pieces lying in the silk scarf between us were real enough.

When I left, Hardy's was wearing its evening hush, only essential lights burning, and the security man at the side door had settled to his evening paper and his meat-pie supper. I took the suitcase from him at the door. "You'd better decide to come back from holiday, Jo. We'll be forgetting what you look like soon."

I went back to the Mini feeling slightly bewildered. From the excitement of talking with William Hudson as if I might one day be his equal in knowledge and experience, I was back with the chilly reality of a rainy spring evening and of being tired and hungry. If the world of Thirlbeck seemed remote and unreal, a mixture of fairy tale and nightmare, then for some strange reason which I couldn't explain, in these weeks I seemed to have taken a step away from Hardy's also.

* * *

I drove the Mini up a block to Jermyn Street, and there was a parking place near an Italian restaurant where I often ate. I felt my whole body dragging along the pavement, and then there came the warm, sensuous smell of drink and food when I opened the door. I was on my way through the bar to the dining section when the voice called to me.

"Jo—where have you been? We hear tales of you living it up with the Jet Set somewhere. How's life? Have a drink."

In the darkened area where the drink tables were I recognised two young men from Hardy's, though at the moment it was difficult to put a name to either of them. They were flanked by two young women, neither of whom seemed much interested in me. I didn't think, after all those hours on the Motorway, after the time which had gone by since I had heard Nat Birkett's Land-Rover go up the valley that morning, that my appearance posed much threat to their fresh London elegance. With a faint sense of shock I realised I was wearing the anorak I had bought in Kesmere. I dropped down into a seat beside them, and then my mind began sorting out the special departments they both worked in, and the things they excelled in.

The Scotch was put in front of me before I could frame the thought. "Peter—you speak Spanish, don't you?"

"Yes, a bit. But don't send me to take any exams right now."

"Just hold on—please. I'll be back." Then I called back over my shoulder: "And don't let them take my drink away."

I returned quickly, having once again searched the suitcase for what I wanted. We had to ask the bartender to bring a candle from one of the dining tables so that Peter Warner could look at what I had brought to show him.

He examined it closely, a kind of minor variation of William Hudson's behaviour over the Sung bowl. "Lord, Jo, where on earth did you come across this?"

"It doesn't matter, Peter. All you have to look at is what's written under her name. Can you make out any of it?"

He looked up at me. "It's an extremely beautiful *Horae*, Jo. Worth quite a bit. It probably wasn't made for her, was it? I think it was a she, from the handwriting."

"It was a she," I admitted. "You see her name there. I suppose it was given to her. But what is written under the name? Can you make it out?"

"Well, she was pretty young, I'd say—from the handwriting again. Well enough educated, but a bit spottily—which might well have been so for any lady at that time. The Latin and Spanish is all mixed up, and the spelling—well, the spelling is what it was in the . . ." He shrugged. "I'd guess the sixteenth century."

"What does it say?"

"Give me a chance." He took his time, sipping his drink, tapping his fingers on those parchment pages. I saw one of the girls at the table look at the other and give an exaggerated shrug. I realised then I hadn't even waited to go through the formality of being introduced to them.

"*What*, Peter?"

"I think . . . I *think* it says, the sense of it is, roughly, 'When I am dead, of your charity, offer nine Masses for my soul.'" He looked up. "That's about it, I think. It's typical enough. The Spanish are always brooding about death."

"Thanks, Peter." I finished my drink quickly, and fended off the questions about Thirlbeck. Then I went and sat alone and ate cannelloni, and had a half bottle of wine. And as I ate, Juana Fernández de Córdoba's Book of Hours lay on the banquette beside me, wrapped in several sheets of paper, and a final covering of plastic. I suppose I had no more right to it than to the miniature in my handbag, and I would have to return it to Thirlbeck. But as I ate, the misspelled words of the little exiled Spanish girl came echoing through the centuries, her loneliness and her premonitions of death. *When I am dead, of your charity, offer nine Masses for my soul.* No one knew where she was buried, or if she indeed had a grave at all. And no one, I thought, had offered nine Masses for her soul.

I started for my flat in Chelsea, but when I got to Knightsbridge I just kept going west until I reached Kensington High Street, and the turn up into Church Street. It was probably madness to do what I was doing in this state of fatigue, but it was something I knew I could never do in the cool calmness of an early morning. I had needed the Scotch and the wine, even the feeling of languor after the food so that there should be some insulation against the shock of visiting Vanessa's flat for the first time since her death. I had avoided going there on the few days after my return from Mexico. Gerald was executor of her will, and he had told me that I was the only beneficiary. It was understood between us that when the estate was settled, there might be very little to inherit. Vanessa had been recklessly extravagant in giving her time, her money, and her patience to a host of friends who suffered reverses of fortune; she had been the first call for all the lame ducks. Gerald had deplored the tendency, telling her she was being "used," and yet he had loved her for it. We both knew the chaotic state of the books she kept, or tried to keep, of the antique business she owned. She had had one employee, Mary Westerson, who still kept the shop open, hoping to sell off its contents for the eventual settlement of the estate. Mary Westerson loved beautiful things, which was why Vanessa had employed her, and was just as hopeless as Vanessa herself in keeping books that would make sense to an accountant at the end of the year. Between them, they had enjoyed the business they ran, had made enough money to live, and that had been all Vanessa had cared about.

I found a parking space near the mews flat around the corner from Vanessa's shop. She had been lucky that, on Gerald's advice, she had bought long leases with low ground rents on the two properties more than twenty years ago—before the property market in London had gone soaring. Probably she had borrowed against them; Gerald had thought that when her affairs had been gone into, we would find them heavily mortgaged.

And then I thought of the Hilliard miniature of the third Countess of Askew, carried now, as always, in my bag. That would have to be declared as part of the estate also—or should be. And if I declared that, what else would I be declaring about Vanessa? That she had stolen it? A good quality Hilliard could now be worth as much as twenty thousand pounds. At the time it would have left Thirlbeck it might only have been worth hundreds. I stared up at the darkened window of her flat, the open curtains with the blackness behind them speaking of a terrible emptiness within; my heart ached, and the puzzle of Vanessa's unrevealed presence at Thirlbeck all those years ago nagged and tugged with growing urgency. I suddenly knew why I had come this night. Somewhere in the chaos of Vanessa's personal possessions, in the labyrinth of her papers, there might be revealed the reason for her silence. There was little chance I would uncover much—but now, the urgency of the unanswered question translated itself into the urgency to re-establish contact with Vanessa herself, the glowing spirit of the woman which had not died with her body.

Gerald had given me keys to the flat, as well as duplicate keys to the shop. There was even the smell of emptiness about the place when I entered, the smell of closed windows, and most acutely for me, the absence of the smell of flowers, which had always been here, and were one of Vanessa's great loves and great extravagances. It was a small flat—just one long room on the ground floor which was a combination sitting and dining room, with a partly screened-off kitchen at the end, and above it, two small bedrooms. One of the bedrooms had been mine when I was growing up; it was now used as an overflow office for the shop, crammed with papers, catalogues of sales, reference books, the whole paraphernalia of Vanessa's jumbled existence. It would be there, if anywhere, I would find some reference to the summer and autumn she had spent at Thirlbeck. Did Vanessa ever keep a diary? I doubted it—that would have been too orderly a habit for her. Then, with my hand on the bannister ready to mount the steep stair, I turned away. Up there was also Vanessa's bedroom, as strongly personal a room as I had ever seen, stamped indelibly with her character, her charm, her sensuous nature. I wasn't ready for that yet.

So I went into the sitting room, turning off the light in the hall as I went. The flat had an opaque glass panel with wrought iron across it in the front door, and whenever I had approached it at night, it had seemed too exposed to the street outside. So I turned off the light in the hall, and closed the door to the sitting room. Then I drew the curtains on the street side. It immediately became the warm and charming room it had been in Vanessa's time—the orange carpet, the gold curtains expressions of her own vibrant nature. Vanessa had never favoured blue. I looked again at the favourite antiques she had gathered into her life, the beautiful small tables, the mirrors, the Chippendale chairs. And with these pieces she had mixed comfortable sofas and easy chairs, upholstered in yellow; she had never let the antiques dominate the comforts of life. What it needed was the scent of flowers.

It was all dusted and tidy. I wondered if it had been Gerald or Mary Westerson who had arranged for the cleaning woman to come still, whose duties now would be so vacant and empty. I went into the kitchen and drew the curtains against the darkness of the opposite brick walls. Now it was almost the cosy world of Vanessa's making, lacking just the scent of the flowers and the crackle of a fire. So I turned on the substitute electric fire. There was no way to make up for the flowers.

I brewed some coffee. The refrigerator had been defrosted and cleaned out. There was coffee, tea, sugar, but no milk. Biscuits were still in their canisters—all looking unnaturally tidy because Vanessa had not been there to disturb their order. I stood by the stove while the coffee perked, and hardly let myself think. It was just enough, for the moment, that I had been able to come here. Then I poured the coffee and went to the chair beside the telephone.

It was a shock to hear Harry answer almost at once. I was so used to the voice of the manservant, telling me that Mr. Peers was elsewhere. "Hello, luv," he said. "Where've you been? Back in London now, aren't you?"

"Yes, how did you know?"

"Difference in your voice. Up there, you always sounded as

if you were off somewhere in cloud-cuckoo land. A bit absent, you know."

"It's a long way, Harry."

"Sweetheart, you don't know what a long way means. A long way is Australia—or the moon."

"What have you been doing, Harry?" I wasn't going to argue our differences on the level of miles.

"This and that. I bought a house, for one thing."

"A house? I thought you were always buying houses."

"Luv, you don't know anything. I buy properties, I don't buy houses. But yesterday I bought a house. A house for *me*."

"You're giving up the flat, then?"

"Well, what do you think? What would I need one a half a mile away from the other for? I'm good at throwing money around, luv, but not absolutely crazy."

"So you've bought a house, Harry. Where? When are you going to move into it?"

"When you do."

I was silent a moment. "Harry, I don't think I need to move into it. I have a flat."

"Crazy, girl—crazy. Do you expect us to bring up our kids in that two-by-four place you live in? Our kids are going to have nurseries and nannies, and the whole razzmatazz. They're going to be wheeled in their prams in St. James's Park. All that common old lot get pushed around in Hyde Park, but our kids are going to wave at the Palace Guard every day."

"Our kids, Harry? *Our* lot?"

"Who else's? Nothing too good for them. I've bought a house in St. James's Place. It's the last building that will ever be a private house. Nice and convenient for us both. And the kids. You can get to Hardy's in two minutes flat—no, three, allowing for the crossing. I don't want you to get run down. And I can nip along to St. James's Square and kiss you good-bye on the steps of Hardy's on the way. You can keep on working right up until each kid is born, almost, and then be back again before they've missed you. And you'll end up being a director of Hardy's."

"Who says that, Harry? That's not something even you can

guarantee." I don't know how I got the words out; he was preposterous and overwhelming, as always, and at the centre of my excitement there was a dead cold calmness.

"I don't have to, luv. You're good, you know. Other people know it. You just need a few years, and a little bit more confidence. And I promise you our honeymoon can be any place in the world you want to go to look at bits and pieces of china. Any place. I'll even get you a visa into China itself. Just so long as you make *my* half of the honeymoon a beach in Bali. It's all done, Jo. The house is bought. It has to be fixed up a bit, but you could move in here until it's done. It won't take nine months. All we have to do is arrange to get together in person instead of by telephone. So . . . when will it be?"

I spoke very deliberately. "I think I need to come and talk to you, Harry. There's so much to talk about."

"What's there to talk about? We're going to get married. There's nothing so odd about that. People do it every day. We can do it any time we want."

"I'll come and see you tonight, Harry. I'm at Vanessa's flat. We have to talk—"

"Nothing to talk about, and especially not tonight. Tonight —in fact right this minute—I'm due at a meeting. It's at my office. These guys have come over from New York. It'll be a late session."

"Harry—"

"Sorry, luv. No business meeting, no trips to China. It's that simple. Just think about it. Take a walk along there. Take a look at the house. You can't miss it. It's the one tucked back beside Duke's Hotel. There's a discreet estate agent's sign on it, and a whopping great vulgar SOLD sign tacked across it. Go and take a look. I'll call you. Bye, luv."

I sipped the coffee, and because I needed it, I went and poured some brandy from Vanessa's stock. I noticed my hands shook a little, and still that strange calmness was upon me. I had just been handed the world, and it didn't feel as I had expected it to. I could have my job at Hardy's and kids too— Harry's kids. I could have China, and a beach in Bali. I was being given time and the chance to become what I had dreamed of, the one whose name could authenticate almost any piece of ceramic that came to hand. It was the world on a golden plate. I should have felt like champagne, but instead I needed the brandy.

I didn't notice how long I sat there. Outside the mews became quiet, the traffic on Kensington Church Street took on its late-evening sound. I sat in the stillness of the room, with just the one lamp lighted on the table beside me, and I thought about Harry—about Harry and Vanessa. I had believed that if this time had ever come I wouldn't even think, that pleasure could drive out any thoughtfulness. It was what I had wanted—more than I had dreamed of. And still I sat on in the quiet, sipping the brandy, and strangely I was taking out once more the Hilliard miniature, turning it between my fingers, watching the light play on the tiny features of the woman who suddenly seemed even more to resemble Vanessa. The light fell on the damaged gold frame, and gave life to the diamonds. I wished Vanessa were here, sitting across from me in her usual place; she would have drunk three brandies to my one, and made all the better sense for it.

I don't know when I first became aware of the sound—the slight scraping sound from the hall. It didn't last long, and I thought it may have been going on for some time before I became aware of it. Then there was the murmur of a man's voice, quiet, authoritative, unhurried. I reached up and switched out the light on the table beside me. Then the door opened, and the beam of a torch swept the whole room quickly, passed over me, and did not pause. I remained in the chair; I couldn't have moved, even if I'd known what to do. The man pressed the switch beside the door, and the chandelier over the dining table sprang to life.

"Good evening, Mr. Tolson."

He looked in my direction uncertainly, peering through the pebble glasses, not quite sure of what he saw.

"Dad . . . ?"

"All right, Ted. Just close the door. Miss Roswell and I know each other well enough." The younger man came through into

223

the room, and I recognised one of the Tolson sons from Thirl-beck.

I deliberately took up the brandy glass, and was pleased to see that my hand wasn't shaking any more. It was as if something I had been waiting for for a long time was beginning to happen. I fingered the miniature for a second longer, and then slipped it back into my handbag.

"You seem to know your way, Mr. Tolson."

"Yes—it took a bit of finding, though. I've only been here once before. London's changed since then."

He was the heavy immovable mountain of a man he had always been. If I could have seen beyond the pebble glasses, I might have known something of his feelings, but as always they would reveal nothing.

"But you didn't expect to find me here—or you wouldn't have come?"

"If I'd known, I'd have waited till you were gone," he answered calmly. "I knew you haven't lived here for a long time."

"Well, here I am. And here you are—and your son. I notice you didn't have any difficulty getting in."

He shrugged. "Ordinary locks aren't difficult for Ted."

"Convenient for you to have a son like Ted. Are you going to tell me why you're here?"

He moved farther into the room, slipping off the raincoat he wore. All at once his movements seemed those of an older man than I remembered, someone fatigued by the journey, stiff and cramped in his limbs. His son stood behind him, his eyes, sheathed in glasses only a little less heavy than those his father wore, shifted constantly between us two.

"I think you'd better sit down, Mr. Tolson. You must be tired. I am. Would you like a brandy? It's there in the cupboard, and the glasses are in the kitchen. Coffee just needs to be heated —there's sugar but no milk."

Tolson nodded to his son, and we waited in silence while the brandy was brought to him. Then Ted went back into the kitchen, and I could see the flare of the gas go on under the coffeepot. He wouldn't find it as good coffee as Jessica made.

"Why are you here, Mr. Tolson? I shouldn't need to ask, but you don't seem ready to volunteer any information."

"I don't volunteer anything until I know how much the other person knows. Now with you . . ."

"Just assume I know nothing. I *don't* know why you're here. I don't know what you've come for. And I didn't expect you. It wasn't anything to do with Jessica this morning? Or the bowl?"

"In a way, nothing directly. But it brought matters to a head, let us say. I've been putting off making this visit—Lord Askew's presence at Thirlbeck was unexpected, and it compelled me to be there constantly. But I've known that the moment would come when I'd be confronted with an unwelcome situation. Mr. Stanton's illness has merely postponed that inevitable time. But once I knew Lord Askew was returning and that people were coming up from Hardy's I knew that the moment would come. Your breaking the bowl this morning, and from the way you handled the pieces and took them off to London with you made me realise you were on to something we had overlooked—or rather Mrs. Roswell had overlooked. Rather more searching enquiries were going to be made, and even before the experts came up to look at the picture. That bowl was very valuable, I suspect. We didn't know it, of course, or it would never have been in the kitchen. But I knew through it you would be on to all the rest of the things . . . that you would start asking questions, and in turn Lord Askew would start asking questions. It is very unfortunate Mrs. Roswell was killed—"

"*Unfortunate!*" I slammed the glass down in anger. "Unfortunate! Mrs. Roswell was my mother! It was more than unfortunate for her—and for me!"

He sipped at the brandy. "I beg your pardon. Very clumsy of me. For us—my wife and I—it was a blow as well. In more ways than one. We grew quite fond of her over the years."

"What are you talking about—*over the years!* My mother hadn't been at Thirlbeck since 1945."

He sighed. "That isn't quite true. In about the last sixteen or seventeen years we've seen her there quite frequently. Several times a year, in fact. Scouting expeditions, she used to call them."

"Scouting for what—for *what*, Mr. Tolson?"

He took off his glasses and rubbed his eyes as if they were weary. Instead of the naked look that most people who wear glasses have when they are removed, his features came into sharper focus. The strength that was implied by the sheer bulk of his body was reinforced by the sight of his eyes, a grey so deep they seemed almost black; the black sprouting eyebrows now shaped a natural frame to the formidable eyes, and the gaze fixed on me seemed even more transfixing because it was myopic. I would only be a blur to him now, sitting in Vanessa's yellow chair. He replaced his glasses. His son came and put a cup of coffee on the table at his father's side, and then he himself retreated to the dining table and drew out one of the chairs and sat down. Obviously he would have no part in what would be said.

"It will be easier," Tolson said, "if I tell you the whole thing. Any questions you have to ask, I'll answer. Perhaps you will be able to answer one or two for me."

"Try me—I expect I will have some questions myself."

He took another sip of the brandy, and then reached for the coffee, stirred it, and drank. I thought his mouth puckered a little at the taste. "I sought out your mother when the difficulties first arose at Thirlbeck. Until then—almost seventeen years ago—it is true that she had not been back to Thirlbeck, but in trying to find a solution to my problem I thought of her because I felt I could trust her—"

"*Trust* her! You were the one who called her a gypsy—you implied that both she and my father were fly-by-nights, spongers, almost. You've revised your opinion?"

"You must realise, Miss Roswell, that when I heard a friend of Lord Askew's was coming up from Hardy's, I didn't expect he would be accompanied by *you*. I realised that you must be wondering why your mother had never spoken of Thirlbeck, or anything it contained. So I—well, I suppose I emphasised her more . . . her more raffish qualities, shall we say, when you asked if I remembered her. At that time I hadn't quite given up hope that Lord Askew would grow bored at Thirlbeck, and simply go away. It wouldn't have ended my problems, but it might have delayed the exposure of what I had been doing. Time itself might have helped me. No one ever expected him to come back, you see. *That* was where all the plans came unstuck. I never believed we would ever see him again at Thirlbeck, and it was entirely possible that he would die without ever knowing what had been taking place. But inflation in these last years has beaten us all. He needs more money, and every day in the papers there are reports of art sales at record prices at auction. I suppose it was inevitable that he would start to think of what he had left at Thirlbeck, and to think of what he could do with the money."

"What exactly are your problems, Mr. Tolson? Have you been stealing from Lord Askew, and now he's going to find out?" I felt a kind of deadly cold anger in me which helped to keep my voice very even and nearly toneless. "Are you going to tell me that my mother had been stealing with you?"

"Not that, Miss Roswell. If there's been stealing, I have done it. Your mother was the means to dispose of what I had—well, what I was advised should be disposed of from the estate. It started in a rather small way about seventeen years ago, but as the demands from Lord Askew have grown and grown, we have had to increase the robbing Peter to pay Paul, so to speak."

"So to speak—*nothing*, Mr. Tolson. Please don't quibble any more. You were stealing, and you somehow induced my mother to be party to it, used her channels to get rid of what you had stolen. And all the time you despised her."

He took up the brandy again and drank. "I'll try to tell you again, Miss Roswell. I came to your mother all those years ago because I *did* trust her. And I trusted her because she loved Thirlbeck. We weren't much of the same kind, your mother and my family. We were all country people, and we've lived and worked on the Birkett estate for generations. We've had positions of trust. I believe we haven't betrayed that trust. Now your mother—yes, she was different from us. But that summer and autumn she was at Thirlbeck I saw her often enough to know that she loved it. Yes, she did love it—the house, everything that was in it, the valley, the privacy of it, the wholeness. She knew that the Birketts owned property outside the valley, quite a lot of it. Land. And that was part of it too. Before there were any of the pretty little knickknacks you see in the house, there was the land. The Earls of Askew were powerful because of the land they held, amassed through gifts of the sovereigns in the beginning—from Henry the Eighth after he dissolved the monasteries, and then grants from Elizabeth. Judicious marriages brought other properties—farms, mines, all the rest of it. Before there was Thirlbeck itself, there was land, and it has always rested on land. People can create other things—pictures, furniture, bits and pieces of china and silver. No one can make any more land. I judged, I think rightly, that the land was more important to the future of the Birketts than their other possessions. And I believed, from what I knew of her, that your mother felt the same way. She was a romantic, your mother— well, you knew that, but you didn't know her at the age she was when she was at Thirlbeck. She felt very strongly about the story of the Spanish Woman. The death of the Spanish Woman, if the old story is true, was the price the Birketts had to pay to keep their gifts from Henry and Elizabeth—if Thirlbeck had been turned back to Catholics, it would have been forfeit. Well, she also knew where its strength lay. People like your mother often do understand such things. Even though she loved everything that whole house contained, she understood that once the land was gone, everything was gone. So when I had my first important decision to make, I traced her in London—I knew she had gone back there and was probably dealing in antiques because she had said that was what she wanted to do. I knew she would never go to Mexico, as Jonathan Roswell was talking of doing. It was quite plain to see that summer that they would not stay together. I expected to find her in London, and I did. My great fear was that she might have remarried, and I'd never find her under another name. But she hadn't, so I found her, and asked for her help."

"What sort of help? What could she do for you, Mr. Tolson?"

"I wasn't sure she could or would do anything. But I put it to her, half thinking she might refuse completely, or she might get in touch with Lord Askew. But she did neither. She came up to Thirlbeck, looked at what was there once again, and she went away and brought back another man, a Dutchman. They spent the best part of a week there, never going outside the place, never letting themselves be seen by anyone in the district. And when they left, they took only one picture with them. A small picture. Its sale satisfied the Earl's demands for a time. That's how it started, and it went on like that."

"Like *what?* For God's sake, what were you doing?"

He went on, ignoring my question. "It had to be one thing or the other. When the rents from the tenancies of the farms owned by the Birkett family failed to reach Lord Askew's demands, he wrote and told me I should start selling off the farms. He didn't care which ones—I was to sell, preferably to those who were already the tenants, and on fair terms. I wrote back protesting at the selling of land, making my arguments for keeping the land as strong as I could. I should have known he would see it differently. He didn't at all mind the break-up of the estate. It fitted his life pattern. He had no children, and even if he had I doubt it would have made much difference. He always had some sense of guilt about people being his tenants. He said the time for all that kind of thing was over. They were all strange people, the present Earl, his father and his grandfather. Each very different in their way. The quarrels he had had with his own father influenced him deeply. He hated his time at Eton. And then there was his time in the International Brigade in Spain. He saw so much of an old society crumble, and being shored up again, artificially, he thought. Then the death of the young Spanish woman he had married, and his only son. After the time in prison, he was changed forever. Even his refusal to take a commission in the Army, not even to accept the rank of corporal, was part of it. He became a Socialist—but one who could never suppress his own taste for luxury. So the break-up of the estate didn't matter to him. He gave me instructions to sell land that was not specifically included in the entail, whenever I had to, and not to bother him with the details.

"I chose to disobey his instruction, Miss Roswell. I borrowed money to buy time, and I sought out your mother. I had some idea, of course, that the house contained valuable things, but it had never been catalogued, and I was no expert. Oh, yes, a list *does* exist of what the Earl's grandmother brought to Thirlbeck. And you would have searched 'til Kingdom Come before you found it. But I had no idea which of the paintings might be of value, except, of course, the Rembrandt. Even the Earl remembered the Rembrandt. It was my effort to persuade him to sell *that* instead of the land seventeen years ago which finally made up my mind that I had to go against his instructions. If he preferred to sell land before pictures, then I judged him not in a fit mental state to know exactly what he was doing."

"So *you* decided for him, Mr. Tolson. Weren't you rather playing God with his property?"

"I don't see it that way," he answered calmly. "Land represents the strength of the Birketts. The pictures and such things are just happenstance acquisitions of the family—marrying the right person from time to time. After the present Earl there will be other Birketts. Nat Birkett and his sons. I judged it my duty to turn over to the next Earl the estate as nearly intact as I could. If it were pictures or bits and pieces of art which had to go, then that was how it would be. I still think I made the right decision for the Birketts—and I may well end up in gaol because of it."

"And did you never think my mother could have ended up in gaol with you?"

"That was a risk she seemed prepared to take. And for nothing more than her expenses. I was prepared to give her a percentage of whatever we realised, but she refused. It seemed I had judged her feelings well all those years ago. She had a dedication to the ideal of a place like Thirlbeck. I never cared to probe her very much on this. It was enough that she had it."

"The things," I said, ". . . the things she handled, they would have had to be disposed of to private dealers or clients. They couldn't have gone to public auction. Not through Hardy's or anyone like them. They want to know whose property it is. If my mother—or anyone else—began to offer too much through those channels they would start to ask questions. If she had offered anything really important, there would most certainly have been questions. She couldn't handle them through her own shop—she was only in the minor leagues of antique dealers. She would have been suspected almost at once of handling stolen property."

"She pointed this out to me. And since there was not the sort of money among English private buyers to make the sales we needed, she said she would have to take the items abroad. She had contacts . . ."

"*Abroad* . . . without an export licence? You mean she smuggled art out of this country?"

"She said she would have to, to get a good price. She was prepared to take the risk. Once it was in Switzerland, it could be taken without export licence into America. She said that was where the money was—the museum directors and private collectors asked few questions so long as they were convinced of the authenticity of the painting—or whatever else."

"My God, how many times did she do this?"

He shrugged helplessly. "I've lost count. The items had to be smallish—there were the Chinese bowls and vases and scent bottles. And the snuffboxes. She said those were easy, and most of them were best sold as a collection. The furniture, of course, was impossible. That had to stay."

"And the pictures?" I asked, my voice very faint and cold with fright. "Did she take more than one?"

"Over the years—I expect she took about twenty. The Dutch expert said they were a very fine collection."

"Can you remember any of the artists?" I had to ask it, but I was afraid to hear the answer.

"Some I'd never heard of before. Others I was vaguely familiar with. I remember there was a van Ruisdael—or was it two? A Seghers, several Hobbemas. There was a—a Steen? Would that be right?" I nodded, unable to speak with the sudden dryness of my mouth. "There were several small panels by Rubens—"

I gestured to make him stop. "That's enough, Mr. Tolson. Those names—they're quite enough. I find it difficult to believe that Lord Askew does not know what was in his possession.

That my mother could have believed he did not know. It was more than a fine collection. Any museum in the world would have been proud to own them. And you still say he doesn't know?"

"He doesn't know, Miss Roswell. He's mentioned nothing but the Rembrandt. Even a schoolboy would remember that. But the rest—he wasn't interested. If he'd known there were two Rubens, he probably would have remembered, but no one knew they were Rubens until your mother brought the expert. Remember that the estate was assessed for death duties during the war. The thing was hurriedly done, and incompletely, your mother guessed. I went to see him in gaol and tried to talk to him about the estate taxes, but he didn't want to hear. "Pay them," he said, and that was all. He wasn't interested. None of the family had been. Pictures of cows and windmills and sailing ships—there were two by someone called van de Velde that your mother prized highly. But *he* didn't know. They'd been on the walls of Thirlbeck all his life, and he wasn't interested."

"My mother would have told him—that time she was there. She would have known those names."

"She never saw them. Neither did your father. I had made one safe room for them all when the Ministry requisitioned the house. They're still there. I simply left them there when the war ended. It was one room where I could keep a fairly even temperature—keep the damp from getting to them, but not so warm that they might crack. I knew *that* much. I went to the Museum in Glasgow to find out about it—just mentioned that I had charge of a small collection and wanted to make sure it was properly cared for. Of course they were on to me at once to see it, hoping for something good, I suppose—and perhaps a loan to the museum. I simply said I was the caretaker and knew nothing about their value. I gave them a false name. I invented a house that didn't exist, and I said I'd be in touch with them. They've waited a long time."

I sat, my stomach churning in a queasy turmoil as I thought of what Vanessa had involved herself with. And for no profit? It was difficult to believe she could have taken the risk for no gain. And yet, it was still more difficult to believe that Vanessa was a thief—that she had stolen, even in a small way, from Tolson or anyone else.

"And when Lord Askew asks for that room to be opened, Mr. Tolson? Even he has to notice that frames are missing—even if he never knew what was in those frames."

"The frames are still there, Miss Roswell. And canvases are still there. What they contain is quite different. Remember, I never expected Lord Askew to return. But we—your mother and I—felt it should appear as if nothing had been changed. They wouldn't have deceived an expert, your mother said, but they were very good."

"Very good, Mr. Tolson? Very good? You mean they were very good copies. Like the Rembrandt?"

He raised his eyebrows. "So Mr. Stanton wasn't deceived? I didn't think he was. The artist . . . well, perhaps the artist hoped he might deceive an expert, but really all we were planning for was the unlikely eventuality that Lord Askew might return. We wanted very good copies of anything he might remember to be there. But if it came to the moment of his deciding to sell, I knew I would be undone. I would probably go to gaol, even though the value of the land I had saved was more than equal to the value of the art works I had disposed of. About the Chinese stuff, and the gold boxes, I had no worry at all. *He* didn't even know they were there. It took your mother to ferret them out. And as art prices evaluated, those little pieces raised the price of quite a number of farms I would have had to sell. It's been a constant wonder to me all these weeks Lord Askew's been back that he hasn't found out how much land he still owns. But then he hasn't been anywhere, hasn't talked to anyone. No one even knew him by sight when he went into Kesmere, otherwise there would have been a lot of heads turned to look at the biggest landowner in the district. But he's a very private man, Lord Askew—in some ways, still quite like that shy boy I remember . . ."

I halted his reminiscences. "The artist, Mr. Tolson—well, let us give him his real title, the forger. Who was he?"

"Van . . . something. I never met him. He never came to Thirlbeck."

"Van Meegeren? No—not van Meegeren. He didn't ever copy pictures. He invented his own. Vermeers. There are quite a number of museums in the world who think they have Vermeers, but they're purely inventions of that one man. He went to gaol in the end. Now who was your forger, Mr. Tolson?"

"You would have had to ask Mrs. Roswell that. I never met him. Wasn't really interested in who he was. Mrs. Roswell would carry out a canvas which would fit into her bag, and, in time, back would come a canvas which, to me, looked exactly like the one which had gone." He suddenly dropped his formal tone. "It makes a nonsense of the whole art thing, doesn't it? Whose signature is it, Miss Roswell? If someone is able to do such an exact copy, why do people pay these mad prices?"

I leaned back in the chair, wearied beyond thinking, almost. "Don't ask me, Mr. Tolson. I don't understand. Ask me why people pay those prices for a lump of carbon, because it glitters. Like La Española. They wouldn't pay it for a piece of coal. But in paintings there's usually something more than the signature. Forgers make exact copies. Van Meegeren was different because he made his own pictures. Forgers . . . well, you can copy, but it's very unlikely the result will ever have the quality of the original. Whatever it is we prize about the original, it's unlikely you'll ever find it in the copy. Expert, yes. But not inspired. But if the forgery is very good, you'll likely sell it to an unsuspecting client, who is simply told what it is, and experts, experts who can be bought, have vouched for it. It's happened often enough. There are tests—X ray and spectrograph—but not every collector requires them. Why should they? They become a little vain about their own ability to judge, or they've grown to trust their dealers too much. Now that Rembrandt . . . you can stand in front of it—it looks like a Rembrandt, it speaks to you of someone who understands what Rembrandt is all about. It deceived me. But to people like Gerald—Mr. Stanton—it isn't a Rembrandt because it lacks the quality that Rembrandt would have given to it. There really is no explaining it, but no expert would authenticate that picture, Mr. Tolson."

For a second or two he bowed his head, as if in acknowledgement. "We really didn't expect that, Miss Roswell. Your mother warned me often enough. That was supposed to be a signed self-portrait, and according to the papers we have, it was that. So when we substituted a copy, we knew that if anyone with real knowledge ever saw it, it wouldn't stand up. And it was a modern forgery—not something the Earl's grandmother could have brought along with her as part of the parcel of paintings she had. So . . . we knew. And I was determined if anything was ever called into question, your mother's name should never be connected with it. If I had to go to gaol, there was no reason why she should."

"You really thought that, Mr. Tolson? You were really so naïve? You were using her as a smuggler. If they had really cracked down on you, there would have been ways to trace her, the handling of money . . . and so on. If you went, Mr. Tolson, she would have gone with you."

He was silent. Once more his head went down. There was a restive stirring from behind him. But Ted took his father's silence as a command.

"So . . . she took out the Rembrandt, Mr. Tolson. And many others. To Holland? To Switzerland? Van something you said his name was. There's a man called van Hoyt. He's been in gaol —as van Meegeren was. Could it have been van Hoyt, Mr. Tolson?"

"It might have been. I don't know."

"You left an awful lot to trust, Mr. Tolson. For a man like you. How did you know Vanessa wasn't cheating you? You couldn't very well verify the price she got. It couldn't go to public auction, where you would have got a much better price because more people have a chance of bidding for it. Everyone who touched it must have known it was stolen, except, perhaps, the eventual collector. And even he might have known—been prepared just to put it in a bank vault as something that was as good as gold. But if my mother was handling all this for you, how did you know she wasn't taking a cut of the price for herself?"

In my hurt I was deliberately striking out at him, forcing

him to recall those things he had said to me about Vanessa when he had virtually denied any knowledge of her.

"In the beginning . . . well, rather naturally the question was raised by my brother. He didn't know your mother well, hadn't my reasons for trusting her. He insisted on a check. There are ways and means of finding out if someone has more money than they should. People as untidy in their transactions as your mother are rather easy to check on. We found out that she seemed perpetually on the edge of bankruptcy—always big overdrafts, and never a sign of any sums of money that couldn't naturally be accounted for. No, she wasn't stealing. I thought I'd made that quite clear."

He faced me directly as he said that, his tone not apologetic; he knew he was facing my anger and he did not turn away from it.

"Thank you—for *that*. She wasn't stealing. But she was taking risks for you. And you let her. Can you imagine what it feels like to walk past a customs officer when you've got a Rembrandt in your suitcase?"

"It was her style. In an odd way, it appealed to her. People like your mother often have an idealistic streak, and quite a lot of daring. She knew what she was doing, and why she was doing it. And, at any rate, as to the Rembrandt itself, it was to be the last thing. She had spent almost a year arranging the sale. The agent and the buyer were coming to Zurich, the purchaser was bringing two experts with him for authentication. Your mother never told me the purchaser's name—she said it was safer not to know. But he wasn't the sort who would pay that kind of money for something that his own people hadn't examined minutely. An uncatalogued Rembrandt—something dug up in an obscure country house in England. Never been exhibited. There was reason for caution. Your mother brought the copy to Thirlbeck even before the sale was completed. I was nervous about not having the one painting I was certain Lord Askew would remember, so we changed the usual procedure. Then your mother went back to Zurich, where she had lodged the real painting in a bank vault. She had to be careful. People watch the meetings of art experts, and known collectors. The

Dutchman who did the copying went to Zurich himself. He wanted to be paid there, to leave the money in a Swiss bank. That was to be his last contact with your mother. The buyer was going to pay a million two hundred thousand pounds if the experts agreed the picture was genuine."

"A million two," I repeated. Then added: "You know it could have gone for twice that amount if it had been sold at public auction. Had you thought of what Lord Askew would have said to selling his property at knock-down prices?"

He gestured to indicate to me that it was a useless question. "I made my decision long ago. This last sale would surely keep pace with Lord Askew's needs for the rest of his life. The man who did the copying was to have his cut. I had earmarked fifty thousand pounds to put a new roof on Thirlbeck and a few other essential repairs. The Swiss agent was to have a cut, and the rest was to be invested through Switzerland. I had always paid Lord Askew through Swiss banks. My brother used to arrange all that sort of thing. He hired and advised the accountants who looked after the estate business. It's been more difficult since he died. But Mrs. Roswell had learned her way around. But this was really why we decided on the Rembrandt— a sale big enough so that all of us could stop this business."

Now he seemed to be talking about a stranger—a stranger to us both. Vanessa, moving quietly—taking trips to Holland and Switzerland, going up to Thirlbeck, directing a porter to carry a suitcase which contained two million pounds' worth of art. She could have done it, of course. There had been many times when she had gone on short trips, trips into the country looking for things for the shop, attending country sales, trips to sales outside England, though these had been rarer. She had never had the money or the market to buy widely in the international field. I wondered how often Gerald or I had believed she was spending her weekend with a man, the latest flirtation, when in fact she had been at Thirlbeck or flying to Holland. It was hard to imagine this devious Vanessa, the one who could lie with such skill, who knew how to keep her secret. I had a baffled sense of hurt, of having been shut out. "I wonder *why?*" It was really a question to myself.

Tolson didn't try to answer. "It all blew up, of course, the day I got the cable from Lord Askew asking me to get the house ready for him and the Condesa. It was totally unexpected. It came while your mother was in Zurich. I knew the hotel she was staying at, and I telephoned the minute I got the cable. She had already checked out. So I knew the sale had gone through, and I had no way of stopping it. I needed the Rembrandt back at Thirlbeck. Of all the pictures there, that was the one I needed. I needed it more than I needed the million-odd pounds in a Swiss bank. Now I have neither."

My head jerked up. "You haven't the money? Where is it?"

"I would dearly like to know, Miss Roswell. But it was a numbered account, opened by your mother especially for this sale. She was to give me the name of the bank and the number. We had done this with other accounts. She would put the proceeds from the sale of a number of items into one account, and then it wouldn't be used again except to transfer money to Lord Askew. So I waited for her to telephone from London which she usually did immediately on returning from the trip, to give me the information. It would be something, at least, to be able to tell Lord Askew that the money was there. Then we heard about the plane crash on the 6 o'clock news. When the papers came in the morning her name was listed among those killed. So . . . I had no Rembrandt, and there was a million pounds sitting in some Swiss bank which none of us would be able to touch."

"Then why have you come *here?* What did you expect to find?"

He sighed. "What? I really don't know. Just the faint hope that she might have left some indication of which bank, at least, she intended to use. She might have made notes. There might even have been something recovered from . . . well, there might have been something left after the plane crash which would have been sent here. A forlorn hope, I know. But I can't put off telling Lord Askew the whole story any longer. I have been nearly desperate these last weeks. The whole of my stewardship of Thirlbeck has gone for nothing. Oh, yes, I have all the land intact, and that has appreciated as much as the paintings have. But now I have defaulted by a million pounds, and more."

He reached for his cup again, but it was empty. "The affairs of the Birketts have never been small. That jewel I have to guard . . . the estate to hold together. A collection of pictures and furniture which your mother thought was almost matchless in this country, and which had to be kept hidden and safe. If the Earl himself had even been an ordinary man . . . but he was born in a mould which caused him to do things like kill his own wife and son, and then win a V.C. If he had been a quiet man, content to stay at Thirlbeck, none of this need have happened. But he is driven by some kind of devil, and he has no rest. The Birketts are not a lucky family—"

"Stop it! *Stop it, do you hear?* Do you expect me to weep for the Birketts, or for you! I know it doesn't mean a thing to you, but I loved my mother. And because of you and your insane ideas about the Birketts being something special, something above other people, she's dead. I don't know how you managed to drag her into all this, and to keep her in it for almost seventeen years. But you do know, in the end, she died while she was carrying out a mission for you—for you and the Birketts. For *what?* *Why?* In God's name, why?"

He breathed deeply and waited for a time before replying. "I thought I hardly needed to explain to you. Because you're just like her. Thirlbeck has taken hold of you, too, hasn't it? I can see you going about there, almost exactly as she did, exploring it all, touching the things she touched, falling in love with it."

"Oh, no! Not that! I'm not falling in love with anything. Don't start trying to drag me in too. Haven't you done enough? Must you have *me* as well?"

"I was trying nothing, Miss Roswell. What has happened to you happened of its own accord. But we won't discuss that. I take it that you will not give us permission to look among your mother's belongings. There just may be the faintest chance . . ."

"No! You'll not touch anything. When someone looks, it will be myself. And I'm not going to look now. And you may forget about there being anything left from the wreck of the plane. There was nothing—*nothing*. My mother is dead. That's all."

He sighed, and struggled heavily to rise. "Then we must be on our way back. Tomorrow—that is, today—I will have to speak to Lord Askew. I can't delay any longer. I'm sure you will see reason and try to co-operate in looking among your mother's belongings. I'm sure Mr. Stanton would think it wise."

"Don't—! Don't start on me! I've heard enough. Don't try to speak for Mr. Stanton. He'll feel as I do. He was very fond of my mother."

He was putting on his raincoat. "I know that. And Mr. Stanton is very fond of you. He was very restive today after you left so suddenly without any real explanation. Lord Askew didn't tell him about the Chinese bowl. But Mr. Stanton knows that something is coming to a head. I will have to be back there as fast as Ted can drive me. I have a feeling that this is the day Mr. Stanton is going to ask to look at the paintings. I will have to have spoken to Lord Askew first."

"That's your concern, Mr. Tolson. My concern is how to keep my mother's name out of it. If Lord Askew decides to prosecute, her name will be as much blackened as yours. Think about *that*, Mr. Tolson, while you drive North again."

"If I can help it, Miss Roswell, your mother's name will never be mentioned. But they'll know I must have had help with this. I don't know how I'll explain not knowing where the money is. Lord Askew will press me, but I'll try to see that your mother gets no blame."

"How good of you—*now*, when she's dead. What a miserable lot you all are up there, hugging your great estate to yourselves. It's really all been for you, hasn't it, Mr. Tolson? The Tolsons have been there as long as the Birketts, haven't they? You've had stewardship for so long it really belongs to you—that's what you think. And if you can't inherit legally—you or your sons— then you'll have Nat Birkett so brainwashed he'll do exactly as you tell him. That's what you think, isn't it? And can you be really comfortable in your own mind that you didn't indirectly contribute to the death of Nat Birkett's wife? Are you quite innocent of that death? *Are* you, Mr. Tolson? You remained silent, and so did Nat Birkett, for the sake of you all. There was no real blame on Jessica—only the all-important fact that she neglected to tell you where Patsy Birkett was that night she died. An omission—not an act. And after all, Jessica hadn't been well. A lapse like that might be forgiven. Jessica is highly strung—and highly intelligent. A little unbalanced, perhaps. But she's been a good, quiet, well-behaved girl these past years— cured of all her problems. You really see no reason why she shouldn't, eventually, marry Nat Birkett. If you just all press on him hard enough, he'll go down. Jessica is beautiful, after all—and who can really believe she knew what she was doing then? So you wouldn't object if she married Nat Birkett, would you? Your stewardship would be justified. Things would take their proper place, wouldn't they? Nat Birkett has two sons, but if their luck runs its usual course, it's just possible that your great-grandchildren—or your great-great-grandchildren—will inherit Thirlbeck and the Earldom of Askew. I don't accuse you of it—you couldn't have been so evil as to plan it that way. But now, as things are, it's possible, isn't it, Mr. Tolson? And you wouldn't stop it. No. You wouldn't stop it."

He was at the door, and Ted, moving before him switched on the light in the hall.

"You're very tired, Miss Roswell. So am I. Those are harsh words you have used. I think we had better both forget them. Perhaps we won't meet again. It would be better if we didn't. I'll do everything I can not to involve your mother. If I can help it, no one will ever hear her name. But . . . if you should find anything . . ." He shrugged, and half turned away. "Well, if you should find anything that might be of help, you could communicate with me through Ted. Good-bye."

He had moved out into the hall, and was almost gone before I called him back. It was something that all my training, all my years at Hardy's had given to me, and it could not be stopped.

"Mr. Tolson!"

He returned, betraying just a shade of eagerness. "Yes, Miss Roswell?"

"Those pictures—the ones that are left. And the ones my

mother took away. Would you remember . . . would you possibly remember anything about an El Greco?"

His disappointment was plain. "El Greco? Spanish, wasn't he?" He was shaking his head. "No, everything I know about those pictures is that they're all Dutch, of one period or another. El Greco . . . no."

"I see. I just thought I'd ask."

"Strange, though . . . your mother once had some such notion. She searched the whole of Thirlbeck—but she never found anything . . ."

He waited a while longer, perhaps with hope, which wasn't fulfilled. I stared at him, my anger giving me a hardness I had never possessed before. I had said hideous things to him, accused him, almost, of unthinkable things, which in my bewilderment and fear, had suddenly become thinkable. I did not recognise the self which had leaped out and hurled abuse at him. In the roughness of my words a different person spoke. I felt as if something had been rending inside of me, and had finally burst. The remnants of the old person lay about me. I had no screen from the knowledge of myself any more. I did not much like what I saw of myself, and yet I could not, then, recall the words I had spoken, take them back; I could not bring myself at this moment to offer help to this man whom, I believed, had destroyed Vanessa.

He had waited, and perhaps saw the struggle reflected on my face. He must have recognised its outcome. He sighed and turned away. I heard them slip out quietly into the mews. Later I heard a car start. If I measured Tolson rightly, they would drive all night up the Motorway, and he would be there at Thirlbeck by the morning to tell his tale to Robert Birkett.

Vanessa's little Louis XIV clock on the mantel chimed the three-quarter hour. A quarter to one. I thought of the smashed and burned wreckage on the mountain slope, the baggage lying broken in the dirty snow which was becoming clean again in a fresh fall. Spring snow. Perhaps by now the spring grasses were already covering the raw scars in the earth. All the wreckage would have been taken away. There had been no suitcase I had been able to identify as Vanessa's among those assembled for inspection in the village school, no single object or article of clothing other than her handbag. And her handbag had contained nothing that would have helped Tolson. I thought bitterly that there would be no reason for Robert Birkett not to think that Vanessa, in this last mission she had undertaken for George Tolson, might not have deliberately concealed the location and number of the account she had opened with the sale of the Rembrandt. Why should he agree with Tolson's idea of a woman he had known for only one summer so long ago? Why would he not press and press Tolson until the man divulged the name of the person who had helped him? What would happen to Vanessa now that she was dead and not able to defend herself—if the story came out there were enough people to say she had been capable of what she had done, and much more. Vanessa had had only friends or enemies—hardly anyone in between. Anything that anyone wanted to say now, or infer, could be believed because she was not here to speak for herself.

I sat in the chair and the tears of anger and pain and fatigue rolled down my cheeks unchecked. They brought, in time, their own sort of relief, a temporary thing, but welcome; I felt myself slip towards sleep. When I woke the clock was striking two.

III

I started for Chelsea once again in the Mini, and once again I ended by going somewhere else. It was only a couple of minutes' drive in the almost totally deserted streets; it wasn't raining any more, but the roads still had their slick greasy sheen under the lights. The streets around St. James's were vacant and silent—a single taxi dropping someone at the New Cavendish, a police car on a slow patrol which made me slow down also. I followed it along King Street and into St. James's Square. The two constables in it were watching me, and stopped their car, so that I had to pass them. Strange how guilty just being watched made me feel. If either of them had asked me what I was doing there, I wouldn't have had an answer. Over on the other side of the square I stopped also. The top floor of one of the modern blocks was still brightly lighted. At the kerb were two large dark cars with uniformed chauffeurs fighting off sleep and boredom. And between them, preposterously rakish beside their solemnity, was Harry's Jensen. And Harry was still up there on that lighted top floor. I sat and looked up at the lights for a few minutes—there was a sense of restless power there, a driving energy which expressed itself in these glittering symbols of success, and of talk which went on until the small hours of the morning. From that lighted top floor seemed to come a kind of urgency which disturbed the quietness of the great square. I started the Mini and drove down into Pall Mall.

When I turned up St. James's Street it was totally deserted. The few restaurants had closed, the clubs offered discreetly lighted porter's desks behind the closed glass doors. I turned into St. James's Place, and then made the turn into the tiny yard where Duke's Hotel was. There was the house Harry had bought—tall, narrow, elegant, its paint glistening, bay trees in tubs each side of the door. The SOLD sign was bright and fresh across the agent's board. Hard to think what Harry must have paid for it. And he was right; even with traffic at its thickest, it was barely a three-minute walk from Hardy's, and only a few minutes' walk beyond that to St. James's Square, and the lighted top floor. Harry had made his plans swiftly, and with great precision.

As I sat there staring up at the house, another car, a large one, turned quietly into the yard, and stopped before the house with the SOLD notice. A chauffeur came around and opened the back door; in the light from the car's interior I saw him assist a woman to the pavement, a slender, elegant woman wearing a long evening coat, a woman as carefully groomed as the façade of the house which she was entering. She was alone, and I watched as the chauffeur took a door key from her hand, opened the door for her, handed back the key, and stood with his hat under his arm until she had closed the door behind her. In the quiet of the little yard I could even hear the other locks being secured, and the chain being dropped into place. The crystal chandelier which I could see through the beautiful Georgian fanlight remained alight.

As the chauffeur gently turned the car and edged through the narrow entry to the yard I felt his careful scrutiny of me, in much the way I had felt the watchful eyes of the police in St. James's Square. Suddenly this man, his face shadowed beneath his peaked cap, could have been either one of the other chauffeurs waiting in the Square. He was all chauffeurs, and the woman could have been myself some few years from now, entering that house alone, and waiting, always waiting, for a telephone call from Harry.

As I headed once more for Chelsea, I remembered that the last time I had been conscious of lights burning in the early hours of the morning had been as we had followed the ambulance to Kesmere, and the lights had shone on Nat Birkett's hill. He and a vet had worked through the night, and a calf had been born.

* * *

I was at Hardy's early the next morning, but I didn't go directly down to the ceramics department. I really didn't know if I should be there at all. Probably Gerald was expecting me to return to Thirlbeck, and probably I should go, but I didn't want to. I was conscious of the need to break with that world, to return to what was familiar and understood. And yet hadn't what Tolson had told me the night before shaken the foundations of this familiar world? If it became known that Vanessa had assisted in smuggling works of art out of this country, would it be possible for me to remain here? Perhaps the name of Roswell might become notorious in the art world, instead of mildly famous, as my father had made it. I stood for a moment at the bottom of the stairs gazing through the inner double glass doors to the street, watching St. James's take up its daily rhythm, watching a few taxis and cars arrive and people hurry up the steps from the street with a salute from the commissionaire. Many carried catalogues of what was on view that day, and they moved past me purposefully; others would arrive later for the sales scheduled for that day, catalogues already marked with items they intended to bid for. The little hum of noise was growing; Jackie Flemming came out of the press office and went to the notice board where she pinned up the clippings from papers all over the world that had reported recent sales at Hardy's. These days it was usually the report of a record price for some item or other—prices never went down, and all over the world people would start looking at objects they owned, and wondering what they were worth.

"Dreaming a bit, Jo?" Mr. Arrowsmith was beside me, wearing his usual quizzically benign look.

"I suppose I was, Mr. Arrowsmith. I was really wondering if I shouldn't just go downstairs and get to work. Except that I don't feel like it . . ."

He asked me about Gerald, and I told him, trying to skirt around the fact that I didn't know whether I was supposed to return to Thirlbeck or not. I ought to go and see Mr. Hudson, my director. It was something we had not discussed last night. The pieces of the Sung bowl were still in my possession. It was to be my task to ask Lord Askew if he wished them mended, and offered for auction. Until this was clear, and the paper signed, Hardy's insurance did not begin to operate. I was floundering in a state of fatigue and bewilderment, and nothing seemed to sort itself into a decision.

Mr. Arrowsmith seemed to sense some of this. "Well, if you don't feel like it, don't go down to your old hole. No one's expecting you, are they? Tell you what, take an hour on the Front Counter. Jenny's not coming in this morning until half-past ten. It'd be a help if you could put in a while." I knew he had no need of help at that hour of the morning—a swift look at the Front Counter showed me that it was well staffed, and enquiries didn't start to flood in until later. But in the spirit in which he oversaw every part of Hardy's operation, Mr. Arrowsmith felt for its employees also. He had been very fond of Vanessa, and he had a kind of affectionate reverence for Gerald. "You're looking a bit peaked, Jo. I thought you were getting plenty of fresh air up in that place you've been staying."

"It's my own fault if I'm looking that way, Mr. Arrowsmith. There hasn't been much to do up there—really nothing except to go through some papers. Mr. Stanton has Jeffries with him, and a lovely titled Spanish lady who seems happy to fetch and carry for him. And Lord Askew doesn't want him to leave . . . I've been hanging round doing nothing, really. We hope there'll be a sale—Lord Askew has some wonderful things." Then I blurted out, because this man had been a kind of father confessor to every young person who appeared on the Front Counter: "I don't know if I'm supposed to be up there or not. I had to come back yesterday . . ."

He seemed to think I had said enough. "Well, while it's being decided, just you be a good girl and help out on the Front Counter. Sharpens you up a bit, you know. Haven't much time for worries when you're dealing with the public."

It was an exercise in tact and public relations. People came in off the street carrying things they thought might be worth putting up for auction. Some were surprisingly good, some worth almost nothing. In each case someone was called from the appropriate department, the client was assigned a private interview room with its built-in green-baize covered table; a rough valuation was made, a reserve price suggested. The client either accepted the estimate of the valuation which was made, and the appropriate sale at which it might be offered, or they left, dissatisfied, unhappy, perhaps, because some dream or hope had been shattered; or it could be that they believed the people at Hardy's were fools, and didn't know their business. After just an hour I was caught up once more, fascinated, feeling the throb of this inexact and, at the moment, soaring market that dealt in people's hopes and fears, the skill of craftsmen both living and long dead, the judgement of what was beauty, and what was the price of beauty in the market place. I was sorry when Jenny Struthers arrived and relieved me, and I was at a loose end again.

Instead of going down to the ceramics department I went upstairs to the salerooms. In the central area was a display of English pictures on view. In two of the side rooms the morning sales had just begun. It was early in the season, and the really important auctions of the year were still weeks away; this morning there was silver and Chinese ceramics; the public attending were mostly dealers, and a few interested collectors. In both salerooms the real bidders sat around baize-covered horseshoe tables, so that they could examine items that came up for bid. They were both small and attentive audiences. I watched the silver sale for a while, listening to the auctioneer, one of the directors of Hardy's, as he made his expert way through the catalogue, knowing most of the dealers by name, recording price and buyer in the Day Book, and always moving at a deliberate pace, never sounding excited, pleased, or disappointed by the prices made. Some lots were bought back into the house when they failed to make their reserve, others went for prices well beyond the reserve. Whichever way it went was never registered on the auctioneer's face. The little hammer fell at the end of each sale, and the next lot was brought out for display. I went on to the sale of Chinese ceramics.

Here, in the West Room were the familiar faces from the ceramics department. It seemed much more than a few weeks since I had seen them. The bidding was brisk, the prices good—very good. But nothing half so beautiful and exciting as the Sung bowl was on offer; I ached with guilt once more at the thought of it lying in pieces in my silk scarf. Mr. Hudson was taking the auction. I would have to wait until it was over before I could talk with him. Mr. Arrowsmith appeared beside the rostrum; he had a bid commissioned for a certain lot, and he had an uncanny knack of gauging within minutes when the lot would come up, and he was always on time. In this case it went beyond the price he had been authorised to pay, and he made his way from the room, smiling at me as he left. I turned back to look at the rostrum.

I suppose it was fatigue. The night had been too long, and there had been too much to try to absorb, too much to think about—Harry, Vanessa, Tolson. For a few seconds the room seemed to swim in a blur of faces and voices. A new lot was being brought out—a jade carving too small for me to see from my place at the back, passing along the baize-covered table and dealers looking once again at something they had already seen during the viewing days. The bidding went on—rising, rising as the auctioneer judged the interest of his audience, pacing the rise to meet the competition. "Against you on the left . . . I'm offered four thousand pounds . . . four thousand five hundred . . . against you on the left." The hammer fell, the record went into the Day Book, the next lot produced. But this time, instead of the K'ang Hsi bottle which the porter was carrying on his baize-lined tray, I seemed to see the fantasy shape of a great eagle, majestic, awesome, fierce, a rich dark brown, tawny-streaked, with neck and crown of gold, perched on the ledge of the rostrum. And the auctioneer's voice saying quietly, "What am I bid . . . ?"

And the room was abruptly silent, because everyone knew there was no price for a golden eagle.

I turned away quickly, and at once the low hum of sound through the room resumed. I looked back, and everything was as it should be, the K'ang Hsi bottle making the round of the table, the bids being placed, everything as it always was. And no golden eagle surveyed the scene.

I left then, almost running down the stairs and out into the street. A taxi was being paid off at the door, and the commissionaire held it for me. He was as old a friend as anyone at Hardy's. "Are you all right, Miss Roswell?" He looked doubtful, and even more so when I gave him the address to relay to the driver. I turned back to look at him as the taxi moved away. He was staring after me, and I saw him give a slight shake of his head. I wondered what he would have thought if I had stopped to explain that golden eagles were not for sale.

* * *

A young man in a habit showed me into one of the reception rooms. It wasn't at all like Hardy's. There was a bare polished floor, four straight-backed chairs, a small table rigidly in the centre of the room. There was a single crucifix on the wall. The window looked onto an inner square garden, shared by the Jesuit priests who lived at the residence at Farm Street and by the houses and flats which faced out onto Mount Street. It was very quiet, the traffic noises muted and far away. A nanny sat on one of the garden seats watching a solitary child chasing pigeons. I had come here because it was the only place I could think of quickly. Sometimes I had come to the church itself to hear the singing on a Sunday morning with Gerald, or to listen to one of the more famous Jesuits preach. Gerald had an intellectual interest in such things, though he wasn't a Catholic.

I stood up when a young priest entered. He held out his hand. "I'm Father Kavanagh. Please sit down." I told him my name, and then I couldn't seem to say anything else.

"Is there some way I can help you?" They must be used to all kinds, I thought, all sorts of requests, every kind of story.

"I'm not a Catholic," I said.

He smiled, and the too-serious face relaxed. "It's still very possible you'll get into Heaven."

"Well, I wondered if it's possible to offer Masses for someone who's been dead a long time?"

"Of course. Is this person some relation—some friend? Would you like to talk about it?" He thought I meant some time in the recent past—a few years, maybe.

"It's a very long time. Almost four hundred years."

"Yes—I see." He didn't show any wonder. "No prayer is ever offered too late—if the intention is right. You would like a Mass offered for the repose of the soul of this person, I take it?"

"Yes—that's it," I said eagerly. "For the repose of her soul." That was what she had written in that still childish handwriting. "*Offer nine Masses for my soul.*" "But I would like nine Masses said. Can you do that?"

"Yes. We'll offer a novena of Masses. Was this person a Catholic? It doesn't really matter. One can still pray."

"Oh, yes. She was a Catholic. She probably died because she was a Catholic."

He raised his eyebrows. "A martyr?"

"No—not officially a martyr. Just a young girl who died a long time ago." I spelled out the name for him, surprised at how easily it came off my lips without referring again to the Book of Hours. "Juana Fernández de Córdoba, Mendoza, Soto y Alvarez."

He wrote it all down, and then he said, "I expect the Lord will know whom I mean if I just say 'Juana.'"

I didn't know how much money to offer him. "Anything will be acceptable," he said. And he smiled once again. "I'll say the Masses myself. The soul of your little Spanish girl will be comforted by the fact of someone remembering her after nearly four hundred years."

"I hope so." And then I added, although he couldn't have understood my meaning: "It's all I can do for her."

* * *

I went and sat in the church for a while, seeking for a moment its quietness to still my own racing mind. I had never seen it empty before; there was only one other woman besides myself. Someone was playing the organ very quietly when I entered, perhaps just practising, or warming up before a lunchhour recital. It was almost twelve o'clock.

The little peace and sense of relief I had bought with the request for Masses for the Spanish Woman seemed to ebb away too swiftly. I was back with the bewildering, frightening thoughts of Vanessa and George Tolson. By now he would be back at Thirlbeck, had probably already told Lord Askew. I wondered if Gerald knew yet; would Gerald be disappointed in me that I had not wanted to face Askew again? Would I succumb to the final weakness of having the Sung bowl mended at my own expense and posting it, and the *Horae* of Juana Fernández de Córdoba back to Thirlbeck? What would Nat Birkett think of someone who had left him so swiftly, almost in flight?

It was nearly by force of habit now that I had the miniature out, and played with it between my fingers. More than ever I saw Vanessa in the vital, intelligent features of the third Countess. The other woman in the church got up and left; I watched her go, not wanting her to go. The organist had stopped playing; he seemed to be spending his time arranging sheets of music. Then I looked back at the miniature, once again placing the broken piece of the frame where it belonged, making it whole again. But I saw something else then, something I had never seen before. A kind of churning excitement caught at my stomach. I almost didn't want to think, to reason it out because reason might destroy the hope that had so quickly built. Yes . . . yes, it was possible. It fitted. It could be tried, at any rate. It was something to try.

I went out quickly into the lunchtime crowds, going all the way down to Curzon Street before I found a taxi. It took nearly half an hour to get down to Chelsea. I hesitated a moment before deciding against ringing Tolson. No matter what he said now, whether he agreed with my reasoning or not, I was going back to Thirlbeck. I repacked the big suitcase, putting the pieces of the Sung bowl and the *Horae* where they would be best protected by my clothes. Just as I was leaving the flat the telephone began to ring. I listened to it ring as I locked the door. It could be Harry—it could be Gerald or Tolson. I let it ring.

IV

I stopped the Mini just before I entered the birch copse. I had not thought it would all feel so familiar, as if I were returning to a place I had known all my life. I had come by the back way, by the North Lodge, using the keys I still carried with me, coming through the larch wood over Brantwick, and now the hard, bony upper slopes of Great Birkeld lay revealed in flinty moonlight. I traced the outline of the mountain against the sky. I might have lost my life up there on those slopes if the dogs had not brought me down, and yet the sight of them now brought no shiver of fear; I almost felt as if I had come back to something respected, known, and loved.

I took the Mini slowly through the birch copse, half expecting to see the white shape of the great hound that had confronted me on that first journey. The trees were now almost completely in leaf, and it was dark beneath them; when I had come first to Thirlbeck they had borne only the catkins of early spring. The valley widened out, the house now was visible. There were no lights anywhere. By habit I looked across the dark mass of trees where the shelter was built, wondering if anyone was on watch. It was past two o'clock, but a night of bright moonlight and no mist might have tempted out someone who badly wanted the eggs of the golden eagles. There was no light at the shelter, no sign of a cigarette glowing in the dark, or the little sterno stove heating water for coffee. Now I was down in the floor of the valley; the dark shapes of the cattle were visible, and the smaller white flecks of the sheep and lambs. It was utterly still and silent—not even a slight breath of wind stirred the mirror surface of the lake. A silent, enchanted world, frozen in the moonlight, a place which my senses recognised as if from a long time past.

I drove around to the back of the house. I knew that the dogs had heard the car and come downstairs. They must have pushed their way past the green-baize door, because I could hear the scrape of paws against the wood of the back door leading to the kitchen passage, and the strange sort of huffing sound that they all made when they were together. And yet they did not bark. I felt the same prickle of gooseflesh I had known on the night I set off the alarm system. I pushed the bell at the back door, and heard it ringing somewhere inside the house, somewhere, I judged, in the Tolsons' wing. I hoped it would not wake Gerald or Lord Askew. The morning, with a few hours of sleep behind me, would be time enough for them.

Tolson came very soon, wearing a heavy, shapeless woolen dressing gown; I guessed he had been sleepless, perhaps sitting before the warmth of the aga in the kitchen. He opened the door without hesitation, as if he knew from the dogs' behaviour who was outside. Light streamed into the passage from the kitchen as he held the door wide.

"You should have told me you were coming," he said simply. "I could have had a meal ready." For the first time I heard no implied hostility in his tone.

"I had thought of waiting until a decent hour in the morning," I answered, "but then I was so close, so I thought I might as well just come on."

He nodded, and motioned me inside; as I walked in all the dogs turned and went with me. I put my hands on the upthrust heads that offered themselves, and there was a turmoil of long, spikey, wagging tails.

"I'll make some tea," Tolson said, without consulting me. "Sit down. You'd probably like some toast—something to eat."

"Please, don't trouble."

"No trouble."

I sat at the kitchen table while he made tea, and toasted thick slabs of bread. I shovelled the toast into my mouth and gulped the tea. Around me the dogs sat, two circles of them, fanning out like some exotic adornment.

Finally the hunger was gone, and the tea had warmed me. I felt my body relax. I leaned back in the big chair, and my hands went naturally to the heads of the dogs nearest me. Their rough tongues scraped my hands as they had done up on the mountain. I wondered how I had ever lived without dogs before.

I straightened. Somehow this lessening of tension had made my journey seem less important. But Tolson still waited.

"I think I have something to show you. I *hope* . . ." I brought the miniature from my handbag. Tolson's massive dark head bent over it as I explained. Then he drew back, but in that large body I sensed a kind of quiet relief, a release of pain and despair.

"Could be," he offered.

"You've already told him?"

"Yes—I've told him. He acted as you would expect a gentleman to act."

"I'll see him in the morning, then," I said.

"Yes, if it suits you. If that's what you want."

"Yes. That's the way it should be."

We sat silently for some time, drinking more tea from large mugs. A strange companionship existed between us, where before there had only been unease. The things I had said to him the previous night, and his own hostility towards me, were past. The dogs lay sprawled on my side of the table. I had almost come to take them for granted.

He spoke at last. "It's late. You'll need some sleep. I'll fill some hot-water bottles."

I didn't protest. When we went beyond the green-baize door the dogs followed us. I led the way, carrying two hot-water bottles. Tolson carried my suitcase. The dogs moved ahead on the staircase, and went on before us to the Spanish Woman's room, as if I had lived there always.

"I didn't have the bed stripped," he said as we entered. He put on the only electric light. "I had a feeling you'd be back. You'd only used those sheets two nights . . . we have to watch economies, you know. Such big sheets for that bed." He put the suitcase on the chest where I could unpack it. I opened the two cupboards and the clothes and possessions I had left in the last hurried packing were there, like the sheets, untouched. Tolson had already put a match under the freshly laid fires in the two fireplaces. "It'll warm up in a bit," he said. "Don't shut the door—I'm going down to get you some brandy from Lord Askew's stock. It'll help you to sleep."

He came back in a few minutes and wordlessly laid the brandy on the big table in the window. I halted him as he was about to leave. "We'll see him together in the morning," I said. He nodded. We had entered into some unlikely compact, the two of us. A long bridge of compromise had been walked in these two nights when neither of us had slept very much.

After I had undressed and washed quietly in Gerald's bathroom, I sat up in bed sipping the brandy. I had my cigarettes close by, but I realised that it was now a long time since I had smoked the last one, and I did not really need this one. I sat there, pillows propped against the carved headboard, feeling the warmth of the bottles against my feet and side, watching the light of the two fires thrown up to the ceiling. It hardly even seemed strange to me now that two of the wolfhounds had stayed; they lay with their great lengths stretched on the rug before one fire. I thought I could even distinguish them from the rest—two males who must have been brothers, or father and son, the leaders of the pack, and still able to live at peace with each other. "Thor . . . Ulf . . ." I whispered. The ears bent back, and the big heads raised. They gazed at me with their questioning, solemn eyes. A flicker ran along each tail, and then they settled to rest again. After a while I heard one of them begin to snore gently. I put the glass aside, and slid down between the sheets, and slept.

CHAPTER 7

I

I had not thought it possible he could seem so changed. Askew faced me now across the desk in the study, Gerald at his side, Tolson, who refused a chair, standing slightly behind him. He seemed much older—or perhaps he merely appeared the age he was. The boyish nonchalance, the flippant grace, were gone. I did not see him now as the natural companion of a much younger woman, but a rather worn man, made too suddenly aware of his years and a weight of responsibility whose acceptance he had not been any longer able to postpone or put aside.

I had told him of Vanessa's part in taking the paintings from Thirlbeck, that it had been she who had introduced the Dutch expert to examine them, she who had carried canvases through customs, who had carried whole collections of Chinese ceramics, of perfume bottles, of snuffboxes, and found buyers for them. Tolson had produced a notebook, and in Vanessa's hand there were lists and descriptions, rather vague, but good enough to give us an idea of the treasure this house had once held, and now was dispersed forever, to nameless buyers.

"Did she ever bring anyone here to look particularly at the Chinese things?" Gerald asked Tolson.

"She once brought two gentlemen—one an Oriental. He said very little, I remember. But after that Mrs. Roswell carried away anything that was small enough to go easily . . . The prices she got seemed very high to me."

Gerald examined the book again and sighed. "They would be much higher now. Most of these were sold quite some time ago." He studied the list for a while, his lips puckering; he stabbed the list at various points with his pen. "*Vase . . . fifteenth-century Mei P'ing, white dragons on blue ground . . . Square baluster jar, Ming Wu Ts'ai, red dragons, green clouds, 7½ inches.*" He looked up. "If it was a good one, Robert, I have to tell you that last season we sold something of this description for about seventy thousand guineas. And here . . ." Again the pen stabbed the paper. "*Ming Fa Hua Baluster Kuan, blue ground, turquoise peacocks, fifteenth century.* Hundreds of pieces . . . on and on. Vanessa's descriptions leave a lot to the imagination, but from the prices she got from probably dubious sources, I'd guess that these were of very high quality." Then he gave a soft moan. "Oh, heavens . . . *Kuan-yao bottle, 8½ inches, Southern Sung Dynasty.* Robert, we sold something of this description for ninety thousand guineas." He reached the very end of the list. "This last piece I hardly like even to think about. Perhaps I shouldn't tell you. *Fourteenth-century wine jar, Yüan Dynasty, 13½ inches, applied moulded flowering chrysanthemum, tree peony, pomegranate, camellia . . .*" His tone lowered as he went through the rest of the description. "If this is accurate, we might have sold almost a twin of that for two hundred and ten thousand guineas. Robert, do you hear what I'm saying? *Two hundred and ten thousand!* That's the highest price ever paid for any work of art sold at auction except a painting. And Vanessa did very, very well for you, considering it must have had to be a very private transaction. She sold it only two years ago."

"Yes," Tolson said. "She left it until last because its size presented difficulties. Finally she found one of those sort of square cases ladies carry about that was big enough. She packed cotton wool balls around it—those things you buy in bags in the chemist, and she filled the inside of the jar with plastic cosmetic jars, hair curlers, all that sort of thing. Ingenious, I thought."

Gerald looked at Tolson as if he had been going to try to explain the enormity of what had been done, but decided against it. Tolson would never be convinced that what he had done was not the right, the best thing, for Thirlbeck. So he merely said, "This list was just for you—so that you could identify the pieces as you remembered them?"

"That was all," he said. "Mrs. Roswell didn't pretend to know all about them. She made a list when she brought the Oriental gentleman that time. It was for her own guidance, too. There were so many of them—saucers, bowls, little jars. They seemed to me to bring very large prices—for what they were. Just all the stuff that came over from Major Sharpe's house after he died. Up in the attics it went, most of it. I felt rather sorry about that, because his will made special mention of leaving his Chinese things to the Earl of Askew. But that was a long time ago, and they couldn't have had much value then. The Countess, I remember, was rather annoyed at having to store them. A few bits and pieces went into rooms through the house. Mrs. Roswell tried to replace with modern copies some of the things she took away—so there shouldn't be too many blank spaces."

Miserably I was remembering the nineteenth-century prunus vase in the library. I was watching Gerald's pen go up and down the list. "She couldn't have taken all that out by herself."

"No—most of the Chinese things were disposed of in this country—perhaps they're still here, or they've gone out gradually. But the important pieces she held onto as long as she could. She said the value was going up every day. The snuffboxes went all at one time, to a single buyer. Someone out of the country."

Gerald looked at Askew, who had remained silent and seemingly not very interested in the details that were being pressed upon him. "Did you know about the collection of snuffboxes, Robert?"

He seemed to drag himself out of a daze. "Of course I knew. Just as I knew about Major Sharpe's Chinese stuff. We never took it seriously. I don't think many other people did then,

either. I'd forgotten about it until Jo brought the bowl to me
. . . Well, who would think—"

"The snuffboxes, Robert," Gerald pressed him.

"Yes . . . the snuffboxes. Seemed an odd sort of a thing to
collect. They came to the family by descent. Wife of the . . .
well, I suppose it must have been the thirteenth Earl—was the
daughter of a publisher, a London publisher. I only remember
that part of it because there's a picture of him somewhere about
the place. Bit of a dandy, I'd say—holding a snuffbox. Snuffbox
Johnny, I used to call him. I haven't an idea what his name was,
though. I remember the boxes. They were all displayed in a
glass case, the sort of flat thing you see in museums. It used to
be in the library. One day when I was about eight I was practising strokes with a cricket bat in there—it was pouring rain outside. It was a bigger bat than I'd ever used before, and the damn
thing sailed clean out of my hands and smashed down on the
glass over the top of the case. My mother was upset about my
breaking it, and got it moved out of the library at once before
my father saw it. I don't think he ever missed it. He never said
anything. I don't know what happened to the boxes."

"Nor do we, now," Gerald said. "Vanessa did a good job on
selling this lot—and why not? If they were really up to this
description, they must have been very fine. *Louis XV gold and
enamel rectangular snuffbox—Jean-Marie Tiron, charge of Julien Berthe. Early Louis XV enamelled oval box, Noel Hard-
villiers, charge of Julien Berthe. English chased gold snuffbox by
George Michael Moser.* Great names, all of them." His pen was
running down the list, his lips moving silently. Then he said,
"Twenty-four of them in all. The best names of the finest period. As a collection, this could have been a connoisseur's
dream. If they were as good as I think they may have been, the
whole might have gone at better than two hundred thousand
pounds. Vanessa didn't achieve anything like that amount, but
she didn't do badly, either, considering the time at which they
were sold, and the circumstances. Whoever got them must have
known they couldn't be sold openly—"

He stopped as Askew's hand suddenly slammed down on the

desk. He turned a troubled, angry face from Gerald to Tolson, and then looked back at me.

"Can't we stop this?" he said. "Can't we remember that we're talking about someone who didn't steal these things, but who ran considerable risks to sell them quietly, and out of the country, most likely. Remember we're talking about Vanessa Roswell. Remember that!"

Gerald answered him slowly. "I *am* remembering it, Robert. In fact, I haven't yet quite taken the dimension of the situation, all its aspects." I watched him very closely. His voice was firm and decisive; he showed no trace of that tranquil invalidism which had hung on in the days after he left hospital. It was as if this shock—this news of Vanessa's total involvement in Tolson's regular plunder of the treasures of Thirlbeck—had shaken him back to full life, as if he were fighting once more, fighting to save what he could of Vanessa's reputation and fighting to save what could be saved for Thirlbeck. And in this metamorphosis back into a healthy man, he had also resumed his cool, professional air, the man of the world of art, the man of the world of prices, who could calmly assess his situation before he moved on. "I am indeed remembering Vanessa.

"I'm remembering her in every aspect that I knew of her." His tone was thoughtful, and Askew's anger seemed to fade. "I knew her as a woman who enjoyed city life, someone who functioned best surrounded by people, and talk, who thrived on the rumours and gossip, the in-fighting of her business. She had a very quick eye, Vanessa, though not always a true one. When she saw the best, she always recognised it. If it was doubtful, she also was doubtful, not certain in the area of second-best. What is taking time to adjust to is the Vanessa I didn't know—the person who recognised the best in ideals, as well as objects. Obviously she believed passionately that what Tolson had set out to save was the best, and so she worked with him and others to sacrifice what must be sacrificed to keep this ideal whole. To do this she has dealt with objects, perhaps one or two objects that are among the greatest works of art our civilization will ever know. It takes time to adjust, Robert. I have to adjust to a different Vanessa—one who could keep her secret to herself over all these years." He shook his head, and sighed. "An old man's vanity, if you like, but I always flattered myself that Vanessa told me everything. And now I find that she made many journeys when I didn't even know she was out of London —that she kept secret what she knew I should never know. She would have known that I would have had to put a stop to it one way or another—the easiest would simply be to have informed you. If she had ever wanted to unburden herself, the quickest way would have been to tell me. But she chose to remain silent, and work on alone, which wasn't in character, as I saw her. Well, that's another dimension I have to get used to. In the meantime, I must just try to evaluate what exactly was taken from here."

"To what purpose?" Askew said. "Why try to put numbers and figures on it all? It's gone, isn't it? And Vanessa was the go-between in it all. None of us will ever understand why exactly she did it—though Tolson probably understands better than any of us. *Did* you understand, Tolson? It certainly wasn't for profit . . ."

Tolson stood there, his glasses masking his expression, his big frame seemed to block the light from the window. "Once she had agreed, I never asked her why. I find it difficult enough to explain why I did it myself. I asked for her help, and she gave it—far more than I had expected when I first approached her. We asked very few questions of each other. She never asked to see the farms that the money she brought had saved for the estate, and I never asked how she came by her contacts and arranged all the deals she did. I had made up my mind about her when she was here all those years ago, and my opinion didn't change. I never mistrusted her in any of these transactions, though my brother did, in the beginning. After a while even he was convinced. Even he stopped puzzling over why she did it." His tone was so even he could have been talking of some ordinary transaction, a legal bill of sale, some trifling act of commerce, not a systematic act of smuggling and forgery on a grand scale. He had lived with it so long it was a fact of life to him.

Gerald tapped the desk with his pen. "Well, we all know

that smuggling goes on constantly. We all know that there are buyers always ready for what they know must be smuggled and probably has been stolen. But there's always some old family somewhere in Europe who are prepared to swear that that particular work of art has been with them hundreds of years. Someone will furnish provenance, even where it doesn't exist. I would guess that for every painting that Vanessa took out of the country, her contact in Switzerland had a Hungarian prince or a Prussian count in exile who was willing to give it some sort of provenance. Exactly the kind of thing that happened here— the family who has treasures on their walls and are simply not aware of them until they are 'discovered.' Oh—" he shook his head. "The art world is full of such tales, and lots of them true. If the article offered with the dubious provenance is itself genuine, all the experts have to do is see such things, and there's no problem of selling. If you find a source like this to tap, the demand will exceed the supply."

He turned sharply to look up at Tolson. "That was why she dared the Rembrandt, wasn't it? You had run out of all the other things, and of the good pictures which were small enough to leave this country in a suitcase."

Tolson nodded. "I don't know anything about pictures. But she said we had taken all the really top class ones that could be taken. There was only the Rembrandt left. We hesitated for a long time about that. The man . . . the one who did the copying didn't want to take it on. Mrs. Roswell told me he had grave doubts about his ability to reproduce such a painting. Mrs. Roswell persuaded him. It was the money, I suppose. He was getting old, he'd been in prison for forgery, and the only employment he'd ever had after that was working for a firm of picture restorers. He wanted to be finished, to retire. So he agreed, when she convinced him that no one would ever see the copy—that no one but Lord Askew ever knew of its existence. You see, it all rested on my belief that Your Lordship would never come back here again. This was to be our last sale—well over a million pounds. I thought even Your Lordship would hardly need more than that. We would be in peace. No more trouble for Mrs. Roswell. And the estate would be safe."

"The forger," Gerald said. "The man who'd been in gaol—would it have been van Hoyt? He's the only copyist I'm aware of good enough to have done that." He nodded towards the shadowed picture on the wall. "He went to gaol for forgery about fifteen years ago. I should have thought he was dead."

Tolson shook his head. "It could have been him. Perhaps he went under another name. Mrs. Roswell was very careful not to talk of names of people she had dealings with. I've been trying to remember a name ever since Miss Roswell asked me that question. I seem to remember something like Last . . . perhaps it was Lastman. It seemed a sort of madeup name to me. Something Mrs. Roswell used to avoid mentioning his real name. She had been in contact with him for about ten years. That was after we sold off most of the Chinese things, and the snuffboxes, and after that first painting—which I was sure you'd never remember because it was hanging in our wing—was gone. Your Lordship asked for money which I couldn't possibly supply without selling several farms, and it was then Mrs. Roswell said she'd try to find this person . . . this Lastman."

Gerald leaned back in his chair. "Perhaps it was a madeup name. Just the sort of bitter jest that a man who had been in prison for forging Dutch masters might make. You perhaps remember that one of the early teachers of Rembrandt was Pieter Lastman, no inconsiderable artist himself, but best remembered for that single fact. It could have been a supreme irony for van . . . for Lastman to have made his final copy a self-portrait of Rembrandt himself—" He stopped abruptly. "Are you all right, Robert?"

Askew waved his hand impatiently. "Perfectly all right, Gerald. Perfectly. As well as anyone can be who finds out what other people have been doing in his name—*for* him, at risk, for a very long time."

"My lord . . ." Tolson began.

Askew cut him off. "Tolson, just one more favour, please. Would you mind bringing me some brandy? Thank you."

Tolson left the room. Askew nodded after him. "It is pretty shameful to come back and find that one man's stewardship has been better than I could possibly deserve, much more than my treatment of him and this place merited. It shames me that he has borne this alone, and never came to me to tell me what straits my own negligence had placed him in. What an opinion he must have of me that he thought me incapable of responding to an appeal of desperation. Strange . . . strange to think that he and Vanessa were some kind of superpatriots, in their fashion. So determined to hold onto this little bit of England, to keep it intact, that they both took unbelievable risks. One doesn't see Vanessa that way—I agree with you in that, Gerald. Tolson, one understands better. After all, he was born to this place. But then, so was I. I simply failed to live up to it. *They* took the risks for this thing I inherited, and I—well, I got the medals. They make it easy for one to get medals when there's a war on. But what sort of awards would there have been for Vanessa and Tolson if they had been found out in any other sort of circumstances than these?" His lips twisted upwards, but no smile came; his skin had a greyish tinge. "The Queen's Award for Industry, perhaps? They were very industrious, weren't they? Holding together nearly nine thousand acres of land—in this valley and outside of it—and a lot of it good arable land. Some of it, Tolson tells me, is now within zones with building permission. Even Tolson couldn't have foreseen the rise in the value of land, almost any sort of land, when he first began this business. He just stuck to the principle that land mattered, and other things could go first."

"He didn't foresee, either," Gerald said, "that there would be such an astronomic rise in the value of just about everything in the art market."

"Well, he made his choice, didn't he?" Askew answered. "After all, until Vanessa brought her experts here, he wasn't sure that there was much of value here. It was just the instinct that somehow—no matter what demands I made of him and of this place —that he would hold the land together. As it happens, I now think he made the right choice. I might have possessed some half-baked socialist principles, but I obviously haven't lived by them, have I? What shames me most is that he had to do it as he did—not telling me, and not daring to sell openly. If I had been here . . ." He shrugged. "But I wasn't here. That's the whole point. I was not here where I suppose I should have been. I chose to walk away from all this, and leave him the responsibilities. Can I complain about his management? I don't have the right to."

I licked dry lips. "You don't intend to prosecute . . . ?"

I thought I saw beads of sweat stand out on his upper lip. "Prosecute? For God's sake! The man hasn't stolen anything! It's all here, isn't it? The land's here, everything accounted for. What *I've* taken from Tolson's life I can't say—when I think of what he's endured in worry all these years, I owe him. And prison, what will that do?—I know, I've been there. He won't come out a reformed character. I see no reason why he should reform. And Vanessa—I can't send her to prison. She's dead now, and if it hadn't been for me, she wouldn't have been on that plane—" He shook his head violently as I tried to cut him off. "Well, can you expect me to feel any differently? Yes, I know it could have happened any other way, but it happened *this* way. And because of me. Directly or indirectly, it happened because of me. Sending people to prison doesn't change any of that."

Gerald rapped his pen again on the desk. "Don't dwell on it, Robert. It does no good. What might have been . . . whose fault it was. You've got to live with the here and now. I must confess again that Vanessa's part in this astounds me. Not because I don't believe she would have had the daring to do it—she had more than enough. But that she was so possessed of the idea of holding all this together. That she and Tolson should have become partners in this. They really are a very unlikely pair. *Very* unlikely. I can't think how Tolson ever brought himself to the point of asking for her help."

"When you're desperate, you do desperate things, Gerald. You'd think Tolson never could get his tongue around the sort of things he had to say to Vanessa at one time. But he did. Having taken that first step, having got her co-operation, I imagine both of them went deeper and deeper into it, hardly noticing. It's a very tight little world up here. Tolson has complete loyalty from all his family—however many of them knew anything about all this, no one would have questioned that he wasn't doing the right thing. It's possible Tolson never was able to imagine what Vanessa had to go through to get those things out of the country. My God, *I* can't smuggle a packet of cigarettes . . ."

Tolson had returned with a tray, three glasses, and a bottle of brandy. I noticed that Askew's hand trembled as he poised the bottle over the glass, looking at me. I shook my head; then he turned to Gerald, who also declined. He poured a large amount for himself, and drank quickly, and I was reminded of the first night I had spent at Thirlbeck when he had sent me for the brandy, and his face had had the same ashen colour. After he put the glass down he said to Tolson, "For Heaven's sake, do sit down!—sit down and have some brandy."

Gingerly Tolson drew his swivel chair closer to the big desk and sat down. I saw his heavy, thick fingers, those fingers I could somehow never imagine toiling over ledgers, twine and untwine themselves. He paid no attention to the invitation to pour himself a brandy.

Askew motioned to me. "Like the gentleman he is, Tolson refused to tell me yesterday who had managed to get rid of all the things . . . who had disposed of them, how they had been copied. Nothing but the fact that they were gone. I still don't understand why you had to come back here and tell me what Tolson had refused to tell. So, it was Vanessa . . . surprising as it is to Gerald and myself, it was Vanessa. Now, *why* did you have to come here and give us this information? For Gerald it's painful. I've already said how it affects me. I can't imagine it's been easy for you to come back here in order to tell us these things about your mother."

"I didn't intend to. After Mr. Tolson and I . . . after we met in London, I thought I could never bear to come back here. Then something happened to change my mind. Because I knew Mr. Tolson would have had to tell you he has not received payment for the Rembrandt. It was lodged in a Swiss bank in a numbered account—which bank and which number, Mr. Tolson doesn't know. So you're missing more than a million pounds for the Rembrandt, Lord Askew. And only Vanessa knew where it was."

266

Gerald leaned forward anxiously. Tolson had not stopped clasping and unclasping his hands, waiting to see how the information I had given him last night would be judged. "Have you found something, Jo?" Gerald demanded. "Have you?"

"I think so—I hope so."

I took the miniature from my handbag, and passed it to Askew. He tensed visibly as he saw it, and seemed reluctant to take it from my hands. Gerald edged his chair closer, peering to see. It was actually he who took it from me. His mind, working more quickly than at any time since his illness, must at once have placed it as the miniature missing from the set of five in the velvet frame upstairs. "This is . . ." He looked at me, his eyebrows raised.

"It was in the handbag Vanessa was carrying when the plane crashed," I said to Askew. "I couldn't identify any other piece of luggage as hers—a lot of it was completely destroyed. But I knew her handbag. Her passport was in it, and other things I could identify. I had never seen this before . . ."

There was heartbreak now in talking. I had not thought it would be easy, but the agony of sifting through the pathetic possessions of the victims laid out in that school hall of the mountain village was back in its full force. And as I spoke I saw Askew's hand go slowly towards the little portrait of the red-haired lady now lying on the blotter between himself and Gerald. He took it in both hands and turned it between his fingers, as I so often had done. His expression had altered subtly; I saw some reflection of my own pain there. Then he laid it down and reached for his brandy glass.

"With her, you said? It was in her handbag?"

"Yes. I assumed she had bought it in Zurich. Vanessa often was lucky in running across finds in people's houses, or junk shops. There was still a price tag on it. A rather new price tag."

Now I looked at Gerald. "It suddenly came to me that it wasn't a price tag at all. Look at it! I haven't really *looked* at it all these weeks. To me it was just the price she had paid in Swiss francs. But it couldn't be that. It's all wrong, isn't it?"

Gerald turned the tiny piece of white cardboard on its thin

red string. "SF 13705," he read. He looked at me enquiringly. He still did not speak of the miniatures upstairs.

"In Vanessa's handwriting—I don't know why I never wondered about *that* before. It couldn't have been the price marked on it in some shop. And in Swiss francs it just doesn't make sense. Not for a miniature like that. If it *is* a Hilliard that means it would have sold for only, well, let's say for rather less than fifteen hundred pounds. Even if a junk-shop dealer had had it, he wouldn't have let a diamond-studded frame go for that price. And at any rate, it would have been the most unbelievable chance that she had run across it during that very short visit—"

Askew shook his head. "She didn't run across it. I gave it to her. There is a set . . ." He didn't finish.

I nodded. "I never wanted to believe that she had stolen it. Then when Mr. Tolson told me how often she had come to Thirlbeck I knew that it hadn't been picked up somewhere, just by chance." I reached into the little leather pouch that had covered it. "See . . . the little bit of broken frame is here. It must have broken in the crash." I had almost forgotten what I meant to say as I watched Askew's fingers place the broken piece against the whole, as so often I had done. Gerald's voice recalled me.

"Jo, what *is* it you're saying?"

I took a deep breath. "It wouldn't have been like Vanessa to trust her own memory on figures. I searched every single thing in that handbag for some number—something that would relate. There wasn't any sort of notebook. I went through her whole passport looking to see if there was some number that didn't belong with a stamp. But there wasn't anything. I looked at the plane ticket stub. I even looked inside the packet of cigarettes to see if she'd written anything there. Before I came up here I went back to her flat and checked the post that had arrived during these past weeks, in case she had posted the number to herself in London. I checked at the shop with Mary Westerson. There was nothing—nothing at all but the numbers on the price tag that didn't make sense in Swiss francs—not for something like this." I gestured towards the tiny picture on the blotter.

Gerald rapped his pen on the desk again. "It's possible, Jo. It's possible." His calm voice was shot with excitement. "The Swisse-Française Bank. Almost the largest there is. Hardy's often use it. The bank—and the number, 13705." Then his excitement died. "It's possible—but not good enough. What branch? It has hundreds. Swiss banks don't disgorge information just because someone has an idea."

I turned to Tolson. "Do you know where she stayed that time? Did she always stay at the same hotel?"

He shook his head. "She changed around. That time it was the St. Gottard."

"On the Banhoffstrasse," Gerald said. "And so is the largest branch of the Banque Swisse-Française. It's a starting point. We could produce a death certificate, and the passport."

Tolson cleared his throat. "If you really think that is the number, Mr. Stanton, then I might be of help. Without a number I couldn't begin anywhere. No Swiss bank would have given that information just on the production of a death certificate. But with the number . . . well, it's more hopeful."

"What do you mean?" Gerald said.

"Well, Mrs. Roswell had made it a practice always to designate me as the person who had access to the account—on production of the number. She left instructions that while she might make further deposits, only I could make withdrawals or transfers. She wanted nothing to do with the transfer of money from accounts she set up, to Lord Askew's bank. While my brother was alive, his name was also included in the account, and in fact it was he who carried out all the business of transfers to Lord Askew. It's been more difficult since he died. I was glad this was going to be the last time. Mrs. Roswell made a practice of telephoning my brother as soon as the account was opened, and telling him the bank, the branch, and the number. This was the first time we had ever handled this business with a new account—this one solely to receive the proceeds of this sale—since he died. It didn't work as smoothly as it had in the past. This time—well, we missed each other."

"Missed each other?" Gerald questioned. I kept watching Askew as the talk passed between the other two men, and he hardly seemed aware of it. He sipped very often from the brandy glass, and with the other hand he kept turning and turning the miniature.

"You see, I'd been trying all day to reach Mrs. Roswell. I'd just received the cable from Lord Askew that he was returning, and I guessed the question of the Rembrandt would come up. It was the most easily salable thing in the house—possibly the only thing he really remembered. Mrs. Roswell had warned me that the copies wouldn't stand up to expert scrutiny—most particularly the Rembrandt. If Lord Askew intended bringing in experts, the Rembrandt was the one picture above all the others that *should* be here. I was desperate to stop the sale. When I telephoned the hotel that morning they said she wasn't in. But she hadn't checked out, so I left a message for her to telephone here—urgently. By that time, though, I was beginning to think I was already too late to stop the sale. It was a busy time here, starting to get the house in order for Lord Askew. I was up in the attics going through the things there, wondering if Lord Askew would notice the absence of so many of the Chinese items. I heard the telephone ring, and I hurried down. I was going to take the call in Lord Askew's room. But by then Jessica had answered the phone down in the service passage, and said I wasn't here. The child didn't know where I was. Mrs. Roswell wouldn't leave the message about the number and the bank with anyone but myself. So she left no message at all—and she didn't know why I wanted to get in touch with her. I rang back to the hotel immediately, but they said she had just left for the airport. I didn't think she had planned to fly back that night, so it only could have meant that the sale had been completed. It must all have been done—the picture sold, the money deposited—more quickly than we judged. It's possible that she got on that plane . . ." He turned and looked directly at me; it was an acknowledgement of the pain the words must bring. "She must have wanted to get to London quickly to have taken a plane that had a stop-over in Paris. My own belief is that she was a stand-by passenger for that flight. When they reported the crash, there had been no vacant seats."

Askew's face crinkled into a mask of lines. We all were silent

as he reached again for the brandy bottle. This time, as he motioned to me, I nodded, and I thought as I watched him top
up his own glass, that he shouldn't have been drinking. I wondered if he'd had enough breakfast to be able to drink that
much. But then, what was I doing with brandy at eleven o'clock
in the morning on too few hours of sleep? In those moments
of silence I looked away from Askew, not wanting to see too
closely what his face revealed, looked down at my own hands
which also trembled slightly. I thought of the tumult of these
last two days. How long since that radiant dawn when I had
been with Nat Birkett in the shelter at the edge of the woods?
How far in my life had I travelled in these few hours? I raised
my eyes and looked cautiously at Askew again, and he was staring at me. I had thought I would never return to Thirlbeck.
Now I wondered how I was to find the strength to leave this
world that Vanessa had given so much to; how was I to leave
this and Nat Birkett as well? The agony in my own mind
seemed to meet a like agony in his gaze.

I said something that had nothing to do with the chance
flight that Vanessa had caught, in a hurry, from Zurich. I was
thinking of that last telephone call. "Did . . . does Jessica
know?—about all this?"

Tolson sought his words with caution. "She knew . . . yes,
I have to say she knew. None of the details. I never discussed
them with any of the family. But Jessica's very sharp. She has
stayed here so often with my wife and myself that it was impossible to keep it all from her. She is so familiar with the house
. . . she knew almost at once when some of the items were
taken. I didn't let her see any of the pictures. I was the only
one who ever went into that room. But she knew about Mrs.
Roswell's visits. And then, by accident, she saw the copy of the
Rembrandt when Mrs. Roswell brought it here. She saw it out
of the frame. It was our custom to bring the copies here as
soon as this man—this Lastman—had completed them, even
if the arrangements for the sale were not complete. Mrs. Roswell often left one of the originals in a bank vault in Switzerland for some weeks until the right people had come together
to look at it. We had a similar arrangement as with the num-

bered account. I and my brother always knew where the picture was, and we could have access to it on proof of identity. It was . . . unfortunate that Jessica saw the canvas that one time. She is, well, let us say she is very fond of all the things at Thirlbeck. She didn't like to see any of them go. She must have guessed a great deal about what we were doing with the pictures after just that one glimpse."

"And so, when my mother telephoned from Zurich, wanting to give you the bank and the account number, answering your call to telephone urgently, Jessica said you weren't here. And the message wasn't passed. And yet you had waited all day for the call . . ." I stopped. It was wrong to add further to his misery. Jessica, with some kind of unhappy genius, had seemed to spin a glittering and terrible web between these two last tragedies of Thirlbeck. I thought of Patsy Birkett, dying alone, and I thought of Vanessa's last telephone call—the call that would have given Tolson the vital information he needed to prove his good faith. And Jessica had lied about her grandfather's presence in the house, had hung up before he could reach the extension—probably because she had disliked Vanessa and feared her influence here at Thirlbeck. Tolson had paid a cruel price for his love of his granddaughter.

I looked at the faces of all three men about me, and only Gerald's was free of anguish, only he now seemed competent of managing what new developments my suggestion had thrust on them.

In a fashion he now took over, as I had thought he would. "Well, we have somewhere to begin. At least a number. If we present ourselves at enough banks we will find what we are looking for. I know one or two well-placed legal men in Switzerland who may be prepared to advise us. It will have to be done with discretion. I will have to stay as much as possible in the background. It wouldn't do to involve Hardy's in any way with this. But you, Jo, should go—and Tolson, of course. You must have every piece of proof the bank may need. I could make a quick trip to Switzerland. As Vanessa's executor, my reasons for being concerned in her death would seem obvious . . ."

He straightened in his seat, and I thought, looking at him,

that this crisis had seemed to restore years of living to him. He was managing, and the rest of us sat and let him do it, and that pleased him. The executive abilities that had made his position at Hardy's were now back in full flood. In a little while, if he thought there was a good chance that in the end we could recover the money from the numbered account, he would almost be enjoying himself.

"As for the rest . . . well, I shall see we don't have any of Hardy's geniuses near the place until it has been gone through thoroughly. I have already had a look at the pictures that remain. There's a man I know . . . someone I can trust to be discreet, who will come and verify my own opinion. And after that, if Robert wishes, we can go ahead as we planned, and Hardy's can come in to do a complete assessment. No need to worry about the bad copies of the ceramics—every family collects things like that. What is missing is just missing. No one knew about it. No one will be the wiser. Many things are gone, but, as Tolson so sensibly says, the land remains. It might seem a fair exchange. What we have to be sure about before letting anyone but my friend, who will keep his mouth closed, near this house, is that not a single copy by van . . . by Lastman remains. They will have to be destroyed, not just hidden. Can you imagine the . . . well, to some people it would be the most delicious scandal of the decade if nineteen or so modern copies—all by the same hand—should turn up among the legitimate treasures in a remote English country house. I can just see my associates in the art world purring over my discomfiture, or getting apoplectic over it. Imagine the anxious calls of the collectors to their dealers wanting them to verify once again that what they have is the genuine thing. Imagine the real horror of those who bought the originals on learning that very clever copies of their particular work existed. Lastman did a splendid job. If it were not for the list, I would have let some of them slip through myself. Really, Vanessa might not have done her job so thoroughly. It's rather unlike her to see things through to this extent. Yes . . . the copies will have to be destroyed. What remains is very easily sorted. We can—"

I broke in. "Gerald, you know what you're saying? I mean you're involving yourself . . ."

"My dear Jo, there's no need at all to tell me what I'm involving myself in. I'm involving myself, quite deliberately, in the aftermath of what is considered a criminal act. If it is ever discovered, my position is a very bad one. An act of smuggling on a grand scale has taken place. I am assisting in covering it up. Robert here says no act of *theft* has taken place, so all of us are now concerned in a lesser, but still a serious situation." He sighed. "Well—what else can I do? Robert is a capable man, but in the art world, an absolute innocent. He didn't know what was in his own house. If I walk away and leave it to him, he'll betray himself, and the whole situation, out of hand. Can't help it. He just isn't that cunning. And if I walk away from here, leaving all these marvellous things behind, and someone other than Hardy's handles the sale, then people will *know* something is wrong. I have a duty to Hardy's. I have a duty to Vanessa, I have a duty to Robert and yourself, Jo. Now, to discharge those duties I have to step on the other side of the law. I've never been on that side in my life. I will have to sail along in the belief that what is gone is gone, and no effort on our part can bring it back. Undoubtedly, even sitting here with you has made me a part of a conspiracy. And you, Jo—you were an innocent bystander until you thought of the price tag on the miniature. Then you involved yourself. Why?"

"Well . . . I . . . Because of Vanessa . . ."

"Yes," Gerald said crisply. "A great deal of this story is because of Vanessa. A strange and fascinating woman. I hope I don't find myself in serious trouble because of her. But according to her lights, she did her best. Somehow, wherever it leads me, I don't feel like betraying her."

He began to discuss quickly the plans for what we would do in Switzerland. "I'll have to make a few telephone calls first. But we should get it over as soon as possible. It might be as well to travel separately . . ." He began making notes, setting down the order of things as he thought we should do them. It was the Gerald I had known all my life, and still my senses didn't take in that we were now all involved in a criminal act—

274

a conspiracy, he called it. Nothing had been stolen, since Askew would bring no charges. But works of art had left the country without an export licence, illegally. As Gerald had said, if the truth about the forgeries were known, it would make the art scandal of the decade. And here was Gerald calmly making notes as to how we should act to go deeper into the conspiracy, taking him with us. "Well, if you don't do something to recover it, some Swiss bank is just going to be sitting on more than a million pounds forever. I don't entirely disbelieve those stories of fortunes deposited before the Second War whose owners didn't survive, and which will never—can't—be claimed. It's Robert's money, after all." He said as an aside to Tolson, "I hope all is in order with the tax people as far as Lord Askew is concerned. *That* would be a complication we wouldn't like."

"I believe so, Mr. Stanton. My brother was very careful that all expenditures of the estate were recorded—and the usual taxes paid. Lord Askew's personal taxes were another matter. We recorded a certain income paid to him from the estate. The extras that were paid from the Swiss accounts—that's in a doubtful area. My brother arranged all these things."

Gerald frowned. "Pity we don't have him to work on this. But still we must manage . . . Robert, are you all right?"

"Yes . . . yes." Askew sipped the brandy before he spoke again. "It's so damn complicated, isn't it? I've always hated this sort of thing. From time to time I get little notes from the Inland Revenue asking what periods I've spent in the U.K. . . . and where I've been last Tuesday week. I've paid taxes in Switzerland, I know—but only when Edward Tolson told me to. Since Edward died, I don't think I've answered an official letter—from anyone. It didn't seem to matter very much. Funny . . . when I was in the Army things were much easier. Easiest of all was just to stay a private. No responsibility. No forms to fill out. No reports to make. Just stick to the rules, go by the book, and they took care of you. Easy, really. Never had it so good, I expect. No decisions . . ." His eyes seemed to have taken on a glazed, faraway expression; I caught a glimpse of the man who had fled from Thirlbeck and its responsibilities twice in his life, the man who, until this morning, had seemed to me to have retained much of the spirit and outlook of the boy who had grown up here. In his terms, even the decorations for outstanding bravery became understandable. He had believed he was just going by the book—but it had been very much his own book.

Gerald looked at him with faintly disguised impatience. "Well, I'll go ahead with all this, Robert?" It was hardly a question at all. "After we've been through the Swiss tangle, we'll give our attention up here. I take it you don't intend to stay on indefinitely? I mean, there's no point. Now that I understand the situation, Tolson is perfectly capable of coping with all the things that arise when the Hardy people come. It's quite a long business . . ." He was urging Askew to leave, afraid, perhaps, as he had said, that he was not capable of sustaining the façade of innocence which would be needed. It would be so easy for a slight slip of the tongue to indicate to the busy, careful young men of Hardy's that much more than they saw had once been in this house. When Askew seemed unwilling to reply, Gerald went on. "The furniture would make a 'highly important' sale just by itself. But we must catalogue it very carefully, and see that the right people know about it. One loses a great deal by being in too much of a hurry. And the pictures— well, they should be held until the important Old Master's sale next season."

"Yes . . ." Askew said, but I don't think he heard.

I looked at Gerald. "Important? But I thought Vanessa had taken all the good ones . . . ?"

Now a smile of real pleasure broke on Gerald's face. "She only took what was portable, Jo. It's rather difficult to take a Cuyp measuring about three-and-a-half feet by five feet out in a suitcase. You'll love it, Jo. It's a beautiful thing. There's a Hobbema that's of very fine quality. Two Jan Steens. A magnificent Jakob van Ruisdael. A Nicolaes Maes. Some are signed. There are a couple of beautiful canvases that are not, so I'm just making guesses as to the artists. But there are some exceptionally fine pictures there."

"All those . . . still there?" Perhaps he knew what I was thinking. Last season a Cuyp had gone at auction for over six hundred thousand pounds. There was no name among them which flashed a signal light of instant fame to the whole world, such as the Rembrandt, but to the art world this could be a collection of enormous distinction and importance. "Not catalogued? . . . Not known?"

He shook his head. "All by descent from the van Huygens family. Mixed among them are the usual number of respectable and fairly nondescript canvases. And there's the Birkett contribution of country-house portraits which aren't at all good. The van Huygens must have acquired all their stock of pictures in the seventeenth century—almost hot off the artist's easel—and never added to the collection. They all fall within that one great period of Dutch painting. I suppose they'd filled their walls by then, and never bothered acquiring later artists. Once we've destroyed the copies Vanessa brought here, we'll bring in the big guns to give their opinions. But I haven't any doubt that it is . . . well, what everyone like myself dreams of. In my opinion it's a major art discovery."

"When did you see them? I would have liked . . ."

"Jo, you weren't here. After Tolson told his story yesterday morning, well, I stopped putting off going into the picture room. Tolson had a list of the copies, and had always kept them separated. We've been through the rest, and I've already sorted the good ones. It was quite a task—just physically moving them all, and looking. I must say Tolson was very determined to guard every single picture the house held. There are engravings, there are flowers pressed under glass—and watercolours which look as if someone's governess executed them," he added unkindly.

Tolson made a defensive gesture with his hand. "You do understand how it was, Mr. Stanton? With the requisition order on the house I had to be very careful. All I knew was that one picture was supposed to be a Rembrandt. What did I know about the others? You can't be too careful. If those scientists had ever really come to take over the house, I would have moved the whole lot—pictures, furniture—everything but the very heavy stuff—into my sons' houses. We had cleared out rooms to get ready for it. Even some outbuildings. I was afraid of the damp though. You remember we couldn't get building materials during the war. A single leak in one roof—well, what did I know about the damage it could do? It was hard enough just to keep going during the war—to keep the farms up—never mind looking after all these delicate things."

His gesture with his large splayed hand was final; he had had this charge, he had done the best he could. He had saved everything without discrimination. It was up to others to sort the good from the inferior and the bad.

"You acted very wisely, Tolson," Gerald said soothingly. "We went through—"

Once more I interrupted him. "We? Was the Condesa there? Does she know?"

Since Askew didn't seem inclined to answer, Gerald did. "You realise, Jo, that the Condesa came here with Robert, believing, as he did, that there was a Rembrandt in the house. Now, of course, it became quite impossible to conceal from her that it is a copy—but a signed copy of a self-portrait. She is an intelligent woman . . . she guessed that if there was this one copy, there were probably others. She understands, and she will not betray what happened here. The choice between the land and the art works was just as clear to her as to Tolson. It will not, I think, be necessary to tell her the part Vanessa played in all of this. The fewer people who know of that the better. But . . ."

"But," I said, "she is a member of this . . . this conspiracy also."

"Yes," Gerald admitted. "Yes, I suppose she had unwittingly become one."

"And Jessica," I demanded. "Was she also with you?" I was aware immediately of the slump of Tolson's body in the chair. I had touched again, harshly, on the weak spot.

"I had realised it was unwise to involve Jessica any further. There is a limit to the responsibility which should be placed on the child. So I sent her home to the South Lodge. I would think she suspects something is stirring, but so long as she doesn't know exactly what, then I think we are quite safe to carry on."

Quite safe . . . quite safe. The words had a great feeling of security. I looked at Tolson's large intractable figure, the very image of a man unshakable in his loyalties, his conception of duty. Yes, one could leave it to him. I looked between Gerald and Tolson in a kind of daze of fatigue. Two men, infinitely capable in their own spheres. With the handing over of the miniature I had laid down most of my own problems. Then I looked again for the miniature. Askew was turning it still in one hand, while he sipped steadily at the brandy. I wondered how much of the conversation he had really attended to; he was lost in a world that was Thirlbeck, but still a part of Thirlbeck none of the rest of us seemed to know.

I made an effort to focus my mind. "You went through all the paintings—*all* of them?"

"Yes—all of them."

I turned then to Tolson. "You did say you had gathered up *every* picture in the house? Every one? There aren't any in your part of the house—not on staircases, or out-of-the-way places?"

"Everything except a few watercolours that Jessica did. She's quite talented. I had the best of them framed . . ."

"No . . . well, I really didn't think . . ."

"What is it, Jo?" Gerald asked.

"Oh, nothing, really. Just some odd idea I had, but it really couldn't mean anything. I suppose in everything you looked at yesterday you didn't come across anything that might remotely look like . . . might be an El Greco?"

"Remotely? Jo, you know as well as I do that there is no such thing as a painting that is remotely like El Greco. It either is an El Greco, or it isn't. He didn't have any imitators. Why do you ask?"

"I'm sorry, Gerald. Please forget it. I know it sounded stupid. So much has happened, I . . ."

He was nodding his head absently, his thoughts evidently on the business at hand, not on my fantasies. "After all, Jo, finding an El Greco in the middle of a collection of Dutch Old Masters would be rather a cuckoo in the nest, wouldn't it?"

"Of course," I said. I got to my feet. "Do you need me for a while, Gerald? I thought I might go and take a walk. My head feels as if it's packed with cotton wool. I never did manage very well on missing sleep . . ."

"No, nothing right now, Jo." He looked at Askew. "Robert, I'll have to monopolise the phone for a while. A call to Hardy's, just to tell them that I'm still alive. A hint of good news to come. But I'll tell them I'm not prepared to leave for a week or ten days yet. That will give us time to get to Switzerland. And about you, Jo. You'll have to go to Zurich with us, so I'll say you'll be back with Hardy's in a few days. I'll say I need you here to help with some preliminary sorting. And, Robert, I'll start the telephone calls to Switzerland. Can you be prepared to go at any time, Tolson, once I've made the necessary connections? Your passport, and all that . . . ?"

"I've always kept my passport up to date. Mrs. Roswell made sure of that. We never knew when it might be necessary for me to go either to Amsterdam, where the . . . the copier worked, or to Switzerland, in case she was herself unable to go."

"Very good," Gerald said briskly. "Then I'll start the calls, Robert. Robert . . . ?"

Askew stirred, and seemed to shake himself back to awareness. "What? Oh, the calls. Yes . . . yes, of course, Gerald. Handle it whatever way you want. You'll do it better than anyone . . . Yes, of course."

He rose, and then rather unexpectedly addressed himself to me. "Mind if I go for a walk with you? My own head could stand a bit of clearing. Things to think over . . . All right?"

"Yes . . . yes, of course. I'll just go upstairs and get my jacket. I won't be long." I was conscious of a sense of disappointment. I hadn't realised until he made his request, that in fact I had been intending to walk to Nat Birkett's house. I had told myself all through the drive up here that I would merely say what I had come to say, offer the evidence of the miniature, and then I would go. I had meant to leave Nat Birkett free of any sense that I was reaching out to hold him, to bind him in the fashion that the Tolsons bound him. We would both have our memories of that radiant dawn in the shelter by the woods, and if it were no more than a memory, then we would let it be so. But when Askew spoke I had to acknowledge to myself that I had intended to take the road along by the South Lodge and climb the hill to Nat Birkett's house. I knew that pride or independence had no place in what I remembered of that morning.

But then I had looked fully into Askew's face, and had known that even that walk along the valley to Nat's house must wait. The face of this man who had seemed to age overnight was the face of a man desperately lonely. He wasn't even trying to cover it; I thought of the whole span of his life—the life of the boy who had lived here, and the brief periods he had spent here as a man. I sensed that whomever he had had with him as his companion and lover during this long absence, he had still been lonely, and a part of him had always been homesick. He had come quite suddenly and cruelly to the realisation of it in this past day. I couldn't refuse the quiet plea of his loneliness now.

I walked slowly across the room as Askew held the door for me. Tolson followed. As I reached the door Gerald's voice came again, musingly.

"Lastman . . . Lastman . . ." We all turned. Gerald was staring at us, his brow creased. "I remember it now. Some place I had encountered that name very recently—and not as a signature to a painting. You won't remember it, Jo. Why should you remember what happened to the others? I stayed on there in Switzerland for a day after you left with your father—to take care of certain formalities. By that time most of the relatives had left—either taking their dead with them, or having buried them there. One man only had not been claimed. He had a passport—and therefore an identity. But the authorities in Holland were unable to contact relatives. He seemed to be a man quite alone, they said. His name was Lastman.

"I suppose it's conceivable that neither he nor Vanessa had any idea they would each take that flight. He was waiting in Zurich for his share of the money, waiting to deposit it in a Swiss bank. It came sooner than anyone expected. So he and Vanessa may have found themselves unwittingly on the same plane—something they would never have done if either had known. Stand-by passengers. Yes . . . his name was Lastman."

Gerald's face crumpled; he picked up his pen and bent swiftly over the notebook once more. I felt Askew's hand on my shoulder propelling me through the door. I heard his voice, low, close beside me.

"We can't help it, you know—the way we have to die. It's just best to remember that we all do, sometime."

* * *

Upstairs I washed my face in Gerald's bathroom, splashing the cold water into my stinging eyes. My face, without make-up, looked back palely at me from the mirror. Pale lips, pale grey eyes, pale blond hair, the tan of Mexico had almost gone. Strangely, the face I saw seemed to have altered subtly. I looked older. There was a twist to the mouth I had never noticed before—if it had been there before. I saw a face that did not look at all like Vanessa's. Perhaps I had never even remotely looked like Vanessa, but I had tried to. It almost seemed as if I had stepped out finally from behind her shadow and declared myself to be my own self. Perhaps it had happened when I had sat there in the empty church, studying the miniature, and in those moments had decided that I would return to Thirlbeck—as if in throwing in my lot with Vanessa's own decisions, I had truly become my own self, not her shadow. Or perhaps it had happened in the instant I had stood at the door of my own flat, and refused to answer the insistent ringing of the telephone, when before I would have flown to it in the hope that it was Harry calling. Perhaps it had happened most clearly when I had entered Thirlbeck once again in the early hours of the morning, had seen the whole valley bathed in its white moonlight. It might have happened in the moment of my stepping across the threshold, greeted by the hounds as if I had been known all my life. It could have been all of those things, or one. Most strongly it could have happened when I was received, as if by a ghostly presence, back into the room of the Spanish Woman. Perhaps it had come to me in my exhausted sleep, as the sun had risen over Brantwick, and gradually stole down the fierce, barren slopes of Great Birkeld, and the young priest had robed himself to say the first of those nine Masses.

But strangely when I went back to the Spanish Woman's room to get my anorak I was at once aware of an alien presence. As before the room had always welcomed me, now the ambience was distant, almost warning. I looked around, but everything seemed as I had left it. I had made the bed, and tidied the possessions I had scattered around the night before, my clothes were hanging just as I had left them, the suitcase with the silk scarf with the pieces of the Sung bowl, and the wrapped Book of Hours of Juana, seemed quite undisturbed. I bent to smell again the captured scents of last summer in the bowl of potpourri. All was the same. I turned at the doorway, my anorak over my arm, and looked back. I had expected to see her, there in the chair by the fireplace—or was that her shadow thrown on the floor by the sunlight? But she was my friend, and whatever, whoever had recently entered here, was not. I thought of the sugar-spun fairy who had danced about on that morning I had first wakened at Thirlbeck. Jessica. No—not Jessica. Jessica had been sent home. But home was only a mile down the valley, the South Lodge. And Jessica had inhabited Thirlbeck all of her life. No prohibition by her grandfather could keep her out.

I looked once again at the empty room, the empty chair by the fire, the empty chair at the long table. Once, long ago, a young Spanish girl had sat there. She was there no more. I shook my head and closed the door. Once I had re-entered Thirlbeck, it had become possible to believe in ghosts.

II

Askew had not really intended to take a walk, or his resolution had faltered. He was there, where so often I had seen him with the Condesa and Gerald, on that mown patch of grass, the long view of the tarn exposed, with an ice bucket and the long-necked bottle of champagne embedded in it, placed ready on the wooden table. He waved to me, almost a replica of the youthful gesture he had always used. But I was conscious that this time it was a replica, a studied thing. And he knew it also.

"Thought we might enjoy the sun," he greeted me. "Sheltered here." Even the words and sentences were cut short, as if he had no strength for unneeded effort.

There were three glasses on the tray. "I called up to Carlota, but she doesn't seem to be about yet. She'll probably appear some time soon. She has a marvellous instinct for timing. You'll have a drink?" It was scarcely a question. He was already pouring it.

I thought of the brandy we both had drunk, and now the champagne. It hardly seemed to matter. It was the sort of day that I would never live again.

"Yes—yes, thank you."

He poured for both of us, and eased himself into the deck chair close to me. We made a slight inclination to each other with our glasses, but exchanged no words of salutation. As with each situation here, I was beginning to believe that I had been doing it for a long time. I believed it also as Tolson approached from the gravelled area through the mown path of grass, walking purposefully, but not hurrying. It was probably the combination of fatigue, of brandy, and the first heady sips of champagne, but I thought I saw him walking out from centuries past, Tolson in all guises, in all dresses, always a Tolson come to serve a Birkett.

But it was to me he spoke. "There's a telephone call for you, Miss Roswell. It's Mr. Peers. I told him you were out of doors, but he said he'd wait. Mr. Stanton told me he's quite ready to leave the study for you . . . otherwise there's the extension in Lord Askew's room, or the one in the service passage."

I put down the champagne and started to rise; then I dropped back in the seat again. "Thank you, Mr. Tolson. Would you . . . would you mind telling Mr. Peers that you can't find me, but you'll deliver the message when I get back?"

He nodded. "Of course, Miss Roswell."

When Tolson had gone, Askew said, "You could have gone. I don't mind . . ."

"I wasn't certain . . . no, I'm sure I didn't want to go. For once, Harry will have to wait. He won't wait very long," I added. "After a while he won't call any more."

"Isn't that a rather unfair way of getting rid . . . well, I'm sorry, it isn't my business, and it may not be what I think it is."

"Unfair? Not just at the moment. Oh, I won't just let him go by default. But I'm too tired now to talk to him. I will talk to him when I'm sure that I'll sound as if I'm sure. Harry is used to a rather different person—someone not quite sure, ready to be told what to do. I want him to understand I know what I'm talking about, that I mean what I say . . ." I looked across at Askew. "No, you really don't know much of what it's about. But for the first time I'm sure about what I want to do. I don't want to drift into something because it's easier than making some other decision and living by it. I don't think Harry would care for that sort of person. It's only fair to tell him. Have you got a cigarette?"

He gave me one from the gold case I remembered, and lighted it before taking one for himself. We sat in silence for some time. The wind from the tarn was gentle, and sun-warmed. There was the sound of bees engrossed in the blossom of an old apple tree that had survived the jungle about it. I sipped the champagne and smoked, and wished that, for some time, life could stay just like this. All I needed was a little time. A time to get used to the creature who had broken from the chrysalis; the wings yet were feeble and uncertain. I knew what I had just done. I had handed back the world on a golden plate that Harry had offered. Gerald would be disappointed—and surprised. He would have enjoyed that house in St. James's Place; he would have enjoyed my and Harry's children, and enjoyed the fact that I would go on working at Hardy's. He would never want to see me repeat the untidiness and chaos of Vanessa's life, her impulsive rashness. I would have been safe with Harry —safe and empty. As the years passed I would have grown into the person Gerald had hoped for, the expert who would have written, eventually, scholarly monographs on ceramics, the expert Harry had not just hoped for, but planned for. I would have borne him children, and waited for him to come back from his trips, or waited for those late-night meetings to finish. And then I suppose that I would have stopped waiting in my heart, and accepted the fact that Harry had acquired me, a home, children, all in one well-executed move, and he would expect us all to function with the clockwork regularity and precision of his own efficient staff. I would have been his best girl—but one like my own china figurines, relegated to a shelf until wanted for use or inspection. And what would I have in place of Harry? I didn't let myself think of that. What was important was that the new uncertain person who had broken out of the mould must stay outside. It seemed odd that in stepping away from the shadow of Vanessa to which I had clung, I had in some respects become more like her. But now, instead of standing behind her, I could turn and face her.

Then I suddenly realised that I could turn and face anyone —anyone at all.

I said to Askew, "What will you do now? Are you going to let Gerald take over everything? Are you going to go away and let him arrange a sale of everything that's in the house? If we recover the million pounds will you go off and just spend it?"

"I don't see how I can, do you?" He flicked the ash of his cigarette towards the ashtray, but the breeze carried it off. "Too many people have paid too high a price because I have refused my responsibilities here. I'm thinking now . . . I'm thinking that I shall stay. It may be a decision made late. But at least it's a decision. I may even be able to do something to ease Nat Birkett's burden. All this land that Tolson has saved for the estate . . . it'll be worth a good deal of money, and demand a hell of a lot in death duties. I probably should stay here and see if some of it can't be fashioned into some sort of trust— only for that I shall have to try to stay alive another seven years, I suppose. I could try to make friends with my heir, however unwilling he is. There are a lot of things I could do . . . should do. It begins to seem now that I must. That people have been willing to risk prison, that Vanessa had died while carrying out an unpaid commission for the sake of holding Thirlbeck together, finally places a responsibility on me that has always been there . . . but I've never been able to carry it before. Never wanted to. So . . . probably I shall stay on. Does that answer your question?"

"Not quite. What will you do? Just sit here in the sun? And indoors when it rains? Who will keep you company?"

"Not Carlota. Is that what you're asking? No, you wouldn't ask that. But Carlota won't stay. This isn't her place. In time she'd shrivel and die here. In time I shall, too—but at least I know what I have finally come back to. Very belatedly, I shall have to learn from Tolson what I must do—how I must act. He will know. I don't know how to live this sort of life. But I haven't been very successful at any other sort of life, and here at least I can try. Does that satisfy you?"

I sat silent for a while, thinking about what he had said. "Why does it all have to be sold? Why does all the furniture and pictures and books have to go? You could open it to the public. Or just the house alone, even if you had to strip it of the most valuable things—just the house alone is worth a dozen visits. You're used to it—you were born here. But when I first saw it, I thought it had grown out of a fairy tale. It's very beautiful—all of this valley. All of this valley that you keep people out of. This is a very crowded little island, Lord Askew. I wonder if it's right that people like you—and Tolson, I suppose—should be allowed to keep quite so much to themselves. This whole region is one of the few National Parks we have. And you own a slice in its very heart. Do you really have the right to keep it all to yourself?"

"You're talking about my going into the Stately Homes business. That just isn't on, you know. I could never do it. I don't feel much pride in this place, or much identification with it. It will be hard to stay, hard to learn to be something different at this stage in my life. It would be impossible if I had to encounter strangers walking through my house, and set up souvenir stalls, and all that. No, for my time, at least, it will have to stay as it is. When Nat Birkett's time comes, he'll have to make his own decisions."

"By that time," I said, "the boot of the furniture and the pictures will be gone. The things that help draw people will be gone. What's left of the garden will be lost . . ."

"Look," he said with an air of wearied patience, "there has to be a choice. I have to put several hundred thousand pounds into Tolson's hand to do what needs doing about this place. You can see for yourself that it needs a new roof. Have you noticed the outbuildings?—they're falling down. Tolson and his sons need new tractors and farm equipment—yes, even if they're tenants they've a right to some help. With as much land as there's still left there could be some sort of co-operative for machines and all that stuff. There's areas that should be drained—much of it could make good pasture. There are fences —miles of stock fencing that need attention. It's got to be paid for with something. Have you noticed how well-managed Nat Birkett's farm is? He's in debt to the bank for a lot of that, but he's got the best farm in the area. What will he thank me for most? A flourishing estate, well run and productive, or a few Dutch pictures and some spindly legged tables? There'll be enough left here—the big stuff that no one could sell. I doubt that he'll want to open the place though—he's not one bit keener on swings for the kiddies and car parks littered with cigarette packs than I am. Quite a touch of the eccentricity of the Birketts, Nat has, even though he's so distantly related. Must be something that happens to you when you know one day you've got to be the Earl of Askew. Poor devil, he won't like it one bit better than I do."

"Have you suddenly become a farmer yourself?"

He shook his head. "Do I sound converted? I really don't understand half of what's really needed. If I stay here, it will be to relieve Tolson of the financial problem of supporting me elsewhere. He seems to think there's some symbolic value in my actually being resident here. I think I'll only be a nuisance to them all . . . but I'll have to give it a try."

"When did he say all this?"

"Last night. Last night, after our day of revelations about the pictures and the other things, after that session Gerald held in the picture room, he and I had a long talk alone. Or at least I listened to him talk. I wondered what he would do with the money if he had it to spend here at Thirlbeck. He gave me a lot of talk. Breeding better beef cattle for the Common Market— but it takes years to do that. We should have a completely au- tomated milking parlor for the dairy herd—and that stock needs improving, too. We should be looking out for prize rams for the sheep. And that's just the Home Farm. If there was money, he says, he could get good qualified help if he could build decent cottages for them, and pay them more than the minimum rate. It sounds fair, doesn't it? You forget that half the agricultural labourers in the country don't have running water in their houses, and no means of transport to the nearest town. Makes it hard on the wife and kids. I never thought of it that way. My father and grandfather had plenty of help about the place. But most of the cottages they had were picturesque hovels, and they've fallen down, which they deserved to do—like the North Lodge. A model farm, Tolson paints it as—with me, belatedly, as the model landlord. Of course I won't be. I'll sit here and he'll run the show. But I'll try to sit here, just the same."

"Gerald once described you as anti-Establishment before anyone really knew what that was. And now you'll be living an almost feudal life . . ."

He stubbed out the cigarette and immediately reached for another. "I had half-baked ideas on Socialism. I dashed off to Spain to fight for the common man and his rights. I didn't notice that the common man on my father's estate wasn't doing all that well. Somehow one only thought of the poor in England in those depression years as being in cities and in the mines. I forgot my father owned mines, and the labourers' wives carried water from a pump. I saw it rather more clearly after the war. But I wasn't professing to be a Socialist any more. I wasn't professing to be anything. I'd reached the age when ideals flicker and go out unless there is something to nourish them. I didn't seem to find it here, so I went away and left it all to Tolson. I thought when I told him to sell the farms at fair prices to the sitting tenants I was doing my bit for my own little system of land reform. It never occurred to me that Tolson would see it all in larger terms—that the Birkett estate should be one big co-operative. Paternalistic, I call it, but Tolson seems so damn right about his figures. If a man only farms eighty or so acres, how the hell can he afford to run a tractor? In his small way Tolson had been running a sort of co-operative with the Home Farm and the farms his sons have tenancies of, but he has schemes so grand I can't even imagine how he'll work them. But I don't have to. All I have to do is sit here, and that will make Tolson happy. He'll know I've given my tacit approval to all the schemes he's worked out. In fact, I'm so completely in his debt that there's no chance of ever repaying him. And as for Vanessa . . . well, she'll never know that I'm even trying.

"It's an England," he continued, "that I don't know any more. I'll have to try to know it. I can ride here a bit, and shoot a bit. I suppose we could straighten out the house a little, and I could have a few people to dinner. I could join some London clubs—finally. That would give me a reason for shooting up and down the M6 to London every so often. After all, I don't suppose it will be so very different from what I've been doing all these years. Except that this time I'll be an Englishman, doing all these things in England—and just as much a stranger as I've ever been in all the wild and lonely places I've visited.

"I might even," he added, with a curious shyness, and a covering dry laugh, "I might even read a book or two. I didn't have much education, you know. I was always bottom of the class."

Why should my heart ache for him? And yet it did. I wished I could say something, but there were no words of reassurance. He was a stranger in a strange land, and struggling, in his sixties, to make it his own. He would try to stick it out, but I thought he would very often be making the headlong flight down the Motorway, and then, restless and bored in his London clubs, making only a superficial life for himself there, he would be heading back North on the Motorway, to meet the same stranger here at Thirlbeck.

"I hope you and Gerald will come sometimes," he said. "I'd be glad if you would."

"We'll come, of course."

"Good! I'm glad to know that. I don't know quite how to start all this. It isn't that I can just pick up where I left off— things have changed too much for that. And I'm not young any more. It's rather bad when the excitement—even the hope of excitement goes. It will be very bad indeed once Carlota goes."

"Are you sure she will go?"

He nodded. "Yes, in time she'll go. She's a rare and exotic bird, Carlota. It wouldn't be fair to expect her to settle down like a little broody hen. She will be sad about going, I know. She will talk about coming back. Perhaps she will come back a few times. And each visit will be shorter and shorter . . . and I will be older."

This time it was I who rose and poured more champagne. "I'll come back if you really want me to. Yes, I will come back." I handed the glass to him, and the smile he gave me had so little resemblance to the smile of the man who had come down the steps to greet us on that first night that once again I hardly recognised him. The charm was still there, but he was so vulnerable; he couldn't often, I thought, in the years since he had grown up and left Thirlbeck and his father, have had to ask for friends, for company. And yet what did I really know of him? I knew little, and should judge less. But in these last few hours we had grown rapidly closer—closer in thought and age, much closer in understanding.

It was hardly a shock then when the miniature came out of his pocket. Often as we had talked I had noticed that his hand went there, and he touched something, as if for reassurance. I saw the tiny thing suddenly exposed in the sunlight; the diamonds, dulled a little in their aged setting, sprang to life.

"I didn't think it mattered if I took it. Gerald has the number. He doesn't need this."

"Do you?"

"Perhaps." He sat and looked at it for a moment. "Perhaps I shall ask you to lend it to me for a while. It really belongs to you, but do you mind if I keep it? Just for a while?"

I couldn't deny it to him. At once I had the sense that of all the treasures Thirlbeck possessed, this was perhaps the only thing he really wanted. "No, you keep it. Keep it as long as you want. Perhaps Vanessa might have liked that best—having it go back to you. She must have thought it very special. It was in the zippered compartment of her handbag, as if she rarely was parted from it. And yet I'd never seen it in my whole life before."

"I wish she would have taken much more from me, but she never did—or would."

"Did you really expect her to? This is truly a very special gift. A Nicholas Hilliard miniature, and one of your own family."

"That part of it didn't matter. It looks like Vanessa. That's why I gave it to her. I hadn't forgotten about it, but still when you brought it out this morning, it was as if someone has thrust me back all those years. Red-haired and beautiful, Vanessa was —and a little bit wild. Just the way I imagined the woman in this portrait was. I remember when I was a boy I used to look at this quite often, and wish I had known her. When Vanessa came, it was like seeing the lady in the portrait come to life."

I was pouring the last of the champagne. Could we really have drunk this much? It was too late for the Condesa to come now. The droning sound of the bees seemed hypnotic, or was this sensation of being totally relaxed with this man merely what champagne drunk in the sun will do? I watched the long reeds in the shallows of the tarn sway lightly in the breeze.

"Shakespeare called miniatures 'The Manacle of Love,'" I said softly. "People used to carry them then the way we carry special photographs now—very precious, personal things. Do you think she carried it in that way?"

"I hope she did. If she did, I suppose it is evidence of how much she was prepared to do for Thirlbeck. But I hadn't expected her to remember or care about it for such a long time. Vanessa was very independent. After she and Jonathan left Thirlbeck, I never saw her again."

"Tell me about it—what it was like then, here at Thirlbeck? The three of you . . ."

"The three of us. Yes, that's what it felt like—just the three of us. We had all come through a different sort of war, and at that time it felt as if survival should count for something splendid—if we had survived it meant it was for some special reason. Vanessa achieved her special thing in her own way—Jonathan found his. I'm the one who can't find anything significant in the years since then . . . so, because of Vanessa and because of Tolson, I'll stay. There's a little time yet . . ."

"But tell me," I insisted. "Tell me about it then."

"Then? Well, we were all young—that's the first point. At least we *seemed* young. I was in my thirties, and that seems young to me now. Vanessa was only about twenty-one. Jonathan, I suppose, was twenty-seven. It was very isolated up here then. At times it seemed as if we were the only three people left alive in the world. No doubt we were very selfish. The Tolsons all were here, and life wasn't one long game for them, the way we made it for ourselves. Every fine day was an excuse for a picnic. Mrs. Tolson was a splendid cook, and a baked rabbit was a feast. Funny . . . how I remember the food. We were still rationed, of course, but with the war over, a bit of black market didn't seem such a crime. After the Army food I used to look forward to every meal. I used to go and gather the eggs from the hen run myself, and I was very greedy with them. I used to shoot too—out of season, and all. But the valley was so overstocked, it had to be done. I shot deer, partridge, and pheasant. We had venison and jugged hare, and trout. Once in a while we'd have salmon. There were salmon about, if you knew the streams. Most of it illegal, but we didn't care. Vanessa and Jonathan eventually ate most of their meals here—I wanted their company. Any reason was good enough to bring up the best wine from the cellar. Having been through one war, we saw no reason to save anything for the next time around. It began to seem like one long party, and we gave Jonathan very little chance to work. It used to make him angry sometimes, and he'd keep to himself for a day or two. But he wasn't well and he wasn't working well. So he'd be back with us, and the party would go on.

"Then all of a sudden it seemed as if we'd come to the last of the wine. We knew we couldn't go on like that forever. It was autumn, and Vanessa and Jonathan went—quite suddenly they went. So I went too. Vanessa had left an address in London, but when I went there, I found out that they'd never been there. That was when I knew Vanessa didn't want to see me again."

"But you had given her the miniature, and she had taken it. That must have meant something."

"I had hoped it meant something. But obviously it didn't mean what I had hoped."

What had seemed difficult before now was easy. I asked my question directly. "Did you love her? Did she love you?"

"I loved her. I believed I loved her. I really believed that.

But perhaps she didn't believe it herself. Perhaps she never loved me. She never said she did. I remember . . . she never actually said she did."

We looked at each other, and there was knowledge in the look, and a kindliness, a shared awareness of Vanessa and each other. "And now," I said, "you know that she did love you. She must have loved you, even if she never said so. *That* was why she was willing to do so much for Thirlbeck, and kept so quiet about it. It was something she wanted to tell no one. I wonder . . . I wonder if my father knew she loved you."

Askew sighed. "I don't know. I probably was blindly selfish about that, too. She and Jonathan were married during the war. He was captured soon after, and was in a P.O.W. camp right until the surrender. They'd spent so little time together. Renting the Lodge here was some sort of effort to get to know each other again. War does more than take time out of your life. It had taken Jonathan's health, and his sureness about being able to paint. He wanted to get both back again, and Vanessa as well. They tried terribly hard, both of them, but they should never have come to a place like this. The quietness suited Jonathan, but the climate didn't help him at all. Vanessa tried to bear it—the quietness was hell for her. She kept us all laughing, I remember, but I had the feeling that she was afraid to stop laughing because of what she might hear. So, when I went to the address in London, and they were not there, I decided that I should leave them alone. Without me hanging on, they might have a chance."

"They really didn't have much of a chance," I said. "They stayed together until I was born, and then my father went to Mexico. Vanessa could never have survived there. There seemed to be no bitterness. It was a marriage that went wrong, and they both knew it. As soon as he started selling some paintings, he always sent money. Vanessa tried to refuse it at first, and he was hurt—so she let him put money in the business. Investing, he called it, but they both understood that it was a nonrepayable loan. He kept arguing in letters that living in Mexico was very cheap, there wasn't anything to spend money on—except his hobby of collecting some vintage cars after he began selling really well. He wanted the money to be put to work. I suppose it was a polite fiction they had. When I got old enough Vanessa used to show me his letters. He sounded nice. When I finally did meet him, he turned out to be nice—rather more than just nice. But I couldn't picture him *married* to Vanessa. She was a bit too much for most people, except in small doses. Gerald, for instance. In his fashion he adored Vanessa, but I don't think he could have spent a solid week in her company. Perhaps she knew that about herself. Perhaps that was why she went away and never saw you again. Do you think that might have been the reason . . . do you?"

He sighed. "If it was, then she was wiser at her age than I guessed. Perhaps I pressed her a little before they left . . . pressed her too much. She used to say she couldn't compete with a ghost. I suppose she meant my wife . . ."

I didn't try to answer him. It could have been that Vanessa had meant rather more than the vague image of Askew's young wife who had died even before she had reached Thirlbeck. But who knew now what she had meant?—the spirit of the little Spanish girl that I sensed here was to me a friend. But who could tell what Vanessa had experienced at Thirlbeck—who knew what ghosts, friendly or not, had waited in other rooms, other places? Or had she used that phrase only as an excuse so that the independence she had always fought for so fiercely would still remain hers. In my time of growing up, Vanessa had always been supremely her own woman; even that young, still-seeking woman must have known this was how it had to be for her. For this reason, probably, she and my father had parted. They both had been rare spirits, and neither could have long remained subordinate to another. Askew himself had probably given this same kind of heartbreak to some of the women who had loved him, and whom he had not married in all these years. In a sense, they had been three of a kind, Vanessa, my father, and Askew. He had said it in his own fashion . . . "At times it seemed as if we were the only three people alive in the world."

I rose from my chair and walked the few yards to the crumbling stone balustrade which separated this part of the garden from a lower terrace which led down to the lake. The surface of the water was golden-bright in the sun, the green marshy places near the crumbling jetty seemed deceptively firm. I watched the long grass blow about that tall thin slab of stone which recorded the Spanish Woman's name.

"There are all sorts of ghosts, aren't there? Do you think she thought at all about the Spanish Woman? Do you think that's why she called me Joanna?"

"Who knows what ghosts anyone sees? They're different for us all, aren't they? Joanna's a good name, even if it wasn't taken from the Spanish Woman. Vanessa was highly imaginative, but was she fanciful?"

"Fanciful? No, I don't think so." I turned back towards him, and as I did so the whole pack of hounds started a joyful rush along the cleared avenue between the trees. Even the older ones ran like puppies, but still at the head of the pack, and still keeping the younger ones in their place. It was only when they came close to us that I was aware again of the formidable size of them, the long tongues that lolled over the big teeth, those wise, wistful eyes that seemed to look at me from my own level. They fanned out equally between myself and Askew, the sea of moving tails reminding me of the long rushes that swayed down in the shallows of the tarn.

"Strange, isn't it, how they've taken to you?" Askew said, "They've always been very gentle, but all the hounds I can remember from my childhood—the ancestors of this lot—have always been a bit reserved. This lot seemed just like them, until you came along. I know it infuriated Tolson. He's always believed he had a quite invincible force of watchdogs whom no one could cajole or tempt away from their first duty. But if they were the sort who rolled over to have their tummies scratched, I do think for you they'd roll over like spaniels."

"I didn't think so the first time I saw them. I was terrified —frozen. If you hadn't come, I couldn't have moved from the car. And especially after what happened up there at the birch woods."

"At the birch woods?" Askew straightened himself and leaned forward. "What happened at the birch woods?"

"Nothing—that's it. I always feel foolish whenever I think of it. You remember we came over by Brantwick that first evening? Well, I thought I saw one of the dogs. In fact I was *certain* I saw him. He ran right in front of the car—seemed to leap over the wall and spring out of nowhere. I slammed on the brakes, and we went into a bad skid. Well, I got the car under control, and looked back and just saw the last of the dog going through the trees towards the larch plantation. I could hardly see him—it was dusk, and he was just a whitish shape. That wouldn't have been so strange except that Gerald didn't see him. He didn't *see* him, Lord Askew. He wondered why on earth I'd braked like that, and risked a crash. Then he pretended he had dozed off, but we both knew he was wide awake. And then when we got down to the house you said all the dogs were with you at that time—and there were no other wolf-hounds around." I reached out and patted a great head that was upthrust to my face. "It wasn't you, Thor, was it? A ghost of one of your ancestors, perhaps? They must have run all over this valley hunting deer at one time . . . I hadn't thought I was fanciful either, but now every time I see one of these, I remember that dog. Sort of . . . oh, well, like something out of a dream."

Askew reached out and jerked the edge of my sleeve. His face, to which some colour had seemed to return as we sat in the sun, and on which the tension had appeared to ease as we had talked of Vanessa, was once more grey and strained.

"Are you sure? Are you absolutely *certain* you saw a white hound up there at the birch copse?"

"Yes . . . but I tell you Gerald didn't see it. He saw nothing at all. I could have killed us that evening—"

Askew slumped back in the chair. "And I did," he said. The perspiration once again beaded his upper lip. I had to bend towards him to hear the next words. "I *did* kill my wife and my son. There—at the same place. The day I came back from Spain to take over at Thirlbeck—the day before my father's funeral. That white hound—straight in front of the car. Completely real to *me*—but it never existed. When I pulled myself out of the wreck and ran down to the house for help they told me that all the dogs had been there, in the house, at that time. No one believed me, you see. No one. I'd been drinking—yes, I'd had some drinks before I could face Thirlbeck again. But I wasn't drunk. *I wasn't!* I couldn't stand up in court and say that a phantom hound had caused the crash—but because of it my wife and little son were dead. I couldn't say that so many times in the Birketts' history strange things had happened at that place, there where the birches begin. There are tales that the Spanish Woman used to go to that point in her walks, waiting always for news from Spain. I wonder if one of the hounds was her companion . . ."

He brushed a hand that trembled across his mouth. "Well, that's no defence in a court of law, is it? You just can't say those things, and I *had* had a few drinks. But my wife—I never knew if she saw the hound, because she never spoke again. But you —*you* saw it. It is something that happens to Birketts—and sometimes to those who threaten them in some way. 'Who Seizes, Beware.' But you—you'd never been here in your life, never knew that Vanessa had." His hands tightly gripped the arms of the chair. "Jo—you're Vanessa's child. Are you *mine?*"

We looked at each other for a long time, face examining face, eyes suddenly familiar, which each recognised in the other. A terrible weakness struck me—and the beginning of joy.

"I wonder . . ." I said softly. There would be no way to prove it, but that didn't matter. I thought that we both knew. Then above us there was a faroff, but powerful thrust of wings. I thought I could almost feel the motion of the air as they moved. All the dogs and I raised our faces, and across the sun came the shape of an eagle—one of Nat Birkett's golden eagles in that soaring, swooping flight that was heart-stopping in its wild wonder and beauty. For an instant the shadow of the great wings seemed to cross us, but it couldn't have been; the bird was far distant, and leaving us farther behind with every second. I knew I wanted to cry out to it not to leave us; the moment of grace was precious, and soon gone.

I looked down at the man beside me. He had collapsed in the chair, and a stain of bright red blood had trickled from his mouth and already spread evilly across his shirt and jacket.

CHAPTER 8

I

We didn't wait for the ambulance or for Dr. Murray. Askew had vomited blood once more before we got him stretched on the back seat of Gerald's Daimler. The Condesa was driving, and I took the seat beside her, unbidden. Jeffries thrust a pile of towels into my arms, and I knelt on the seat and took the soiled ones away as they were used. The elegant leather upholstery was stained with the bright red blood, and there was blood on the grey carpet. Tolson had been on the telephone almost at the moment I had reached the house, calling the hospital to tell them that Askew was on the way, calling about to try to locate Dr. Murray on his rounds. Gerald stayed behind. "I might be of more use here. I'll follow in a bit, Jo. Take care of him. God, how awful . . ."

I didn't want Gerald to look at Askew any longer. His own face had taken on that terrible look of strain and fear I had remembered from the night I had found him half fallen from his bed.

Tolson had telephoned ahead to the South Lodge, and the gates stood open. Jessica's mother was there, giving a half-fearful salute as we went through. The Condesa drove quickly, and yet with great skill, seeing, almost before they appeared, bumps in the road, avoiding them, speeding up on the straight, smooth stretches. At each junction she managed to get us through without stopping—even at the outskirts of Kesmere, where the traffic had begun to thicken with holiday crowds. The delicate tap on the horn, and something that was an inspired blend between a command, and a message of pleading urgency in her signals—and perhaps most of all the anguish of her face—got us round the lorries, and the caravans, and the usually selfish driver. In the narrow streets of Kesmere, at one bottleneck, I left my seat and went to the head of the line of traffic; I didn't know what gave me the courage to stand there at the junction and wave the Condesa on against the traffic, holding up the other lane myself. At one set of traffic lights we waited three minutes; kneeling on the front seat and bending towards him, I saw Askew's body give a convulsive shudder, and there was more blood.

"What . . . ?" I whispered to the Condesa. "What is happening to him?"

Her reply was almost savage. "You saw it happen to him before. But not like this. He has been warned it could happen. The duodenal ulcer. Too much drink, too much smoking—the wrong food, or not enough food. And now the massive haemorrhage. The upset of these last days . . . that Tolson man—I could kill him! Why not to leave well enough alone? Why not to do what Roberto had instructed him? Pray God Roberto does not lose too much blood before they can help him . . ."

We went to the emergency entrance of the hospital, and they were waiting for us. I knew it angered the Condesa to see Askew suffer the indignity of having to be handled as he was to get him onto the trolley, but she said nothing. She simply took his hand as they wheeled him inside. I stayed and folded the towels and put them in the trunk. Then I drove the car to a place in the parking lot.

From the emergency entrance they directed me down a long corridor I remembered from the night Gerald had been admitted in this same fashion; then another glass corridor connected to a smaller wing of the main building. Here, on a long seat, was the Condesa. Someone, Jeffries perhaps, had put her needlework bag into the car. She was tugging at the strap in anguish, and then reached into its depths to find cigarettes. She had none, and snatched, without thanks, at the packet I offered. I handed over the keys of the Daimler.

"What are they doing?"

"He has lost a lot of blood. They must make a transfusion." Her tone was sharp, almost angry. She looked around at the plain, pale green walls with a kind of loathing. "He is very ill, they say. In shock . . . God, why can't they *do* something? He's in that room there." Then suddenly she seemed to become more aware of me as a person, and her anger and fear transferred itself to me. "*You* don't have to stay. What use for the two of us to be here?" In her stress her English was not quite as flawless as before, and her slight accent became stronger. Her face too had altered, the high Spanish cheekbones more pronounced, her warm olive skin now tinted to sallowness. There was something now much more elemental in her than I had ever glimpsed before. The sheen of sophistication had slipped from her. The sense of the drama of life and death that lies close to the surface in every Spaniard was breaking through. She could not accept the seeming inactivity behind the closed door.

"Let me wait a little, please. I would like to take back some news to Gerald. I would like to know . . ."

"To know!" She flung her hands wide. "They tell you nothing. He is closed in there, and I cannot see him!"

"Give them time. They have a lot of work to do—" A sister in her starched apron came sweeping down the corridor, barely glanced at us, and went into the room where Askew lay. The Condesa regarded her retreating back with hatred. "You see! You English . . . ! Roberto is vomiting up his lifeblood, and no one will tell me anything. They just come and go in their white coats."

As she spoke a young man a doctor, I guessed—came out of Askew's room with a covered kidney-shaped vessel in his hand. The Condesa jumped to her feet. "Please, you will tell me—"

"Not now, madame. I'll come and talk to you when I have time." He half ran along the corridor. The sister came out of

Askew's room, and for a second I had a glimpse of another sister working there with two nurses. I couldn't see Askew, but I saw the sphygmomanometer being used. Then one of the young nurses came out with Askew's clothing in her arms.

Once more the Condesa jumped to her feet. "Give me those." Her usually soft voice was gratingly harsh. She snatched the clothes from the girl as if the bloodstained bundle were precious and personal, not to be touched by other hands. We waited for long minutes after that, and then the young doctor came back again, took no notice of us, and went into Askew's room. He reappeared again almost at once. In the doorway he encountered an older doctor who had come down the corridor at that sort of flying march that seems to herald an emergency in a hospital.

"Tough one, sir," the young man said. "Just about as tough as they come." He glanced over at the Condesa and his voice dropped. We couldn't hear the next words. The older man disappeared into Askew's room, the young man went to a room almost opposite us whose door stood open, an office of some sort, with a desk, files, a telephone. Probably the sister's office, I thought. At once he was on the telephone. As eagerly as the Condesa I strained to hear his words. The call was to a hospital in Penrith.

". . . done the group and cross-match. Unless I've lost my mind it's . . . Yes, I know. Impossible. Well, you've got a list of donors, haven't you? All right . . . I'll hang on. But for God's sake hurry." There followed long minutes, and I saw the Condesa once again tearing at the handle of her bag as if she might shred it. The doctor tapped his pen on the blotter. He seemed for the moment to have forgotten us. Then his voice again. "No one? No one at all? Well, damn—to be expected, I suppose. I'll try Carlisle. Thanks."

He put through another call. The first sentences were blurred. Then I heard him clearly as his voice rose in frustration. "Yes . . . that's what I said. ABRHDU. Yes—ABRHDU. All right, so I know it's as rare as hen's teeth! *Have you got a donor?* We've got a bloke here who's vomiting it up as if he can't get rid of it fast enough. Well, look, will you? I'll hold on." During the time he waited I looked down at my own hands and they were as tense as the Condesa's. We heard the doctor's voice again. "Have you? Good. On the telephone? Just pray he's not on holiday, or out at the pub, or something. How long do you think? I don't think *we've* got much time unless we can control the haemorrhaging. Yes, I'm sure. While I'm waiting I'll do the tests again, but I'm *sure*. This group's so damn rare I double-checked. *ABRHDU*. Make it as fast as you can, will you? Alert the police and they'll give you an escort—fine on the Motorway, but these bloody mountain roads . . . well, do your best. Thanks . . ."

He hung up, and for a moment that young body in its stiff white coat sagged. Then the rap of the pen on the blotter was violent. "Damn!"

It was as if his last expletive suddenly had broken through my own numbed reflexes. The letters that had been spelled out so many times translated themselves into the typed symbols on a card I carried with me always. I got up and went to the doorway. "You said *ABRhDu?* That was what you said?"

He turned with weary impatience. "Look, I'm sorry, we are busy. I'll explain it all to you later . . ."

"You need a blood donor of that group." I was shuffling the few credit cards I had in my wallet—the wallet that now, like everything else I had, seemed to live in the pockets of the anorak instead of a handbag. "Here's my donor's card. I'm registered with St. Giles's in London."

He sprang to his feet and grabbed the piece of pasteboard from me. "God Almighty . . . !" Then he looked at me sharply. "You related to this . . . to Lord Askew?"

I looked at him very directly, and then shook my head. "No—just coincidence that I'm here."

"God Almighty . . ." he said again, and now his voice was like a whisper. "You're sure about this? I mean absolutely *sure?*"

I was getting angry. "As sure as St. Giles's is. I've been called three times for emergencies. I give blood routinely a few times a year. If you doubt *them* . . ."

He let out a sort of whistle. "No, I don't doubt them. Look, I'll just have to do my own group and cross-match on you. It won't take long. I just can't take the chance of a mistake. You know what happens if you're an incompatible donor?"

"Yes, I know. It will be rejected."

"He'll destroy the transfused blood, and there'd be a severe reaction. He could die. O.K. Well, let's get going."

He took the routine blood sample in a room off in another wing. "O.K. Go back to where you were, and when I've checked it, I'll be along. Don't leave the hospital . . . O.K. I'm sorry. One gets so used to people being stupid about these things. General health O.K.? Nothing I should know about? I haven't got time to test for syphilis. How long since you donated blood at St. Giles's?"

"A few weeks."

"O.K. I'll take their word for it."

When I got back to the seat beside the Condesa her angry, hurtful hand gripped my arm. "What is happening? What have you to do with him?"

I explained as well as I could; I told her about the years of donating blood in London. She didn't believe it. "Why can't I give him *my* blood? I'd give him all of it. *All!*"

"He can't take it, Condesa. He's of a very rare blood group. It's useless to him. Rejection . . ."

"*Rejection!*" Her voice sunk away on a low wail, the sound of ancient mourning and grief. She bent her head, but she did not weep.

The young doctor came back; there was a few moments' delay while he talked with the older man in Askew's room. Then he came back to the door and beckoned me.

Askew's bed was now surrounded by screens, but I could see the oxygen tank, the mask being used. It would normally have been a small ward for two people. The other bed was empty. The older doctor nodded to me.

"You know all about the procedure. I understand you donate blood regularly." I nodded. I peeled off the anorak again, rolled up my sleeve, kicked off my shoes, and lay down on the empty bed. I automatically clenched my fist to give them the vein sharp and clear, and felt the prick of the needle. The tubing was attached to the bottle and the suction set going.

After that it was a matter of waiting, and trying to relax my muscles deliberately, not to strain too hard to hear what was going on at the screened-off bed. The voices were low. "Morphine . . . saline drip . . . venous tourniquet." A half-litre bottle was taken from me. They put the next in place. It all seemed to take a long time.

I had never gone beyond this point before. I didn't care. The sounds from a few feet away told me Askew still continued to vomit up blood. The bottle of my own blood was now suspended on a stand above him; I continued to pump more blood into the waiting vessel next to my bed. The voices at the other bed seemed lower. "One hundred and forty . . ." Was that the pulse? I turned my head, and I saw the blood pressure was being monitored constantly. "Sixty," the sister said.

People came and went. For a few seconds I heard the Condesa's voice in the corridor, angry, frantic. They closed the door. Time passed me. I didn't know time any more. There was a blankness, a kind of coldness creeping over me. The second half-litre bottle was taken away. Someone came over to me—took temperature, blood pressure, pulse.

"Are you able for some more?" Now I recognised a voice that I knew—though in the dizziness that seized me his face was a blur. I struggled to remember the name, but couldn't—it was the man who had taken care of Gerald that night when I had waited in the same place.

"For God's sake," I said, "go on. I'm all right."

I watched the blood mount in the third bottle they attached to me. It was getting much colder. The shapes began to fade before me. And through it came the voices and the movements from around the next bed. The bottle was almost full, and they were taking it away, to suspend on the stand above the other bed. I seemed now to be struggling for breath; it was very cold. The needle and tube connecting me to the receiving bottle was disconnected. Another blanket was pulled over me. I was only dimly aware that someone was pulling at my tights, and I struggled and was hurt unnecessarily. The needle bit deep into my buttock.

I tried to cry out, to beg, but my voice came only as a whisper through the cold and the faintness. "Go on! For God's sake, go on! I've got more blood . . ."

The voice I recognised said gently in my ear, "You've got no more to give. If we take more now, you'll die. Go to sleep now. You've done your best."

I found the strength to stretch out a hand and pull at his sleeve. "But if he doesn't have more *he'll* die . . ."

The face moved away. Before the drowsiness took possession of me utterly, before the last remnant of spirit I had to fight the drug departed, I heard the soft, measured tone from the other bed. "Blood pressure fifty, Doctor."

He was going to die. I wondered, through his shock and weakness, while those doctors had battled for his life with my blood, had he been aware of my presence in the room. I supposed the instant of recognition had come when I had confessed the vision of the phantom white hound which had greeted my arrival at Thirlbeck, and he had matched that with his own experience all those years ago. I realised, as I faded towards unconsciousness, that the real gift I had given him was not just the chance of life, but the release from the guilt he had carried through those years for the death of his wife and son. Two Birketts, at least, had seen that sight. The release, and the shock of recognition that Vanessa's child was also his, had started the fatal haemorrhage. The proof, the bond of this same rare blood group we both were cursed with, lay in the bottle still suspended above his bed. I hoped he had known it was my blood, and that I had tried to give it back to him.

They seemed to have forgotten my presence. The screen had been moved aside to let them work more freely. I saw his face between those white-coated bodies. It was colourless, and very still, the lips blue-tinged, as if he no longer responded to their feverish efforts for him. The coldness that must have been in his body was in mine also, but it was for him a fatal coldness. "Pressure forty-seven." Time passed, and I held out against the effects of the drug, somehow believing that while I kept my senses, he would keep his life. Then that activity seemed to cease around his bed. The doctors stepped back, and the nurses took over. They remembered me, and saw that my eyes were still open. They replaced the screens, and the last thing I saw was the empty bottle being unhooked from the stand.

He was dead. My father, Robert Birkett, eighteenth Earl of Askew, was dead. And all the blood my body had been able to give to him had not been enough to keep him alive. I closed my eyes.

II

I woke in a room by myself, a room with a single bed, and a window that looked out towards the car park. Almost at once a nurse came, and there was the routine of temperature and pulse, blood pressure. She wrote something on a chart, and I noticed that the shadows were growing longer outside. It must now be late afternoon. The nurse went, and the sister came at once.

"How are you feeling?" It wasn't a social inquiry.

"All right. Can I go now?"

"No, of course you can't. You don't seem to realise—you've given up just about as much blood as anyone can and still be alive. You've got to rest, and wait for it to make up a bit. You can probably leave here tomorrow, but it'll take weeks before you're quite fit again. We've been trying to locate that donor in Carlisle but he's a sales representative who travels around this area, and his wife isn't quite sure which town he's in today. You really should have a transfusion. Not so easy with your blood group, as you know."

I turned my head on the pillow. "But it didn't save him, did it? He's dead."

"I'm sorry—yes. He just kept haemorrhaging as fast as we gave it to him. You mustn't fret—you did more than anyone could expect."

"I'd like to go," I said.

"You can't go. You don't seem to realise. You've had treatment for severe shock—oxygen, a dextran infusion, hypocortisone. If you tried to get up you'd probably faint. Give it twenty-four hours, Miss Roswell. We'll see how you're going then. Perhaps we'll have located the donor by then . . ."

I didn't answer her. I just lay there, and thought about my father—the father I had discovered in the last hours of his life, and who had discovered me. And I also thought of the other man who had made himself into my father in the hours and weeks after Vanessa had died—the man in his remote Mexican retreat who had given to me a most precious gift of intimacy, knowing, as he must have done, that I was not his child. He had gathered me to himself, as he had gathered all that huge Mexican family, knowing my need. Both men had loved Vanessa, but she and Jonathan had known whose child I was. I wondered at her own courage and independence that she had never revealed this to Askew, and I marvelled at the generosity of Jonathan Roswell that he had let me, in name, and finally in fact also, be known as his child. I knew quite surely what Askew would have wanted to do if he had known Vanessa was bearing his child, and she had known, with equal sureness, that it would have been a useless and empty thing. If they had married, they would not have remained long together. She had chosen the hardest, and the best way. And I knew also quite surely that she would have told all this to Jonathan Roswell. I now read things in his attitude which I had never seen before —his gentle protectiveness, the assumption that if we were lucky we would be friends—and we had become friends. I must have seemed to him like one of those Mexican *niñas*—only blonde and grown-up, and now, as I thought of it, with the colouring, if not the face, of Robert Birkett.

So I had had, in the space of a few weeks, two fathers. And I thought, before my eyes closed again in sleep, that few people could have had that experience and been so lucky as to have made friends of both of them.

* * *

A dim light flicked on in the growing dusk of that small room. The sister's voice. "Lord Askew is here to see you, Miss Roswell."

308

I struggled half-upright on my elbows. "Lord Askew! Lord Askew is dead!"

And then Nat's voice. "Hush, Jo. Things change, you know. They will insist on these things . . ." The sister was gone, and he was bending over me. "You all right, Jo? I wanted to come earlier, but they said you had to rest."

I looked up at him; he seemed different, and for a while I couldn't make out why. Then I realised I hadn't seen him dressed in a suit before. "Nat, you know all about it?"

He pulled a chair over close to me. "I've talked with Gerald Stanton. I knew about the blood transfusion—the rare blood group. Not really a coincidence, is it, Jo? Stanton told me about your mother having been at Thirlbeck. You're part of the family now, Jo. You and I are cousins sixteen times removed, or something stupid like that. Only I haven't got the right kind of blood to give you. It's strongly hereditary, a blood group, they tell me, but only in close relations. Sixteen times removed is too far. Dear Jo, I'd give it all to you—the way you tried to give it to him—but it isn't the right kind." His roughened hand lay on mine. "Jo, you look so pale. Are you all right?"

"Yes, I'm all right. But I'm sorry about—about him. I wanted him to live. I think he wanted to live, Nat. He was going to do things . . . we were talking about it . . . He could have done so much for Thirlbeck—for you. He said he needed to live seven years to make the proper sort of trust fund, but he didn't live seven hours beyond that. He guessed about me—before the blood thing came out. He knew, and I think he was glad. It might have helped him to know he had a child. He seemed so lonely . . . and I was in the room when he died."

"Hush, Jo . . . hush. You're tiring yourself."

"There was so much to do. He would have made himself stay at Thirlbeck, and I could have helped him. Well, it's over now."

The pressure on my hand increased. "You've talked too much. We'll find that donor, Jo, and you'll have a transfusion. There must be some in a blood bank somewhere—surely in London. They could send it up."

"But I'm not in danger, Nat. Not the way he was. The blood replaces itself in time. You have to keep the emergency supplies for people who have accidents and burns—the ones who are bleeding. I'll be all right." Then I fingered the dark material of his jacket. "Why are you dressed like that, Nat? You look so strange."

He shook his head. "I never have liked suits. But well . . . there are times when you feel you have to wear them. They're . . . Jo, they're moving his body from here to the church in Kesmere this evening. I have to go. The Tolsons are going. It's been hard on them. It was on the six-o'clock news on the radio. Because of him being a V.C., and all that. All the stories will start up again . . . poor devil. Well, he's out of it now."

"Yes . . . he's out of it. And if he'd been given a chance he might have wanted to stay in it. I think he was just beginning to want it, Nat."

"Jo, don't distress yourself. He hasn't known any real peace or sense of accomplishment all his life. Could he have started now—feeling as he did about Thirlbeck? It might have been just another charade for him to play."

"He was going to try, Nat. He was going to try to make things as right as he could for you. Sometime I'll tell you—sometime I'll tell you everything that happened today."

He smiled. "I'd like to hear it. Yes, I would. I don't know what sort of mess I've inherited. There are shocks enough, even if you know what's coming. What I didn't expect was the story Gerald Stanton told me, about what your mother and Tolson had been doing. The strange thing was that Askew had been here all these weeks, and not found out about the land still being his. If he'd behaved like an ordinary man—gone about a bit, talked to people, he pretty soon would have found out that he was still a big landowner. But once he got back here, he settled into the privacy of Thirlbeck just like his father. It must have been a wretched time for Tolson—wondering just which way Askew would find out that he still owned this farm and that farm, places he must have supposed were sold years ago." He shrugged. "Well, suddenly today *I've* become the landlord, and with a pile of death duties to find, somehow. And young Thomas there is now Viscount Birkett. It's crazy, isn't it—this hereditary system? The only thing Thomas asked me was did we *have* to go and live in Thirlbeck, and I said no, we *didn't!* That helped him. But Tolson, of course, has swept them up into that great maw of the family. Young Thomas is now heir to Thirlbeck. And you, Jo—well, for Tolson you're something very special. You're Robert Birkett's own child, even if the rest of the world doesn't know it. If there was justice—which there isn't—you'd be inheriting all the estate which isn't entailed . . ."

He was quiet a moment, staring into the growing dusk outside. Then in the stillness we heard the Kesmere church clock striking. Nat got to his feet. "I'll have to go, Jo. We're keeping it all as quiet and simple as possible. No one but myself and the Tolsons know that he's being taken to the Kesmere church this evening. The vicar's been very helpful. He knows Askew hated publicity all his life. A private man should be buried in a private way, he says. Of course we're bringing Askew back for burial in the private ground at Thirlbeck, but the service tomorrow has to be in Kesmere. No hope of keeping the public out of *that*. It's their church, after all . . ."

He was scribbling something on a paper. "This is a phone number. The telephone company's been ruddy marvellous. They've rigged up a new line and a new number so that we can call in and out of Thirlbeck without using the old number. Even the old one was unlisted—trust Tolson for that—but still a few people had it, and more would find a way of getting it. The newspapers have started ringing. They've even started ringing my house. Questions about La Española. You'll see some crazy stories in tomorrow's papers, stories about the wretched curse. A man can't die a natural death but they'll make something of it. I hope to God no one on the staff here remembers a Roswell renting the North Lodge, or, if they do, they keep their mouths shut about who was the blood donor. The papers would have a field day. Oh, hell—why *now!* Why just now?"

"Why not now?"

"Because we haven't had a chance. I thought when you took off that morning, in such a rush, for London, that you were running away from me. Stanton told me about the bowl, and all that. Well . . . this isn't the place to talk, and I've got to go back to Thirlbeck to collect the boys. Stanton says he'll come to see you when it's over, later this evening."

"No—don't let him! He shouldn't come here, Nat—he mustn't. Nat, take care of him. I need him now. I've lost— I've lost enough."

"Yes, Jo—I'll take care of him."

As he reached the door I called to him: "Nat, come back and take me home—take me back to Thirlbeck. I don't want to stay here."

"Tomorrow, Jo. Tomorrow you'll be stronger. They might have found the donor by then."

He was gone. The church clock struck another quarter-hour. Tears of frustration and weakness brimmed in my eyes.

III

They brought me clear soup and toast, and a boiled egg. I ate some of it, and then got out of bed. I found I could walk quite steadily, with only a sense of woodenness in my legs, and a slight blurring of vision. I found my clothes hanging in a cupboard and dressed. It seemed to take a long time to dress. Then I went to the door and opened it. I was in a part of the hospital I didn't remember seeing before. A young nurse was standing at a table built against the wall, writing. She looked up in surprise.

"Oh, you're up! I don't think . . ."

"Please, I'd like to go. I'm perfectly well. I wonder if there's some way I can get a taxi to Thirlbeck? I want to go back."

"I'm sorry, Miss Roswell. I don't think you should go—and I haven't the authority to let you go. I'll have to call one of the doctors."

"I'd like to discharge myself. I don't need to see a doctor for that."

"Sister's off duty . . . if you could wait . . ."

It took some insistence and another nurse came along and tried to persuade me to go back to bed. In time they produced the proper discharge form, and I signed it. Then I asked the same question as before. "Is there a taxi service I could call to get back to Thirlbeck?"

The younger of the two nurses glanced hesitantly at the other, then spoke to me. "I'm going off duty in ten minutes. I live in that direction. It wouldn't be any trouble to take you on. I have a car . . ."

I thanked her, and waited. I fingered the keys to the North and South Lodges of Thirlbeck, still in the pocket of my anorak. I seemed to need to get within those gates. I thought of the quiet there, the safety from questions which lay behind those gates.

The young nurse came, hardly recognisable out of uniform, her long hair falling freely down her back. Her car was a Mini, just a little older than mine. "It's good of you," I said. "I hope there won't be trouble for you."

"Oh, no—I don't think so. All one can say is that the sooner you're back in bed the better, and since you were determined to go . . . You're sure you'll take proper care? Have some hot tea as soon as you get there, and see that there's plenty of hot-water bottles . . ."

It was all she said until we reached the gates of the South Lodge. "What do I do? Blow the horn?"

I gave her the key. "I don't think anyone will be there. They've all gone . . . Lord Askew's body was being taken to the church this evening. They wanted to do it as quietly as possible."

She used the key, drove through, and as carefully closed the gates again, but leaving them unlocked for her return. "I wouldn't care to be locked in." She drove on slowly. "I'd better confess I've always wanted to come in here," she said. "You know how it is—when you're kept out of a place you always want to see what's behind the walls. Once my father and I climbed Great Birkeld up to the ridge. That was the only time I've ever seen into this valley—we could see the house through glasses. A sort of fairy-tale place, I thought. And then the mist came down. It was rather rough getting back down again. We've never climbed that high since." She added: "The odd thing is that Lord Askew is our landlord. We've never seen him." We were driving through the park now; it was getting too dark to see the cattle except where the headlights struck them; the sheep were grey masses in the gathering darkness beneath the trees. We were coming close to the house, where the maze of rhododendrons began. The pace became slower, and I felt an impatience rise in me.

"It's all right, isn't it?" the girl said. "I mean—there will be *someone* here?"

"It doesn't matter if there isn't."

"You mean you don't mind being alone in that house? What about the dogs? I hear they're very fierce . . ."

I stifled the first words that came. She was only expressing what I had felt that first time I had approached Thirlbeck. "It will be all right," I said. "If there's no one there, there soon will be. Don't worry about the dogs. They know me."

A single light burned above the front steps. I was about to direct the girl to the back door, suddenly realising that I, in fact, didn't have a key to the house itself. I didn't know what I would do now. I knew I wouldn't be able to persuade her to leave me sitting on the back-door step. I began to feel, also, that I needed that hot cup of tea.

Unexpectedly the front door opened. I should have known that Tolson would not leave the house unattended. The dogs streamed down the steps, their tails wagging a silent welcome. I felt the girl stiffen in the seat beside me. "God!—they're monsters!" and then, "Oh, look—who's that?"

For an instant she seemed hardly different from the first time I had seen her—the slender figure in silhouette against the lighted hall, her face shadowed as it had been then, the fall of thick, shining hair. But now she was wearing pants and a jacket, and there was no sense of languor in her stance.

"She—she is a friend of Lord Askew's. The one who died," I remembered to add. "She's been staying here." The dogs were all around the car, and the girl didn't want to move. I started to get out, and the weakness attacked my knees. The girl rolled down the window and called to the Condesa. "We need some help."

The Condesa came down to the car. "I didn't know it was

you," she said. "I had to be careful. Tolson told me to be very careful." She was helping me out, her hands surprisingly gentle after the savagery of that morning. She had an almost unnatural calm, as if she were deliberately imposing it upon herself. The girl took courage from the silence and friendliness of the dogs, and came around to help me. I was grateful for the support on each side. I hadn't imagined my legs would feel like this. The girl was talking to the Condesa. "She insisted on discharging herself from the hospital. She should go to bed at once. Hot tea and hot-water bottles . . ." We had reached the top of the steps and entered the hall, and the girl's voice faded. I could feel her check, as the great extent of the hall and the staircase was revealed. And once again I was reminded of how it had first struck me. The girl found her voice at last. "Would you . . . would you like me to help? I'm a nurse—from the hospital. I could at least see her to bed. Or make tea—or something."

I expected the Condesa to accept. I didn't think she would relish the role of nurse, the carrier of tray and hot-water bottles. But she shook her head. "You are most kind. Thank you. But I'm sure I shall manage. The others will be back soon. I did not go." She addressed herself to me now. "You understand that I could not go to—to *that*."

I felt ashamed. In my own grieving I had not thought too much of hers. "I'll go then," the girl said, in a rather flat, small voice. She was disappointed; she had wanted to stay, to see more. "If you'd just see that the dogs . . . ?"

"Of course," I said. I sat on a chair, and the dogs crowded about me. "They *do* know you, don't they?" the girl said. Then she gave a last long careful look about the hall. "I'll go then," she repeated, and began to walk slowly towards the door. The Condesa was there before her, the door already open, as if she were impatient for her to be gone. "Can she have brandy?" she asked the girl.

"I'm not really sure," the girl replied. "She's over the worst of the shock now—but giving alcohol is always chancy. Better not, perhaps. If you could get her to eat something . . . she's very weak." She paused at the doorway, and looked back at me. "Well—I hope you feel better soon. Good-bye."

I raised my hand to her. "Thank you—thank you very much." Even as she walked down the steps the Condesa had closed the doors behind her and begun thrusting the bolts home. I thought at least she might have waited until the girl had reached the car. I had a sudden wish that the girl had not gone. I wished I had asked her to stay, though I didn't know why. The aloofness of the Condesa was disconcerting. I didn't want her to help me; the house was so silent as the sound of the Mini faded in the distance. Comfort came from the rough heads of the dogs as I laid my hands on them.

The Condesa came towards me briskly. "I'll help you up the stairs, and then I think some brandy—" She cut me short as I began to protest. "Ah, what do *they* know? At that hospital they are all fools. Once you are in bed, it will be all right . . ."

I could feel the athletic strength of her body as she helped me rise; I wondered why I ever thought her slenderness denoted weakness, when she could hold a horse with such ease, and handle a gun, manage a powerful car. As we mounted the stairs I thought of something else. I had seen her handbag on a chair in the hall, and the jacket she was wearing was leather, as if she were dressed for travel. I was conscious of the smell of her perfume, and all at once I was also conscious that now she was a woman very much alone.

I said, "Will you stay—I mean, will you stay for the funeral?" Perhaps it was the wrong thing to say, but she seemed on the point of departure.

"Roberto is dead," she said flatly. "I have no need to take part in his burial. For me, he is dead, and I am no longer part of his life."

"I tried . . ." I began.

She cut me short. "I know you tried. The grief for me is that I was not permitted to try." Then the calm of her voice broke. "If we had been elsewhere—if we had been in London or Rome or Paris, Roberto would have lived. I know it! There would have been better people, better treatment."

"I don't think so," I answered. "No matter what they had

done—and they did try awfully hard. He just couldn't keep the blood they were transfusing—he was haemorrhaging as fast as they gave it to him. His heart may have given out in the end . . ."

"If they could have found that other donor. The fools—they did not try hard enough." Then she cried out in fury, as one of the dogs pressed too close. "Oh, damn these dogs! I have stood them for Roberto's sake, but to me they are damnable. Ugly brutes . . . why must they always be in the way?—like having horses in the house! I have been trying to get into the study to use the telephone to make plane reservations, and they stand there, and will not let me pass. Pests—yes, pests, they are!"

I realised that I felt sorry for her, a new experience, and that some jealousy had crept into her attitude towards me, which until now had been one of indifference. I wondered if she suspected that my relationship with Askew had gone closer than the coincidence of the same blood group. She was much more alone than I. I had never imagined ever feeling sorry for this silken creature, this aristocrat bred to horses and guns, and yet preserving her fine-boned wrists and ankles.

"I think . . ." I didn't want to admit that I had ever explored the house so fully. "I think there's a telephone extension in Lord Askew's room."

"Yes . . . so there is." Her tone was curiously flat, as if that information was not what she sought. "But still those dogs . . . they follow one everywhere. Why do they do it?" Her tone became harshly nervous.

So I turned on the stairs and said gently to the dogs, "Stay! Thor . . . Ulf . . . Oden. Stay!" They halted, and the pleasured wagging of their tails was stilled. I felt sorry I had had to say it—their presence gave me comfort. But the Condesa was trying, in her fashion, to be kind, and the dogs annoyed her. So I left them behind. "I hope they'll just stay there," I said, "and then they won't bother you."

"I hope so."

We reached the Spanish Woman's room. I slumped into the chair by the fire. I saw that since the time when the fires had burned out as I slept after that late return to Thirlbeck, and the conversation with Tolson—God, had it only been that morning?—someone had been in and cleared the ashes, and relaid the kindling and the wood. They were ready for a match to be set, but it didn't seem to occur to the Condesa to do that. I thought that all her life someone else had been doing such things for her. I also thought that I should have been capable of doing it for myself, but it seemed too much trouble. I didn't want to move.

"You'll be all right?" she was saying. "You have the nightgown and the robe? You should get undressed and into bed. I shall bring brandy." She didn't offer to get these things for me. She wasn't the kind of person to handle other people's clothing —and yet I recalled how she had snatched Askew's clothes from the nurse that morning. I didn't have the strength then to ask her what had become of the miniature which had been in his pocket, or to argue for its possession. I would wait until she returned with the brandy.

"Yes . . . I can manage. Thank you."

She was gone, and I was alone, wishing more than ever that I had asked the nurse to stay. It was easier for the Condesa to bring brandy than to fuss with tea and hot-water bottles. I wondered how long it would be before Tolson came back. I wished I had a cigarette, I wished the fire were lighted. I saw matches on the rim of the candle stick, but it was too much of an effort to bend down to the fire. I stood up at last and went to the cupboard where my clothes hung. I took off the anorak, and immediately shivered in the chill of the room. I hung it up carefully—carefully because all of my movements seemed to require great care and precision. I was like a person drunk, knowing that each action had to be performed with great exactitude and concentration or the whole focus would slip into a blurred fog. I was reaching for my nightgown, hanging on one of the heavy oak pegs on the back wall of the cupboard when the focus seemed momentarily to desert me. I was falling, and I grabbed at the peg as a support. I hung there, swaying, fighting off the blackness that threatened. The earth itself had seemed to move with me; I had slipped sideways, and the strain on my arms became too much. I felt myself falling, and the oak peg itself seemed to have gone, and the very back of the cupboard was no longer there to support my body as I slipped down. I fell into blackness in a tangle of my own clothes which I had wrenched from their hangers. I fell into blackness and the smell of ancient dust.

I don't know how long the blackness remained—it could have been minutes, or only seconds. I could open my eyes, and I started to disentangle myself from the clothes that had come down with my fall. The faint light from the bedside lamp did not reach into this space—a new space, I was beginning to realise, not part of the hanging cupboard, but an extension of it. I got to my hands and knees. Exploring, groping, my fingers encountered the feel of rough bricks and crumbling mortar. The dust on the floor where I knelt was a thick, muffling sheet. The smell of the ages was in this recess. I crawled backwards out of the space, and pulled myself to my feet by holding onto the door of the cupboard.

I rested with both hands on the mantelshelf for a few minutes. The fall had knocked the breath out of me, and I waited for a while to recover it. My hand still trembled violently as I struggled to light the candle on the mantelshelf.

I went inside again, kicking aside the clothes that had fallen. I stood there with the candle burning steadily in that draughtless space, and I saw what had survived of the Spanish Woman for almost four hundred years.

That short body, now a skeleton, had been laid with due reverence, on a carved oak chest. It was dressed in a gown of yellow silk which might once have been white, as might the yellow lace of the ruff, and the lace of the cap that was tied about that narrow little skull. The hair held in place by the cap was black. The gloved skeletal fingers had been intertwined about an elaborately jeweled crucifix. A heavy signet ring had been placed over one of the gloved fingers. The gloves were embroidered with silk and seed pearls, as were the little slippers. I put out one finger cautiously, afraid that the glove might crumble to dust at my touch; it remained intact. I traced the initials on the ring. *J.F.C. Juana Fernández de Córdoba.*

319

I felt no horror at what I saw. That little face might once have been beautiful; all I saw was the skull with small, unde-cayed teeth exposed. She had only been seventeen, they said. Someone—and no one would ever know who—had recovered her body and somehow managed to bring it back here, dress-ing her in what might have been her bridal gown, giving her her crucifix, laying her in an attitude of repose. I didn't doubt that in the oak chest on which she lay were some of the posses-sions which she had brought with her on that long journey from Spain, other gowns and slippers, the baby clothes she would have been stitching for her unborn child. I stood and wondered why she had been brought here, and laid in this place. Had there been more Catholic sympathisers in this place than any-one had known of, or guessed?—those too frightened to appear openly to befriend the widowed second Countess of Askew, but roused to pity for that unburied body? Perhaps they had brought her to this place with the thought of eventual burial, and the chance had never come. Secret places such as this were no novelty in a house built in such a period of history. Had this been intended as one of their priest's holes? Had indeed the first Earl remained secretly Catholic, and heard Mass, and been prepared to give shelter and succour to any hunted man who fled and defied Protestantism? I wondered if it were even possible that her supposed murderer, the third Earl, had had her body laid here—he too fearful of giving a Catholic a grave in the family burial ground, at that time when the Birketts must have been under the cloud of Elizabeth's displeasure. When the tarn had finally given back her body, had he ordered it brought here secretly, her possessions gathered about her, and the door locked against the world until the Spanish Woman would be finally forgotten? But who, then, had dressed her this way, with tenderness and compassion?

I thought of the tiny portrait of the third Countess, the woman Vanessa so much resembled, and hoped that it was she who had possessed the courage and spirit to defy what orders her husband might have given, and instead of a body hastily bundled in a cloak or blanket, had felt pity for this friendless soul in death, and dressed her according to her station, with the insignia of her family and rank. What had been the ultimate plan for this body we might never know; the oak chest might give back no secrets of whom the Spanish Woman's friends had been—to leave written evidence itself was dangerous. If someone had intended eventually to bury this body with appropriate ceremony the chance had never come, and the secret of the Spanish Woman's hiding place had died. But her spirit had spoken strongly and with great force over the centuries to some of the people who had inhabited this house, this room, myself among them. *"When I am dead, of your charity, offer nine Masses for my soul . . ."* I remembered that this day the first of the nine Masses had been offered. If Juana's Book of Hours had lain here instead of forgotten among the other manuscripts of the period, I would never have known of that pathetic, fearful, last request.

I raised the candle higher and looked around the little chamber. The rough brick my hand had encountered was probably the brick of a chimney flue—part of the huge one that led up from the fireplace in the great hall below, and also served the fireplace here in the Spanish Woman's room. It was very dry; the chamber itself was dry, which could have accounted for the state of preservation of the clothes of the Spanish Woman. Just the right amount of heat had reached this chamber to offset the dampness that would have caused those silken and lace garments to rot. If she had lain in any other chamber, not near a flue which had been in constant use, there might have been nothing to identify her except the jeweled crucifix and the monogrammed ring.

A rush of excitement seemed to give me strength once more. I held the candle higher and saw the only other thing the chamber contained. It was propped against the brick wall at the back of the oak chest—a smallish rectangle, but too wide to allow it to fit into the chest, completely dust-covered, but with elaborate carving on its delicate frame. I put down the candle and reached across the little skeleton, wondering which of her possessions this had been. It was heavier than I expected. I hesitated after lifting it only a few inches from its place; I rested it back again where it had been, and in doing this, my hands removed some of the heavy dust. A faint reflection glowed back at me from the candlelight. I knew then that it was a mirror, rare in the days of the Spanish Woman, and surrounded, I thought, by a silver-gilt frame. I put down the candle and stretched out both hands to lift this precious thing over the obstacle of the chest and the body of the Spanish Woman.

It was too much for my strength. As I was about to lower it to the floor beside me it slipped and crashed down. The old Venetian glass shattered, and two large fragments fell from the frame. I sighed in agony at the thought of what I had done. Why hadn't I waited until I had help to examine it? Why, having made this discovery, hadn't I had the patience to wait until someone else could help me? I had destroyed, once again, something very valuable, something that belonged to the history of Thirlbeck. Then another thought came, the memory of the words, the translation written in Vanessa's hand, ". . . *this our likeness, a mirror of conscience* . . ." The prickling of excitement ran through my body like warm wine. I wondered if what I saw was again a blurring of my vision, my focus. Where the large fragments of shattered glass had fallen away, I saw something else—not the wooden back I would have expected for the mirror. A canvas showed behind the jagged edges of glass. With a kind of frantic excitement I began to pick at what remained, being very careful now, fearful that I might pierce the canvas with the jagged edges. Reason told me to wait, but instinct and emotion overrode it. Piece by piece the glass came out; some fell from the frame. In the nearly four hundred years the canvas had stayed in that place, it had been protected from dust by the mirror, had been given almost ideal circumstances for its preservation from both extremes of heat and damp. I gazed at the face I saw—knelt down and lifted the candle so that the light fell upon that painted face. The remembered face of Philip the Second of Spain, painted, in his own words, *"by the hand of Domenico Theotokopoulos."* It was unmistakable. No one in the world had ever painted in this quite individual style. No one in the world—certainly not in the time when he had lived, most certainly not now when his fame was universal —would ever have attempted to imitate it. I gazed at it in awe.

"By the hand of Domenico Theotokopoulos." Pursued, envied, grasped at by every museum in the world, absolutely forbidden an export licence from Spain under any circumstances. Priceless. The greatest treasure Thirlbeck contained. A hitherto unknown painting by El Greco.

And then, my body seeming to pulse with the joy of this discovery, began to feel cold and weak again, and I didn't understand the meaning of the warmth against my hand until I looked down. In picking away the fragments of the mirror, I had gashed the palm of my hand. The blood was starting to trickle down to the end of my fingers.

I tried to get to my feet. I grabbed one of my dresses which was lying on the floor of the cupboard and wrapped it tightly about my whole hand. I stayed for a while as I was, trying to gain strength for the effort of rising. It didn't come; I couldn't summon it. Then I remembered that the Condesa was coming; very soon she would return with the brandy. With that thought I let myself lie down, lie down beside the remains of the little Spanish Woman.

I probably had moments of unconsciousness. There was no way to mark the time until I heard the footsteps, the hurried footsteps through the room as if I were being sought, the shadow that fell even into the darkness of that inner chamber. For a second I thought it must have been Jessica. The sense of hostility was strong, a sort of chemistry I had felt many times in my days at Thirlbeck. But no, not Jessica. This time, not Jessica. Before she spoke I had the scent of her perfume.

"What . . . ?" A very long silence followed. I had expected her to touch me, but no hand was laid on me, no hand attempted to raise my head. But she had picked up the candle; its light was nearer, and higher. "So . . . so . . ." The voice was well known, a kind of harsh triumph in it now, the sort of fierce excitement I had known in the moment of discovering the painting. "You have found it! And I had searched all these weeks at Thirlbeck. I have even taken Tolson's keys and searched in the picture room when they believed I was having the siesta . . ."

"Please . . ." I whispered. Why did she do nothing? I could

feel the warm blood seeping through the rough bandage; I raised my hand so that she might see it. I tried to raise my head but could not. I could see nothing but the dim blurred focus of the candle flame.

"She is ours." Now the tone had softened, as if the Condesa spoke to herself, musingly. "The Spanish Lady and her possessions are ours. For many generations in our family we have known of the existence of this painting—as we have always known about the jewel. She was of our family, this Spanish Lady, sent in marriage to England by Filipe. The knowledge of the El Greco was our tradition. If this painting still existed anywhere in the world, it could only have been here at Thirlbeck. And *you* have found it when I had begun to believe that it must have been destroyed."

I shifted my head, but all that came into focus was the edge of her slacks. "Help me!" I whispered. "For God's sake help me! I'm bleeding again. I can't lose any more blood. Please . . ."

She didn't seem to hear me, or if she did, it made no difference. Whatever anguish and rage she might have felt at Robert Birkett's death now seemed to have been submerged, transferred almost, to the triumph of winning what she had come to Thirlbeck to seek. She was no longer a woman alone, no longer a woman who had lost everything that day. "So . . . I take it now, since it does not belong to the Birketts, but to us. And I am the last of my family. But it will not go back to Spain. It will go to the highest bidder. Very private . . . and for a great deal of money."

"Please . . ." What was meant to be a cry came only as a whisper. I doubt she even heard it. I never knew if the ultimate crime was her intent—she may have believed I would be discovered, but the real horror of what she was doing only came after I felt the canvas in its elaborate frame removed from my side, and then the candle itself was withdrawn. I wanted to scream as I smelled the acrid smell after it was blown out. I made one last feeble attempt to stop her when I sensed, from the noises that came to me, that she was tugging back into place the panel which had sealed the dark little chamber and its secret. I had to pull back my fingers as the panel squeezed them. Then I could only lie there and listen to the sound of the cupboard door being closed. I felt the tears of frustration and despair prick my eyes, but there was no energy to weep or cry out. Muffled noises continued for some minutes in the room beyond. I could feel the vibration of her footsteps, and then all sound and movement ceased. I felt my lips form a word. "Please . . ." But there was no sound.

In the silence and the darkness I pulled the rough bandage tighter, and closed my fist to hold tight against the cloth. And still the gentle ooze of blood continued; my body was growing very cold. That stuffy chamber was suddenly as cold as death. For four hundred years this silent, dusty place had been the tomb of the Spanish Woman. And now I shared it with her.

IV

The sounds came from very far away—I wondered if this was some sort of prelude to death, if in the grip of this frightful cold, sounds came back that were part of life, and if they would fade as life faded. I heard no voices; I remembered words, phrases, people—but I did hear the sound of the dogs, those strangely haunting sounds with which they had called to one another that day in the thick mist on the mountain, the sounds they had used which gave me the courage to follow them through the denseness down into the clear. Strange, that in a whole lifetime of people's voices to hear and remember, the last thing I should be aware of were the cries of the great hounds of the Birketts.

Then some sense returned, and I knew the sounds were not imagined, but real—and near. Were they beyond the door of the Spanish Woman's room, setting up that massive chorus, giving full strength to their big voices? They kept on, insistent, demanding, a new note, almost frantic. Was there anyone in the house to heed them, or would they shepherd them away from the room because they believed I was still in the hospital? The dread and the hope were equally mixed. "Oh, God . . ." Was I praying? It was a silent prayer and a cry for help from the tomb of the Spanish Woman, whose burial place only I had ever discovered. But I was so cold—they said the tomb was a cold and lonely place. Stop thinking, just remember the dogs, and hold the strength to will them to do what they were doing. Will them to insist and demand, and not to give up until someone should obey the demand of their clamour.

There was another period of blackness, and then the sounds were much nearer. The dogs had been let into the room, and now all eight of them must have taken their stance before the closed door of the cupboard. "Quickly . . . quickly," I whispered in the darkness. The door of the cupboard was open. The incredible din the dogs made would have drowned out any cry I might have made. But there was no strength to cry out. All I was conscious of was the wish that I would not die; in these moments I wanted very much to live. "Live . . . live . . ."

To answer my wish came the frantic pawing and scraping of their claws on the other side of the panel. Whoever was there understood and respected the dogs—knew the peculiarities of their attachment to members of the Birkett family. Whoever it was didn't waste much time trying to find which niche or peg had to be pressed or pulled to release the panel that held me prisoner. Then I heard voices, not imagined, but real; I heard the blessed splintering of the wood. Someone was using something—a poker, even an axe, perhaps, to beat and tear their way to me. I pressed my body as close as I could to the oak chest on which the Spanish Woman lay. We would come out of the darkness together.

One of the dogs was through first, the great head thrusting into the dark hole trying to lick life and warmth back into me. He was forcibly withdrawn, and the chopping recommenced, but with more deliberate care. A strong beam of light was now shining on me.

I felt myself being lifted with great gentleness, and the dogs fell silent. I was cradled in arms that were familiar. Nat's voice was close to my ear as he carried me.

"You're going to make a rotten farmer's wife. You know that, don't you?"

* * *

Through the drive to the hospital Nat's arms cradled me still. "Hang on, Jo. The hospital's just telephoned. The donor got back to Carlisle, and now he's on his way to the hospital. Where you should have stayed . . ."

Tolson was driving, and I knew that Gerald was there in the car with us, but there were frequent moments of blackness; in the times of consciousness I grew aware of the tightness of something about my arm. They had tied a tourniquet there, and frightening numbness was present all though my arm. The dizziness and coldness persisted. I framed words to speak, but few would come out.

"Gerald—the Condesa . . ." It was the lightest whisper, and Nat caught it.

"Yes, Jo, we know . . . we know she's gone. Don't try to talk. For God's sake save your strength."

I tried again, but it was no use. I was aware of the lights when we reached the hospital, the strangeness of staring face-up at the lights in the corridors as I was wheeled along. Then the wound was quickly stitched and bound, and the tourniquet released. I was aware of pain as the blood slowly began circulating in that arm. Then some time later—I didn't know how long because the times of blackness kept returning—the transfusion began. I never saw the donor, not until much later. They gave me the blood of this unknown man, and made preparations to put me to sleep. I had only the strength to demand that Nat and Gerald return. I could tell from the nurses' manner that they thought me a difficult and unco-operative patient. Ungrateful, too.

I tried to talk when they brought Nat and Gerald. I had believed I had the strength, but when I tried the words, once more they failed me.

"The Condesa . . . she has . . ."

It was Gerald who put his fingers on my lips. "Please, dear Jo, don't try to talk. We know all about it. The Condesa has gone, and so has La Española. Now, please—everything is being done, and you are to sleep. You were nearly dead, you know."

"That makes it twice today." Nat's voice. "You look like a ghost."

"La Española . . ." I whispered.

"Jo, stop it! What are you bothering about it for? Tolson has told the police. The ports and airports have been alerted to watch for her. For myself, I hope she gets clean away with it. I hope she manages to get it cut, and the damn thing disappears forever, and I hope they never prove she took it." He sighed. "But I don't suppose we'll be that lucky. I don't really believe we're through with it at last. I think it will come back, that damned thing. It always has, to cause ruin, and trouble . . . and death."

"Nat, please . . ." Gerald's voice was cautioning him. "Jo needn't worry about any of that. Everything's taken care of. Look, there's the nurse with an injection. You *must* rest, Jo . . ."

I licked my dry lips. "An El Greco . . ." But the words had no form, and no one heard. I could feel the rising panic in me. Thoughts, confused and jumbled, whirled within me, and I couldn't seem to find the right sequence. I had to warn them, somehow—but Gerald was telling me it was already too late. None of them knew that the Condesa had taken the El Greco as well as La Española. None of them would realise that by telling the police they were placing themselves in terrible jeopardy. How did I tell them that if the Condesa were caught, not only with La Española, but with the El Greco canvas, she could claim that she was merely one more of the couriers who had left Thirlbeck with a precious canvas, that on the Earl's death she had volunteered to take out of the country an even rarer treasure than the Rembrandt. If she was caught at all, she would talk, and the world would know the secret Vanessa and Tolson had kept so faithfully. She would implicate Gerald, and possibly Nat. The tears of frustration rolled down my cheeks as I thought of it, and could not say it. And even if I could say it, what would be the use? They had already told the police La Española was gone. Nothing, now, would stop the inexorable sequence of events if the Condesa failed to get clear. But once she was out of the country, and she had disposed of the jewel and the painting, the danger would recede for all of us. So I didn't try any more to tell them. It was too difficult to find the words, and already useless.

I felt the jab of the needle. In the last seconds before the blackness came again I managed to touch Nat's hand. He bent towards my lips, but I didn't know how the words came out. "You have to get me in the morning. Must be there, Nat. Must be there when they bury him . . . Promise . . . ?"

He had heard and understood me. "I promise, Jo. Go to sleep now."

Like him, I felt it was no use. La Española would return to Thirlbeck. What had been the Spanish Woman's, would remain hers. And whatever ruin followed, we would have to bear. But still the opposite thought persisted until the oblivion of the drug took hold. To me, she was a friendly spirit, the Spanish Woman.

CHAPTER 9

I

He came quite early, but I was dressed and waiting for him. I had asked one of the nurses to telephone Nat's house to make sure he was coming. He entered the room with his brows settled into a frown that seemed too permanent.

"Jo, you know this is madness. You should stay at least another day. Give yourself a chance. You only got a bit more than a pint of blood from that man. They couldn't risk him collapsing, you know. Both you and he have some making up to do. You need time . . . and rest."

I shook my head. "I'll be better there, Nat. I'll rest—I promise. But I have to be there."

He acknowledged the inevitable with a shrug, but insisted on using a wheel chair to take me to the car. He was driving Gerald's car. "It won't shake you around like the Land-Rover," he said. "And it's heavy enough to take a bash from someone else without feeling it." But still he drove with exaggerated care, stopping completely at every junction, slowing down to ten miles an hour at each bend. "All I want is to see you safely back in bed," he said. "I don't care how long it takes to get to Thirlbeck."

We passed Kesmere church. As early as it was, a few people were wandering around the churchyard, and gathering on the porch. "Mostly press, I suppose," he said. "You can't keep them away. It *is* the parish church. When they bring him back to Thirlbeck to be buried it will be quite private. Just us—and the family."

Through the slow drive I didn't speak to him of the fears I was trying to beat down. He said nothing about there being any news of the Condesa. I had listened to the early news bulletins on the radio, and there had been no mention of her. I wondered how long the wait would be. Later—later, after they had buried the Earl—I would have to talk to Nat and Gerald and Tolson, tell them about the El Greco, the danger that the Condesa posed to all of us. But for the moment it served no purpose to lay further burdens on Nat, who could do nothing to prevent what might be inevitable.

We reached South Lodge, and Jessica's mother was there to open the gate for us. She looked at me with an interest that now was tinged with concern, and I sensed the kind of enfolding possessiveness that characterised the family's attitude to all that touched Thirlbeck, the thing that Nat railed against, and yet, in the future, would not be able to do without. I knew that I also was now included in this.

As we drove on he said, "You know, I think we have to say that it was Jessica who possibly saved your life."

"*Jessica!* How?"

"She saw you in the car when you came back to Thirlbeck last evening. She didn't want to go to the service at the church, and she'd seen you pass the South Lodge in a strange car. When it came back again quite soon she got concerned. She knew that the Condesa was at the house, but she doubted that the Condesa could do the right things for you—see you to bed, and so on. So she walked to Thirlbeck, and was in time to see the Condesa drive off in Askew's car—heading over Brantwick. It was dark, but she was practically certain you weren't in the car, and when she went into the house the dogs were kicking up an almighty fuss, and trying to get into the Spanish Woman's room. The door was locked, and there was no key—at least not on the outside. She called, and couldn't hear a sound. So then she telephoned the vicarage to get a message to me and

Tolson to come as quickly as we could. The service was over, and we were actually in the vicarage when the call came—we were discussing arrangements about today's service, and all the rest of it. She said she thought you were inside the Spanish Woman's room, and she couldn't get in, and you didn't answer when she called. She told us the Condesa was gone. We just about burned up the road getting back here. Of course we didn't know then that you were bleeding again, but Jess somehow conveyed that something was very wrong. She said she'd never heard the dogs go on like that . . ."

I was silent, thinking about it, recalling the events of the night before, this sudden new knowledge of Jessica slow to sink in. The high, heraldic frieze of Thirlbeck was in plain view before I spoke. "Then she did the exact opposite of what she did with Patsy. When she could have spoken before, she didn't. This time she took more on herself than she need have done. Nat—oh, Nat, do you mind very much? She could have saved Patsy—but she saved me. I suppose she was ill then—but this is a bitter sort of twist for you. Three years ago, it could have been Patsy."

His hand touched mine, the very roughness of it somehow reassuring. "I can't begin to weigh you and Patsy in the same scales, Jo—and don't ever think it. Patsy was sweet and lovely, and I loved her. Now I love you. I have to leave behind what Jess did or didn't do in the past. Last night I think she saved your life. Now I'm in her debt, and always will be. When Tolson realised what Jessica had done last night, he looked like a man who'd had an intolerable burden removed from him. God knows, he still has plenty of troubles to face—yes, he's told me the whole thing about him, and your mother—everything. But now, at least, the worry about the person he loves most in the world seems to have lifted. He can face anything now. And so can I. And so will you . . . and the family."

I had little time to get used to this new idea. It was Jessica who opened the door at Thirlbeck. She was standing there at the top of the steps as we drove up, and she came forward at the same time as all the dogs. Involuntarily, I felt myself stiffen at the sight of her. And Nat's voice came gently. "Easy, Jo. We have to give her a chance . . ."

The first greeting was lost in the surge of the dogs, lifting their faces to me, their tails waving in a frenzy of welcome. Jessica had opened the door of the car before Nat could get around, and stretched out her hand to help me. I wanted to refuse it, and yet I knew I must not refuse it. "I waited until you came to cook breakfast," she said, "but coffee's ready."

She took my arm on one side, and Nat held me on the other. We moved slowly up the steps into the hall, the dogs following. There was a blazing fire in the dining room, and a sofa had been brought from somewhere and placed before it, heaped with cushions. "Grandfather and I brought it in here," Jessica said, as she motioned Nat to take me to it. "Dr. Murray is furious with you for leaving hospital so soon—so I had to make it look as if you're going to be quite all right here." I found myself, without protest, being put on the sofa, my legs up, cushions piled behind my back to support me, a rug spread over me. Jessica brought a small table to the side of the sofa. I watched her then as she moved to the sideboard to pour two cups of coffee. I wasn't mistaken about what I had first sensed. She was in some way older; her body did not seem to dance through its tasks, as if they were some graceful game she played. She didn't smile, and the shining blond hair was not shaken for Nat's admiration. When she had placed coffee on the table beside me, and a cup before Nat who sat at the dining table, she stepped back and said, "There's news, Lord Askew."

Nat answered her quickly. "Cut the rubbish, Jess. My name is Nat."

She shook her head. "Oh, no. Not any more. Everything's changed. No one can help it changing. It just has changed."

He sighed and stirred his coffee. "What's the news, Jess?"

"This morning—very early this morning I went up to the shelter to take your watch on the eagle's nest I knew you wouldn't be able to go. Grandfather isn't letting any of the volunteers in from outside. He's afraid of newspaper people. Well—when it got light, I started watching the eagles with the glasses—you know how you watch them flying just to ease the strain of watching only the nest. I put the glasses over the whole valley, and I saw something up there by the birch copse—something I'd never seen before. I went there as quickly as I could. It was Lord Askew's car—it had run off the road, broken through a wall, and crashed down among the trees. The Condesa was in it. I was . . . I was much too late to help her. They think she must have died almost at once. At least from what Dr. Murray can tell at this time. He thinks her neck was broken."

"God . . . !" Nat looked from Jessica to me. He shook his head as if to escape from some violent dream. "Dead? . . . she's dead!"

"There wasn't anything I could do," Jessica said softly. "I did try. Honestly, I did try. But even I could tell she'd been dead for quite a long time. It was . . . it was rather horrible. There's a lot of broken glass. She wasn't wearing a seat belt. She was jammed against the steering wheel, but Dr. Murray still thinks she died from a broken neck. She was a little cut, but she can't have lived long, Dr. Murray said, or there would have been more bleeding. One of the car headlights was still shining. If the car hadn't dived so far down into the trees below the wall, we would have seen the light shining up there last night. She had the key of the North Lodge in her handbag. And La Española . . ."

For a moment Nat's head sank; he too, like Jessica, seemed to have aged and altered. The changes of these last hours had been thrust on all of us, and we had reacted in our different fashions, and none would ever be quite the same again. The closeness that existed between Nat and myself had broadened to include even Jessica, and she in her turn had opened out, so that she seemed no longer to dwell exclusively in her own precious, tight little world. We had all accepted some part of the responsibility that Robert Birkett's death had laid upon us.

"That damn jewel! I was hoping—yes, I *was* hoping she would get away with it. I was hoping it was gone forever. If I'd had my way, Tolson would never have told the police last night—but he pointed out that we would have to report its theft or the Revenue people would want to know why it was gone—and how long ago. So they put a watch on all the

334

ports—and she, the Condesa, poor devil, never even got out of this valley with it. I was hoping La Española would simply cease to exist. But it didn't even have to be brought back. La Española never left."

I grasped the coffee cup between both my hands to force stillness upon them.

"Did you find anything else, Jessica?"

She looked at me closely. "Yes . . . yes, I did find something else. So that was why . . . yes, *that* was why she shut you in that place with the Spanish Woman. It had to have come from there. You found it—and she'd taken it."

"What the hell are you talking about?" Nat demanded.

Jessica turned to him. "In the back of the car I found Miss Roswell's big red suitcase." She wasn't at all abashed at knowing my possessions so well. "When I found her dead—the Condesa—I decided I'd bring down her handbag and the suitcase. It seemed so strange that she should have taken one of your suitcases, and left all her own behind. Hers were so expensive . . ."

"But mine was tough. Rather cheap fibre glass, but tough. Was the painting in it, Jessica?"

She nodded. "It was all packed about with your clothes—a protection, I suppose. My grandfather had never seen it before. He woke Mr. Stanton. Mr. Stanton was much more pleased about that being back here than La Española."

Nat interrupted. "Would you mind explaining? I'm beginning to feel even more dense than usual."

I sank back against the pillows; perhaps I was weaker than I knew, or the worry had been greater.

"It's all right now, Nat. It was a painting by El Greco." In a low voice I found myself explaining what I had not been able to say last night. A sense of relief, of reprieve, was surging through my body.

"She was of the same family as the Spanish Woman, you see, Nat."

Jessica broke in. "It's true, you know. It's there in the passport. Her full name is Carlota de Avila, Fernández de

Córdoba, Mendoza, Soto Alvarez y Alonzo. Part of that is the name of the Spanish Woman."

From the doorway, Gerald's voice. He had entered very quietly and had been standing behind us, listening. "Fernández de Córdoba . . . one of the most distinguished names in Spain —and joined to others almost as distinguished. How are you, Jo?" He came around to inspect me, putting out his hand, brushing the hair from my forehead. "You shouldn't be out of hospital at all, but I'm glad to see you, Jo, dear. You still look like a ghost—and you nearly died there with the Spanish Woman."

I started then to tell them what I hadn't been able to say the night before, the words the Condesa had used. "She must have believed that if the painting still existed, it was most probably still here at Thirlbeck. She said . . . I remember she said that she had been searching for it. Even in the picture room. And none of us knew it. Well . . . she had no success, no more than Vanessa had." I told them about the scrap of parchment signed by Philip the Second, and the translation in Vanessa's hand.

"She was all ready to go when I got back to Thirlbeck. She was ready to leave just with La Española—and I made a gift to her of the El Greco as well. I even made it possible for her to take La Española. Until I came, the dogs wouldn't move away from the door of the study. When I came, they wanted to be with me. I made them stay on the landing . . . left her free to take what she wanted, once she'd switched off the alarm system. It's all so terribly easy once one knows this house well, and the dogs are taken care of."

"The dogs saved your life," Gerald said. "The dogs and Jessica. We had to break the lock of the Spanish Woman's room to get in, but without the dogs we wouldn't have found the little chamber where the Spanish Woman was laid out. I don't pretend to know what it is those dogs have bred into them, but it is something that primarily concerns the Birketts." He looked around at the three of us. "That is something that all of us know about, even if we don't understand it. It's something that will never be spoken of outside this family. It is best forgotten, if it can be." His tone was grave and musing. "Thank you, my dear," he added, as Jessica placed a cup of coffee in his hand.

"What has happened to the painting?" I asked.

"Grandfather kept the suitcase and the painting here. We returned La Española and the handbag to the car. It had to be there when the police came, otherwise I'd be accused of tampering with evidence. We're just to say—when it's time to announce it—that the painting was discovered in the little room with the Spanish Woman. Nothing more. No need to bring the Condesa into that at all . . ."

Gerald sipped his coffee appreciatively. He perched himself on the end of the sofa. "It was one of the most exciting moments of my life, Jo," he said, "when I looked at the picture and knew what it was. That was what you had asked about before, wasn't it? I thought I heard you say something about it last night at the hospital, but I just assumed you were rambling a little. I should have known better . . ."

"It *is* Philip the Second, isn't it?"

"I'd say so. El Greco has made him look more spiritual than any portrait I've ever seen of him. Strange—how Philip neglected the one artist who catches the spirit of Spain more truly and fundamentally than any other—and yet he was a stranger in Spain. Well, it's a splendid portrait. Almost as moving, in its way, as that wonderful *An Unknown Man* in the Prado. He has taken the face of the most powerful man in the world, and made him appear almost humble, Hapsburg lip and all." He made a little smacking noise with his own lips. "What a sensation! What a sale it will make!"

"Will it pay its own taxes?" Nat asked. "Forgive me for not sharing quite all of your excitement, but there are very practical matters to think of."

Gerald's brow puckered. "With a picture like this, all kinds of arrangements are possible. It might be possible to avoid a great deal of tax by making a gift of it to the nation. We'll have our export at Hardy's go into that one. He practically wrote the laws on how that could be done." But the excitement he felt could not be restrained. "This is the one picture I *don't* want to see leave this country. I can just imagine them—the crowds —lined up outside the National Gallery the way they were at the Metropolitan after they bought the Rembrandt *Aristotle*. When the story of how this was found gets the full press treatment, what publicity! What they'll make of it all—La Española, the young Spanish Woman herself, and now the El Greco."

Then he sighed, and the excitement died. "That poor woman —the Condesa. I wonder if she fastened onto Robert just with the thought of making him come here so that she could search for it? How frustrating to search all these weeks and never find it, and when the picture room is finally opened, there is no trace of it, and no one seems to expect it to be here. She probably only made up her mind to take La Española because there was nothing else left for her. With Robert dead, her world was collapsing about her. Poor woman . . . to be so desperate. I'm sure she didn't mean to kill you, Jo . . . she *couldn't* have understood about the bleeding. Poor Robert. I hope she felt some real love for him. How glad I am he never knew about her . . ." His tone dropped lower, and he seemed to speak to me alone. "How glad, Jo, I am that he knew about *you*. To have the gift of a daughter in the last hours of his life . . ."

He cleared his throat, and went back to the sideboard for more coffee. "There's a nice obituary about Robert in the *Times* and *Telegraph* this morning. They talk about the Victoria Cross and the Military Cross. The other papers are just treating it as a news story—digging up all the old tales about La Española and his being in prison, and all that. Don't read them, Jo. It won't help . . ."

"I get angry," Jessica said. "They're not even giving Nat a chance—I mean, Lord Askew—a chance. He's only beginning and they're already making life miserable. It will be much worse when they find out that the Condesa died here at Thirlbeck, and with La Española in her possession." She turned to Gerald, as if appealing to the one who would have a solution. "Isn't there *any* way to shut it off? Can't the police be made to keep quiet about La Española? Surely . . . ?"

Gerald shook his head. "Once they were told last night that it had been taken, there was no way to bottle up the news. It's

338

part of the freedom of the press, Jessica. They'll get their stories wherever and however they can, and one normal source is the police. At times the police need co-operation from the press. It works both ways."

Jessica turned back to the sideboard and gave her attention to slicing bread for the toaster. "It isn't fair. Not a chance to begin anything in peace." Then she shrugged. "Well perhaps the publicity won't hurt, in the end."

Nat said slowly: "What do you mean, Jessica . . . 'in the end'?"

"Well . . . I suppose in the end you'll just have to open the house to the public, Nat—Lord Askew. There really isn't any other way to pay for it. Grandfather's hung on all these years, but we all know places like Thirlbeck just eat up money. People want to come and see them, and *they* provide the money. I know you won't like it, but it will probably come to that. You could open up the valley just to this point, and leave the rest of it private. Make it a nature sanctuary . . . or something. There'll be some pictures left, surely—some furniture to show off." She flung a rather frightened glance at Gerald and myself. "I mean, you won't have to sell *everything*, will you? Maybe the National Trust—no, you wouldn't like that either. They'd be telling you how to run the place. Well, it'll work out. Miss Roswell would be very good at working it all out, and she's trained to know where to go for advice. I'm sure Mr. Stanton would help. *I'd* help all I could. I know the history of most of the family, and I'd learn the rest. Miss Roswell could write a descriptive booklet. Perhaps the stables could be turned into some kind of restaurant. There might be a craft shop. People like to buy things when they're on holiday . . ."

She stopped, perhaps because the silence had become too heavy. "Oh, well, it's just an idea. You're going to have to do *something*."

The finished slices popped from the toaster, and she put more in. "I'll go and do the eggs now. Dr. Murray will want to see you, Miss Roswell, when he's finished up there . . . the ambulance and police are there too. I'd better put on more coffee . . ."

339

She looked across at Nat. "I suppose the police will take care of getting in touch with the Condesa's family. But don't you think . . . well, it would be a good idea if you sent a message? They probably will want to have her body sent back to Spain. I suppose I could try ringing the Spanish Embassy in London. The address in her passport is some place in Italy. But a family as important as that . . . I'm sure the Embassy people would know where to find them . . . Well, I'd better go and do the breakfast. I didn't want to start the eggs until you arrived. I'll bring more coffee."

She paused in the doorway. "We'll just all have to stick together. If there are reporters, you'll just have to say 'no comment,' Nat—Lord Askew. I've already told all the children they're not to talk. They're all going to the service in Kesmere. Grandfather thought it was right. I don't think I'll go—I didn't want to last night, either. But I'll be here with Miss Roswell, and I'll go to the burial ground when you bring the Earl back. Nat, shall I go and get the Land-Rover? You could drive Miss Roswell to the burial ground in that—it's too far for her to walk." Then the door closed behind her.

After she had gone we all exchanged glances, but it was on Nat's face that the beginning of a smile first appeared. It infected all of us, and we had to laugh. "Well, there you are," Nat said. "Everything laid out nicely. Everything taken care of."

"And the thing is," Gerald said, "the child could be right." He rose and went to pour himself more coffee; then he came back and laid more wood on the fire. When he turned back to us his face was serious again, and he looked tired. He was another on whom Robert Birkett's death had laid an extra burden. "You know, that was as close as I'd like to come again to being really in the hands of the law. It's possible the Condesa might not have told about the rest of it if she'd been caught only with La Española. I had already primed Tolson with the story that it could have been a gift from Robert. Of course, it would have seemed even more natural if we'd known from the beginning that she was of the same family as the Spanish Woman. But when I saw the El Greco I realised that if she'd been caught with *that*, there would have been no mercy for us.

She would have told the whole story—Vanessa, Tolson, everyone would have been implicated. She wouldn't have been stealing it, but simply acting as a courier, as quickly after Lord Askew's death as possible, in getting out the most important item of a fabulous collection . . . Well, thankfully, it didn't happen that way. But I do wonder. I wonder about that place at the birch copse . . ." He shrugged. "Useless wondering about things like that . . . never gets you anywhere."

I shivered, and Nat was quickly beside me. "You cold, Jo?" He pulled the rug higher on me. I was wearing the yellow anorak, which was what they had bundled me into last night before wrapping me in blankets for the trip to the hospital. It was soiled now, and there was some blood on the front of it.

"No," I said. "I'm all right." I wasn't going to say, not now or ever, what it might be that the Condesa had seen at the beginning of the birch copse. Perhaps she had seen nothing. An accident with no apparent cause. But the dying words of the Spanish Woman had once more proved their potency, and La Española would once more be back at Thirlbeck, another shred of legend and tragedy attached to its history.

Gerald took my empty cup and went and brought me more coffee. Nat had taken his place at the end of the sofa. There was the beginning of a smile once again appearing on his face. "If I didn't feel so miserable—and so damn bewildered—I *could* almost laugh. Look at them, the Tolsons. Every last one of them, the family, I'm certain, is planning already for Thirlbeck. What they'll do to fight off the death duties. How we'll all hang together. Incredible, isn't it? There's Jessica now—fighting to redeem herself in some way. She'll give her heart and soul to this place. She'll take over when Tolson begins to falter. When she does marry, you can bet it will be to someone who can, in some way, be of service to Thirlbeck. We've got Jessica and the Tolsons—and Thirlbeck—for the rest of our lives. You know that, don't you, Jo? Can you bear it?" He shook his head impatiently. "Of course you'll bear it. You'll bear it because I need you, and because you're his daughter. My need—and your inheritance, Jo. It's a formidable combination."

He rose and went to the window, looking up the valley to where the white of the ambulance, and the white markings on the police car could just be seen at the beginning of the birches. "I said you'll make a rotten farmer's wife, Jo—that's the truth, and always will be. But you'll be great for Thirlbeck."

Now he looked quite deliberately between Gerald and myself, perhaps even glad that there was a witness to his next words.

"I'm not really asking you, Jo. I'm telling you the way things have to be. You can't leave here now. I've got to take this job on, and I can't do it without you. It wouldn't really matter if you were a helpless dummy. I've got to have you with me. If you decide you're not going to stay, then that's the end of Thirlbeck, no matter what the Tolsons say or do."

Gerald remained motionless, as if he feared that a movement might stop the flow of words that were still to come. Nat began to speak again, rather slowly, making things clear for himself as well as for me. "Jo, if you don't stay with me, I'll sell every damn thing that's salable, and if no one will buy the house, I'll tear it down. It's possible to give up a title, and I'll give up this one. The Earldom of Askew will cease to exist. I have no heart, and no guts for this job unless you are here."

I watched Gerald's face for a moment, saw the faint, almost involuntary nod he gave. I felt incredibly weary. "Nat," I said, "you won't tear down Thirlbeck—no more than you'll give up trying to save the golden eagles. Jessica said it. Everything has changed by this one man's death. You've taken his title and his responsibilities. You'll handle both in a different way from him—but you'll handle them, not throw them away. Yes, I know I'll make a rotten farmer's wife. The rest—I'll do what I can."

I looked down at the bandaged hand. "It's only the beginning, Nat. Gerald knows even better than we do what sort of problems are ahead. You'll have to go soon, and get changed. You have to go to the church and be ready to face the cameras, and the questions, and keep your temper. There's an awful lot to start to learn. We might as well begin properly."

342

I stood at Nat Birkett's side when they brought the body of Robert Birkett, eighteenth Earl of Askew, back to Thirlbeck to be buried. Nat's sons, and the Tolson families, had brought flowers picked from the gardens of the farms, and from the lanes and hedgerows. The daffodils were long over, but the bright flame of tulips was there, and the scent of wallflowers; there were small bouquets of pansies and bunches of pale primroses, and bluebells, already wilting. Some had sacrificed the scarlet and white bloom of azaleas to dress that grave with the flowers of the English spring, to which Robert Birkett had returned.

I looked at the faces about me—at Gerald, with Jeffries behind him, at Tolson and the faces of his sons which now, seen together, had a startling likeness, at the fairy-like Jessica who had grown up so swiftly, at all the faces of the Tolson grandchildren gathered here to witness the end of one era and the beginning of another.

"We brought nothing into this world, and it is certain that we can carry nothing out."

That was what it had all been about—and why it was continuing. We had all, all of us standing here close by his grave, been concerned with the property of a gentleman known as Robert Birkett. Vanessa had unwittingly died for it; Robert Birkett had died in the anguish of knowing what she and others had risked to preserve it, had died knowing that Vanessa had been willing to serve this legacy because she had borne a child to him; Tolson had endured years of punishing doubt and worry to hold this property intact. Up there, on the mountainside, last night another woman had died because she had sought to take away that property. Gerald and I had come to cast a coldly commercial eye over it, and had stayed to become as enmeshed in its saving as any of those standing about us. How much hate and greed and struggle had gone into the amassing of these lands, from the humble beginning in the now ruined pele tower which rose above us, to the further shimmering beauty of the stone frieze that surmounted the house of the Birketts, splendid in the morning sun. The spirit of the little Spanish Woman had marched with their history through the centuries, and the dark spell of the great jewel she had brought to them. *Caveat Raptor—Who Seizes, Beware.*

And I thought also of the other man who had loved Vanessa once, who had given to me his name; I thought of Jonathan Roswell. I thought that one day he also would be buried in a private family burial ground, beside a ruined chapel, and young, dark-eyed children would gather the brilliant tropical flowers that grew around to place on his grave. It would not be a grave among the English rains and mists and green grass, but in the hard, baked earth of Mexico, and the sun would warm his bones, even in death. And the children and the women would weep because they loved him, as we, this correct and controlled English gathering, would not let ourselves weep.

Thinking this, it was all the more surprising then, on that bright, rainless morning of the English spring, to find the wetness on my face, to look across and see George Tolson's head bowed, as if he did not know how to handle his grief, and then to see on the face of Jessica the tears that would make her whole and human. The full realisation of what I must take on with Nat, the responsibility for the lives and loyalties of all these people came fully to me then. Perhaps I wept for myself as well as for my father, Robert Birkett.

III

That same day the priest came out from the Catholic Church in Kesmere and talked with Nat and myself. "I don't know why it should not be done," he said. "Every Christian soul deserves Christian burial—and she has waited a long time." He looked at the burial ground of the Birketts, noted the date set in the arch above the roofless chapel. "I doubt that it ever was deconsecrated," he said. "Of course I'll telephone the bishop, but I can see no reason why it should not be used. After all, we haven't always had our great churches. So often it was Mass under the open sky—and especially in her time. You're certain of her identity?"

"We examined the monogrammed ring she wore very carefully. I don't think there could be any doubt that it is she."

He nodded. "Well, then, we'll go ahead. Let's hope it doesn't rain."

In what remained of that day we set the Tolson grandchildren to clearing the floor of the chapel, to clipping at the worst of the briars that grew against its walls, but we left alone the young birch tree that had sprung up close to where the marble fragments told us the altar must have been. Mrs. Tolson provided a table that could be covered with a white cloth. Jessica brought great masses of flowers in big vases to set about on the sod-grown ground. At the end of the day young Thomas, Nat's son, brought me white violets wrapped in damp paper. "They're for her," he said. "Dad says it's very private, and very early, and I should not come. He said not to think too much about her—but I do. My mother told me the story of the Spanish Woman. I'm sorry she's been up there in that place all these years alone. It must be sad to be forgotten, like that. But she won't be lonely any more. It's a pity she can't be beside her husband. But he was beheaded on Tower Hill—wasn't he?— and he never came back to Thirlbeck."

I shook my head. "I suppose the third Earl, his brother, must have been afraid to claim the body of a traitor."

"It's interesting to have a traitor in the family," he said with the calm matter-of-factness of a child, and he went off, the future Earl of Askew, not troubled at all by the four hundred years that had passed since that time, not troubled by the thought of his inheritance.

Nat sat with me late that night as I rested in the bed of the Spanish Woman. All eight of the dogs were with us, lying before the two fires; they had attached themselves to Nat in the immediate fashion they had attached themselves to Robert Birkett and to myself. He was already growing used to being almost unable to move without them. He looked at them now. "They've split up pretty evenly between you and me, Jo. We'll have to breed some more of them, as well as some kids for ourselves."

"Yes . . ."

He was sitting in the big chair where I so often had thought I saw the shadowy figure of the Spanish Woman. His body filled it to a comfortable degree. A candle burned on the mantel above him, and he had been trying, in a dazed and tired fashion, to make some notes of things needing to be done. He smoked, and there was a bottle of brandy on a silver tray on the table, and we each had a filled glass beside us. In the way we talked, we could have been married for a dozen years.

He was not completely reconciled to the idea of opening Thirlbeck to the public. "What the hell can we do with it, Jo? The National Trust—no, I suppose not. Can we somehow get rid of La Española? Even if they don't find out about what Tolson and your mother have been doing, there's still a hell of a lot of things that will be lumped into the estate. Are we going to be beggars because of this? Will they let us keep anything?"

"Nat, they'll be on to you—the Revenue Commissioners, in good time. They won't put their hand on your shoulder tomorrow. There are things here . . . well, we'll just have to talk to them about it all—and keep quiet about what has already gone. I suppose Lord Askew—Robert—paid tax on his income when he had to. The proceeds from the paintings and other things all went to him. But there's a million pounds sitting in a Swiss bank that should belong to Thirlbeck. I suppose we've all become conspirators in this, Nat. That's the biggest worry—perhaps if we find it, it can be paid into Lord Askew's Swiss account. Then you inherit—and pay the tax. No Swiss bank is going to give out information about where it came from. We'll just have to face it out. There is a difference, though. Now the money will be coming back to England. The Revenue people will have their cut, and then the money can be spent as it's needed. I don't quite see yet how it's all to be done—managed. But Thirlbeck is going to be saved, Nat. If you have to grit your teeth and let the public in, then grit your teeth."

He managed a tired smile. "I've got good strong teeth."

"They'd better be. You'll grind them a lot in the next few

years when you discover how ill-prepared Lord Askew had left you to be heir to this estate. We might have to do as Gerald said and sell the El Greco to the National Gallery . . ."

I couldn't see his face fully, but he seemed almost to be laughing when he spoke. "Yes, Jo—and what else?"

"A lot of the French furniture could be sold. As beautiful as it is, it doesn't belong in this house. It looks like a bow on the head of a middle-aged woman. We should try to keep the pictures. They're a beautiful collection. A minor marvel of Dutch Old Masters. We could specialise . . . Oh, yes . . . and the legend of La Española."

"What about it? Damn, Jo, I'm only a farmer. These things take time to sink into my thick skull."

"Not so long for this one, Nat. The way I think about La Española. It's been locked up for so many years. A fabulous jewel worth at least a million pounds—and yet worth nothing. Because it can't leave here."

"Jo—Jo! I have to pay death duties on it. Can't I just hand it over to the Revenue people? Let *them* take the risks. Let them get killed trying to sell it."

I spoke softly. I was looking round the room, looking at the carving of the panelling, the dogs sleeping before the fires, the light that the candle cast on the side of Nat's face. I looked at the door of the cupboard behind which the Spanish Woman had dwelt for so many centuries.

"It can't leave here, Nat. You know that. The first accident, the first misfortune that strikes anyone who handles it, will half kill you. You'll blame yourself. It stays here. We'll have to make a deal with the Revenue people. You'll pay the tax however and whenever you can manage it. And La Española will become the jewel it was always meant to be. If legend belongs to it— if people want to think there's a curse on it—then let them come and see it. Put it in a secure glass casing. Relieve Tolson— oh, for God's sake we've got to relieve Tolson finally of this hellish responsibility. Put in the best security system—and let people come in and see what the Spanish Woman brought to England. Tell the story—tell it as if she were telling it. Make them weep, Nat. Let them have their few sentimental tears.

The little Spanish girl has been neglected too long. She lived here, she died here—no, she was murdered here. Tomorrow, she will be buried here."

"Jo, do you really know what you're taking on? We could live in half poverty for the rest of our lives just to keep this thing going. Is it worth it?"

"Do we have a choice? I think the question answers itself, Nat."

He put down his glass and stubbed out his cigarette. He came then and sat on the bed beside me. "I'll do it if you say I must. By God, what a child Robert Birkett has left behind in you. You're still as weak as a kitten, and yet you've already begun to fight. You'll fight for every last thing in this place, won't you? You'll give an inch at a time, and argue all the way— and probably win something back. When you first came you seemed such a quiet type—cool and sophisticated, but not tough. Now you suddenly seem as tough as old boots. I don't really understand *your* sort of Birkett. *He* didn't want to fight —except when they put him in a war. I suppose I'd do well to remember that you *are* the daughter of a V.C."

"I'm also Vanessa's daughter," I said. "Stop worrying, Nat. Birketts fight when there's something to fight for. He's left us plenty of that . . ."

He sighed, and slipped off his shoes, lying back on the piled-up pillows that supported me. "Yes, plenty . . . God, I'm tired. I started feeling tired when I saw the newspapers this afternoon. All that horrible muck about the Condesa and La Española. Well, we couldn't expect to have kept that quiet . . . If only we—you and I, Jo—could have started with just my farm. I've never minded a simple fight. Farming's all a fight—but it's fighting things you understand—the weather, crops, sheep—ordinary things like that. A simple enough ambition for a simple enough fight. And what did I get?—you and Thirlbeck. Well—I suppose nobody ever has it easy . . ." His voice trailed off; he closed his eyes, and his body curved against mine as if for warmth and comfort. I drew the eiderdown over him.

"Well, it *is* a start," I said. He didn't answer, and in a few minutes his deeper breathing told me he had fallen asleep as

348

swiftly and completely as a child. After a while he even snored gently, in rather the way the dogs snored in their deepest moments of sleep. We were not like new lovers then, but people long accustomed to each other, facing together the problems of a new and cruelly acquired inheritance. There was going to be no easy way. I thought that the ghosts of Thirlbeck, whatever they were, whatever form they took, would not easily forgive a shrugging off of the tasks laid before us. They had not forgiven Robert Birkett his desertion of his place and responsibility, and in the end they had brought him back to die here. As they had brought me here—to live.

Nat's voice came again, sleepily. He spoke with his eyes still closed. "I didn't tell you, did I?—the great news. One of the eagles' eggs hatched today. And . . . and I put away the Bentley."

In a very little while he was asleep again.

IV

The next morning we were ready very early. Tolson was waiting in the library where the oak coffin rested—the coffin which contained all that remained of the Spanish Woman in her last night under the roof of Thirlbeck.

Nat, and George Tolson with his sons, carried the coffin between them. It was so early the mist had not yet lifted from the tarn, and all we could see was the low white swirling blanket over the water, and rising from it, startling in the early sun, the peaks of Brantwick and Great Birkeld were revealed in their bald strength.

The coffin was laid on trestles in the newly tidied chapel. Mrs. Tolson's table was covered by a starched white cloth. The priest was waiting, with a young boy as acolyte, both robed for the Mass. I noticed that his vestments were the white of joy, not the black of mourning. I had asked him to recite the Mass in Latin. "She didn't understand English," I had said.

And afterwards she was buried among the Birketts. I laid Thomas's white violets on her grave. Who, on that bright morning, could believe in ghosts? What she had brought with her lived with us, now and forever. A sense of peace, of happiness, stole across me. It might be that, with her final laying to rest, the Birketts themselves would know change. Now that she was at last accepted among us, accorded her due place, her spirit would become for all of us the benign presence it had always seemed to me. And she was truly among us. Standing in place above the grave, the results of Nat's labours yesterday with Ted Tolson, was the tall rough obelisk, with the uncertain hand and spelling. *Juana The Spanishe Woman.*

The priest was finished; the holy water sprinkled. *"Requiescat in pace."* For Nat and myself there was an additional blessing, perhaps the beginning of a special grace passed onto us by the Spanish Woman, who lay at last in a hallowed grave. "And may you live in peace."

3471